THE CONFESSORS' CLUB

THE CONFESSORS' CLUB

Jack Fredrickson

This first world edition published 2015
in Great Britain and the USA by
SEVERN HOUSE PUBLISHERS LTD of
19 Cedar Road, Sutton, Surrey, England, SM2 5DA.
Trade paperback edition first published 2015 in Great
Britain and the USA by SEVERN HOUSE PUBLISHERS LTD.

British Library Cataloguing in Publication Data

Fredrickson, Jack author.
  The confessors' club. – (A Dek Elstrom mystery)
  1. Elstrom, Dek (Fictitious character)–Fiction.
  2. Private investigators–Illinois–Chicago–Fiction.
  3. Serial murder investigation–Fiction. 4. Detective and
  mystery stories.
  I. Title II. Series
  813.6-dc23

ISBN-13: 978-0-7278-8488-6 (cased)
ISBN-13: 978-1-84751-594-0 (trade paper)
ISBN-13: 978-1-78010-645-8 (e-book)

All Severn House titles are printed on acid-free paper.

Severn House Publishers support the Forest Stewardship Council™ [FSC™],
the leading international forest certification organisation. All our titles that
are printed on FSC certified paper carry the FSC logo.

Typeset by Palimpsest Book Production Ltd.,
Falkirk, Stirlingshire, Scotland.
Printed and bound in Great Britain by
TJ International, Padstow, Cornwall.

For Jack R. Fredrickson

My guide, my dad

ACKNOWLEDGMENTS

The whole gang – Patrick Riley, Missy Lyda, Eric Frisch, Mary Anne Bigane and Joe Bigane – slogged through the early drafts of this one, criticizing, counseling, supporting. As always, I'm grateful.

Thanks, too, to the ever-patient Sara Porter of Severn House for managing this book, and me, with grace and aplomb.

First, and last, thank you, Susan. Again. For it all.

The gold Rolex Day-Date on his wrist had cost eleven thousand dollars. It was still keeping perfect time, but that would be expected. It was water resistant to a depth far greater than the shallows at the marsh end of the small lake. And it had been engineered to run on the faintest of movements: the gentle lapping of the water through the rushes was more than enough to engage the self-winding mechanism. It was a gentleman's wristwatch, designed for a man who need make only subtle gestures – a wealthy man, a man of nuance.

He had dressed well. His gray gabardine trousers were of the finest wool, light for the warming spring. His white shirt was cut to precise specification, sent over from Jermyn Street in London. His shoes were English as well, lace-up brogues polished by a houseman to a high gloss.

His attire had not fared as well as the wristwatch. The press had gone from the trousers and soft, milky flesh protruded where the water reeds had abraded the wool. The shirt was now a putrid green, mucked by the moss at the shore. And the shoes had puckered and blistered, since even the finest of leathers, no matter how well oiled, are not meant to withstand even partial submersion.

His face, of course, had suffered the worst of it. The part of the forehead closest to the bullet hole had gone, nibbled away in tiny bites by the sunny fish and microscopic urchins that worked the shore of the small lake.

His eyes, though, still commanded. They remained as clear and direct as they'd been in life, demanding that notice be taken, witness be made, to the truth of the horror they had seen.

ONE

Amanda called me two days before what would have been our fifth wedding anniversary.

'Happy almost anniver—' I said, before I slammed my mouth shut on words that bubbled up from nowhere. I hoped.

My remembering had caught her off guard, too. 'Dek, how sweet of you,' she said, after an awkward beat. Then, 'I'd like to have dinner.'

We hadn't spoken in months. 'Surely not to celebrate?' I asked.

'Our divorce?' She managed a little laugh. 'Of course not.'

'I'm good all next week, after Monday.'

'Business has come back so well you're not available until then?'

I hesitated for an awkward moment of my own. 'I'm headed out of town.'

'Not business, then,' she said.

'A mini-vacation.'

'Today?' She knew I'd never taken a vacation in my life.

'Not for a couple of days.'

She paused, then said, 'How about tonight? It's important.'

I paused too, but only for a second. 'I'll pick you up. You're still on Chicago's tony Lake Shore Drive?'

'Did you get shock absorbers yet?'

'They diminish the aged Jeep experience.'

'I'll meet you at Petterino's,' she said. 'Afterwards, we'll go to the theater. My subscription tickets are for tonight.'

It was going to be like old times, for whatever reason.

'A play afterward?' I managed. 'Surely you remember that's over my head.'

'See you at Petterino's at six.' Her voice softened. 'And Dek?'

'Ma'am?'

'Little is over your head.'

Little was over Jenny's head as well, though her calling ten minutes after I'd clicked off with Amanda could only have been coincidence.

'I can't wait to show you Fisherman's Wharf,' she said.

It was going to be our first time together since she had taken the San Francisco television job eight months earlier. They'd been long months, those eight, and we were set to celebrate the wonder of making our new relationship work at such a long distance.

'Picturesque, is it?'

'Just your cup of Twinkies,' she said.

'Real and authentic, old-time San Francisco?'

'You can get a picture of Elvis on black velvet to hang above your table saw.'

'Black velvet would also nicely complement the white plastic of the lawn chairs,' I said, of the turret's first-floor conversational grouping. 'I'm also in need of a really wide refrigerator magnet, maybe of the Golden Gate Bridge.' The avocado-colored refrigerator I'd found in an alley was rusting from the inside out, and I was looking to slow the loss of semi-cold air.

'I've got four days off, time enough to take care of all your needs.' She laughed, hanging up, leaving me with the promise of unspoken naughtiness.

And grateful that I hadn't had the chance to tell her I was having dinner with my ex-wife that evening.

TWO

I've always suspected that a malevolent chicken farmer designed the Goodman Theater complex in downtown Chicago. It's set up like a poultry processing plant. Petterino's is on the corner, a high-glitz restaurant of hooded table candles and deeply cushioned chairs. Good food, big prices. Petterino's is for the plumping and the plucking.

The theater connects through an interior doorway so that patrons, overfed and softly sweating, can be shepherded straight to their seats without being aroused by fresh outside air. Amanda always insisted that the Goodman offers mainstream productions, but to me the plays were confusing. And that, I used to say, is the point. Dulled by overeating at Petterino's, staggering straight into the dim plush of the theater, folks are further numbed by droning actors saying things that make no sense. The audience slips from stupor into sleep; it's the poultry man's intent. The Goodman is for the lulling.

Two hours later, the audience is jolted awake by the smattering of applause at the final curtain. Groggy, now disoriented by the sudden noise and lights, they're herded across the street to the garage, where they're made to wait in lines to pay a credit card machine that mumbles nonsensical instructions in an adenoidal, digitized voice, then funneled into other lines for a chance to push their way into one of the two overcrowded elevators. By the time they reach their cars, they're dripping sweat, their eyes bright with the need for escape. But the final chaos is yet to come. The automobile exit lanes all merge into one, and the flow quickly becomes choked, an impacted drain, backed up all the way to the roof. Trapped, frantic at the stoppage, the drivers whimper and slap at their horns, but the sudden, overwhelming noise only enrages them further. Control vanishes; it's every chicken for himself. They gun their engines, aim recklessly at imagined hair-width gaps in the line. Fenders crumple, voices scream. It is at this moment that they welcome death. The garage is for the slaughter.

And somewhere, unseen, the poultry farmer laughs.

To me, it is not amazing that people pay great sums to do this. What shocks is that they subscribe to do it several times a year.

Petterino's was crowded with pre-show diners. Amanda, now one of Chicago's wealthiest socialites, had been provided a quiet table in the corner. As she'd said on the phone, she wanted to talk.

I hadn't seen her since I'd dropped her into the welcoming arms of her father, his small army of heavily armed security men and, pacing in front of them all like a silvered peacock, her impeccably attired, suitably affluent new beau.

She looked magnificent as always, in dark slacks, a cream blouse and the garnet pendant I'd given her for her birthday.

I, in my blue blazer and the least wrinkled of my khaki pants, looked like a used office furniture salesman.

We ordered drinks and proceeded carefully. 'How's business?' she asked.

A scandal, stemming from a false accusation, had trashed my

business and our marriage. The business was resurrecting, though slowly.

'Two more old insurance company clients are using me again to verify accident information. It's not much, but it's a foot on the road to hope.'

'And the turret?' she asked. We were stilted, awkwardly catching up, but there was something else in her voice. Hesitation. She was stalling, not yet ready to tell me why she'd called.

'I've finished hanging the kitchen cabinets and am awaiting only the funds for new appliances. Now I'm up on the third floor.'

'The master bedroom,' she said. It had never been ours. We'd lived in her multi-million-dollar home in Crystal Waters, a gated community, before my career, our marriage, and then her neighborhood had blown up.

The bed, though, had been ours. She hadn't wanted it, but I'd not been willing to give up. I'd hauled it from her house before it had been reduced to rubble.

'I've built a closet,' I said, with as much pride as another man might say of a new Ferrari.

She sent a bemused glance toward the wrinkles in my blue button-down shirt.

'I don't as yet have hangers,' I said.

She smiled. 'Of course.'

'Any day now, some hotshot commodities trader is going to drive by, see my five-story limestone cylinder, and buy it for millions. The turret is my other foot on the road to hope.'

Her smile tightened. I'd slipped, seemingly into pettiness. Richard Rudolph, her silver-haired new beau, was a wealthy commodities trader, and precisely the sort of hotshot I was trying to snare.

'You are well, you and Mr Rudolph?' I asked of the hotshot, trying for casual. It had been some time since my friend Leo Brumsky had reported seeing their picture in the papers, always at some appropriately charitable event. I'd supposed that at some point, Leo had decided I didn't need to stay current on such news.

'He's in Russia – new opportunities,' she said, perhaps a little too quickly. Then, 'Jennifer Gale, the newswoman?' Her gaze was direct, her eyes unblinking.

We were catching up more pointedly now. 'How could you know . . .?'

'Your photo ran in the papers too, Dek. Some journalism awards dinner. She's as lovely in print as she is on television.'

Jennifer Gale had been a features reporter for Channel 8 in Chicago until she'd been offered newsier television opportunities in San Francisco. With me, though, she was Jenny Galecki, a sweet, solidly Polish girl struggling to mix celebrity and ambition with feelings for me. For eight months, we'd managed to stay involved, telephonically. And now I was about to head to San Francisco.

'She is lovely, yes,' I said.

For a moment, we let silence shelter us. We'd moved on, some.

I veered away, asked about her work. She'd given up teaching at the Art Institute to establish philanthropies in her father's name. Wendell Phelps, head of Chicago's largest electric utility, had come to regret being an indifferent parent, and had offered Amanda the chance to do really good things with really big money. It was an offer she did not refuse.

'He's moving me into operations. I'm day-to-day electricity now, Dek. I liaise with every city and town on our grid, building relationships. Philanthropy hasn't been on the agenda for several months.'

'He's prepping you for great responsibilities.'

'All of a sudden, he's in a rush.'

'He's the major shareholder. It's prudent to bring his only child into the family business. Lots of investment to protect.'

Our waitress came with drinks – a Manhattan for her; a first-ever, low-carb beer for me. As in old times, we ordered the everything-but-the-kitchen-sink salads that had long been one of the prides of Petterino's.

She stirred her drink for a long minute, and I took a pull from the bottle of de-carbed beer. It tasted like it had been run through something alive, perhaps hooved, to get the carbohydrates out.

She removed the cocktail stick, its cherry still impaled, and set it on the napkin. 'I've told my father to hire you,' she said.

'Whoa,' I said, understanding why she'd played too long with her drink. I set down the bottle of carb-less beer residue. 'Me, work for your father?'

Wendell Phelps was no admirer of mine. We'd never talked face-to-face, but we'd argued plenty on the phone after his daughter had been abducted. His arrogance, along with my stupidity, had almost gotten her killed.

'Actually we've discussed it several times. No, that's wrong. I've brought it up several times.'

'What, exactly?'

'He's hired bodyguards.'

'A deranged shareholder or some nut pissed about his electric bill?'

'He won't say.'

'The business pages say he's taking heat because of all the service outages. The governor and the mayor are pushing him for equipment upgrades, but the big shareholders don't want him to spend the money. It's a real tussle.'

I reached for the low-carb but quickly stopped my hand; drinking more might stick the taste to my tongue permanently. 'I also heard his stock price dropped. People have lost money. Maybe some cranky shareholder got wiped out.'

'He said it was nothing like that.'

'What then?'

She shook her head. 'He won't say, other than he hired an investigator to take care of it. The man found out nothing, apparently. My father looks old, Dek; old and afraid and weak.'

'Could that have something to do with his new wife?' Long a widower, Wendell's recent marriage lingered only briefly on the society pages before descending into the gossip blogs. The most charitable of them said the bride was charmingly eccentric.

'You're wondering whether she's driven him into becoming delusional? I don't think so. His fear is real.'

'Cops?'

'He hasn't gone to them.'

'What is it with rich people, so afraid of going to the police?' A bomb-wielding extortionist had assaulted the mega-rich home-owners in Crystal Waters, yet none of her neighbors wanted to call the cops. At least not until people started getting blown up.

'He said he'd talk to you.'

'Because if he didn't, you'd hire me yourself, and then he'd lose control of what I learned?'

She smiled a little. 'Of course.'

'No doubt he pointed out I'm a lightweight as far as investigators go, that I research records for lawyers, chase down accident information for insurance companies. I don't do life or death.'

'You did, for me.'

'I got you kidnapped.'

'Talk to him, Dek. Reassure me he's having some sort of small mental lapse. Tell me he's just feeling too many ordinary pressures.'

I smiled then, too, because ultimately that was what I always did with Amanda. Our salads came, and we smiled through them as well. Our awkwardness was disappearing.

After the play, she told me I'd slept through another magnificent performance. That was too close to old times, too.

THREE

Wendell Phelps's house, stone clad and slate roofed, loomed high, a dark fortress on the bluffs above Lake Michigan. To the south, the Chicago skyline was a blur in the gloom of the late March sky, as though it were a backdrop painted pale and inconsequential to make the magnificent mansion stand out even more. Down below, past the closely mowed lawn and the terrace of tightly trimmed yews, the lake lapped at the edge of the raked beach, gray and vaguely restless.

One of the doors in the five-car garage was open, exposing the tail end of what I knew was Wendell's old black Mercedes and, alongside it, the lighter-colored fender of something inexpensively American, likely belonging to a live-in housekeeper. I drove past the garage and stopped behind a dark brown Nissan pickup truck.

A young woman in her early twenties, wearing a brown sweatshirt that matched the truck, was picking shredded yellow flowers out of the concrete urns at the base of the front steps. Large money bought that; fresh flowers before spring. I got out of the Jeep and smiled at the girl, one tradesperson to another.

'Pigs,' she said, jamming the ruined blooms into a paper yardwaste bag.

'Ah, but they pay the bills,' I said, and walked up the stairs to the massive walnut door.

Amanda told me once that state senators, mayors and business leaders had been summoned to this house, but the only visitor who'd not been made to wait at the door like a pizza driver was the mop-headed former governor of Illinois, now doing prison time out west. Go figure, she'd said, laughing.

An unremarkable man answered the door. Not tall, not short; not dark haired, not blond; not young and certainly not old. Right down to the faint gray stripes in his bland blue suit, he was indistinct, an average man, a medium all around. The best ones are like that: mediums all around. They don't get noticed in a crowd. Only the slight bulge in his suit, under the left arm, gave him away. He was one of the bodyguards Amanda had mentioned, and he was packing.

I showed him my driver's license. 'Dek Elstrom to see Mr Phelps.'

'You're expected.' He pulled the door open all the way.

The foyer was dark, lit only by four small wall sconces. It was only after I'd followed him halfway across what seemed like a football field of black-and-white tile that I realized the walls were paneled in walnut as thick as the front door. That the head of Chicago's largest electric company was wasting none of the company product at home might have come from frugality. Or it could have come from fear.

The bodyguard knocked on a door, stepped aside, and motioned for me to enter. I went into a library as dim as the foyer. The curtains were drawn. The only light came from a yellow glass lamp on the desk in front of the curtains.

'Mr Elstrom,' Wendell Phelps said, rising from behind the lamp.

I'd seen his face in the business news and, of course, in the oil portrait I'd cut to make a Halloween mask in the last drunken days of my marriage. Those pictures were of a younger and more relaxed man. As he came closer, I saw lines deeper than any sixty-three-year-old should have. He wore golf clothes – yellow slacks to match the lamp, and a green knit shirt with a crocodile on it – as though he were about to go hit a bucket of balls in his foyer. The croc's mouth was open, which fit with what I knew of Wendell Phelps.

'Mr Phelps,' I said.

We sat on opposing sofas without shaking hands. A tan envelope lay on the low plank table between us. The only other thing on the table was a small framed photograph of a little girl holding a blue balloon. The picture might have been of Amanda, but it was too small to tell in such dim light.

'What has Amanda told you?' he asked.

'She said you hired bodyguards, one of which I saw for myself, and that you retained an investigator, who learned nothing.'

'We speak in confidence, you and I? You do not report back to Amanda?'

'So long as you're the client, and not her.'

He frowned at the reminder of his daughter's threat, and pushed the tan envelope an inch toward me. 'There have already been three murders.' His hand shook a little as he lifted it from the envelope.

There were three letter-sized sheets in the envelope. I held them up to catch the faint light from the desk. They were photocopies of obituaries from the *Chicago Tribune*, the big, quarter-page kind that ran with photographs when someone important died. Each of the three dead men had been prominent in Chicago business. The first had died of a heart attack the previous October, the second from cancer two months later, in December. The most recent had been the victim of a hit-and-run in February, just the month before. None of the obituaries implied murder. I slipped the three sheets back into the envelope and set it on the table.

'They were murdered,' he said.

'Did your investigator tell you this, or is this a hunch?'

'That man was ineffective, and I try never to rely on hunches.'

'Two deaths from illness, the third from a hit-and-run. Not the stuff of foul play.'

'They were CEOs of major corporations.'

His eyes seemed steady; his focus appeared good. Yet he seemed to be speaking gibbered paranoia.

'CEOs die just like ordinary people,' I said.

'They were murdered,' he said again.

'Because they were CEOs?'

'Don't patronize me, Elstrom.' He turned around to look at the heavy curtains. A thin sliver of light, half the width of a pencil, shone where the two fabric panels did not quite meet. He got up and went to pull them together.

'Yes,' he said, remaining by the curtains as though worried they'd open again on their own. 'I believe they were killed because they were CEOs.'

I stood then, and walked to the desk. Another tiny picture frame had caught my eye. 'For what motive?' I asked, picking up the photo.

It was the same as the one on the plank table: a little girl holding a blue balloon. I wondered whether it was the only childhood photo he had of Amanda.

'I'm hiring you to find that out,' he said.

'To keep your daughter from nosing into it?'

'She need not worry about this.'

'A plot to kill major business executives would surely interest the brass of the Chicago Police Department. They'll investigate for free.'

'A man with my links to the business community would lose credibility if such accusations were seen as unsubstantiated, or worse, just plain crazy. The effect on my shareholders would be disastrous. Gather sufficient information, Elstrom, and then I'll go to the police.'

He handed me a folded check from the pocket of his golf shirt. It was for two thousand dollars.

It was too big a retainer to indulge what seemed like a rich man's delusion, and it was more than I'd made in the last two months. I put the check in my pocket.

He reached to pinch the seam in the curtains, though no light was coming through. Whatever the man's tensions were, they were very real to him. I took the manila envelope and showed myself out into the hall. The Medium Man was waiting, and together we made footstep echoes across the marble to the front door.

The flower girl had almost finished replacing the shredded yellow blossoms with vibrant, dark red blooms. I winked at her as I came down the concrete stairs.

She frowned. 'Pigs,' she said.

FOUR

The Bohemian's offices are on the top floor of a ten-story rehabbed yellow brick factory on the west side of Chicago. The ancient wrought-iron elevator doors opened right into the reception area. Earnest-looking bond and stock-fund sales-people, wearing good suits and carrying thin attachés, sat on the green leather wing chairs and sofas, studying the proposals they were about to pitch to the Bohemian's staff of financial advisors. I crossed the red oriental carpet to the black walnut reception desk.

'Dek Elstrom, wondering if I might have a moment of Mr Chernek's time.'

The receptionist was new, a tanned brunette at least a decade shy of murmuring the word 'Botox.' She flashed a perfect white smile. 'Do you have an appointment, Mr Elstrom?'

I shook my head. 'If you would just ask?'

'Certainly, sir.' She pushed a button on her telephone console and said my name with a question mark into the thin mouthpiece of her headset.

Behind me, I thought I heard the uneasy shifting of good wool. The tailored suits had sensed a sudden intrusion of polyester. Though my blue blazer, with but the merest hint of mustard on the left cuff, had a forty-five per cent wool content, a blend is a blend, and was as out of place in that reception area as a bongo drummer at a chamber recital. Even the grandfather clock in the corner seemed to stop ticking, anticipating my swift dispatch.

Buffy, the Bohemian's frozen-faced, helmet-haired assistant, materialized in less than a minute to hold the door open for me. And a woman in one of the green leather chairs behind me sighed.

In a different life, I couldn't have gotten into Anton Chernek's offices to wash the windows. He's an advisor – a *consigliere* to Chicago's most prominent families, the ones whose names adorn the city's museums and parks, endow its philanthropies, and attend its most fashionable events. I imagined his financial counseling was straightforward enough – the usual recommendations on blue-chip stocks, bonds, mutual funds and such – but it's his role as the go-to guy for other, touchier concerns that defines his real value to the city's ruling elite. When a problem arises that cannot be handled traditionally – a divorce arising from the gamier appetites of human behavior; a scion caught cheating at a prestigious university; an embezzlement within a family firm – the rich summon the Bohemian. He is wise and he is discreet. He makes problems go away quietly, with smiling assurances, packets of cash and, if need be, swift retribution.

We first met when he accompanied Amanda's lawyers to our divorce settlement conference. He'd liked that I'd brought no lawyer and no demands. Months later, he hired me to uncover who'd begun blowing up houses in Amanda's gated community. The case got more gnarly when Chernek was accused of embezzling from his clients. The charge was false, but he was publicly humiliated, and that cost him most of his staff and, for a time, many of his clients.

I knew about false accusations, so I didn't pile on. I kept on reporting to him as though nothing had happened. He never forgot that, or the fact that I never hit him up for freebie financial advice about how to manage the 250 dollars I'd rat-holed in a passbook savings account.

'*Vuh-lo-dek*,' he boomed from behind his carved desk, stretching the two syllables into three. I'm named for my grandfather, a handle that charmed the Bohemian the first time we met. He's been the only one. Not even an animal used to extract carbohydrates from beer should be named Vlodek.

I sat in one of the burgundy leather guest chairs. The Bohemian was around sixty, and a big man, just shy of my six feet two. Today he wore a pale yellow, spread-collar shirt with a figured navy tie that perfectly matched the color of the custom coat hanging on his antique mahogany coat rack. His teeth gleamed; his tan glowed. Not a single combed-back silver hair was out of place.

'You're prospering, Anton,' I said.

'Times are fine, Vlodek. And you?'

'Improving.' I handed him Wendell Phelps's tan envelope. 'I'm interested in these three men.'

He removed the photocopies. He might well have been on

retainer with the men whose obituaries he was now reading, but his face betrayed nothing. The Bohemian respected confidences, even with the dead.

'Fine businessmen, in the heavy cream,' he said, looking up. 'Right up at the top with your ex-father-in-law.' He leaned forward slightly. 'Why do their deaths interest you?'

'A client is wondering if anything about those deaths was overlooked.'

He nodded, respecting my need to maintain confidentiality. 'How may I help?'

'How well did you know these men?'

He eased back in his chair. 'Two of them quite well. The third, Grant Carson, the one who got killed by a car last month, I'd met only at social functions.'

'Have there been rumors about their deaths?'

'None that I've heard. It was no surprise that Benno Barberi died of a heart attack last October. His friends knew he had a bad heart,' he said. 'Jim Whitman's death last December came after a long illness, also as the *Tribune* said. That's true enough, as far as it goes, but technically his was a suicide. Jim was dying, and he swallowed all his painkillers at one time. The papers had the decency not to print that, though it's widely known. As for Carson's hit-and-run, you'll have to check with the police. They haven't found the driver, but I don't believe they saw it as anything other than a tragic accident.' He slipped the papers back into the envelope. 'How is Wendell Phelps, Vlodek?' His smile had become sly, venturing a guess about who had hired me.

I gave back just enough of a grin to keep him wondering. 'How many men in Chicago are like these three?'

'Of their stature in business? Off the top of my head, I'd say perhaps fifty.'

'May I have a list?'

The Bohemian's eyes worked to get behind my own. 'You'll keep me apprised?' Meaning that I'd alert him to anyone I thought might be in trouble. Client safety was always his major concern.

'Of course.' It was a necessary quid pro quo.

'I'll email names,' he said.

FIVE

Traffic was backed up solid on the outbound expressway. No matter the years of supposed improvements, the Eisenhower is almost always a crawl. In my darker moments, I let myself think a secret cabal of oil and communications executives engineered it that way, to trap drivers into burning up expensive gallons of gasoline while raging on their phones, burning up cell-plan minutes. Like my Goodman Theater imaginings, it's baloney – a poor man's cranky fantasy and flimsy as a cobweb – but ever since the Jeep's radio got boosted, it's given my mind something to mull when I'm stuck on the Ike.

I wondered if that sort of paranoia got notched up inside Wendell Phelps. The *Tribune* had seen nothing suspicious in the deaths of Barberi and Whitman, nor had they reported Carson's death as anything more sinister than a typical hit-and-run. More calming was the Bohemian's ear. It was finely tuned, and he kept it pressed to the ground, yet nothing about the three deaths had tripped his sensors. Likely enough, Wendell Phelps had given me nothing more than a dark delusion, except his came with the money to pursue it. Me, I had to get stuck in traffic, sucking auto exhaust, to indulge mine.

I got back to Rivertown as the dying sun began turning the turret's rough limestone blocks into a hundred soft shades of yellow, orange, and red. My narrow five story cylinder is always beautiful at sunset, with its shadows and fiery colors, marked hard here and there with the black stripes of the slit windows, but it can be melancholy then as well, a slim monument in dying light to a dead man's dead dream. The turret was my grandfather's fantasy. A small-time bootlegger with big-time plans, he built it as the first of four that were to connect with stone walls to form a grand castle on the bank of the Willahock River. The one turret was all he got built. He died broke, leaving behind only a corner of his dream.

I walked down to the river to count leaves. When I'd moved to the turret on the first of a November several years before, out of money and out of hope, the spindly purple ash growing alongside the water had already turned its expected autumn purple color and seemed healthy enough. The next July, after a normal spring, it suddenly shed its leaves. By then, that summer had already gone bad. My records research business was struggling to survive and I was trapped in a seemingly hopeless bomb and extortion case that I could not puzzle through. I took the hollow clacking noise the dying ash's branches made, in the wind, in the night, as one more sign the world wasn't spinning right.

I didn't need new signs of bad times. When the next new spring came and the other trees along the Willahock began budding and my ash still resembled nothing but upright kindling, I went out with a pole saw. Better to cut it down than to suffer its death rattle in the night any longer.

I started at the top, sawing and pulling, until all of its brittle upper branches lay on the ground. But as I reset the ladder to cut off one of its two main limbs, I spotted the tiniest tendril of green, no longer than an inchworm, protruding from the bark. I don't know trees but I know trying, and I left that ash as I'd butchered it: a dinosaur-sized wishbone, thrust upright in defiance against the sky.

Several years had passed since then, and it was still slow going for me, and for the ash. Yet once again, in this new spring, the tree was unfurling tiny new leaves like little flags of hope. It was only the end of March, too soon to know how many would come, but I kept count as I had in previous springs, as an act of faith. That night, a fresh sprout brought the new spring's total up to twenty-six.

I take my positive omens wherever I can find them.

I spent two hours on the Internet that evening and found nothing to counter what the *Trib* and the Bohemian's ear had concluded. There had been nothing premeditated about the deaths of Benno Barberi, Jim Whitman or Grant Carson. Still, I planned to give the deaths a long, last mull on the plane west to San Francisco the next day, before calling Wendell to tell him I'd be refunding almost all of his money. Though with that, painfully, would go my hopes to replace my leaking refrigerator.

I took a flashlight into the kitchen, laid it in the refrigerator, shut the door and turned off the lights. A pinpoint sparkled next to where the handle was coming loose; air was leaking out there. As I'd told Jenny, such a small rust-through would be easily contained by a Golden Gate Bridge refrigerator magnet.

Happy times – seeing Jenny, and acquiring a magnet – seemed just around the corner as I reclined in the electric-blue La-Z-Boy, also salvaged from an alley, to watch the start of the ten o'clock news.

And then the Bohemian called.

His voice did not resonate with its usual optimism. 'I started on the list of names at six o'clock. It was fairly straightforward to establish who our prominent businesspeople are, and I was done by seven o'clock. There are forty-six,' he said, then paused. 'No,' he corrected, 'there *were* forty-six, before the three deaths.'

'This afternoon you guessed fifty. Pretty close, Anton.'

'Life is not so much about numbers as it is about percentages, Vlodek. That's why the three deaths are troubling.'

I shifted the La-Z-Boy to full upright and silenced the four-inch television balanced on my lap. 'Percentages?'

'Three is too many.'

'Two of the three were men in their sixties, and ill,' I said. 'The third was fifty-five, not that it matters, and the victim of a hit-and-run. All three deaths seem easily explainable.'

'Remember the heavy cream?'

'You said all three were among the top fifty business people in Chicago.'

'I misspoke. I meant to use the term more narrowly, to define Barberi, Whitman and Carson as being among the very top of the city's leaders, in the heaviest of the cream, so to speak.'

'I don't understand.'

'I just told you there were forty-six top-flight business leaders in Chicago, right?'

'With Barberi, Whitman, and Carson among them.'

'The forty-six was a simple ranking of business prominence. I then filtered that list to include only those individuals prominent in civic, political and charitable endeavors as well.'

'Only those are in the heavy cream,' I said.

'Exactly. I got down to sixteen names.'

'Of which three are now dead?'

'That's troubling. Nineteen per cent of the most influential people in Chicago – three of only sixteen – died in the last four months. Mathematically, that's beyond reason.'

Anton Chernek never indulged false alarm. He was too level-headed, too grounded. And almost always too well informed.

'I'll say again, Anton: two were older and ill. The third, Carson, got whacked by a passing car.'

'Yes, and I was inclined to accept it as an anomaly, an explainable oddity.'

'Exactly—'

He cut me off. 'Arthur Lamm has gone missing.'

'Arthur Lamm, as in head of Lamm Enterprises?' Lamm headed a conglomerate of real estate sales, management, and insurance brokerages. He was very prominent: a political player and a close friend of the mayor. There was no doubt he was in the heavy cream.

'A vice-president of his insurance company told me he's not called in for four days. Do you see what this means?'

I barely heard his voice. My mind was forming the word that I knew he wanted.

'Vlodek?' he asked after a minute.

'Percentages,' I said, giving it to him.

'Arthur's only fifty-one and, from all accounts, he's in peak condition. A marathoner, in fact. If he's met a bad end, he increases your list to four out of sixteen.'

'That's twenty-five per cent.'

He murmured something about emailing me his list of names in the morning and hung up.

I needed fresher air in which to think. I went outside to sit on the bench by the river. A small speck lay on the ground, almost colorless in the pale white light of the lamp along the crumbling asphalt river walk.

It was one of the would-be leaves from the purple ash, curled up, stillborn and dry.

Sometimes I don't like omens at all.

SIX

I woke at five-thirty in the morning, remembering the Bohemian's anxiety about percentages too much to go back to sleep. I put on jeans, a sweatshirt and my Nikes and, stepping around the duffel that lay on the floor, still to be packed for California, I went downstairs.

The Bohemian wasn't having a good night either. He'd emailed me his list two hours earlier.

I printed his list, put on my pea coat and took a travel mug of yesterday's cold coffee up the stairs and then the ladders to the fifth floor and the roof. I like to believe I think best on top of the turret. Even when I don't, the dawn likely as not serves up a spectacular sunrise, and that's a good enough reason to go up on any roof at the end of the dark. I leaned against the balustrade, sipped coffee and looked out across the spit of land at Rivertown, waiting for the cold caffeine and the chilled, pre-dawn air to rouse me from a sleep that never much was.

The town was softly shutting down. The tonks along Thompson Avenue were switching off their flickering neon lights, discharging their last, hardiest customers into the night. The slow-walking girls who smiled into the headlights of the slow-cruising gentlemen were shuffling away too, alone at last. And from somewhere down by the river, the sound of shattering glass rose above the rasping staccato of automobile tires hitting the rub strips on the tollway; a trembling hand had let go of an empty pint. Rivertown was twitching itself to sleep.

The thin hint of orange rising over Lake Michigan was bright enough to read what the Bohemian had sent. He'd drawn a simple grid, labeled it 'H.C.' for Heavy Cream – a wit, that Bohemian, even when troubled. On the left side of the sheet he'd listed the sixteen primo shakers of Chicago in alphabetical order. Across the page he'd made columns for the criteria he'd used to select them: business affiliations, political access, social and civic relationships. He'd assigned letter grades for each person, for each category, like a report card. Almost all of the boxes were filled with an 'A.'

All but two on the list were men. The Bohemian's Chicago, that world of vast money coupled to political and social influence, was still very much a boys' club. The names seemed vaguely familiar in the way that names captioned under society news photographs often seem familiar. Yet if asked, I couldn't have said what most of the primos in the heavy cream had done to achieve their prominence. My own world existed farther down, in the muck stuck to the bottom of what was Chicagoland.

The Bohemian had put asterisks next to the names of Barberi, Carson and Whitman. In the middle of the page, next to the name of the missing Arthur Lamm, he'd first drawn a question mark, then added an asterisk.

Asterisk meant death. It was those four asterisks, those four names out of sixteen, which had kept the Bohemian up in the night.

It was the fifth person on the list, four lines below Arthur Lamm's, who had put me in a trick bag: Wendell Phelps. For that, I now hated the son of a bitch even more than before.

My history with the man was limited. I'd called Wendell's office right after Amanda and I married, thinking it reasonable to introduce myself as the man who'd wed the daughter he hadn't seen in years – and maybe become a hero to my new wife, by effecting a reconciliation between the two.

I never got past the secretary to his secretary. No matter, I thought; there would be time to try again later.

There wasn't. I was soon implicated in a fake evidence scheme, having erroneously authenticated cleverly doctored checks in a high-profile insurance fraud trial. My name flashed dark across the front pages of Chicago's newspapers, there not for the notoriety of the trial, or my sloppiness, but because I was Wendell Phelps's son-in-law. I was soon found to be innocent, but I was guilty of being stupid – and of being Wendell's son-in-law. The publicity vaporized my credibility and killed my records research business. Unmoored, I poured alcohol on my self-pity. I blamed Wendell for my notoriety and found that so satisfying that, with the logic of someone totally lost to alcohol, I spread that blame to Amanda for being my link to him. No matter that she'd been estranged from her father for years. In my twisted, liquored logic, she was a most convenient target, and that was enough for me.

It was too much for Amanda. She filed for divorce and I got flushed out of her gated community – appropriately enough, on Halloween – unmasked as a fool.

I crawled back to Rivertown, the town I thought I'd escaped years before, and into the rat-infested turret I'd inherited from another failed man, my grandfather. Amanda fled to Europe, because she had no good place to go either. As I sobered up, I blamed Wendell Phelps for that, too. No matter that I'd trashed his daughter's life; he could have descended from his executive suite to help undo the damage I'd done.

Amanda and Wendell later reconciled, so much so that he enticed Amanda to quit her jobs writing art books and teaching at the Art Institute to join his utilities conglomerate.

He and I had never had need for reconciling anything. We were done, and that was fine for us both.

Except now he was bringing new breath to old furies. If I misplayed his case, investigated what were delusions too seriously, the press might get wind of it and trigger his public humiliation. Worse, if the Bohemian's fears of percentages were accurate and there really was a murderer out there, targeting Wendell and his ilk, my misplaying the case could get people killed.

Damn the man, Wendell Phelps.

By now, the glow of sunrise had risen above the massive dark shapes of Chicago to touch the top of the turret. Mine is the tallest building in Rivertown, a modest attainment in a town of abandoned factories, huddled bungalows and deserted storefronts. The only grand building in town, a city hall of long terraces, expansive private offices and tiny public rooms, was still in the darkness behind me. It, too, had been built of my grandfather's limestone, but later, by corrupt city managers who saw no shame in seizing most of his widow's land and all of its great pile of unused stone blocks. But those lizards couldn't take the sun, nor change the fact that it always lit the turret first every day. I took satisfaction in that.

I crossed the roof to look down at the river. The sunrise would soon light the butchered, two-limbed ash, causing it to cast a dark, jagged 'V' west along the river path. The shadow would look like a giant, crooked-fingered hex, a Greek *moutza* of contempt, thrust directly at Rivertown's corrupt city hall. I took satisfaction in that, too.

Likely enough, there would be no satisfaction in the direction I was now heading.

Damn the man, Wendell Phelps.

SEVEN

N ews of Arthur Lamm's disappearance had not yet hit the Internet, so I searched for more information on Grant Carson's hit-and-run, the most recent of the deaths in the heavy cream. There was plenty of speculation over the impact his passing would have on his international conglomerate, but there were very few facts surrounding the hit-and-run, and no suspicion that his death had been premeditated murder.

On a day in early February, just after midnight, Grant Carson had pulled his Lincoln Town Car sharply to a curb, got out and was struck by a passing car. He was thrown twenty feet and died instantly. The police noted that by all appearances it had been an accident: Carson had stepped out of his car without checking for oncoming traffic; a car had struck him. Panicked, the driver sped away. The police were seeking anyone who might have witnessed the accident.

I phoned a dozen of my insurance company contacts to learn who'd carried policies on Carson's life. I wasn't interested in beneficiary information; I was hoping an insurance company's private investigation had yielded more than the few facts the cops had released. It was the kind of work I used to do often, before I got tangled up in scandal. I struck gold nowhere, but got promises that others would ask around.

By now it was eight o'clock in the morning in California. I called Jenny. 'I've got a job,' I said.

'A trip-canceling job?'

'More like a trip-rescheduling job.'

'It's life or death, this case?'

'I'm fearing that.'

'What aren't you telling me?' Her newswoman's antennae had picked up words I'd not used.

'Amanda's father is the client.'

'And Amanda – she's involved, too?'

'Only to have steered me to her father. I'm working for him.'

'We were going to have such an amazing four days,' she said, dropping her voice.

'I know.'

'An amazingly lustful four days,' she said, whispering now.

'Oh, how I'd hoped . . .' I said.

'Oh, how I hope you'd hoped,' she whispered one last time, and hung up.

Mercifully, in the next instant I got a call to change the direction of my thwarted naughty thoughts. It was from Gaylord Rikk. He worked for one of Carson's insurers.

'What's your interest?' he asked.

'One of Carson's rich friends asked me to follow up to see if anything new has been uncovered,' I said, trying for casual.

'Ask the cops.'

'I will. What's the status of your investigation?'

'There is none. We've closed our file.'

'So soon?'

'It's been over a month. The police have no leads.'

'The area where Carson got hit is upscale, full of nightlife. It was only midnight. Surely someone saw something.'

'Only midnight,' Rikk agreed, 'in a late-night district that's full of Starbucks, young bucks and sweet girls.'

'Nobody was headed home after a late last purple cocktail or out walking a designer dog?'

He gave me the sort of long sigh one gives an idiot. 'Remember a few years ago, some young woman hit a homeless guy with her car, knocked him up over her hood and half through the windshield?'

'Everyone remembers that.'

'She drove all the way home with the guy stuck, head first, through her windshield. That was at midnight, too, when there were other cars on the road and people out walking. She pulled into her garage with the poor bastard still alive, his head and upper body leaking fluids into her car. He pleaded with her to get him help. Nope. She left him as he was and went into the house – though at the trial she assured the judge she did come out several times to apologize profusely to the guy for ruining his day, or whatever.'

It was the kind of thing I thought about, up on the roof in the middle of the night. 'The guy finally bled out.'

'The point is that she drove through town with the guy's ass sticking out of her windshield, and nobody reported anything. She got caught only when she asked a few friends over to help remove the body. It was one of them who called the cops.'

'Was is mechanical difficulty that forced Carson to the curb, or was he drunk?'

'Neither. No mechanical problems, other than a right front wheel bent from hitting the curb. His blood alcohol was under the limit. He wasn't drunk.'

'You think he was forced over?'

'And got out mad to confront another driver who'd stopped, or just to inspect his car for damage? Possible scenarios, both of them.'

'Why get out at all? If his car was not drivable, why not call AAA or someone else for help?'

'We don't know. He had a cell phone. He didn't use it.'

'What about paint from the car that hit Carson?'

'No sample was recovered from his body or the smashed-back driver's door. Don't trust what you see on TV. Paint doesn't always transfer. Plus, the point of impact could have been glass or stainless or chrome-plated steel, or the car could have had one of those front-end bra things.'

'One of those vinyl covers yuppies used to put on the fronts of their BMWs to protect against stone dings?'

'You still see one, now and again,' he said, 'though most everybody knows they do their own damage, flapping against the paint. All I'm saying is there are all sorts of reasons why paint doesn't transfer.'

'The cops played it by the book, sent out alerts to body shops?'

'Ideally, but there again, those bulletins work mostly on television. Hit-and-run drivers are ordinary people who freak out. They panic, stick the car in the garage and don't open the door for anything. After a day or two of dry puking and no sleep, they get the idea to dump the car in a bad neighborhood with its keys in the ignition and report it stolen. It almost always works; the car gets boosted and stripped. Hit-and-run cars never get brought to legitimate body shops.'

'Where did Carson have dinner?'

'Somewhere north, I suppose, near where he was killed. He lives up that way, in Lincoln Park. The payout's being processed, Elstrom. The case is dead.'

I called the Bohemian. 'Any news on Arthur Lamm?'

'Perhaps there's been much ado about nothing. He has a camp somewhere up in the piney woods of Wisconsin. He does the real outdoors stuff: small boat, small tent, eating what he catches swimming in the water or crawling on the ground.' The Bohemian's tone of disgust made it sound like Lamm dined on roadkill. 'Anyway, Arthur has some guy who stops in from time to time to check on the place. He said one of Arthur's boats is missing.'

'Meaning Lamm is off somewhere camping.'

He offered up a chuckle that sounded forced. 'I might be imagining evil everywhere, in my old age.'

I asked if he could put me close to people who knew Barberi and Whitman.

'I'm not just imagining, Vlodek?'

'I like to be thorough.'

'I'll call you back.'

He did, in fifteen minutes. 'Anne Barberi is at home. You can go right over.'

'You told her what I'm looking into?'

'Here's the odd part: I didn't have time. She interrupted, saying she'd receive you immediately. She's anxious to talk.'

EIGHT

Anne Barberi lived at the Stanford Arms, a tall, upscale gray brick-and-granite building across from the Lincoln Park Zoo. While the upper floors surely provided magnificent vistas of

Lake Michigan, I imagined the lower apartments occasionally offered troubling views of coupling chimpanzees, and suspected that those units were equipped with electrified, fast-closing drapes. Even when living the good life along Chicago's Gold Coast, the rich had to be vigilant.

A parking valet leaning against a Mercedes straightened up with a pained look on his face, likely soured by the clatter of my arrival. I thought about pulling in to give him a closer blast of my rusted exhaust, but the thrill wouldn't have been worth the parking charge. I drove on, found a spot on a street four blocks over, and hoofed back.

The lobby was enormous, dark and deserted except for two potted palms and two potted elderly ladies, slumped in peach-colored velvet wing chairs, sipping fruited whiskies. The oily-haired man behind the oak reception counter scanned my khakis, blue button-down shirt and blazer like he was looking for resale shop tags.

'Dek Elstrom to see Mrs Barberi,' I said to the oiled man.

'Photo identification, sir?'

I gave him my driver's license. As he studied it, and then me, the corners of his mouth turned down, as if he were wondering whether the blue shirt in the photo was the same one I was wearing. Such was wealth, I wanted to tell him. Even I didn't know; I had three.

'A moment, sir,' the man said, handing back my license. He picked up the phone, tapped three digits and said my name. Nodding, he hung up. 'Mrs Barberi is expecting you.'

I turned and almost ran into a burly fellow who had noiselessly slipped up behind me.

'Mr Reeves will show you to the elevator,' the oiled man said.

He meant Mr Reeves would show me only to the elevator, and nowhere else. We walked to the farthest of the three sets of polished brass elevator doors and Mr Reeves pressed the button. I stepped in and the doors closed before I could ask which floor was Anne Barberi's.

There was no need. The elevator panel had only one button, and it was not numbered. After a short whir and the merest tug of gravity, the doors opened directly into a rose-colored, marble-floored foyer. A gray-haired woman wearing a lavender knit suit stood waiting. Likely enough, she hadn't strung the jumbo pearls around her wrinkled neck from a kit.

'I'm Anne Barberi,' she said, extending a hand that was as firm and in command as her voice. I followed her to a small sitting room. She sat on a hardwood ladder-back chair; I sat on a rock hard, brocaded settee. Freshly cut yellow flowers sat just as stiff between us, on a black-lacquered table.

'Mr Chernek tells me you have questions concerning my husband's death,' she said.

'I'm afraid they're not very specific.'

'At whose behest are you conducting your inquiry?'

I'd considered inventing a lie, but decided simply to stonewall to protect Wendell's identity. Truths are always easier to remember than lies. 'One of your husband's associates,' I said.

'Within Barberi Holdings?'

'No.'

'Fair enough, for now.' She folded her hands in her lap.

'I understand Mr Barberi had a long history of heart disease,' I said.

'For twenty years, he'd been careful, monitoring his choles-terol, exercising under supervision, watching his diet. At work, he chose very able assistants, young men and women who could shoulder much of the stress. My husband was cautious with his heart, Mr Elstrom, which is why I am interested in what you are doing.'

'I'm merely gathering facts, for now.'

She studied me for a moment, realized I wasn't going to offer more, and went on. 'As I said, Benno kept a tight lid on the pres-sures of his job. Until the night he died, when he lost control. He came home from a dinner furious, literally trembling because he was so upset. I tried to get him to sit and tell me what had happened, but he would not. He went into his study, and a few minutes later, I heard him shouting into the phone.' She looked down at her hands. She'd clenched them so tight the knuckles had whitened. Pulling them apart, she looked up. 'I found him in there the next morning, slumped over his desk.'

'Do you have any idea who he'd called?'

'I assumed one of his subordinates, but I really don't know.'

'No one thought to question what set him off?'

'Come to think of it, no.'

'Can we find out?'

'Surely you're not sensing something deliberate, are you?'

'I like to check everything out.'

'His secretary might be able to help.' She reached for the phone next to the vase and dialed a number. 'Anne, Joan. Fine, fine,' she said, brushing away the obligatory questions about her well-being. 'I've asked a friend, a Mr Elstrom, to find out something for me. I want to know with whom Benno was speaking on the phone, the night he died. It was about some matter that upset him greatly.' She paused to listen, then said, 'I'll tell Mr Elstrom you'll call him to set up an appointment.' She read the number from the business card I'd given her, then hung up.

'Joan was Benno's secretary for years,' she said. 'She knows things she'll never tell me, but she's always been loyal to Benno. And unlike me, she did think to inquire with whom Benno was speaking the night he passed away. He'd set up a conference call with two of his subordinates. She'll make them available to you.'

She walked me into the foyer and pushed the elevator button. 'It was not like Benno to allow himself to become so upset, Mr Elstrom. I won't ask again what you're pursuing, but I expect the courtesy of a report when you're done.'

I said I'd tell her what I could, when I could. As I stepped into the elevator, it seemed likeliest that Benno Barberi had simply lost control as accidentally as had the driver of the freak passing car that had smacked Grant Carson. But as the elevator descended, I imagined I heard the Bohemian's voice intermingled in the soft whine of the motor, whispering urgently about the certainty of percentages. And by the time the door opened, I almost knocked over the burly Mr Reeves in my haste to get out. I hurried across the tomb-like foyer, silent except for the ancient ladies gently snoring beside their drained whiskies, and out into the daylight.

I called the Bohemian from the sidewalk. 'Any luck on getting someone close to Whitman to talk to me?'

'He was a widower. I left a message, and your cell number, for his daughter, Debbie Goring.'

'She'll call soon?'

'My God, Vlodek, do I detect urgency?'

'I don't know.'

'You've seen Anne Barberi?'
'I just left her.'
'And?'
'Call Debbie Goring again.'

NINE

I was stuck waiting for the Bohemian to set up a call from Whitman's daughter, Debbie Goring. I could do it pacing the planks at the turret, or I could indulge in the illusion of exercise at the Rivertown Heath Center. I chose illusion.

The health center is a stained, yellowish brick pile that used to be a YMCA, back when young people came to work in Rivertown's factories and needed rooms, and running was considered exercise instead of a means of fleeing the police. Nowadays, the health center still has a running track and exercise equipment, and it still offers rooms, though now the equipment is rusted and the rooms are occupied by down-and-out drinkers working only half-heartedly to stay alive.

I knew those foul-smelling, dimly lit rooms. After being flushed, drunk, out of Amanda's gated community, I spent the night at the health center, as vacant-eyed as any of the grizzlies who puddled the upstairs halls. Waking the next morning in a room still damp from the pine-scented cleaner used to mask the death of its previous occupant, I looked up and recognized rock bottom. I moved into the turret, clear-eyed for the first time in weeks, and began inching my way back to life.

I still come to the health club. The exercise doesn't hurt, and the sting of pine-scented cleaner in my eyes and nose is a fine reminder not to slip that far again.

I eased over the potholes and parked in my usual spot next to the doorless Buick. As always, the lot was empty except for a half-dozen thumpers – high-school-age toughs in training – leaning against the husks of several other abandoned cars. I made a show of leaving my door unlocked. There was no sense in making them rip the duct tape from my plastic side curtains only to see that the seats had already been slashed and the radio boosted from the dash.

Downstairs, I changed into my red shorts and blue Cubs T-shirt quietly, pretending not to disturb the towel attendant pretending to sleep at the counter. Authentically, he was even drooling on the short pile of stained towels. Nobody minded; nobody dared use them. As with the Jeep, I left my locker door unlocked. The attendant need not dull his bolt cutters only to see I'd not left my wallet or keys inside.

Normally, raucous laughter from the exercise floor echoed down into the stairwell – chatter from the men in their sixties and seventies, retired from jobs that no longer existed, who came not to exercise but to laugh and sigh and share old stories. Not so today. The stairs to the exercise floor were eerily silent.

I understood when I got to the top. The regulars were all there – Dusty, Nick, Frankie and the others – roosting as usual on the rusted fitness machines like crows on felled trees. But that day, nobody was joking. They were staring across the exercise floor.

'Purr,' Dusty said softly.

'Doo,' Frankie murmured, almost worshipfully.

The others nodded, staring, just as transfixed as Dusty and Frankie. Big, yellow-toothed grins split their wrinkled faces.

Across the floor was a woman. She was no ordinary woman. She was a big woman, a jaw-droppingly huge woman, the biggest woman I'd ever seen. She was at least six-foot eight and three hundred pounds, but she packed no fat. Every ounce of her was perfectly proportioned, solid and muscular. And she was beautiful, with golden skin and long, dark hair. She was stretching and bending with the grace of a tiny ballerina, curving her body in such lazy, perfectly fluid motions that I could only imagine what long-smoldering embers were being fanned into a full blaze in the minds of the exercise room regulars.

She turned, so that her back was towards us.

'Purr,' Dusty said.

'Doo,' Frankie added.

The Amazonian goddess wore black collegiate exercise shorts, emblazoned with the university's name in yellow letters across the rump. Those kind of printed shorts are designed with a gap in the middle letters, to allow the fabric in the center to curve into the cleft of the buttocks, yet still be read as one word. But her shorts, probably a man's double extra-large, were stretched so taut that the name read as two distinct words: 'PUR' and 'DUE'.

I left the old men to the frenzy of their imaginations and ran laps.

Amanda called my cell phone that evening. 'Still in town?'

'Yes.'

'Is that worrisome?'

'Tying up little loose ends, is all.'

'My father said you stopped by.'

'Yesterday.'

'How come you didn't then call right away to say he's delusional?'

'I'm trying to be thorough, dot my "t"s, cross my "i"s.'

'Don't dodge with cheap humor.'

'I report to your father, not to you.'

She took a breath. 'You think there's something to his fears?'

'Probably not.'

'Now I am worried.'

'Don't be. There are just a couple of wrinkles I want to check out.'

'*Wrinkles?*'

Too late, I realized she remembered my hot word. A wrinkle was my slang for something troubling enough to require being checked thoroughly.

I tried to joke. 'The older I get the more I'm like an aging beauty queen. Even the smallest wrinkles demand more attention than they're worth.'

She let it go because she knew I wouldn't say more. We tried other, smaller talk but it was stilted, like the stuff of two people passing time, sharing a cab. After another moment, I invented an excuse to get off the phone. She didn't try to find an excuse to stop me.

I supposed that, too, was a wrinkle.

TEN

Benno Barberi's secretary called just before nine the next morning. I'd been up since five, varnishing wood trim for the third-floor closet and thinking about men dead in the heavy cream. She asked if I could meet with Barberi's two assistants at one o'clock. I said that was convenient. She said fine.

Barberi Holdings, Inc. was headquartered north of Chicago, in a concrete building sunk low, like a bunker, into the rolling close-cut grass alongside the Tri-State Toll Road. The interior was just as hard – concrete walls and a blue quarry tile floor. The receptionist took my name and motioned me to wait on one of the immense, curved white leather sofas. As I sat, my left blazer sleeve grazed the sofa cushion. And stuck. I tugged it free and turned it for a look. A smashed drop of varnish sparkled next to the spot of yellow mustard I'd forgotten to rub off.

I draped my sticky left arm high on the back of the sofa and used my right hand to leaf through a *Forbes* magazine. The issue featured the 400 wealthiest people on the planet. Their brief biographies were disappointing. None of them had made their fortunes rehabbing architectural oddities.

A young man named Brad came for me after five minutes. He wore a blue suit and had an impeccable haircut. He brought me to a small conference room where another young man, this one named Jason, stood waiting. He also looked to have recently visited Brad's barber. His blue suit was the identical shade of Brad's, as was my blazer. But mine, I guessed, was the only one sporting a shiny speck of varnish and the merest blush of yellow mustard.

We sat at the round table and Brad began. 'We understand Mrs Barberi is interested in the problem we discussed with Mr Barberi the night he died?'

'She told me her husband took great care to control stress, yet that evening he came home very upset about something. She thinks that triggered his fatal heart attack.'

Jason spoke. 'Mr Barberi called me at home; I conferenced in

Brad. Mr Barberi was worried someone was making a play for equity in the company's stock.'

'Isn't Barberi Holdings a publicly traded company?' I asked. 'Can't anyone buy its stock?'

Jason's gaze had dropped to the sleeve of my blazer. He'd spotted the varnish, or perhaps the mustard. For a second he seemed to struggle to raise his eyes to focus again on my face. 'How technical do you want me to be?'

'A short answer will do.'

'Yes, BH is a publicly held corporation. Anyone can buy its stock. The night Mr Barberi died, he learned that a company he'd never heard of had acquired an insurance policy on his life. He was afraid the insurance payout would be used to acquire BH stock when he died.'

'And gain control of the company?'

'Hardly.' Jason's eyes had begun to stray again, down to my sleeve, but he stopped them cold and looked back up. 'It would take many, many such insurance policies for that. Still, it was an agitation, and he wanted us to look into the matter.'

'Look into what, exactly?'

'He wanted us to find out who had taken out the policy.'

'Even though such an individual could do no damage?'

Jason looked at Brad. Brad shook his head. 'It's complicated,' Jason said.

'You're thinking I won't understand business talk?' I said, too fast. It was the Rivertown chip that occasionally throbs on my shoulder, reacting to two condescending, over-barbered MBAs. I smiled like I was making a little joke, to cover it.

'Anyone who acquires stock can have a voice at the annual shareholders' meeting,' Jason said. 'Someone who owns a large block can have a louder voice, and that can be disruptive.'

Brad cleared his throat. 'It's pointless, now.'

'Because Mr Barberi is dead?'

Brad nodded.

'Mrs Barberi will not be pleased if I come back empty-handed, so I'll ask again: Did you look into the company that took out the policy on Barberi?'

Jason said, 'As Brad said, it was pointless. Mr Barberi was dead.'

They both stood up. They were concerned about their own futures, not the king. The king was dead; long live the king. And I was an inconsequential interloper with varnish and mustard on his jacket. They walked me to the lobby, went through the charade of telling me to call anytime with more questions, and breezed me out into the sunshine.

Before getting into the Jeep, I took off my blazer to lay it on the back seat to dry. As I opened the door, I happened to look back at the building. Brad, or perhaps it was Jason, was standing in one of the windows at the side of the lobby, watching me.

Or perhaps it was neither, but another well-barbered MBA, taking an innocent look outside. The place must have been lousy with them.

Then again, that was probably just Rivertown talking.

ELEVEN

There were two messages from Wendell on my cell phone. I returned neither. I hadn't learned enough to dismiss his suspicions outright, or enough to interest any cop.

I called the Bohemian. 'Arthur Lamm?'

'No news might be good news, if he's simply out in the woods, eating insects. Debbie Goring?'

'No news is irritating news. She hasn't called.' Then, 'How common is it for a company to insure the life of the CEO of another company?'

'It's done sometimes when a shareholder makes a big investment in the CEO's company. The loss of a chief executive can be catastrophic to the investment, hence the insurance policy.'

'Is the CEO, whose life is being insured, notified when a policy is taken out on him?'

'Almost certainly, because medical history and perhaps even an actual physical will be required. Plus, CEOs are always in touch with their big shareholders. They need their support at shareholder meetings. Where are you going with this, Vlodek?'

'I have no idea.'

'Do you want me to call Debbie Goring again?'

'No. Give me her address. I'll stop by.'

Debbie Goring lived in Prospect Park, a few miles east of O'Hare airport. Hers was a beige bi-level in an older mix of ranch houses and other bi-levels.

A green Ford Taurus station wagon with its tailgate up was parked in her driveway. A short, squarish, dark-haired woman in blue Levis and a plain black T-shirt was pulling grocery bags out of the back of the car. The T-shirt wasn't long enough to cover the death's head skull tattoo on her lower spine. I parked the Jeep in the street and walked up.

'Debbie Goring?' I said.

She straightened up, a grocery bag in each arm, and turned around. Most of her was in her early forties, but the skin around her eyes was deeply wrinkled, as though she'd spent sixty years squinting distrustfully at the world.

'Unless you're from the Illinois Lottery, bringing a check for a million dollars, she's not home.' Her voice was raspy from too many cigarettes.

'I'm Dek Elstrom,' I said. 'I'm not from the lottery.'

'No shit,' she said.

'An associate of mine, Anton Chernek—'

She cut me off. 'I've gotten Chernek's messages. I'm not interested in talking to any more insurance bastards.'

'I'm not an insurance bastard.'

'What then?'

'A freelance bastard, with questions about your father's death. Can I help with the bags?'

She hefted the bags closer to her chest and started to walk towards the front door. Tops of four cereal boxes – two Cheerios, two Cinnamon Toast Crunch – protruded out of the brown bags. Oats and sugar seemed a sensible mix; she must have been a sensible woman. 'Adios,' she called over her shoulder.

'I'm serious about investigating your father's death.'

She stopped and turned around, hugging the bags. 'For who?'

'I can't tell you, but it's not for an insurance company.'

She lifted her chin. 'My father was murdered.'

I held out my arms for one of the grocery bags.

She shook her head. 'There's another bag in the car, and two gallons of milk. And slam the back lid.'

I went back for the bag and the gallons, closed the tailgate and followed her to the front door.

She led me through a living room that smelled faintly of old cigarette smoke. Pictures in gold frames of her with two young boys were on a spinet piano against the wall. 'My boys are six and ten,' she said as we walked into the kitchen. I set the milk and the last of the groceries on the counter and stood by the door as she put them away.

Without asking if I wanted any, she poured coffee into two yellow mugs, nuked them for twenty seconds and, after turning on the kitchen exhaust fan, brought them to the table. She lit a Camel from a crumpled pack and dropped the match in a cheap black plastic ashtray. 'When I heard Chernek's messages on my answering machine, I thought, "I'm not doing this crap anymore."'

'What crap?'

'Trying to get deaf people to listen.'

'About your father being murdered?'

She blew smoke towards the exhaust fan. 'I was in an abusive marriage, Mr Elstrom. My husband took off, leaving me dead broke. My father bought me this house, so I would have a place to raise my sons. He was a very wealthy man, but he expected me to make my own way in the world.'

'Yet he bought you this house,' I said.

'He drew the line at his grandsons doing without.' She took a long pull on the Camel. 'My father had pancreatic cancer; he knew he was dying for quite a while. He had plenty of time to get his affairs in order. He'd arranged for his stocks to be donated to various charitable causes in which he was involved, and had just finished cataloguing his art collection for museums. That, too, is set to be donated.'

'Nothing for you?'

'Not true.' Her face was defiant. 'Insurance was for me. He told me he had a two-million-dollar life insurance policy, naming me as sole beneficiary.'

'He died from painkillers,' I said.

Her eyes tightened, daring me to say the word.

'Suicide,' I said.

She stubbed out her cigarette. 'No payout for suicide.'

'Bad pain can make anyone desperate for relief.'

'I was his only child. We didn't get along great, but he adored his grandsons. If he'd been in the kind of pain where he needed to end his life, he would have changed his other bequests to make sure I got money for my sons.'

'Still, sometimes pain—'

'Please,' she said, lighting another Camel. 'His pain was being managed. He went to the office every day, kept up his schedule. For him to come home and swallow a bottle of pills is too much to believe.'

'What do you know about the day he died?'

'I was told he got to the office about ten in the morning, looked at his mail, and went out to lunch with his attorney. He had nothing pressing because, by this time, my father had shifted his responsibilities to others within the firm. Like I said, he had plenty of time to take care of things.'

'Time enough to make sure there would be money for his grandsons.'

'You got it. After lunch, he talked briefly to a few of his managers about small things and was driven home about three o'clock.'

'Your father had a chauffeur?'

'A hired driver was on standby for the last months, in case his pills made him woozy.'

'And when he got home that day?'

'He took a nap. According to Mrs Johnson, his housekeeper, he got up at six, watched the news as he got dressed to go out to one of his dinners. He left about seven.'

'Do you know where he went?'

'No.'

'What time did he get home?'

'Eleven-thirty, according to Mrs Johnson. And then he went into his study and died, still in his evening clothes.'

'Not in bed?' It was a wrinkle. I'd always assumed pill swallowers laid down, for the wait.

She'd caught the question behind my eyes. 'At his desk,' she said, a little too loudly.

'There was no note?'

'A pill bottle in his pocket doesn't have to mean suicide,' she said. 'He didn't even pause to take off his suit jacket, if the bullshit is to be believed.'

'A medical examiner must have conducted an investigation.'

She stabbed the ashtray with the Camel. 'Haven't you been listening? What the hell kind of person sits at his damned desk, writes no note, and swallows pills knowing his adored grandsons won't get one damned dime?'

I asked if she knew the name of Whitman's chauffer.

'We can get it from Mrs Johnson.' She looked at the clock on the wall. 'I have to pick up my boys from school,' she said. 'Be here tomorrow morning at eleven. I'll take you to her. She'll tell you about my father and my boys.'

At the front door, she said, 'I'll give you a hundred thousand dollars if you can prove it wasn't suicide.'

'I already have a client,' I said, ethical purity spilling from my mouth like gospel washed in Listerine.

'So you said. And just who the hell is that?'

I shrugged.

She smiled, softening the wrinkles at her eyes. 'Tomorrow morning, eleven o'clock. Mrs Johnson will tell you.'

I walked to the Jeep morally intact, true to my first responsibility, my client Wendell Phelps.

And all the way to Rivertown, I fantasized about what I could do with a hundred grand.

TWELVE

The next morning, before heading off to meet Debbie Goring, I drove across Thompson Avenue to Leo Brumsky's house. Leo has been my friend since grammar school. He is brilliant, and eccentric. He makes upwards of five hundred thousand dollars a year authenticating items for the big auction houses in New York, Chicago and LA; he drives Porsche roadsters that get jettisoned at the ten-thousand-mile mark; he wears designer suits when he must, and he dates a beautiful research librarian who is younger and taller but has the same genius IQ. All that could fit him into a rare, high social niche except he lives with his mother in her brown brick bungalow. He has an aversion to anything smelling of social snobbery, and buys his casual clothes at the Discount Den, a place where thirty bucks acquires a whole outfit, so long as one is not picky about color, style or size. Since Leo is barely five feet six inches tall, and weighs a spare one-forty, his casual attire is invariably several sizes too big, and makes him look like a malnourished dwarf with an oversized pale bald head, wearing someone else's clothes.

He is the smartest person I know, but more importantly that morning, Leo knew the art market in Chicago. Likely enough, he knew of Jim Whitman.

I noticed the black BMW as soon as I pulled away from the turret. It was parked on the short road that leads from my street to the dingy string of honky-tonks, hock shops and liquor stores that is Thompson Avenue. It was one of the smaller BMWs, the sort junior pretenders drive until they can afford one of the more dramatic models.

A car parked on the stub road was no oddity after dark; lots of johns looking to enjoy fast, last-of-the-night bargains often linger in that exact spot. Never, though, had I seen a car parked there in sunlight.

Odder still was the speed with which the driver's head slid from view, as if it belonged to someone who did not want to be seen watching me.

I did not continue on toward Leo's. I swung left on Thompson and headed east toward Chicago. The BMW appeared in the rear-view mirror two times, hanging far back, but by the time I got to the health center lot and parked next to the doorless Buick, it seemed to be gone.

Still, to be certain, I went straight into the exercise room. It was too early for Dusty and Frankie and the rest of the regulars to be roosting; too early for the Amazonian Pur Due to be stretching her magnificent bulk as well. Except for one poor soul in stained street clothes sleeping on the barbell press bench, I was alone. I walked to the window that looked out over Thompson Avenue and watched for fifteen minutes. No black BMW came into sight. I gave it up and motored over to Leo's.

His yellow Porsche roadster was parked out at the curb, meaning not only that he was home but that likely he'd already been out. And that might mean, if the fates had properly aligned, that he'd been to the Polish bakery.

I walked up the cement stairs. One of the front windows was open a crack, and the sound of people stage-whispering lustful things came through the screen. I pushed the doorbell button twice, trying to time it between the moans coming from Ma Brumsky's softly erotic cable television program.

'Yah?' the old woman's voice shouted above the fast breathing.

'It's Dek, Mrs Brumsky,' I yelled.

'Who?'

'Dek Elstrom!' I screamed. Leo's mother has known me ever since her son brought me home, like a stray cat, in seventh grade.

She thumped the floor with her cane, almost in time with the thumping coming from the television. Leo's office is in the basement. 'Leo, the UPS man is here,' she yelled above the TV voices.

A moment later, the sound of footfalls came through the window screen, the front door opened and an assault of bright colors appeared behind the screen door. Today's rayon Hawaiian shirt was a medley of chartreuse palm fronds and yellow parrots. It was shiny and huge and hung in folds down his scrawny chest, sagging the parrots into something more closely resembling snakes.

'You working for UPS now?' Leo grinned.

'You've been to the bakery?'

'Nothing wrong with your sniffer.' He opened the door and stuck his head out. 'And it's warm enough for the stoop,' he said, and disappeared back into the dark of the bungalow.

He came out a moment later with a long white waxed bag and two cups of coffee in scratched porcelain mugs. The mugs had been scratched even before Ma Brumsky swiped them from the lunch counter at Walgreen's. When we were twelve, Leo had told me, proudly, that all of his mother's plates, cups and silverware came from Walgreen's. I told him I'd figured that out already, since everything had 'Walgreen's' etched on its handles or imprinted into its porcelain. I didn't mention what he had yet to figure out, that Ma had swiped it all on lunch breaks when she worked downtown, before he was born. Nobody wants to think of his mother staggering away from a drug store lunch counter with a purse full of dirty dinnerware.

Leo knelt so I could take a mug, and then sat down. He slid an end of the raspberry coffee cake out of the bag, pulled a steak knife from the front pocket of blue knit pants that coordinated not at all with the blinding chartreuse rayon, and cut me a slice.

'This coffee cake cost more than your shirt,' I said, eyeing the half-sleeve that drooped almost to his wrist. It wasn't even good chartreuse. It reminded me of stomach contents, perhaps de-carbed.

'I should hope so,' he said. 'I wouldn't put a shirt like this in my mouth.'

For a minute, we ate coffee cake and looked at the row of brown bungalows across the street, every one identical to his, like we'd done a thousand times since we were kids.

'I drove by your place yesterday afternoon,' he said, carving me another slice. 'The Jeep was gone, and the turret was locked up as it should have been, since you're supposed to be in San Francisco, indulging fancies with the luscious Jennifer Gale.'

'I'm working on a job,' I said.

'Must be important, if you dusted off Jenny.'

'Wendell Phelps.'

Leo raised his eyebrows. Most of the time, the dark fur above his brown eyes languishes in boredom. But when he laughs, or his enormous intellect charges at something, his eyebrows come alive and cavort like crazed caterpillars across the pale skin of his forehead. The caterpillars danced with abandon now, frenzied with curiosity.

'Yes, I finally spoke to the great man, face to face.' I cut myself a third piece of coffee cake. Chicago is known for its wind; one must maintain ballast.

'He called you?'

'Amanda was the one who called.'

'You cancelled Jenny for Amanda?' He liked Amanda and he'd liked us together just as much as he now liked the prospect of Jenny and me together.

'Postponed, not cancelled.'

'I haven't seen Amanda in the papers lately, with that commodities trader, Rudolph,' he said.

'She didn't seem to want to talk about him, other than to say he's in Russia, investigating opportunities.'

'Did you mention Jenny?'

'I didn't need to. Amanda had seen the photo of us at that network correspondents' dinner.'

'The one where you're wearing that cheap, too-small rented tux?' He laughed.

'I should have tried it on at the rental place. Anyway, Amanda and I are strictly business now.'

'Where did you meet her? Someplace dimly lit?' The eyebrows waited, poised high on his forehead.

'Petterino's, and then the Goodman for a play.'

'Just like old times.'

'Wendell thinks somebody is trying to kill him.'

'Jeez.'

'Amanda is hoping her father is simply stressed, imagining things.'

'But you don't.' He didn't ask it; he said it. Since we were kids, Leo could see into my head like he was looking through glass.

I told him about Grant Carson's hit-and-run and Benno Barberi's fatal heart attack. 'You've heard of these guys?' I asked.

'I recognize the names. Movers and shakers, for sure, though I'm not solid on what they moved and shook.'

'Then there's Jim Whitman.' I eyed the coffee cake, thinking it wouldn't take running but a few laps to justify an incredibly tiny small fourth piece.

'I knew Jim.'

'Actually, he's why I'm here.' I removed a three-inch width, fully intending to get back to the health center soon.

'No doubt,' he said, watching me heft the wide new slice.

'How well did you know Whitman?' I asked through the pastry.

'I helped value some of the paintings he was going to leave to museums.' Leo's eyebrows began to move, restless with a new thought. 'His death wasn't understandable?'

'He went out for the evening, came back, sat at his desk at home and up-ended a bottle of painkillers. It was understandable to the medical examiner, given Whitman's terminal condition.'

'But?' Leo at his most terse is Leo at his most probing.

'His daughter doesn't buy it. His suicide nullified an insurance payout to her, money intended to provide for his beloved grandchildren.'

'I remember Jim mentioning his grandchildren. He was very

proud of them. And, for a man facing death, he seemed very businesslike, very much in control.'

'Suicide that nulls provision for his adored grandchildren doesn't sound businesslike.'

'How much?'

'Two million to her.'

'No. I meant how much did Whitman's daughter offer you to prove her father's death was no suicide?' His lips started to tremble with the beginnings of a smile.

'I told her I already have a client.'

The grin widened into a smile that split his lips.

'Damn it, Leo.'

He smiled broadly, exposing eight hundred big white teeth. 'How much?'

'A hundred thousand.'

'All wrapped up around a case involving Amanda.' He raised his scratched Walgreen's mug, satisfied.

'I love quandaries and ethical dilemmas,' he said.

THIRTEEN

Debbie Goring was leaning against the back fender of her Taurus, smoking, when I got there at eleven. She looked to be wearing the same blue jeans, but her T-shirt that day was orange and had a Harley Davidson logo on the front. She took a slow look at the silver tape curling off the Jeep's top and side curtains like a spinster's hairdo gone wild in an electric storm, flicked the cigarette butt into the street and said she'd drive. I took no offense.

Ten minutes later, we pulled into old streets lined with big trees and what used to be considered substantial houses. Used to be – because the teardown phenomenon was now changing the definition of substantial in Deer Run, her father's town. On every block, at least one huge new house hulked across an entire lot, dwarfing its neighbors.

'Teardowns are big here,' she said, braking as a flatbed truck ahead stopped to unload a bulldozer. 'Any property worth less than five hundred thousand gets pushed over to build something for a couple million or more.'

'That would buy an entire block of houses where I live,' I said.

She backed into a drive and turned the Taurus around. 'People want to live here, for the charm of an old town, but they don't want the modesty of an old house. Better to knock it down, they think, and put up something flashier and bigger in the middle of all that old charm.' She shook her head. 'You should see these new places at night. They've got lights everywhere – under the eaves, on the railings, beneath the shrubs. After dark, some of these streets look to have a whole bunch of starships landing.' She shot me a sly grin. 'All that need for showiness makes me wonder if there's something wrong with their personal parts.'

She stopped in front of a Spanish-style stucco two-story home with a red tile roof, across the street from the Deer Run Country Club. It was a nice enough house, but not the kind of place I'd been expecting for a multi-millionaire. My respect for Jim Whitman went up a level.

I looked at her.

'Sure to fetch a half-million as a teardown, if Mrs Johnson sells,' she said, getting out.

'The housekeeper inherited his house?'

'While his grandchildren got nothing.'

We walked up to the front door and she rang the bell. A minute later the door was opened by a trim older woman in gray pants and a black sweater. The woman smiled.

'Hello, Mrs Johnson.' Debbie's voice had turned soft and I wondered if the butch rasp she'd been using, talking to me, was an act for when she felt threatened. She introduced me to the housekeeper and we walked into a cool central hall.

The living room had a brown glazed tile floor and mission-style, black metal windows. Lighter rectangles on the beige stucco walls showed where pictures had recently been removed. Several cartons were stacked in the corner. We sat on wide, well-worn, nubby fabric chairs.

'Forgive the mess,' Mrs Johnson said to Debbie. 'I'm boxing up the last of the bequests he left to the museums.' She said it almost apologetically.

'Thank you for seeing us,' Debbie said.

Mrs Johnson reached to squeeze Debbie's wrist, and turned to me. 'I understand you're going to help with the insurance.'

I nodded. It saved me from explaining I had another client who was seeing murder. 'The day Mr Whitman died, he came home in the middle of the afternoon, took a nap, then watched the evening news as he dressed to go out?'

'Yes,' Mrs Johnson said.

'How were his spirits?'

'The usual, no worse. Mr Whitman tried not to let his troubles show.'

'Did he appear to be in pain?'

She pursed her lips, thinking back. 'No. His pills seemed to be working as always.'

'What time did he go out?'

'At seven. Mr McClain, his driver, came by early and we had coffee in the kitchen while Mr Whitman finished getting ready.'

'Do you remember where Mr Whitman went that night?'

'I'm sure it's written in his appointment book. Is it important?'

'I like to get all the details.'

'Let's find out, then.' She stood up and Debbie and I followed her down the narrow stucco hall to a small study lined with bookshelves. The Spanish motif of the rest of the house had been continued in the carved mahogany desk and the tooled red leather reading chair.

'I've thrown nothing of your father's away,' Mrs Johnson said to Debbie as she picked up a blue leather planner from the desk. She opened the book, flipped the pages to the back. She stopped at December thirteenth. It had been a Tuesday.

I looked over her shoulder. 'What is "C"?' I asked.

She shook her head. 'I don't know. Mr Whitman abbreviated everything,' she said, slowly fanning a few more pages so I could see.

The pages were filled in with one- and two-letter abbreviations. For someone dying, James Whitman was a busy man.

'Most of them I can decipher,' she said, looking down at the book, 'but "C" has me puzzled.'

'His driver would know where he took him.'

'Of course, especially since that was the night Mr Whitman died,' Mrs Johnson said.

We went back to sit in the living room.

'How did Mr Whitman seem when he came home later that evening?'

'Very fatigued, but he tired easily, the last few weeks. I was putting away some things in the hall closet when I heard the car pull up. I'd been listening for him because he was out later than usual. I looked out, saw him get out of a different car—'

'A different car?'

'Mr McClain usually drove a black Cadillac, but that night he brought Mr Whitman home in a tan-colored car,' she said. 'When Mr Whitman came in, I asked him if he needed anything. He said he was tired and was going to get something in his study and then go to bed. I said goodnight and went upstairs.' She pulled a tissue from the pocket in her pants.

'Do you have a card for Mr McClain?'

'I have his telephone number memorized,' she said, reciting it.

I wrote it down and asked, 'You were the one who found him?'

'The next morning. He was always an early riser, even at the end. I made coffee, and brought a cup for him to the study. It was then . . .' Her voice trailed off as she touched the tissue to her eye.

It was all so eerily similar. Anne Barberi had also found her husband dead in his study the morning following a night out.

'What medication, exactly, was Mr Whitman taking?' I asked.

She glanced at Debbie, then back at me. 'You mean, what did he use to end his life?'

'Yes.'

'Gendarin. I'll get it for you.' She got up and left the room.

Debbie turned to me. 'Why is the kind of pills important?'

'It's only a detail for now, nothing more.'

The sound of a cabinet door opening and closing came from upstairs, and then Mrs Johnson came back into the room and handed me an orange vial. 'Gendarin, as I said.'

The vial was full. The label said it contained twenty-eight pills, to be taken one every twelve hours. It was a fourteen-day supply.

'These haven't been touched.' According to the label, the prescription bottle had been filled a little less than two weeks before Whitman died.

'This wasn't the vial they found in his pocket,' Mrs Johnson said. 'This was to be the new supply. He always reordered when he opened a new vial. That way, he always had a full two weeks in reserve, which I kept upstairs.'

'This was the only Gendarin he kept in reserve?'

'It's a controlled narcotic. They won't let you buy too much. I was to pick up a new refill when he began taking pills from this one.'

Something about what she'd just said flickered in the dark attic of my mind and disappeared.

'He carried the current vial he was using?' I asked instead.

'Always. The police made much of the vial they found in his pocket, but I told them he didn't want to risk being someplace without his pills.'

'He occasionally took extras, when the pain got severe?'

'Not that I know of. Carrying the pills was mostly a precaution.'

'Do you know where that vial is now?'

'I imagine the ambulance people took it.'

Debbie leaned forward in her chair. 'My father would not have left me without insurance.'

'Of course not,' Mrs Johnson said, shifting to look right at me. 'Mr Whitman was a meticulous person. He had his insurance man over here several times in the last year, going over this and that. He wanted to make sure everything was in order.'

The room went quiet. Both women leaned forward, attentive, anticipating, as though I might pop out a theory that would correct everything. I had no theories. I stood up. Debbie Goring and Mrs Johnson exchanged glances, then got up too.

At the front door, Mrs Johnson said, 'I feel so bad, Debbie. Your father left me a wonderful bequest. I don't have to work again if I don't want to. But you . . .' She reached for her tissue.

'It's all right, Mrs Johnson,' Debbie said. 'Elstrom here is going to set things straight.'

I didn't look at either of them as I walked to Debbie's station wagon and got in.

Debbie got in a second later, started the car and we pulled away. Lighting a cigarette, she spoke in the same small voice she'd used in front of Mrs Johnson. 'That didn't help, did it?'

'I don't know,' I said. I seemed to be saying that a lot lately.

'You won't help me?' she asked, her voice rasping now.

'I don't know how, yet.'

We drove the rest of the way in silence. She pulled into her driveway and we got out.

'I'll call his driver,' I said over the roof of her car, but it was to her back. She was already walking away.

FOURTEEN

The main drag through Deer Run was noisy with traffic. I pulled into a cemetery, parked next to a granite Civil War sentry who looked like he might welcome company, and called the chauffeur's number. Robert McClain answered on the first ring. He sounded eager for company, too, but said he played bridge until three o'clock. I told him I'd see him then.

I hadn't eaten since the modest half of a long coffee cake at Leo's. I drove into Deer Run's business district, hunting for a fast-food restaurant with the right kind of windows. I got lucky right away. A storefront across from the train station was papered with window banners advertising chili dogs, half-pound hamburgers and cheese fries. The promise showed in the sharpness of the red letters on the white signs. They were not sharp. They were blurred. I cut the engine and got out to make sure. Right off I spotted a fly stuck to the inside of the window, proof enough that the faintly fuzzy signs weren't the result of sloppy brush work. The blur came from the glass. I went in.

Kings, Kentuckys and Macs are never my first choice because their windows are invariably spotless. The joints I seek have glass made opaque by the inside air. If the windows are filmy with grease, the chef is using properly fatty meat and real lard – sure signs he's not cooking to some bland, committee-crafted, offend-no-one formula. I see it as my obligation to support such efforts by visiting those grease blots as frequently as I can, for they are highly flammable and regularly explode into black smoke.

I ordered a hot dog, onion rings and a Diet Coke and took them to a Formica counter to look at the blur of the world outside. My first bites validated my greasy window theory once again. The hot dog was properly slippery, topped with pickle, tomatoes, peppers, mustard, chopped onions, dill salt and absolutely no trace of catsup. The rings were strong, sure to delight for the rest of the afternoon. And the Diet Coke . . . well, the Diet Coke, like every diet soft drink, was there simply to dissolve calories.

I puzzled again over my earlier sense that I'd missed something when Mrs Johnson talked about Whitman's pills. And in a moment, I had it: Whitman had been about to crack open the reserve vial of pills she'd showed us. That meant his current supply, the one they found in his pocket, should have been almost depleted if he'd been taking his pills in the dosage prescribed.

I swallowed the last bit of hot dog and turned around to ask where the police station was. The man behind the counter shrugged and said something in Spanish to the woman who'd taken my order. 'Three blocks up the street,' she said. 'It's in the basement of City Hall, opposite the park.'

I stepped almost lightly outside, sure of my wisdom in selecting a hot dog and onion rings for lunch. Like an automobile, my brain functions best when it's freshly greased.

I decided to hoof the three blocks. Crossing the first street, I spotted a junior-grade black BMW parked down the side street, just like the one that had tailed me for a time earlier that morning. I continued on to the middle of the next block, and stopped as if to look in a store window. No black BMW or well-barbered head on feet had followed.

Deer Run's city hall was red brick and white pillars. Walking down to the police department in the basement set the onion rings to barking. I slid three breath tapes into my mouth. The tapes were generic; I get them at the Discount Den in Rivertown, at the same place I get the duct tape to mend the rips in the Jeep's top and Leo gets his shiny Hawaiian shirts and fluorescent pants. I aimed a test breath at the painted yellow block wall before opening the metal door at the bottom. Nothing peeled. Encouraged, I went in.

'I'd like to talk to someone about Jim Whitman's death,' I said to the desk sergeant.

He scooted his chair back a yard, making me wonder if the Discount Den's breath tapes were as unreliable as the duct tape that curled from the Jeep every time it rained. I slipped my hand surreptitiously into my pocket and thumbed loose another tape.

'Your business?' he asked, looking off to my right where, perhaps, there was better air.

I held out a card. It says I do insurance investigations. He scooted forward, grabbed it, and again retreated fast. I slipped the new tape into my mouth.

He frowned as he studied the card. 'I thought you insurance guys closed your file.'

'I'm just filling in a couple of blanks.'

The sergeant swiveled around. 'Finch, get the Whitman file,' he yelled to the empty hallway behind him. Turning back, he motioned for me to sit by the door, on the plastic chair farthest from his desk.

Officer Finch came out in five minutes. He was young, maybe twenty-five, and carried a brown accordion file. 'How may I help you, sir?' he asked.

'I'd like to know how much Gendarin Jim Whitman swallowed the night he died.'

Finch looked to the desk sergeant, who nodded. Finch took a sheet of paper from the file and said, 'Approximately twelve hundred milligrams. It was enough to send him to the moon twice.'

'You're sure it was Gendarin?'

Finch took out a clear plastic bag. Inside was an orange pill bottle identical to the one Mrs Johnson had showed me. It rattled as he held it up to read the label. 'Gendarin,' he said.

'May I?' I asked.

'So long as you leave it inside the plastic bag,' he said, and handed it to me.

The pill bottle rattled again as I held the bag up to the light. 'There are still pills in there,' I said, like I was surprised.

'Two,' Finch said.

'This vial was found in Whitman's suit jacket?'

'Yes.'

I read the label through the bag. Just like the reserve supply Mrs Johnson had showed me, this vial had contained twenty-eight pills, eighty milligrams each, prescribed at two a day. It had been filled almost a month before Whitman died. That made sense, calendar-wise. It had been kept in reserve for two weeks before

Whitman had begun taking pills from it, at the prescribed rate of two a day, not quite two weeks before he died.

Which meant the vial I was now holding should have contained but a few pills, the end of a two-week supply.

Which meant it could not have contained enough pills to kill him.

'You're sure the medical examiner found twelve hundred milligrams of this stuff in Whitman's system?' I asked.

'Approximately.'

'Isn't it odd that two pills remain inside this vial?'

'Whitman would have known just a few would do the trick.'

I gave him the arithmetic. 'Fifteen pills were needed to put twelve hundred milligrams in his system.'

'OK,' the desk sergeant said slowly, not comprehending where I was heading.

'That's over half a vial. His reserve supply at home was untouched.'

'What are you saying?'

I rattled the vial in the plastic bag. 'He took pills from this vial exactly on schedule, two a day. Where did Whitman get fifteen pills to swallow all at once?'

Finch grabbed the bag back. 'From this—'

'No,' I cut in. 'There weren't enough left in there.'

The desk sergeant cocked his head, motioning Finch to leave. 'You'll have to check with the medical examiner,' he said to me.

I gave it up, and walked up the stairs. I took a long look through the window in the door before going out. I saw no black BMW or sharply barbered MBA outside, but I'd just seen plenty inside.

I crossed the street to a drug store and bought a pack of Listerine breath tapes. They were stronger than my generics, and got rid of the taste of onions right away.

But they didn't mask the bile that had risen in my throat.

FIFTEEN

Robert McClain was in the parking lot behind his dark brick apartment building, dry wiping a shiny black Cadillac Seville. He looked old enough to have been driving when roads were made of dirt.

'I like to be ready, in case I get a call,' he said, smiling.

I asked him about Jim Whitman.

'Working for Mr Whitman was a real pleasure,' he said. 'Most fellows would have insisted on a younger driver, but not Mr Whitman. He was always real polite and regular, always sat up front with me. He tipped really well.'

'Do you remember the night he died?'

'Like yesterday. I knew he was ill – he was straightforward about it – but he didn't act like a man about to kill himself.'

'His spirits were good?'

'Considering what he was facing, yes. As usual, he talked about his grandchildren all the way into the city.'

'You picked him up about seven?'

McClain nodded. 'Went in, had a spot of coffee with Mrs Johnson while Mr Whitman was getting ready.'

'Do you remember where you took him?'

'Corner of Michigan and Walton, downtown.'

'I meant which restaurant.'

'No restaurant. Dropped him at the same corner, as usual.'

'You'd taken him there before?'

'Every few weeks. He never did say where exactly he was going from there.'

'And you picked him up later at that same corner?'

'Not that night. He called to say he was catching another way home.'

'You didn't bring him home in a tan-colored car?'

'This baby's all I got,' he said, touching the gleaming hood of the black Cadillac.

'Was it usual for him to find another way home from there?'

'He'd never done it before. Every other time, I picked him up at ten o'clock sharp. He'd be standing on that same corner, waiting.' He picked up his rag, worked at an imagined spot. 'That was the last time I drove anybody.'

'Business slow?'

'I'm old, and I look it. The agency's got younger drivers.'

There was nothing left to say. I left him in the late-afternoon sun, polishing a future that likely had disappeared.

I busied myself cutting the last of the closet trim that evening. I needed simple work requiring clear and logical steps while my mind stumbled about in the fog surrounding Jim Whitman's pills.

For a time, it worked. The cutting, sanding and staining were calming, easy steps in an understandable sequence. But then, well into the evening, it came time for varnishing. Varnishing, done right, requires care: one pass, no over-brushing. Be too fast, and a spot can get overlooked.

And that's what happened with the cops looking at Jim Whitman's death. They'd missed a big spot: they hadn't accounted for his pills. He couldn't have used his current two-week prescription to kill himself because there had been too few remaining. And he hadn't tapped his reserve vial because it was untouched. He had to have gotten his fatal batch of fifteen pills from a third source.

Unless he hadn't. Someone else could have slipped Gendarin into his meal or his drink, knowing that the excess in his bloodstream wouldn't be questioned because it was the pain medication he was already taking. It would have been assumed that Whitman used his own supply to overdose himself.

What I couldn't see was the logic in risking the murder of an already dying man.

The vague thoughts and the pungent smell of the varnish finally made me woozy. I walked down to the river to sit on the bench and breathe in the cold March air. Behind me, the jukes in the tonks along Thompson Avenue were beating out big bass notes, primitive drums summoning tribe members to return. I almost envied those in that dark carnival. They were sure of what they were seeking: a simple tingle from some booze, a few laughs, a rub of rented flesh.

Perhaps it had been that simple for Jim Whitman, that last night. Maybe he'd finished a good meal, enjoyed a few drinks, had a few laughs being driven home by a friend . . . and realized things would never get any better than they were that evening. Maybe he'd rat-holed a stash of Gendarin for just such a time, and asked himself, on the spur of that moment: Why not? Why not check out with a belly full of good steak and good Scotch, and the sound of a laugh still resonating in the back of his throat? Why not?

Except for the grandchildren he'd left without a nickel.

The dim light from the lamp along the riverwalk made a tiny shadow on the ground just beyond my feet. It was another still-born ash leaf, curled and dried on the grass. I looked up at the tree. There was not enough light to see for sure, but I knew in my throat that no new leaves had appeared that day.

I took out my pocket calendar and recorded that loss, too.

SIXTEEN

Two men in loose-fitting gray suits, one carrying a square carton, the other something the size of a wrapped painting, came out of the Whitman house the next morning, heading toward the black Ford Expedition parked at the curb. They stopped when they saw me pull up. The one with the painting gestured at someone in the big SUV, and a third man, also in a suit, got out from the driver's door. All three stood motionless, watching me. I couldn't see the guns, but I knew they had them. Whatever Jim Whitman had bequeathed, it was worth enough to merit three guards.

Mrs Johnson had followed the two men out of the house, saw them tense and stop on the front walk. She turned to look where they were looking. I waved out the Jeep's open side curtain. She squinted, recognized my face. 'We're almost done,' she called. And the world righted itself. The men carrying the box and the painting resumed walking toward the SUV, the driver got back inside, and I settled back to wait.

Ten minutes later, Mrs Johnson followed the armed men out

with the last of the cartons, and watched them drive away. She came over to the Jeep. 'You can't imagine how relieved I am that those things are on their way to the Museum of Contemporary Art,' she said. 'The house has an alarm, but I've not been comfortable there, alone with all those valuable pieces.'

'They'll be exhibited soon?' I asked as we went up the front walk.

'The curator said they'll be catalogued, then stored. In a year, maybe less, they'll be rotated into exhibition.'

'How valuable are the pieces?'

'Millions,' she said, as we entered the house. 'Mr Whitman was a plain man, not the usual patron of the arts. Those pieces were recommended as investments. From what I understand, he profited quite handsomely from their purchase.'

'Yet not even one was left to Debbie.'

The distress on her face seemed genuine. 'Wealthy fathers can be especially difficult on young daughters. And Debbie, as you might imagine, was very strong-willed. But Mr Whitman cared for his daughter, and adored his grandsons.'

'You find it odd that he left them nothing?'

'It's impossible to believe. And now you've come back because you're wondering where he got the pills, haven't you?'

'Yes, and I'd like to see his calendar again. You're certain there was only one bottle of Gendarin in reserve?'

'Certain as I can be. As I said, Mr Whitman wanted to keep more on hand, in case the pain got worse, but his doctor wouldn't go for it. Federally regulated narcotics are so very tightly dispensed.'

'Could he have set aside a pill or two from each refill, to build up an extra supply?'

'That's very doubtful. He truly needed those pills, and skipping one would mean going twelve full hours in pain. And yes, Mr Elstrom,' she said, 'I told that to the police, but they didn't seem interested.'

'Any more thoughts on where Mr Whitman might have gone that last night?'

'Mr McClain was no help?'

'He dropped off Mr Whitman on North Michigan Avenue. Someone else drove him home.'

'In that tan car I saw.'

'Any idea whose it was?'

'Only thing I know it was tan, and it was a Buick.'

'You know cars well enough to spot a Buick?'

'Goodness, no. All cars look the same to me these days, like jelly beans. It's just that when I was young, Buicks had those holes . . .' She stopped, searching for the words.

'Like portholes, on the sides of the car?'

'That's it. Imagine Buick still doing those holes, only smaller, after all these years.'

We went into Whitman's study. She picked up the calendar from the desk and handed it to me. I opened it to the page for December 13, the day he died, and looked again at the half-dozen entries. His first appointment was for lunch, at eleven-thirty. Other names were penciled in, beginning at one, ending at two-thirty. After that, the calendar was blank until the 'C' entry, scrawled across the lines for the evening. I pointed to it.

'As I told you last time, I don't know that one,' she said. 'After you and Debbie left, I flipped back a few months. There are other entries just like it.'

'McClain said the same thing. He dropped Whitman at the same intersection, Michigan at Walton, every few weeks.'

'You think he got the Gendarin there?'

'I can't understand why he'd need to. He had enough in reserve here to kill himself.'

'I went through the whole house, Mr Elstrom. I found no third vial, no trace he'd hidden more Gendarin.' She studied my face. 'You came back because you're thinking what I'm thinking.'

'Two pills remaining in the vial in his jacket, as there should have been? Full reserve supply upstairs, as there should have been? Leaving us to accept he'd gone to the bother of obtaining the pills he needed to kill himself elsewhere, when he didn't need to? Yes, I'm having a problem understanding why he'd go to that trouble.'

'He didn't commit suicide, did he, Mr Elstrom?'

'I can't prove that.'

'Why would someone risk killing him? Why not simply wait?'

'Did he have enemies?'

'Business adversaries, perhaps, though Mr Whitman was not ruthless, not someone who took unfair advantage.'

I started turning back the calendar pages. 'I need to know where he went that evening.'

The appointments looked to have been written by two different people. Most were in a feminine hand. 'Did you make most of these entries?'

'His secretary made those,' she said. 'The ones that are barely legible, like that 'C' for the night Mr Whitman died, he wrote himself.'

Almost every page had an abbreviation for an evening appointment. I started pointing randomly to different evening entries.

'Y?'

'YMCA of Metropolitan Chicago, usually a dinner meeting for the directors, every three months.'

'MP?'

'Millennium Park, the new park on Michigan Avenue. He donated one hundred thousand dollars.'

I came to another 'C' entry, two months earlier, in October.

'That's one of the others I found,' Mrs Johnson said.

Again it was simple and cryptic, scrawled across the lines for evening appointments. Beside me, Mrs Johnson shook her head, offering nothing. I turned back more pages. There were 'C' entries in August, June, April and February.

'Did he keep another desk diary at his office?' I asked.

'This was the only one; he carried it back and forth in his briefcase.'

'Maybe the prior year's book has more information?'

'His secretary kept his old diaries,' she said, picking up the phone. Then, while she was dialing, 'Why would someone murder an already dying man?'

There was no answering that.

SEVENTEEN

Whitman Industries occupied four floors in a high-rise office building just north of the Chicago River. Jim Whitman's former secretary, a trim, efficient woman in her mid-fifties, came to the lobby carrying two blue leather desk calendars identical to the one I'd brought from Whitman's house. We sat in a secluded corner next to a plant.

I opened the calendar I'd brought to December 13, the night Whitman died. 'Do you know what this is?' I asked, pointing to the 'C.'

'I wondered about those,' she said. 'I wrote most of the appointments in his book, and knew almost all of the ones he entered. But those "C"s . . .' She shook her head. 'I never asked, of course.'

'Were there many?'

'Several a year.' She opened one of the calendars she'd brought, the book for the year before last. Turning the pages, she made notes on a small pad. When she was finished, she said, 'The year before last, he attended 'C' meetings on February tenth, April thirteenth, June eighth, August tenth, October twelfth, and then December fourteenth. They seem to have been regular enough, all on Tuesdays.' She handed me the list.

'How about the year before that?'

She opened the other book she'd brought, the one for the third year going back, and, turning the pages, read off the dates so I could write them down. 'Regular thing,' she said, when she was done. 'Tuesdays, every other month.'

'You have no idea where he spent those evenings?'

'No.'

'How did he seem, his last day here?'

'For a man whose life was being cut short – a strong, powerful man who had to give up control of an empire he had constructed?' Her lips tightened, then relaxed. 'Actually, he seemed in remarkably good humor that day. He met with several people, dictated a few letters, mostly apologies for matters he could not attend to personally, and left around three o'clock.'

'Did he keep any extra medication in his office?' I asked.

'You mean pills to kill himself?'

'Yes,' I said.

'I went through his office thoroughly. There was no trace of pills.'

I had no doubt she'd searched immediately, looking to destroy any evidence Whitman had taken a deliberate overdose.

'You wouldn't tell me if there were,' I said.

'I find it difficult to believe he killed himself. In any event, there was no trace of an extra supply in his office.'

I believed her like I believed Mrs Johnson. Whitman had no extra pills.

And that was enough for Wendell Phelps to call the cops.

I called his private cell phone number as soon as I got outside. 'I've got something for you to take to the police. Jim Whitman loved his grandsons, and would have known his suicide would null the insurance policy he'd left for their well-being.'

Wendell said nothing for a moment, and then asked, in a surprisingly weak voice, 'Insurance?'

'He had a two-million-dollar life policy, benefitting his grandsons. Death by suicide nulled it.'

Again he paused. 'Perhaps there were other policies . . .' He let the question trail away.

'If there were, his daughter, Debbie, does not know of them. She got nothing for the care of her kids. You have enough to go to the police, Wendell.'

'The cops will say he was a sick man. Pain doesn't make for high lucidity.'

'He was lucid enough to arrange his other bequests.'

'That proves nothing,' he said, his voice stronger, almost combative.

'Then try this: I can't find the source of the pills he supposedly took. He had plenty at home, but he didn't touch those. If he took his own life, he used pills from a secret stash.'

'Cops will say a secret stash was easy to create.'

'He could have been fed those pills. Murdered, as you suspect.'

'Jim Whitman was dying, damn it. There was no motive for murder. Cops will laugh.'

'Why fight me on this, Wendell? You suspected right away your friends were being murdered.'

'I overreacted.'

'The night Whitman died, he went downtown to a place that begins with a "C." He went there every two months, always on a Tuesday. He was secretive about it. He had his driver drop him nearby, but never directly at the destination.'

He chuckled, but it sounded forced. 'Whitman was a widower. Maybe he went down there to visit a lady friend he didn't want anyone to know about. Hell, she could have been a high-priced hooker.'

'His regular driver didn't come back for him the night he died. Someone else drove him home, somebody in a light-colored Buick.'

'This is all you've got?' He exhaled disgust into the phone. 'There are thousands of Buicks in this town, like there are thousands of places that begin with the letter "C." I'll get back to you if I want you to continue.'

'Go to the cops,' I said, but I was talking to dead air. He'd hung up.

Wendell had become too argumentative. He'd swatted away every red flag I'd waved. For a man who'd been so certain his fellow tycoons were being murdered, a man who'd been frightened enough to stand by his curtains to make sure they didn't open even an inch, his behavior had transformed suddenly from fear to aggressiveness.

The day was breezy and sunny and good for a walk to mull my new confusion. I headed over to Michigan Avenue, where Jim Whitman had spent the last evening of his life.

Measured by glitz and geography, North Michigan Avenue is the middle sparkler in a three-diamond necklace, approximately equidistant from Rodeo Drive in California and Fifth Avenue in New York. Amanda and I used to walk the grand boulevard when we were new to each other. I was charmed by the way she'd look through the store windows for customers who'd mastered a certain curve to their backs and the oh-so-slight rise to their eyebrows that feigned unconcern to the ridiculous prices of the baubles they were inspecting. 'Arch,' the beautiful girl who'd grown up so rich used to call such false posturing. On North Michigan Avenue, Amanda said, life started and ended with false attitude.

I'd brought Wendell validation of his worries, at least about Jim Whitman. He should have pressed me to find out more. Instead he'd dusted me off with impatience and anger. And arch.

I got to Walton Street, where Whitman had been let off. It was one of the grandest intersections in the city, anchored on the northeast by the Drake Hotel. Upscale shops fanned out from the other three corners, lots of vogue for lots of arch. In the distance, past Lake Shore Drive, Lake Michigan rippled blue and calm, already dotted with the first of the season's sailboats.

I stepped close to the curb to see better in all four directions. I wasn't expecting anything obvious like a neon sign flashing a

big orange 'C' or a raven-haired dame in a black dress slit to her
hip, blowing C-shaped smoke rings from an upper-story window.
I would have settled for even the tiniest of mental nudges, but I
didn't even get that. All I saw were sun-washed storefronts and
restaurants offering subtlety at non-subtle prices, and not one had
a name that began with a 'C.'

I turned right, walked east on East Walton Place, toward the
lake, then reversed, and came west all the way to State Street. I
passed the Drake, shiny new storefronts and old three-story graystones – some housing fashionable boutiques and trendy bars,
others housing those who hung out in the fashionable boutiques
and trendy bars. It was a rich, hip, ever-evolving neighborhood,
but mostly it was young, and a seemingly unlikely place for Jim
Whitman to visit six times a year. I got back to the Jeep no smarter
than when I'd left it and considerably less employed.

I drove south toward the expressway. Michigan Avenue across
the bridge is a different place. Gone is the sunny glitz of the
boulevard to the north. Michigan Avenue south of the river is dark.
The buildings lining its west side are tall and close to the street
and shut out the sun from the sidewalk early as it heads away
from the lake. There are no strolling swells swinging little boutique
bags south of the river, just art students and secretaries, store clerks
and podiatrists; people hustling with their heads down just to stay
even. And there are pigeons, often dozens of them, strutting and
worse on the sidewalk. There is no pretense on Michigan Avenue,
south of the river. There is no arch.

But there is often chaos. Unfamiliar drivers heading southbound
are often made crazy trying to find the expressway; the signs
pointing the way are small and placed too far down. Only at the
last moment do the uninitiated comprehend that a left turn is
needed to make the right-hand curve to the expressway. And then
they swerve, panicked, across several lanes of traffic.

That's what happened that afternoon. The driver in front of me
shot across my bow, barely missing my front bumper.

I didn't hit the horn; I didn't raise a fist or a finger. I didn't
even remind myself to stay mellow, that this was normal road life
Michigan Avenue, south of the river.

I did none of those things because the sight of the car veering
in front of me seemed to demand more than that, like I was

supposed to focus on what I'd just seen. It was an ordinary enough car – light-colored, beige or tan, swerving in the same stupid way that I'd seen a hundred times before. Yet somehow this car, at this time, seemed very much to matter.

I replayed the image over and over in my mind as I drove back to Rivertown, but I could make no sense of why the image nagged.

Just like I couldn't make sense of Wendell's arch behavior.

EIGHTEEN

'd just stepped into the turret when a slow ripping creak sounded loud from upstairs. I ran up the wrought iron, knowing, and shot into the kitchen to see for sure.

The turret's craggy, curved limestone walls make for interesting architecture, but they play hell with converting the place into a residence. Hanging anything onto them is a true nightmare. One of the kitchen cabinets I'd just hung was coming loose. I'd arrived home just in time to pull it safely from the wall before it crashed to the floor.

I changed into my rehabbing clothes, which look only marginally worse than my dress duds, and spent the next few hours re-anchoring the cabinet to the wall. By the time I got it to hang right, it was well past dusk, and Amanda had called three times. I'd dodged each call, knowing she must have spoken with her father, and now she wanted truths from me. I didn't want to worry her by saying I suspected Jim Whitman had likely been murdered, and that Wendell didn't want me to learn any more about it.

I walked across what one day might be a hall, and sat at the card table I use as a desk. My cheesy, giveaway black vinyl calendar was nothing like Jim Whitman's leather-bound desk diaries. Though mine was dressed up in gold like Whitman's, instead of mono-grammed initials, mine sported an air-freight company's logo of an emaciated bird. And where his provided an entire lined page for each day, mine offered a stingy small page for an entire month – space enough, the air freight company must have concluded, for people who don't have much going on in their lives. Certainly they'd been right about me. Save for the leaf counts of the ash by the river, and the few hours I'd invoiced so far that spring, my pages were mostly empty.

I switched on my computer, typed in my billable hours for Wendell's final invoice, wrote a check to refund the balance on his retainer, and printed out two copies of the invoice. One went with the check into an envelope addressed to Wendell. The other was for me. Opening the case folder, I saw again the photocopy of Benno Barberi's obituary.

This time, though, the date of his death the previous autumn danced on the paper like it was lit by a strobe: October 11.

I grabbed the notes I'd made just that day. Jim Whitman had scrawled a 'C' in his calendar across the same Tuesday evening Benno Barberi had come home, furious, to die.

I spilled the rest of the file onto the card table, pawing for the newspaper article about Grant Carson's hit-and-run. My hands shook as I read it. He'd been killed on February 15th. It had been a Wednesday, but very early in the morning.

My cell phone rang again. I glanced over. It was Amanda. I let it ring.

I read all the obituaries again, double-checking the dates with my vinyl calendar to be sure. There was no doubt. Benno Barberi, Jim Whitman and Grant Carson had all died on, or just an hour or two following, the second Tuesday of an even-numbered month.

I got out of the chair and went up the stairs to the third floor. I wanted a sweatshirt.

Suddenly, I was cold.

NINETEEN

I called Anne Barberi at eight-thirty sharp the next morning. 'No, I can't remember where Benno went that evening,' she said. 'He attended so many dinners.'

'Who has your husband's appointments calendar?'

'His secretary, I would imagine.'

'Can you arrange for me to look at his appointment books for last year and the year before?'

'What have you learned, Mr Elstrom?'

'I'm casting a wide net, trying to gather as much information as I can.'

'What do you suspect?'

'I'll tell you when what I suspect becomes what I believe. For now, tell me, was your husband taking much medication?'

'Of course; several prescriptions. You're wondering why they were ineffective, that last night?'

I was wondering if they'd been too effective, for a killer, but I couldn't dare say that yet. 'Sort of,' I said instead. 'Can you arrange for me to talk to his primary physician?'

'As part of that mysterious wide-net business?'

'Yes.'

'Benno's doctor is a close friend. I'll have him call you.'

And he did, fifteen minutes later. 'What's this about, Elstrom?'

'Was Benno Barberi taking any medication that, in larger than prescribed doses, could have killed him?'

The doctor paused, as he must have often, in this modern era of high-buck medical malpractice suits. And then he evaded. 'Aspirin, taken in large doses, can kill you.'

'Could Barberi have overdosed?'

'The cause of his death was obvious to the EMTs: massive heart attack.'

'He wasn't autopsied?'

'No need.'

'If there were sufficient grounds, can he be autopsied now?'

'Elstrom, you're inferring something untoward? The EMTs would have noticed anything suspicious about Benno's death, as would the emergency room personnel who pronounced him dead.'

'Maybe they didn't probe because his heart condition was well documented.'

'My God, man; you're insinuating he was deliberately overdosed?'

'For now, it's something to rule out.'

'Who would benefit from his death? I don't believe Benno had any enemies.'

There was no answering that yet, just as there seemed to be no reason to overdose Jim Whitman, a dying man.

'I need your support to exhume Benno Barberi,' I said.

'Summon divine intervention instead. Benno was cremated and his ashes were scattered off his boat in Lake Michigan.'

Benno Barberi's former secretary called twenty minutes after the doctor slammed down his phone. She was as crisp and as efficient as she'd been the first time we'd spoken. She told me I could come anytime. I left immediately.

She was waiting in the lobby. She was an austere but attractive brunette in her late thirties. If she'd been briefed by Barberi's two sharply barbered assistants about my first visit, she didn't show it. Certainly she did not glance down to see if any varnish or mustard remained on my blazer sleeve.

We went to the same small conference room where I'd met Jason and Brad. Two red leather appointment books sat on the small table.

'I recorded all of Mr Barberi's appointments,' she said. 'What are you looking for?'

'Symmetry,' I said.

'I'm afraid I don't understand,' she said, 'but that's not necessary. Where shall we start?'

'The day and evening of his fatal heart attack.'

She opened one of the books and started turning pages. 'That would be October eleventh,' she said, stopping at the page. She turned the book around so I could see.

The page was crammed with entries, beginning at seven-thirty in the morning and ending with a notation at five-thirty that read: 'Emerson.' Nothing was posted for the evening.

'What's Emerson?' I asked.

'Emerson is a fitness trainer. Three times a week, Mr Barberi took light exercise, as prescribed by his physician.'

I pulled out my note pad. 'Where's the health club?' I asked.

She smiled. 'In the basement here. Mr Emerson is on staff for our senior executives.'

'Of course,' I said, like I had the lifestyle that would have presumed that. I pointed to the bottom of the calendar page. 'There's nothing written for the evening, yet his wife told me he'd gone out to dinner.'

'I wondered about that.' She looked down at the book. 'He

didn't tell me of a dinner engagement, and that was a rarity. His evenings were as busy as his days, and he expected me to keep track of his after-hours obligations as well.'

I started turning the pages backwards. She was right; every one of his evenings, Monday through Saturday, had a notation penned in her handwriting. I didn't find a blank, working-day evening until I'd gone back to August 9.

It, too, had been the second Tuesday of the month.

I turned the book to show her. 'Nothing here, either.'

'I guess he forgot to tell me his plans then, as well.'

I continued backwards through the book quickly, growing more certain. And all were there. Or rather, they were not: The evenings of the second Tuesdays in June, April and February had been left blank. I picked up the calendar for the preceding year. It was the same. Benno Barberi had listed no evening appointments for any second Tuesday in February, April, June, August, October or December for two years.

Second Tuesdays, even-numbered months. I closed the second calendar and stood up.

'Did you find what you were looking for?'

'I don't—'

'I know: you don't know.' Her smile was tight and telling. She knew I'd spotted something.

I could only smile back. She walked me downstairs to the fitness center in the basement. Rudy Emerson, dressed in gray sweats, could have been forty or sixty, and looked like he'd never gotten outside a Twinkie in his life.

He remembered his last session with Benno Barberi. 'Of course I knew about his heart. Like always, there was no unusual exertion that day. I started him with easy stretching exercises, we moved to the light weights, and finished with more stretching. Thirty minutes, easy does it. He left here feeling good, looking good.'

'Looking good?' I asked.

'Same suit, but a fresh shirt and a different tie.'

'He sounded good, too? No disorientation, no signs of physical distress?'

'Whatever he ate that night might have killed him, but I guarantee it wasn't the exercise he got here.'

'He didn't happen to mention where he was headed?'

Rudy Emerson shook his head. 'Not for a heart attack, that's for sure.'

Barberi's secretary left me in the lobby. Walking out, I had the thought to turn around and look back. Like the last time I'd left Barberi Holdings, I caught sight of a young man in a dark suit watching me. It could have been Brad; it could have been Jason; it could have been someone else, similarly barbered. Whoever he was, he must have caught sight of me looking back, because he quickly moved from sight.

The Rivertown chip pressed down a little on my shoulder, suggesting a little show. I took a leisurely stroll down the rows of the cars parked in the lot.

There were six of the junior-grade black BMWs, each identical to the one that had tailed me at least twice.

A tailing car need not be driven by a killer, I told myself.

Nor did it need be driven by an innocent, either.

I spent a showy moment in front of each car's license plate, writing its number in the little spiral notebook I always carry. Then, back in the Jeep, I checked my cell phone before I started the car, wanting whoever might still be watching to think I was running the plate numbers I'd just written down. And maybe later I'd get a cop friend to do just that. For now, I had other things to think about.

Amanda had left fresh, furious messages, demanding to know why I had not returned any of her calls. Leo offered to buy lunch. And the Bohemian had asked me to call right away. I thumbed his number.

There was no booming 'Vlodek' to begin the conversation, but there was a chuckle, of sorts. 'Arthur Lamm is still missing,' he said.

'You don't sound worried.'

'Perhaps because his absence has become even more explainable. The IRS began investigating him last fall.'

'For what?'

'Unreported income from insurance irregularities.'

'Insurance? I thought the guy was in real estate.'

'Arthur might have the longest tentacles of those in the heavy cream. He acts as a broker, selling large office buildings. Then he negotiates to become its property manager. To top it all off, he gets the property owner to buy the building's insurance from his agency.'

'An IRS investigation wouldn't make a guy like Lamm run into the woods,' I said.

'Of course, unless his battery of high-priced attorneys told him to get lost until they could work something out with the Feds.'

'Or unless he committed big-time fraud?' I asked. 'Such things can attract long prison sentences. In which case, he wouldn't run off into the woods of Wisconsin. He'd flee the country, go someplace where he can't be extradited.'

'Look, we already know his rowboat and fishing gear are all gone, and that his cottage is on a string of lakes,' the Bohemian said. 'I suppose we could see something clandestine in that. I guess it's possible he could have headed north to Canada, and from there gone overseas.'

'Or he's staged things, leaving a false trail to buy time to leave the country another way.'

'This might be of interest to some of his associates,' the Bohemian said. 'Those in the heavy cream often cross-invest in each other's companies.'

'You want me to look more deeply into it?'

'I want you to be ready.'

TWENTY

Rikk, at Carson's life insurance carrier, sounded half asleep when he picked up the phone.

'Did anybody identify where Carson went, his last night?' I asked.

He yawned, quite audibly. 'You're killing me, Elstrom. You already asked that. Our concern starts at the moment he got smacked. Dinner doesn't matter.'

'Didn't your investigator ask, anyway?'

'Maybe; probably; I don't know. How does knowing where he ate help us?'

'You never know,' I invented. 'Maybe he was fed something that disoriented him, made him step out in front of traffic.'

'And we could sue the restaurant or his dinner companions to recover our payout? You think he was murdered? For what purpose?'

'I don't know,' I said.

'You're reaching.' He yawned, and added, 'As well as holding back.'

'I'm wondering if someone was with Carson, in the car.' I said, thinking specifically of the man in the tan Buick who drove Whitman home.

'Listen, Elstrom, asking these questions helps us only if the passenger was wealthy, had a hand in forcing Carson in front of the kill car, and we could sue to recover. We discussed all this. Vehicular homicides are too chancy. There are better ways to kill.'

'That's what any right-thinking person would think. That's what makes it a clever way to murder.'

'Give me a motive.'

'I don't have one.'

'There were no witnesses, remember? Even if you found a motive, we can't prove anything.'

'At least find out where Carson went, before he got killed.'

'If I call our investigator, will you leave me alone?'

'If you will also check Grant Carson's appointment books for the last two years, to see if he went to that same place on the second Tuesday evenings of every even-numbered month.'

That woke him up. 'What the hell do you know that you're not telling me?' he shouted.

'Help me here, Rikk.'

'How can I rationalize asking for his calendars?'

'With creativity.'

'You're nuts, Elstrom,' he said, and hung up.

I called Leo after I'd gotten on the tollway, southbound. 'You said you're buying lunch?'

'Yes, but I'm dieting.'

Leo's metabolism runs as fast as his intellect. There'd been no change in his 140 pounds since high school. 'You're porking up?' I asked anyway.

'A pound and a half since Christmas.'

'I can achieve that with a lone raspberry Danish.'

'So I noticed on my front stoop, very recently. See you at Kutz's.'

I'd saved the worst call for last. I thumbed on my cell phone directory and clicked Amanda's number. 'Hey, sorry I haven't been returning your calls,' I said. 'I've been swamped . . .'

Her voice was barely audible in the headset I'd bought cheap at the Discount Den. Then again, I was surrounded by trucks.

'I can't hear you,' I yelled, speeding up to get clear of the trucks.

'Do you miss me?' she shouted.

'Like there'll be no tomorrow, Amanda,' I screamed, joking, at last getting free of the trucks.

'Jenny,' the voice yelled, horribly clear. 'Jenny Galecki.'

'Ah,' I said, hearing too perfectly. For sure, jackasses should not be issued speed-dial features, or thumbs, or headsets. Or mouths.

'Talking with Amanda, are we?' she asked.

'It's that case involving her father that I told you about,' I said, fighting the urge to say I wasn't lying.

'Did you get my little package?' There was frost in the words that I couldn't blame on the cheap headset.

'Package? No.'

'I sent you a little something, to keep you thinking of me. It seemed funny at the time.' She clicked off.

In the eight months since Jenny went west, we sometimes went weeks without speaking. Still, an hour didn't pass where I didn't think of her, hoping an hour hadn't passed where she hadn't thought of me. And somehow San Francisco seemed closer.

Now I'd messed things for sure by fumbling my mention of Amanda. San Francisco felt like it had moved to another continent.

The phone rang again as I got off the tollway. 'Listen, Jenny—'

'Damn you, Elstrom,' Gaylord Rikk corrected. It had only been twenty minutes since we'd spoken. I ripped the headset off and pressed the phone to my ear, in clear violation of Illinois law.

'That seems to have already happened.'

'I got intrigued, but only because I'm bored. In some disgusting way, you liven up my dreary existence.'

'You've got something?' I asked.

'It only took two phone calls. Turns out our people did ask where Carson had gone, the night he was killed. No one seemed to know, not his wife or his secretary, and we dropped it because it didn't seem relevant. So . . .' He lingered in silent smugness, waiting.

'So?' I asked, accepting the cue.

He dropped his voice, a secret agent for sure. 'I called Carson's secretary, saying I was tidying up the last of our paperwork, and needed to know where he'd been that night. She said she already told the police she didn't know, which I knew.'

'And?' I asked, anxious. He'd learned something.

'Nothing,' he said.

'You struck out?'

'No, I mean Carson had nothing written on his calendar for that evening.'

'I don't suppose—'

'I caught your drift earlier,' he said. 'I schmoozed. Carson's secretary had his appointment books, five years' worth, right at her desk.'

'And?'

'Nothing was written in for any of those Tuesday evenings.'

'You're sure?'

'Why do you sound so excited?'

'I'll tell you in a minute.'

'His secretary thought it was unusual because he was always busy at night. But she double-checked because I was so persuasive. Nothing had been penciled in for any of those evenings. And that, to her, is inconceivable.'

It was inconceivable to me as well, almost.

'Tell me how this is going to help me sue the beneficiary, Elstrom,' he said.

'Who is the beneficiary?'

'I can't divulge the entity.'

'Entity? The beneficiary wasn't family?'

'I'm sure Carson had multiple policies. We only carried one of them, and the beneficiary wasn't family. It was an organization, a company. Tell me how you're going to help us.'

I told him I'd call him when I learned more, and clicked him away, but not before I heard him swear.

I swore, too, at the bulb flickering stronger in the back of my brain. Grant Carson had been careful to make no notation of where he'd been off to, those Tuesday nights. As had Benno Barberi. Jim Whitman had noted them in his appointment books only with the letter 'C.' Whatever those three men had been doing, they were doing it secretly, and they were doing it together.

Right down to getting killed, one after the other.

TWENTY-ONE

I skidded to a dusty stop across the few stones left on Kutz's gravel lot with what I thought was considerable élan.

Leo was waiting in his Porsche. The top was down, but he'd parked in the shade under the overpass, and he wore an oversized red straw hat that, even without its tightly knotted blue chinstrap, would have looked ridiculous. Thought it was months before the burning rays of summer, Leo was careful; his pale skin burns like an infant's.

'So elegant, your driving finesse,' he said.

'I know the words to that bit of music you're listening to,' I said, through the newly exposed rip in my side curtain. Another curl of Discount Den duct tape had let go on the tollway.

'They're called lyrics, you boor, but Jobim didn't use them in this song.'

He was listening to a piece of Brazilian bossa nova that, for once, I recognized. I didn't know its name, but it was smooth and flowing and getting a lot of play as background in a television laxative commercial.

'No more pressure,' I began singing, warbling with the same solemnity as the singer on TV.

He sighed, shut off the player, and got out of the car.

We walked up to the peeling wood trailer. Young Kutz glowered at us through the tiny order window. Young Kutz is young in name only; he's on the wrong side of eighty, and had been glowering from his trailer long before Leo and I started coming in grammar school.

'Hiya, Mr Kutz,' Leo said.

'What's it today, twerp?'

Leo stretched up to his full five foot six inches so he could line his eyes along the counter. 'The usual six pups, cheese fries, and Big Swallow root beer, of course.'

'I thought you were dieting,' I said.

'The trick is to chew slowly, thereby atomizing all the fat calories before swallowing.'

'For sure you'll drop that nettlesome pound and a half.' I added my one dog and small diet to his order, gave Leo eight singles – Kutz's prices were an outrage, given the quality of the food – and went around to the back of the trailer.

The lunch rush was over and empty picnic tables were everywhere. The snow was long gone, and it hadn't rained at all in March, yet incredibly, I found a table that was almost half free of pigeon droppings.

Leo noticed when he came with the food. 'Partially dropless – nice,' he said, setting down the flimsy tray of hotdogs, fries and drinks with a careful, soft sliding motion of his hands and forearms. Kutz uses ultra-thin plastic trays because they're likely to flex and be dropped, resulting in re-orders as well as queasy pigeons, which then results in excessively spotted tables.

As always, we ate silently for the first minutes, savoring the truck exhaust drifting down from the overpass mingling with the steam we imagined might be rising from our barely lukewarm hot dogs. They were the exact smells of our youth, nostalgia at its purest. Rumor had it Kutz had never changed the hot dog water in all the years he worked the trailer. No need, he'd supposedly once said: grease floats and ends up on the product, to be consumed by customers or pigeons – depending. That meant the hot dogs Leo and I were now eating might have been cooked in part of the very water Kutz used when we were kids. Nostalgia doesn't get any purer than that.

'You may now tap the power of my formidable brain,' Leo said, after his third hot dog. 'How's the case?'

I told him that Barberi, Whitman and Carson had all died on, or right after, the second Tuesdays of even-numbered months.

He slammed the brakes on the sagging cheese fry he was about to propel into his mouth. When I dare eat Kutz's cheese fries,

I use a plastic spoon because the yellowish substance he says is cheese quickly dissolves potato fiber, rendering them too limp for me to hold. Not Leo. He regards Kutz's cheese fries as among life's worthiest adversaries, and while still in high school, mastered the art of arcing them into his mouth with his fingers. He says it's a matter of wrist speed and pride.

Now, all that was forgotten. The cheese fry slid from his fingers to drop, with a soft, gelatinous slap, back into its cardboard tray. 'What have you made of that?'

'Each of the three men took pains to obscure their whereabouts those nights.' I told him of the 'C' notations in Whitman's desk diary.

'They were together, at this "C" place,' he said.

'Until they started dying, one by one.'

'What's premeditated and sinister in a heart attack, an understandable suicide and a random hit-and-run?'

'What if the first and second deaths came from administered overdoses, and the hit and run was deliberate? Barberi came home highly agitated over some insurance concern, but he'd learned to handle stress. A dose of something might have sent his heart into overdrive, but we'll never know; he was cremated. We do know Whitman ingested too many pills, and right now we know there was no good reason for him to go outside his home to get them. If Whitman was murdered, then it's likely Carson was murdered too, pushed in front of an oncoming car.'

'To what end?'

'I don't know.'

'Does Wendell have any thoughts on motive?'

'He fired me.'

The eyebrows came together and stuck, shocked. 'Surely not for a lack of progress.'

'His whole attitude has changed. Instead of being intrigued by my suspicions, Wendell became combative and swatted every one of them away.'

'What did he say about those mysterious "C" notations in Whitman's calendar?'

'No curiosity there, either.'

'He knows what they mean,' he said.

'He spent those Tuesday evenings with Barberi, Whitman and Carson,' I said, 'and I'll bet he knows who drove Whitman home.'

'You've gotten too close,' Leo said.

'Yes.'

'What's next?' he asked.

'Arthur Lamm.'

Leo shook his head, confused. 'The real-estate biggie?'

'He's gone missing, though it might be because the IRS is investigating him.' I told him what the Bohemian had learned.

'What if he didn't take off?'

'Then twenty-five per cent of the biggest shots in Chicago have just been murdered.'

TWENTY-TWO

'**M**y father fired you.' Amanda spoke slowly over the phone, each word precise, distinct, and under control. I knew that control. She was furious.

'Apparently.'

'He told me you'd made no progress, you'd pocketed his two-thousand-dollar retainer without doing anything but mewing around a little bit, and dusted him off by telling him to go to the police.'

'Mewing? Like a cat? He said I was mewing?'

'Don't evade. What is he up to?'

'Actually, I've made out a check for his refund.'

'Don't parse my words, either. What's all this about: the body-guards, the secrecy? Is his life in danger?'

I'd had an inspiration, driving home from Kutz's. 'I want to deliver the refund in person. I'm certain he won't take my call, or see me at his office.'

'You want me to set up a confrontation without telling me what's going on?'

'He's still my client.'

'I ask again: is his life in danger?'

'Get me in front of him, Amanda. If I learn he's in real trouble, I will violate his trust and tell you.'

It was enough, for the moment. She said she'd get back to me.

I crossed the second floor, headed to see how my freshly re-hung cabinet was faring, when the lid on the front door mail slot clanked. I'd installed one that was extra-large, anticipating improved times, but even the junk mailers didn't yet think me worthy. Today though, my mail slot clanked. Mail had come. I clanked, too, beating down the wrought-iron stairs.

It was Jenny's small something, sent in a padded envelope. I ripped it open. An untied purple bowtie was inside, with a note that read, 'It's not so much the look that's sought, but rather the demonstration of proficiency.'

It was a nudge, aimed with a joke, and so quintessentially, marvelously Jenny.

I'd never tied a bowtie. That was the laugh, and the nudge, because she knew I'd wrestle with learning to tie the thing, and think of her every second I was doing it. And I would, along with thinking about my aborted trip to San Francisco and the phone call I'd fumbled just a few hours earlier.

I took my bowtie upstairs. The cabinet I'd straightened was listing. Not much, just a few degrees, and surely no more than the smoke stacks on the *Titanic* had tipped in the first minutes following its collision with the iceberg. I set down the tie and spent the next hour trying to correct the cabinet, but no amount of shimming, leveling, and shaving got it to hang right.

Amanda called. 'We're having barbecue tonight with my father, at five.'

'That's early,' I said.

'With the pig lady,' she said. It was rough, especially for Amanda.

'You mean his wife?'

'Second wife,' she said.

I knew that, of course. It had been in the papers. Wendell, a long-time widower, had married after Amanda and I divorced.

'You'll have time to tell me everything as we drive up there,' she said. 'Everything.'

Amanda was waiting beneath the portico of her lakeside condominium building. She wore exquisitely fitted jeans and a burgundy top that didn't pull all the fire from her eyes. She flashed the rest of it at me as she slid onto the passenger's seat. 'I don't like cagy.'

'For the time being, I have to respect your father's confidence,' I said as I pulled onto Lake Shore Drive.

She gave my invariable khakis and blue shirt the usual quick glance, but lingered at my neck. Her voice softened. 'A bow tie, and purple?'

'Shock and awe.' It had taken me an hour practicing with downloaded instructions to achieve the partially crumpled mess around my neck.

'You want my father to be shocked and awed by your tie, or by what you're going to say?'

I didn't want to say I'd worn the tie to keep reminding myself of who'd sent it, and I didn't want to tell her of the accusations I was going to lay on Wendell, so I said nothing.

She fingered the wires sticking out of the hole in the dashboard where the radio had been. 'You used to have a Mercedes,' she said.

'Bought used,' I said.

'And such very nice clothes.'

'Fortunes wane.'

'Perhaps, but you gave your clothes away, right after we split up. Including that nice camel-hair sport coat I bought you for your birthday . . .' Her voice trailed off.

It was old detritus, and it was accurate. And it was useful, because it beat discussing what her father hadn't told me about Barberi, Whitman and Carson.

'I'd gotten to living a little too fancy,' I said. 'Jettisoning the duds and the car seemed a reasonable way to simplify my life.'

'Along with going to live in a turret?'

'You are demeaning my castle?'

'You have to admit, there's something monastic about your life . . . the turret, the lack of variety in clothing, this . . .' She bent back one of the wires sticking out from the dash, and turned to me. 'Was I part of all your clutter, Dek? Was I too fancy?'

'Too fancy?' I repeated, startled. 'You've never been too fancy, Amanda.'

It might have been from the rapid turns in the road, but she'd leaned closer before shifting away. 'Your new bow tie is a promising addition to your wardrobe,' she said. 'What prompted you to buy it?'

'It was a gift . . .' I stopped, though my abrupt silence spilled the rest of it.

'Ah . . . the newswoman.' Then, 'What are you going to ask my father?' she asked, leaning more toward her door and safer talk.

Or more dangerous, depending. 'I'm going to ask him about Wendell Phelps.'

She turned to look at me. 'What the hell?'

'I'm going to ask him if he fired his previous investigator using the same baloney he gave me.'

I told her I wanted to talk to Wendell before I said anything more, and we fell into silence as she mulled, and I mulled, things each of us didn't understand about Wendell and perhaps, less than fleetingly, about ourselves. I tried to fill the quiet by shifting more than was necessary, working through the rush-hour traffic up Lake Shore Drive to Sheridan Road, through Evanston, Wilmette, and Winnetka. With every mile, the homes got grander and set back farther from the road. By the time we got to Lake Forest, most of the estates were invisible.

I turned right onto Red Leaf Road and followed it as it curved along the shore of Lake Michigan. As I rounded the last turn, brake lights flashed ahead as cars slowed to turn through Wendell's stone pillars.

Amanda inhaled sharply. 'He didn't tell me he was having a party. I'm wearing jeans, for God's sake.'

'Nice jeans, though,' I said. 'And of course, I'm wearing a purple bow tie.'

She didn't laugh.

We passed a bush that looked like it had been ripped in half.

'Pigs,' she said. Earlier, she'd referred to her father's new wife as a pig lady, but now, apparently, she was including Wendell in her contempt.

I followed a black Mercedes sedan into the long driveway and coasted to a stop. Four more dark Mercedes were ahead of the one in front of us. At the head of the line, several blue-jacketed parking valets were waiting for a uniformed security guard to check invitations. It took ten minutes for the guard to get to us.

Amanda leaned across me and spoke through the rip in my side curtain. 'I'm Amanda Phelps. I've brought a guest.'

I found myself holding my breath. Her body weight, so easily pressed against me, felt like the best of our old times.

The private cop's list of invited guests had small photos alongside the names. He peered in at her. 'I'm sorry, Ms Phelps, we don't have your guest listed.'

'I'm Mr Phelps's daughter. That's sufficient.'

The private cop looked a little too long at the gray primed section behind the driver's side door before asking for my driver's license. Amanda had to straighten up so I could reach for my wallet. I handed out my license, and the guard stepped back to speak into his two-way radio.

'Obviously I didn't tell my father you'd be coming along,' she said to me.

I gestured toward the guard reporting my arrival. 'There goes my shock and awe.'

'Maybe not. My father hasn't yet seen your purple bow tie.'

Behind us, expensive automobile engines revved loud and impatient. Finally, the radio crackled and the guard motioned for one of the valets to come over. 'Thank you,' the private cop said, handing back my license.

'Don't let anybody paint over that primer,' I told the valet as I got out, pointing at the gray patch behind the driver's door. He nodded gravely, probably thinking it was a sign of great wealth to have the confidence to drive up in such a heap, particularly wearing a purple bow tie.

A big man was waiting for us by the front walk, his suit coat bulging from a gun. He motioned for Amanda and me to follow him along the flagstone path around the south side of the house. Wendell had sent him out fast when he learned Amanda had brought a most unwanted guest.

A huge red-and-white striped tent had been set up on the lawn. A four-piece combo was playing gentle jazz on the stone terrace as a hundred people, holding champagne flutes, swayed to the music and made appropriate rich people noises. The unseasonably warm weather had held, and the men wore pastel jackets, the women, pastel dresses. All the guests seemed to be tanned, from Palm Beach or Palm Springs or wherever the palms were where they wintered when Chicago got slushy. I supposed I stood out, because I don't get tanned until summer, and even then it comes mottled with spots of white wherever bits of caulk and paint had blocked the sun from my skin.

I looked around for Wendell. Three more men in ill-fitting, too-square suits stood fairly close together at one end of the terrace. Wendell stood in the approximate middle of them, talking with a small group of people. I started to head over but the big man blocked my way. 'Mr Phelps is busy.'

'Not for his daughter,' Amanda said.

'Mr Phelps suggested later,' the big man said.

Wendell had allowed me in, only to box me in.

Amanda was about to head for her father when a bell sounded from a few hundred feet away. The jazz group stopped playing in mid-riff.

'Delores's new baby,' a woman with impossibly white teeth said to Amanda. Delores was the name of Wendell's second wife.

The crowd began to move as a herd toward the far side of the lawn. I looked toward the tent. Wendell had gone.

I grabbed two flutes of champagne from a passing waiter. 'Delores's new baby?' I whispered to Amanda, handing her one. 'You've become a half-sister?'

I'd expected a glare. Instead, Amanda gave me a faint smile and we followed the crowd.

TWENTY-THREE

Only the waves crashing onto the beach below sounded as we moved, hushed like congregants summoned to a secret sunset ceremony, through a tall grass prairie preserve and into a dense tunnel of arched trees that shrouded the path in almost complete darkness. We emerged fifty yards later into a clearing where the last of the day's sun shone again. Some of those ahead of us had apparently participated in such gatherings before, and were forming a broad semicircle facing a lit-up, miniature stone cottage.

A large woman stood in front of the tiny rock house. Her closely cropped dark hair was streaked with gray, and she wore a loose-flowing, multi-hued robe that, in the backlighting from the little windows behind her, made her look like a pagan priestess afire with the setting sun. She held a champagne flute in her right hand, and the end of a leash in the other. I stepped around the people in front to see more clearly. The other end of the leash was attached to a pig.

It was not the sort of small pink pig seen on farms, destined to become bacon. This pig was larger, with brown and white spots, and looked to weigh two hundred pounds.

The woman in the robe raised her champagne. 'Welcome Jasmine, everybody,' she shouted to the sky.

Everyone raised their glasses.

As I raised my champagne, I snuck a glance at Amanda. She was looking directly back at me, her own flute raised, but not toward the pig. She was toasting my ignorance. 'My new half-sister,' she mouthed above the muffled applause, the best the crowd could do while holding champagne.

After a few last claps, and several more shouts of 'Welcome, Jasmine,' the group began to disperse in the direction of the path back to the food and stronger booze. The homage had ended. I turned to follow, when Amanda stepped up and seized my hand.

'No, Vlodek,' she said. It was the first time she'd ever used my given name. 'You must meet Delores, the woman at the center of my father's not-quite-rational universe.'

Her fingernails dug into my palm as she half tugged me to the small group of people clustered around the woman in robes. As we got closer to the cottage, I noticed that the thick Plexiglas windows were deeply scratched and smeared milky, no doubt from snouts.

Just then, the rubber door swung outward and, to the faint strains of classical music playing inside, another pig lumbered out, this one pure black and half the size of the leashed Jasmine. I glimpsed straw on the floor of the rock cottage before the rubber door slapped shut.

Delores spotted Amanda standing at the edge of the little group. The way the two women stiffened simultaneously said it all. Amanda put her arm under my elbow and marched me forward.

'Amanda,' Delores Phelps said.

'Delores.'

People to the left of us stepped back, to make room for the pig that had come from the cottage.

'Peter!' Delores Phelps cried, holding out her champagne flute low enough for the new arrival, the black pig, to insert his tongue. 'Peter just loves Dom Perignon,' Delores said.

Several in the small cluster murmured approvingly, and Peter the pig grunted, a low, long snorting sound, likely in agreement.

Delores turned to me. 'And you are Mr Rudolph, Amanda's most successful young man?'

'Not young, nor successful, nor Mr Rudolph. I'm Dek Elstrom.'

'We're divorced,' Amanda said, of me.

'I believe I did hear something about that,' Delores said. 'Lovely tie, Mr Elstrom.'

Peter nudged Delores for more Dom Perignon.

'Peter is so attached to his mommy, aren't you, Peter?' Delores cooed, lowering her flute to give him another taste. 'Peter is a Vietnamese potbellied pig,' she said. 'He used to sleep in his own bedroom, just down the hall from ours, but after he outgrew his bassinet, he started coming into our bedroom.' She stopped, noticing the look on my face. 'He was mostly potty trained, of course, but still, he did have his accidents.' She bent down again to nuzzle the pig's hairy ear. 'So we built him his own little cottage, and got him some brothers and sisters.' She straightened up and nodded to the pig at the other end of the leash. 'Jasmine's our newest, a Kunekune from New Zealand.'

I looked at my empty champagne flute, simply because I couldn't think of what to say.

Delores noticed, and held out her own flute, swishing the little in the bottom that Peter had not licked out.

I shook my head. 'Thank you, no.' I took a quick look around for Amanda, but she'd disappeared. Only the bodyguard remained.

'It was lovely meeting you,' I told Delores Phelps.

'Likewise, I'm sure.'

'You, too,' I said to the guard, but he made no move to step away. We walked back to the mansion, me in front, him a close two steps behind.

Amanda was talking to her father on the terrace. 'What have you been telling my daughter, Elstrom?' he asked, when I walked up.

'That you've not been forthcoming, and nothing else.'

'We'll discuss your ignorance privately.' Then, to Amanda, 'Just he and I, my dear.'

'I'm part of this,' she said.

'I'll explain later,' he said.

For a moment he stood silent, I stood silent, and she glared. Finally, she shrugged and walked away.

Wendell led us across the lawn, a small parade with him in the lead, me in the middle, and three body guards bringing up the rear. We entered the house through a side door and passed a laundry room with a porcelain-topped table for folding clothes and a kitchen fitted out, wall-to-wall, with stainless steel. A right turn down another hall brought us to the passage that led to his study door. We didn't go in. The three guards moved up close behind me as Wendell continued marching us through the long dark foyer to the front of the house.

'What are you hiding, Wendell?' I asked the back of his head.

He opened the front door. 'Why call the police?'

'I didn't call any cops.'

He stepped back, and two of the three guards came up on either side of me. I took the hint. I pressed Wendell's refund check onto the guard at my right, and stepped outside. The door slammed.

A valet had been alerted to bring up the Jeep. I got in and drove through the gates. I pulled over fifty yards from the house and called Amanda. Her phone went automatically to voice mail. I didn't leave a message because by then I noticed the glint of a familiar bumper parked just past a copse of trees alongside the road ahead. I started up, motored past without looking directly at the driver. It didn't take long to be sure. The car, a black junior-grade BMW, pulled out and stayed far back at every turn, from Lake Forest all the way south and into Evanston.

I found the sort of cul-de-sac I was looking for just before I got to the outskirts of Chicago. I turned in, spun around fast, and was waiting for him when he eased into the cul-de-sac. He slammed on his brakes but he was too late; I'd pulled sideways to block him in. I jumped out of my car.

His window was open, and so was his collar. I reached in and grabbed it.

It was Jason, or Brad. I couldn't tell because they'd been so similarly barbered.

'Tell Mrs Barberi that I'll report when I'm ready,' I shouted. 'And tell yourself that if I see you again, I'll break your snout.'

As I got back into the Jeep and drove away, I realized I'd misspoken. I'd meant to say nose, not snout.

It had been that sort of day.

TWENTY-FOUR

The fellow flashing a badge early the next afternoon had to be one of the cops Wendell accused me of calling. He didn't look like a cop. Blond and fresh-faced, he wore a gray herringbone sport coat, charcoal slacks, a white shirt and a blue-striped tie. Right down to his highly polished burgundy penny loafers, he looked bound for the Ivy League, Princeton perhaps. He said his name was Delmar. I asked if that was a first name or a last name. He said his first name was Delray.

'Delray Delmar?'

'I figured a guy named Vlodek would understand.'

'Like we were joined at the hip.' I invited him in.

'Nifty,' he said, looking around the bare limestone room. First-time visitors are always impressed with the craggy, curved limestone walls and the beamed wood ceiling, though typically they offer up more than one word of architectural praise.

I motioned for us to sit in the two white plastic chairs. Except for those, two cans of varnish and my table saw, the first floor is unfurnished.

'I know how it is, starting out,' he said.

I was old enough to be his father, almost. Mature enough, certainly, to control my temper.

'I'm saving up for furniture, too,' he added after another beat, as if that helped.

I fought the urge to ask if he'd like some chocolate milk. He might have said yes, and I didn't have any. Milk. Or chocolate. So I stayed silent, and stared at the knot of his striped tie.

He cleared his throat. 'You were hired by Mr Wendell Phelps to investigate the recent deaths of three prominent businessmen?'

He was asking two troublesome questions. He wanted me to confirm the identity of a client, something I wouldn't do. And he was asking me to admit to running an investigation, terminology I had to tiptoe around, because 'investigate' is a touchy verb in official Illinois. Investigators – private detectives – are required to be licensed, and that in turn requires law enforcement experience or a law degree. I had neither. But there's a loophole, as there usually is in Illinois laws: a person can operate as an investigator if he's working for a lawyer. It's a gray line, but it's a mile wide. I knew several lawyers, including the Bohemian, who would cover for me if I ever got in trouble. Still, I like to dodge the word 'investigate.'

'Did Wendell Phelps tell you that?' I said, instead of answering.

'I got your name from Debbie Goring, who was delighted to talk to me. It didn't take much Internet research to learn that you nibble at investigating. I also learned you are Mr Phelps's son-in-law.'

'Former son-in-law,' I said.

'Mr Phelps is a friend to many powerful people, including Arthur Lamm,' he said, floating the name while watching my eyes.

The kid had a contact in the IRS. 'I went to see Mr Phelps,' he went on. 'One of his guards said he wasn't home. So now I've come to see you.'

'I'm a records researcher,' I told the lad. 'Mostly I work for insurance companies, though I chase down information for law firms as well.'

'And for Wendell Phelps?'

'I agree with Debbie Goring. I'm troubled by where Jim Whitman got the pills to kill himself.'

'I believe you're also bothered by the timing of the deaths of Benno Barberi and Grant Carson because they, like Jim Whitman, died on or just after the second Tuesdays of even-numbered months.' Young Delray Delmar had also talked to Barberi's and Carson's secretaries.

'Therefore,' he went on, 'you've probably deduced that the three dead men spent those Tuesday evenings together.'

I liked the way he applied the word 'deduced' to my thinking. It made me sound like something other than a schlump who couldn't hang a kitchen cabinet straight.

'By Jove, Holmes, it's an interesting puzzle,' I said.

'Work with me, Mr Elstrom. I'm not interested in Wendell Phelps. You can continue to protect Mr Phelps and perhaps help Debbie Goring. She might even part with some large dollars if you help her gain insurance money.'

'Who are you really interested in?'

He leaned forward. 'Arthur Lamm. What do you know about him?'

'If he's not gone fishing, then he's gone missing,' I said, rhythmically.

'I think he's on the run,' he said.

'From the IRS?' I asked.

'Surely from them, but I'm wondering if he's running from something more. I want to question him about those deaths. Do you know where he might be?'

'No. Do you think he killed Whitman and Carson?'

'All I think right now is he travels in the same circles as the dead men and now he's disappeared.'

'Do you think he's part of that Tuesday evening group?' I asked.

'He's wealthy enough. Do you have any idea where they hold their get-togethers?'

'No idea.' It was true enough. All I had was the letter 'C,' and I wasn't going to share that without Wendell's permission.

'Somewhere north of the Chicago River, on the Gold Coast?' he asked.

'Because that's where Grant Carson was killed?' I shook my head. 'Are you in Homicide?'

'Special Projects.'

'I've never heard of it. How many are in that department?'

'Just me.'

'Why isn't Homicide looking into this?'

'Not enough heat yet.' Delray grinned. 'My boss respects un-official inquiries from powerful men.'

'Someone asked your boss to look into Arthur Lamm?'

'You got it.' He stood up. 'I'm going to take apart Grant Carson's hit-and-run, because it's the freshest death. I'm looking at Whitman, too, because his daughter, and you, can't figure where he got those extra pills or even why he would have bothered. I'm saving Benno Barberi for last, because frankly, I see nothing in his death that suggests murder.'

'And Arthur Lamm?'

'I'm interested in him most of all.' We walked outside. 'Keep me informed, and I'll do likewise. I'll even put in good words to Debbie Goring, help you get a reward. But we do things my way.'

'Who's your rabbi?' In Chicago-speak, a rabbi is a clout guy, somebody connected, a person who can take care of getting whatever a kid in a striped tie needed.

Grinning, he said, 'The deputy chief,' and got into his car.

As I watched him drive away in his long black cop sedan, I saw a young, brash, arrogant guy who knew how to get clouted into a job. He was ambitious, and he had power behind him. He'd be relentless; he'd learn things.

Some of which would lead him straight to Wendell Phelps and whatever he was hiding.

TWENTY-FIVE

The cell number Wendell had given me no longer worked. It must have been a disposable, discarded like me.

I mulled, but not for long. I owed Amanda an explanation for last night, and a warning about the cop who was likely to complicate her father's life.

I called her cell phone six times in three hours and left no messages. She answered the seventh, angrily.

'You dumped me,' she said.

'Your father had me thrown out.'

'He said you stormed off.'

'He accused me of calling the cops. One was just here.'

'Why would you call the cops?'

'I didn't. You know I'd never rat out a client . . .' I paused, a hypocrite, about to do just that. 'It must have been someone else in the heavy cream who called—'

'*The heavy cream?*' she interrupted, almost shouting with impatience.

'They're the people who have risen to the very top, people like your father, who run Chicago. One of them must have gotten scared and called the Chicago police. Delray Delmar, a pup but earnest, caught the case, and came round to ask what I knew.'

'Scared by what?'

'Your father told you nothing last night?'

'Only that you blew up and left. I tried to press him. He mumbled something about talking later and walked away. For the next hour, he kept himself surrounded by others. Obviously he was avoiding me, so I got one of the guards to drive me home.' She paused for a moment, then said, 'You could have waited out on the street, you know.'

'I called you from outside, but your phone was switched off. Then I realized I'd been followed. It was safest to leave you with your father's guards.'

'You're scaring me. Who was following you?'

'Benno Barberi's widow put a tail on me. She knows I'm chasing the case and doesn't want to wait for information. I put a stop to it.'

'Is Mrs Barberi frightened like my father? Benno died last year from a heart attack.'

'Did you know Jim Whitman, or Grant Carson?'

'Benno Barberi died of a heart attack, right?'

'All signs point to that.'

'And Mr Whitman and Mr Carson . . .?' She stopped, understanding. 'This is why my father hired bodyguards? He sees something sinister in their deaths?'

'Yes.'

'But Mr Whitman technically died of natural causes, though he may have swallowed too many pain killers. Mr Carson was hit by a car.'

'There are wrinkles surrounding each death.'

'I ask now for the third time: is my father in danger?'

'He'll be in less danger if he tells the cops what he knows. Do you know Arthur Lamm?'

'Don't change the subject.'

'I'm not.'

'Arthur is my father's closest friend,' she said. 'He handles our corporate insurance, and my father has invested in a couple of Arthur's real-estate ventures. Is Arthur in danger, too?'

'He's dropped from sight. He might have gone camping, or he might be evading the IRS.'

'I heard a rumor about the IRS investigation, but Arthur wouldn't run from that. He's got lawyers and accountants to take care of such things. If he's not around, it's because he's gone camping . . . Right, Dek?'

'I'd like to be sure he's gone camping.'

'You believe my father's not delusional, that someone's out to kill the men in the . . . whatever.'

'Heavy cream,' I said, supplying the words. 'Wendell won't tell me what he knows. Young officer Delmar has better resources than mine, and he'll find out what that is.'

'This can't be real,' she said, but she said she'd talk to her father.

On the stoop, outside his bungalow, Leo went straight for a vein. 'You, pass for a rich guy?' He laughed.

'Just for a night, maybe two. I'll breeze up to Lamm's fishing camp and see if I can sniff out his whereabouts.'

'Because you think that's something Lamm's friends, family, Wendell's previous investigator, the IRS, and most especially your new young cop friend haven't been sharp enough to consider doing themselves?'

'Because I don't know what to think.'

'Your cop is OK with you pursuing this on your own?'

'I promised I'd report anything I find out.'

'Meaning you'll report anything that doesn't incriminate Wendell.'

'I'm sure he understands.'

A sly grin lit Leo's face. 'Merely driving my car won't pass you as rich enough to be a friend of Lamm's,' he said. 'You've got to have the threads, too.' He touched the hem of his tropical shirt like he was caressing imperial silk. 'Red parrots and yellow flowers on blue rayon are the true signs of affluence. They make you look wealthy enough to not give a damn.'

'I want to look like I own the Porsche, not like I stole it.'

He sighed and handed over the keys.

TWENTY-SIX

Two hours north of Milwaukee, the concrete highway softened into rippling blacktop and the barns began fading from freshly painted reds to chalking shades of rose. An hour north of that, the blacktop crumbled and so had some of the barns. Every few miles, I spotted one lying in a bleached gray pile across an abandoned field. Bent Lake was one more hour up. I arrived just before sunset.

It was a one-block town, anchored at the front by a Dairy Queen and the remains of a gas station. The DQ's parking lot was empty, though the red-and-white wood hut was lit up bright with yellow bug lights and looked ready for commerce.

The gas station across the street did not. Its pumps had been pulled and the only visible reminder of its heritage was an oval blue-and-white Pure Oil sign creaking from rusty chains on a pole. The young man working inside on an old truck didn't jerk up, startled, as I passed by, so I assumed the town was accustomed to some degree of traffic.

I drove slowly past storefronts that were boarded up. The only light came from a Budweiser sign in a tavern window in the middle of the block.

A cluster of old, clapboard motel cottages was curled at the far end. Its sign read: 'Loons' Rest. Rooms $30.' The paint on the sign was fresher by a couple of decades than the white flakes peeling off the cottages. A new, shiny blue Ford F-150 pickup truck with a big chrome radiator and pimp lights on its roof was the only vehicle in the lot.

'Forty dollars for the night,' the woman behind the counter said as I jangled the bells above the door, coming in. She was wrinkled and her skin and hair were colored almost the same gray as the collapsed barns I'd passed, south of town.

'The sign outside says thirty.'

'Them's off-season rates.'

I cocked a thumb at the window looking out at the parking lot, empty except for the truck and the Porsche. 'Hasn't snowmobiling season just ended?'

'You from Illinois?'

'Does that matter?'

'I like to know how our clientele finds us.' She smiled, showing me where she needed dental work.

'In desperation,' I wanted to say but didn't. Loons' Rest was the only place around, it was getting dark, and it wasn't hard to imagine insects the size of antelope roaming the deserted old town. I pulled out my Visa card.

'No credit; cash,' she said.

'American currency OK?' I asked as I peeled off four tens.

'That'll be forty-four with tax,' she said.

I added four singles. 'Do you know where Arthur Lamm's place is?'

'Never heard of him.'

'Thank you,' I said.

'Illinoyance,' she muttered.

'Cheesehead,' I said, but only after I'd stepped outside and banged the door shut on the woman and the jangling bells.

It was all so very adult.

My room smelled of the same strong pine cleaner the Rivertown Health Center sloshed about when a tenant expired, and I wondered whether the weak, twenty-six-watt bulb hanging from the stained tile ceiling was meant to conceal as well. Even in the dim light, the knots on the knotty pine paneling appeared troublesome, and I thought it best not to look at them closely, for fear some weren't knots at all but rather shoe-heel marks on top of cockroach splats.

A tufted orange spread covered the mattress, and a disconnected gold pay box for a long-gone Magic Fingers electric bed massager was screwed to the headboard. It never boded well when the Magic Fingers fled a town. For sure I would only stay one night.

I sat on the bed to check my cell phone for messages. It had not rung. The reason was not that there had been no calls or texts. My display showed that no bars of service were available.

I left my duffel tightly zipped on the bed – in case any of the knots jumped off the wall paneling, frisky – and went out into the dusk. Across the street, several teenagers were running along the sidewalk, yelling as they raked broom handles under the ribs of the corrugated metal awnings of the vacant stores. The racket was deafening, reverberating along the deserted street as though monkeys were banging on pans. Every few seconds, shadowy things dropped from beneath the awnings, which set the teens to waving flashlights, jumping up and down, screaming and laughing with delight.

It made no sense. 'What are you doing?' I called across the street.

They stopped and stared at me. 'Stomping bats, a course,' one young girl, pretty in denim and a pale yellow jacket, yelled back.

'A course,' I shouted back. There were worse places to grow up in than Rivertown, I supposed.

I stepped into the center of the street, reasoning that bat splatter was less likely out there than on the sidewalks, and walked down to the neon Budweiser light. Three men in flannel shirts sat at the bar inside, jawing with a bartender who had a red beard.

'Can I get something to eat here?' I asked.

'Pickled eggs which I prepare special myself, and Slim Jims,' Red Beard said. 'Anything fancier, you got to go to the DQ.'

I told him I needed fancier, and would be back for a brew after I'd eaten.

The Dairy Queen's parking lot was still empty, since the town's evening merriment remained underway beneath the metal awnings at the other end of the block. Inside the hut, a teenaged boy and girl were pressed together as tight as a double-dip of soft-serve ice cream jammed hard in a cake cone. The girl saw me appear in the glow of the yellow bug lights and broke the clinch. So long as I only wanted a hamburger, they could serve me dinner, she allowed. I asked what if I wanted two? That froze her face until I said I was making a joke. They both smiled then, sort of, though I suspected they'd discuss it later. No matter. Two hamburgers soon appeared, and I ate them with fries and a chocolate shake at a picnic table facing the road, so I could watch the cars that passed by. There were none. Afterward, I gave them back their plastic tray and walked down to the tavern.

The three flannel shirts and Red Beard stopped talking when I came in. I ordered a beer.

'Up here for some early fishing?' the bartender asked, skimming the head off the beer.

'At Arthur Lamm's camp. Know him?'

The six eyes above the three flannel shirts turned to look at me directly.

'I don't think he's around,' the bartender said.

I put on my confused face which, in truth, is never far away. 'I came up from Chicago a day early. I hope I didn't get the date mixed up.'

'Lamm's car is there, but no one has seen him,' the bartender said.

'Does anyone know where he's gone?'

'Herman says Lamm's off camping. It's caused a ruckus. You guys from Illinois . . .' The bartender's lower lip curled down, following the thought that was dropping away.

I bought beers for the men at the bar, the bartender, and another for myself. It set me back four bucks, not counting the single I left on the counter. It made everyone more talkative.

'Us guys from Illinois, you were saying?' I asked.

'Cops,' the bartender said.

'There was only the one,' said one of the flannel shirts – his was red.

'Young sonofabitch,' said the man next to him. His flannel was green.

'What was he asking?'

'I didn't actually talk to him. I just heard he was up from Chicago, asking for Lamm.'

'Nobody knows exactly where Lamm is, and that includes Herman,' the third man at the bar said, speaking for the first time. His flannel shirt was plaid, half red, half green, which I supposed made him an excellent arbiter for the other two. 'And if Herman's been drinking, he wouldn't have noticed Lamm being abducted in an alien spaceship.'

'Herman works for Lamm?' I asked.

'Supposedly he takes care of Lamm's camp,' Green Flannel said, 'but Herman Canty's never done a lick of work in his life. Herman's what you call an opportunist. He latches on to things.'

'Like Wanda, over at Loons',' Red Flannel said. 'Latched on to that some long time ago.'

'Rockin' the cot, God help him,' Green Flannel said.

That got the three flannels and the bartender laughing.

'She even lets him stay nights, sometimes, when his sister throws him out,' Red Flannel said.

'Not all nights. She's not all dumb,' the bartender said. 'She knows Herman for what he is.'

'A damned user,' Red Flannel said. 'Strikes at every opportunity.'

'This Canty, he latched on to Lamm as well?' I asked.

'Big time,' Green Flannel said. 'Sooner than later, you'll see a new blue F-One Fifty over to Loons'. That's Herman's truck. No one can figure out what he done for it, being as he's never been useful.'

'That truck come out of Chicago, according to the license plate frame,' Green Flannel said. 'He didn't buy it up here.'

'Either somebody died, leaving him an inheritance,' the plaid man said, 'or he's got Mr Lamm paying him way too large for watching his camp.'

The bartender was giving me a long look. 'You say you're a friend of Lamm's, yet you didn't call ahead to say you were coming up?'

'I'm more like an insurance client,' I said, 'but you're right. It's been a couple of months since he invited me. I should have checked before I drove up.'

'Cell phones don't always work up here, anyway,' the bartender said, shrugging. 'We're just yakking; nobody up here knows Lamm. He's certainly been too good to set foot in here.' He gestured at the murky shapes in the cloudy jar on the bar, as if to suggest that the eggs should have been reason enough to lure Lamm in. As if to warn me to not suffer the same loss, he slid the jar closer to me.

I resisted, saying it might incite the milk shake resting heavily on the hamburgers in my stomach, and asked for directions to Lamm's camp.

The bartender drew a map on a cocktail napkin. 'Mind that rickety old bridge on County M. It's a one-laner. Hit it wrong, you'll end up wet. And dead.'

I told them that if Lamm had indeed disappeared, I might want to speak to the sheriff. That got me another cocktail napkin map, and I left them to their pickled eggs and their flannel.

Outside, I envied their flannel. The night had turned frigid, and my pea coat was in Leo's Porsche. I hurried down the center of the street, deserted now, squinting for glints on the dark pavement. Nothing sparkled, freshly splattered, and I got to Loons' with shoes as dry as when I'd set out.

The inside of my cabin was as cold as the air outside. I spent five minutes looking for a thermostat before I realized that the cabin simply had no heat. I took a fast shower with what little lukewarm water could be coaxed from the pipes, dried myself with a towel that had a fist-sized hole in its center, bundled back into my clothes and pea coat, and slipped into bed.

I thought, then, of the newness of Jenny, waiting to warm me in San Francisco. And I thought of Amanda, and the easy, familiar way she'd warmed me, leaning against me in the Jeep, outside her father's house.

I tried to push those thoughts away, finding it easier to think about what I didn't understand about Arthur Lamm, the dead men in the heavy cream, and the frigid air inside the cabin. It wasn't until the middle of the night that I was finally able to shiver and shake myself to sleep.

TWENTY-SEVEN

'I'm in real need of caffeine,' I said to gray-skinned Wanda as I looked around the motel office for the coffee maker. It was six-thirty the next morning.

'DQ,' she said.

I pasted on the best smile I could offer to such a creature. 'You don't have coffee for guests?'

'DQ does egg sandwiches. You could have a whole breakfast.'

'With ice cream, just the thing for a cold morning.' I turned for the door.

'You checking out?'

'I'll be gone by the end of the morning. Check-out is noon?'

'Eight-thirty in season.'

I looked out the window. The Porsche was the only car parked on the gravel lot.

'I imagine you need to hustle to get rooms ready for the next onslaught of visitors,' I said.

'Eight-thirty,' she said.

'I'll leave the key in the room for when you come to make sure I didn't steal either the towel or the hole in the middle of it.'

'Illinoyance,' she muttered as I went outside.

'Cheesehead,' I muttered back, but likely she hadn't heard me, since I'd already slammed the door.

A truck shot from a parking space down the street and sped away. The truck was shiny and blue and I was fairly certain it was the one I'd seen in Loons' lot the previous evening, which meant it belonged to Herman Canty, Lamm's caretaker. If the rumors were true, that he spent his nights at the frigid Loons' Rest, curled beside the gray-faced Wanda, the man was entitled to whatever haste he needed to get away.

I drove down to the DQ. It was closed, though the sign said it was supposed to have opened at six, almost an hour earlier. I wasn't going to wait for someone to show up. I was anxious to speed out of that town, too. Besides, risking a launch of coffee in Leo's meticulously maintained Porsche, as I so often did in my Jeep, was unthinkable. I drove on.

Fifteen minutes later, in the sheriff's office, I regretted not waiting at the DQ. A massive caffeine-withdrawal headache had blossomed, and was pulsing along in perfect rhythm with the slow, doubting drone of the deputy sitting with his feet up on a brown steel desk.

'Tell me again why you're interested in Mr Lamm.' The man's tan shirt was stretched taut across his ample stomach, as though he'd often visited the DQ in Bent Lake.

'He invited me up for some fishing.'

His face was too red, too early in the year, to have come from the sun, and I guessed that his shirt might have been tightened more from beer than soft-serve ice cream. He craned his neck to look outside the window at the Porsche. 'Don't see gear,' he said, like he could see inside the trunk along with being able to smell a lie.

'Arthur said I could use his.'

The deputy sighed and shifted in the chair. 'Nobody seems to know where Mr Lamm has gotten himself to. People from his

office in Chicago called up to report him missing. I sent two guys
out for a day in a boat, and even hired a Cessna for an hour, but
we found no sight of him. Then that damned fool Herman Canty
up and says Lamm likes to go camping around this time of year.
Wish to hell he'd spoke up before we hired a plane.'

'Lamm's family says it's normal for him to be camping for so
long?'

'He's divorced, no kids. Ex-wife's out in California, and doesn't
much give a damn. She got an annuity out of him instead of
monthly income.'

'I heard a Chicago cop was up here looking for him.'

'Some kid, I heard, but he didn't bother to check in with me.'

'Lamm doesn't have a cell phone?'

'I tried. His was switched off.'

'How would I find Herman Canty?'

'Hard to say, especially now that he's getting about in that fancy
new truck.' The deputy tilted forward to sit upright. 'You want to
ask him about fishing?'

'I want to ask him about Lamm.'

'Herman will tell you Lamm's out fishing for muskies,' he said.
'Ever fish for muskies?'

'No.'

'Then what are you fishing for up here, Mr Elstrom?' he asked.

'Something I can sink a hook into, I suppose,' I said, and left.

TWENTY-EIGHT

I followed the bartender's napkin map down roads designated
with alphabet letters to junctions with roads marked with other
letters, and finally came to the bridge on County M that the
bartender had warned me about. It was a rickety, single-lane
contraption of bleached wood and rusted brackets that looked to
be spanning the narrow frothing river below more from habit than
any lingering structural integrity. The bartender said the knee-high
side rails were loose and the whole thing suffered dry rot. I took
his concern seriously, and eased forward in first gear. Even barely

crawling, the old planks shifted and rattled loudly, like I was disturbing old bones.

A fire lane had been cut into the woods one mile farther on. A half-mile after that, an eight-inch white board, with 'Lamm' written on it, was nailed to a tree beside two narrow clay ruts heading into the trees. I followed them to a clearing.

Herman Canty's shiny blue pickup truck was parked beside a dark Mercedes 500 series sedan made opaque from a rain-pocked mixture of dirt and bird droppings. I parked the Porsche and got out.

The log cottage facing the lake looked right for a rich man wanting to pass as poor. The timbers were splotched with moss, the black tarpaper roof was curling at the bottom, and green paint was flaking off the door and window facing the parking area. There was no lawn, just weeds in abundance, some two feet tall.

Capping the rusticity of the entire enterprise was a privy set far enough into the woods to provide splendid opportunities, while enthroned, for the intimate study of thousands of insects. I would have visited such a privy only under extreme distress, and then at warp speed.

The Mercedes was locked. I'd just begun rubbing the grime off the driver's window when a man stepped out of the cottage. He was lean, tall and grizzled with unkempt gray hair and a week's worth of unshaved beard stubble. Without doubt, he was tough enough to get through every word of the entire Sunday *New York Times* in the privy in the woods. Assuming, of course, that the man knew how to read.

'Herman?' I asked.

'Yep.'

'I came up to see Mr Lamm, but I understand he's not here.'

'Yep.'

'People from his Chicago office reported him missing?'

'Yep.'

For sure, the man must have enjoyed old cowboy movies.

'You told the sheriff there's no need for worry because Arthur takes off sometimes, for days on end, to go camping and fishing?'

He said nothing.

'That's a yep?'

'Yep,' he said. 'His business friends called me over at Loons'. Told them the same thing.'

'You didn't know he'd come up until you saw his car? You didn't actually see him?'

He stared off into the woods. 'Mr Lamm likes to take off, is all.'

I looked past him, toward the lake. An orange rowboat, barely floating above the waterline, was tied to a collapsing dock. 'Lamm's boat is still there.'

'Huh?'

'How can Lamm be off camping if his boat is still here?'

He blinked rapidly and licked his lips. After a minute, he said, 'He has two.'

'Mind if I look around?'

There was nothing friendly about the way he was now looking at me. 'What are you doing here, mister?'

'Arthur told me to come up any time for the fishing.'

Herman spat into the clay. 'Sure he did.'

I started walking toward the lake. Herman bird-dogged me from ten paces behind like he was worried I was going to make off with one of the trees.

When I got to the dock, I pointed at the boat. Barely two inches rode above the water. 'You're sure Arthur took a boat like this one?'

'Yep.'

'Must have bailed it out first.'

He spat again. 'I imagine.'

'Why didn't he bail out this one while he was at it?'

Herman shrugged. 'He only needed the one.'

'You're the caretaker here, right?'

'I look after things.'

'Why haven't you bailed out the boat?'

He looked away again.

'When Arthur gets back, tell him I came up to drop a few worms,' I said. I felt his eyes on me all the way to the Porsche. I hadn't bothered to give him a name. More importantly, he hadn't bothered to ask for one, as though he never expected to talk to Lamm again.

I drove the half-mile to the fire lane and pulled far enough into the leafless trees to hope the Porsche would be hidden from the road. The day had warmed. I left my pea coat in the car and doubled back through the woods. I wanted another look at Lamm's camp without Herman's breath misting the back of my neck. I got within sight of the privy when the sound of a loud engine came rumbling low along County M.

The woods hid the vehicle, but I guessed it was a truck, shiny and new and blue. Herman Canty, the man who'd made sure I'd left Lamm's clearing knowing nothing more than when I arrived, was driving slowly, maybe searching into the trees to make sure I had gone.

I held my breath, straining to hear any easing of his gas pedal. The engine loped on, low and steady. He didn't slow at the fire lane and, in another minute, the big-barreled exhaust had gone.

I ran the last yards through the trees and down to the shore. I could see no other cottages or clearings at Lamm's end of the lake, no places where someone could see me prowling around. Several channels split the shoreline across the lake, leading to other lakes.

I stepped onto the narrow dock. The orange rowboat shifted uneasily in the water. The next rain, even if it was light, would drop it to the bottom of the shallows.

I went up to the cottage. It had three windows at the front, facing the lake. The middle one was unlatched. I slid it open and slipped through.

There was one big room, furnished simply with two vinyl sofas, a couple of sturdy wood rockers, a table and four straight-back wood chairs. Two gray metal-frame cots were folded up in the corner. I imagined the sofas would pull out for extra sleeping. A small, butane cook stove stood next to a large, wood-burning heat stove. Burned-down candle stubs stuck in glass ash trays were set beside two lanterns on a shelf above the back window. There was no refrigerator because there was no electricity; a dented green metal cooler rested in the corner, ready for ice or chilled water from the lake.

I went back out the window and down to the shore. The almost-submerged orange wood boat still nagged. Unless it had a hole in it, Lamm should have bailed it when he was emptying the other. Or Herman, simply because that should have been his responsibility.

Unless neither of them expected Lamm would ever come back.

I bent to look closer at the boat.

Something zipped like a bug into the water five feet from my arm. In the fraction of the instant I needed to think it was an insect, rifle fire exploded the stillness around me. A second bullet zipped even closer, not two feet away.

I dove into the murk of the lake.

TWENTY-NINE

I hit muck in an instant. I was too close to shore, too easy a target for a man with a gun.

I clawed blindly at the spongy decay, grabbing madly to pull myself down and away. The water was ink, thick with the sediment I'd stirred up, slimy in my nose, gritty in my eyes. The saw-edged weeds scratched at my face and ripped at my hands as I tugged at them, one handful after another, to get deeper, farther from shore.

My lungs begged for air, but death was a gunshot waiting at the surface. The water was deeper now, clearer. I let go of the cutting weeds and began breast-stroking through the frigid water to stay down, fighting my lungs, counting, ten more strokes, then nine and five and then no more. I lunged up for air, my eyes shut for the crack of gunfire, the burn of a bullet.

No explosion came. No burn, no pain. I gulped air, dropped back under.

Ten new strokes, and ten more, then up again, gasping, pawing at my face to clear my eyes. Lamm's cottage was two hundred yards away.

My jeans and shoes were lead, tugging me down. I let them pull me under, and breast-stroked below the surface toward the center of the lake until I could do no more, and came up to look. The brown log cottage was lost in the blur of the trees at the shoreline. I made wide circles with my arms, staying up, watching for movement. Nothing moved at the shore.

A thousand iced daggers pricked deep into my legs. My strength had gone; my shoes were dragging weights. I needed to untie them and let them fall away but, barefoot, I wouldn't have a chance of outrunning anyone in the woods.

A thought struck, so perfect that I hugged it like I was hugging life: *A killer would have killed.* I'd been a plump target at the shore and then swimming the first yards away. Anyone close could have easily put bullets into me. But there had been no more gunshots after the first two.

It had been some fool hunter, sure. I was way up north in the land of the gun-toting free, where everybody got armed at birth and shooting wild was a part of life. Hell, by now my hunter was probably a mile away, resting on a termite-infested log for a mid-morning bite of bratwurst and cheddar, perhaps even lifting an ear flap on his plaid cap to scratch his pointed head and wonder why he never hit anything.

Damned fool hunter. Damned fool me.

I'd panicked over nothing.

Cramps hit, great contorting pulsations that dug into my legs with iron fingers. I dropped under the water, doubled over to knead my knuckles into my right leg, then my left. The cramps dug back deeper, relentless in the frigid water.

Damned fool me. I was going to drown if I didn't get out of the water.

I kicked for the trees, flailing my arms at the water as the great electric curls of pain wrapped tighter and tighter around my calves. My hands as well began to cramp, too weak to do anything but slap at the water. Swallowing water, I went down.

Incredibly, a foot grazed the bottom. I pushed up, saw sky, disbelieving. I was still yards from shore, but I'd touched bottom. I wanted to laugh, for the mercy of it. I screamed instead. From the cramps twisting deep into my legs.

I half dog-paddled, half-stumbled to the narrow ribbon of slick moss at the shore and crawled out on my belly. I collapsed face down on to the mud, shivering, sucking in the cool musk of the shore with ragged breaths.

And cursing. I swore at everyone I could think of. I cursed wedge-headed, cheese-worshipping, damned-fool inbred hunters. And their mothers. And the women who ran places like Loons' Rest. And their broom-beating, bat-stomping offspring.

I cursed Arthur Lamm, who might simply have been off camping. I cursed the lead-headed Herman Canty, stoic Northwoodsman, for not telling me anything definitive.

But mostly, I cursed myself. I'd almost died, not from gunshot, but from drowning in stupid panic.

A branch hung low above my head. I reached up and pulled myself up to stand. My legs wobbled and then calmed under my weight. Breathing came easier. After a moment I dared to let go of the branch, and bent to retie my shoe laces, loosened and slimed by ten thousand years of decayed plants and fish.

I started into the trees. The damp rotting carpet of last year's leaves muffled my footfalls as I pushed my legs to move quicker. My hunter might still be in the woods, about to spray a last few thousand rounds into the trees before heading home.

Even stumbling fast, whole swarms of stinging insects found me, chilled wet meat, pulsing with blood – a smorgasbord of lake muck and sweat served up in a thick residue of fear. I didn't slow to learn if they were mosquitoes, flies or gnats. They all stung like they were on steroids. Everything liked to hunt up in those piney woods.

Sooner than I hoped, I caught a shimmer of bright yellow through a thinning in the trees. Leo's Porsche, designed for the autobahn, hunkered low on the scraped clay of the fire lane, as out of place in those woods as I was. I dipped my hand into the pocket of my jeans, came out with the keys. Water dribbled from the little electronic remote. I ran up to the edge of the fire lane.

And stopped.

The sloped nose of the sleek German car was too close to the ground. The right front tire was flat. As was the rear tire. I backed deeper into the dark shelter of the woods and dropped behind a massive oak, to think, to understand.

Two tires, flat, immobilizing the Porsche.

Someone wanted me trapped, defenseless, in the woods.

THIRTY

My cell phone was in the glove box, and not worth the risk of a sprint to get it, even if it did work in that particular patch of woods. It wouldn't do any good anyway; the Porsche would never make the crawl out of the woods on flat tires.

I needed to run – run through the trees, run up the fire lane to the road, to the town. But a small part of my brain knew to beg to be rational. A man of the woods, used to tracking running prey in dark places, would expect that. He'd be waiting.

I scrambled to my feet and ran the other way, down to the lake. Every whisper of the wind came cold like the breath of a mad man with a gun; every creak of a dry limb the snick of a sliding rifle bolt; every snap of a twig the first crack of sudden gunfire. I got to the water and ran along the shoreline until it broke to feed the river. The water was rushing too fast to cross there. Only one direction remained now.

I ran up the bank of the river, to the rocks below the rickety bridge, and crept up to the edge of the road. It seemed deserted in both directions, but that's what he'd want me to think.

There was no choice. I pounded onto the rotting planks, my footfalls jouncing loud on the loose timbers. If my shooter was within a half a mile, he'd know exactly where I was.

I got across in an instant, ducked into the woods and got snagged by a barky vine lying like a snake beneath the blanket of rotting leaves. I crashed down hard. Then, pushing up, dazed, I started to run only to get tripped again. Up once more, my legs were now too weak. I could only stagger from tree to tree in a kind of palsied shimmy, dodging vines when I could, falling when I couldn't. Sweat burned my eyes. Horseflies, bigger than I'd ever seen, bit at my cheeks and my neck. Sometimes I swatted at them, my hand coming away bloody. Mostly I just let them bite. I had no strength.

Somehow, I kept moving. An hour and a half later, I got to the used-to-be gas station across from the Dairy Queen.

Both service bay doors were open. A man wearing dark blue coveralls straightened up from the front bumper of a rusting green Chrysler minivan to eyeball the blood, dirt and bits of bark and leaf shreds that clung to my skin and wet clothes.

'Jesus, mister,' he said. He was young, in his early twenties.

'I had an accident,' I said.

'I guessed that already,' he said, grinning.

'I've got a car with flat tires in one of the fire lanes off County M. I need you to go out and fix the tires.'

He cleared his throat. I would have too, if I'd been confronted with someone bloody and slimed head to toe with lake muck and compost. 'Is the car in the water?'

'No.'

'Then how did you get so—?'

I took out my wallet, extracted the bills, damp and stuck together like a thin sheaf of steamed cabbage, and peeled off a fifty. I laid it on the van's fender. 'It's real money, just wet.'

He looked at the limp bill, then back at me. 'How many tires are punctured?'

'I don't know. I'd gone for a walk. When I came back to the car, at least two of the tires were flat.' I peeled off another fifty, pasted it next to the first one. 'Do you have a gun?'

'I hunt,' he said.

'The second fifty is for you to bring it along.'

He looked at my clothes and then at the two fifties, and then he shrugged. A hundred was a hundred, no matter that it was offered by a crazy man demanding he bring along a gun. He unpeeled the two fifties, went into the office, and came back with a shotgun. We got into his dented, powder-blue tow truck.

'You up here on vacation?' he asked as we rumbled down the road.

'I came to see Arthur Lamm.'

He laughed. 'I guess everybody knows him, leastways his car. Drives a hundred thousand dollars' worth of Mercedes Benz.'

'Seen him lately?'

He shook his head. 'There's a story going around that someone in Chicago reported him missing to the sheriff, but Herman Canty says that's nuts, that Lamm's just gone camping. On the other hand, that Mercedes has supposedly been sitting idle, collecting bird drops, out at Lamm's camp for quite some time.'

'Do you know Herman well?'

'Nobody knows Herman well, except maybe Wanda at Loons' Rest.'

'Herman drives a nice new truck.'

'Noticed that, huh?' he asked, a wide grin on his face. 'Herman ain't never worked much, yet here he is, driving an expensive machine. Somebody must have died for him to afford a rig like that.'

He came to a full stop at the bridge on County M. Shifting into low, he eased the truck onto the timber planks like he was rolling it onto eggs. 'One of those fifties is for risking this bridge,' he said, as the loose old wood shuddered beneath us.

We got to the fire lane a couple of minutes later and bounced up to the Porsche.

'I'll be damned.' The tow driver made a show of looking at me with new respect. 'I'm sorry, mister; I didn't figure you for a Porsche.'

I picked a fleck of leaf off my shirt and flicked it out the window. 'Understandable,' I said.

I stayed in the truck when he got out. He walked over to the driver's side rear wheel and squatted down. Pulling out a pocket knife, he picked at something stuck to the side of the tire, then got up, and moved around the car, bending to flick at each tire with his knife.

He came back to my side of the truck, smiling. 'No need for my gun.' He opened his palm, showing me four bits of twigs. 'You been pranked, is all. All four tires. Kids jammed these into your valves to let the air out. I'll have you on your way in no time at all.'

He started the compressor on the truck bed and uncoiled a long hose. Moving around the Porsche, he inflated each of the tires.

I got out, but had to lean quickly against the door. My legs were still rubber.

He gestured at my filthy wet clothes. 'Be a shame to sit like that in such a nice car.'

'I'm going back to the Loons' Rest to get cleaned up.'

'I probably owe you some change, mister,' he said, coiling the hose. 'This wasn't a hundred-dollar job.'

'It was a bargain,' I said, as much for the company of his gun as it was to fix my tires.

'Fair enough, then,' he said, climbing into his truck.

I led us out of the woods and we drove back to town. As he turned into his old station, I gave him a wave and continued down to Loons'. The parking lot was just as empty as when I'd checked out that morning. I grabbed my duffel from the trunk.

Wanda frowned as the bells inside the door danced.

'I need to get cleaned up. I'll pay for another night, though I'll only be a half-hour.'

'We're full up.'

I stared at her for a couple of seconds before I pointed a finger at the empty parking lot outside. 'There's nobody here.'

'They're out sightseeing.' She looked away from me, and out the window at the parking lot. She wasn't just being deliberately rude; there was something in her eyes. Fear, maybe.

'And I suppose it's your friend Herman leading them around, in that new pickup truck I've been seeing absolutely everywhere?'

She kept looking out the window, as though waiting for someone to pull in. 'Full up,' she said.

It had been no kid with twigs and a gun back in those woods. It had been Herman. I was being warned.

'Tell that son of a bitch I'll see him again,' I said at the door. It was true enough.

THIRTY-ONE

I drove several hours, almost to Milwaukee, before my subconscious quit tensing for bullets whizzing past my ear.

An enormous truck stop just north of the city had showers and a dour-looking cashier who expressed no surprise when I asked to use the showers. I rewarded him with a much fresher smelling me when I emerged in changed clothes, looking and smelling like the Porsche driver I might have been, had I learned more lucrative career skills. I bought paper towels, leather cleaner, carpet shampoo and, as a particularly elegant touch, a three-pack of little air fresheners that looked like flattened pine trees and smelled like urinal cakes. I scrubbed and patted and daubed the driver's side of the Porsche's interior in the parking lot. An hour later, satisfied that the car's interior would heal, given time, air and prayer, I took my little three-pine forest on the road.

I called Delray Delmar's cell phone when I got to the Illinois state line. There was truck noise in his background. I had to shout to ask him where he was.

'In my office,' he yelled. 'Lousy office. Trucks outside. Let's meet tonight.' He named a restaurant we both knew, five miles southwest of Rivertown.

I would have shouted back that any place at all would have been fine, so long as it wasn't in Wisconsin, but I didn't have the strength.

Since it was dark when I set out from the turret, I figured I could head over to Leo's, leave his keys under the mat and switch the Porsche for my Jeep unnoticed before I went to the restaurant. I'd gone over the interior once more after I got back to the turret, even rubbed the three little pine trees together to release more of the fresh, Wisconsin urinal cake smell before throwing them out. As a provenance specialist for high-end auction houses, Leo made his living searching for small inconsistencies, but I was hoping that he wouldn't go into the car until the next day, when the carpet might be dry and the lingering scent of the tiny flat pines had eradicated any last lake muck smell. I parked the Porsche in front of his mother's bungalow, found my own key under the Jeep's mat, and was gone like a bandit in less than thirty seconds.

The notion that I'd pulled off the switch unnoticed lasted barely fifteen minutes.

'Did a bear pee in my Porsche?' Leo demanded when I answered my phone.

'Does it smell like a bear peed in your Porsche?' I countered, trying to sound offended.

'My car looks and smells like a bus station men's room. The floor is wet and it stinks of urinal cakes.'

'There you have it, then,' I offered, smooth as greased glass. 'Bears don't use bus station restrooms, even in Wisconsin.'

'What the hell are you talking about?' was all he could finally sputter, and even that took a number of seconds.

By then I'd gotten to the restaurant, a dark, beef and brew place. I told him I'd call him tomorrow, and added he ought to lock the Porsche's doors, in case any bears had followed me south.

'Nasty bites,' Delray observed as I slid into the booth in the corner farthest from the door.

I'd daubed clear ointment every place that itched, and I glistened like the sidewalks of Bent Lake at nightfall. 'Wisconsin offers more than just cheese,' I said.

Our waitress came and we ordered beer and cheeseburgers. As

she started to walk away, I called out, telling her to hold the cheddar. I'd had enough of the notion of that.

Delray grinned. 'What did Wisconsin offer you, exactly?'

'No more than you learned up there,' I said, testing to see how much he'd reveal.

His expression didn't change. 'Tell me anyway.'

I told him about Arthur Lamm's car, seemingly abandoned at his camp; Herman and his shiny new truck; an orange row boat that should have been bailed out; the Porsche's deliberately deflated tires. And I told him about getting shot at.

'Shot at, but not getting shot?' he asked.

'I've come to realize the difference.'

'You were being run off.'

'It worked.'

'I'll bet. But it was a cheesy way of doing it . . .'

I groaned.

'Forgive the pun,' he said. 'You're guessing the shooter was Herman?'

'He was nearby.'

Our burgers came. Delray squirted a massive glob of yellow mustard on his fries, as I remembered kids did in high school. 'The question is why Herman wanted to run you off,' he said.

'So I wouldn't find Arthur Lamm.'

'Maybe, or maybe not,' he said, playing with a smile.

'Herman Canty need not have worried,' I said, not understanding. 'Too many lakes; too many trees. Even with an army and a fleet of boats searching for him, Lamm might be able to stay hidden up there for years, if he didn't go to Canada.'

'Think harder. Go back a little, consider what else Herman might have been up to.'

'After Lamm's Chicago people called, the sheriff started looking him. It was Herman who remembered Lamm always went camping this time of—' I stopped, remembering a thought I'd had, talking with the Bohemian.

'Do you see?' Delray asked.

'Herman established that Lamm is up there, when perhaps he's not up there at all.'

'Herman wasn't afraid of what you'd find, but rather what you wouldn't find.'

'No Lamm,' I said.

'Exactly. Herman could have driven the Mercedes up there, let it sit until Lamm's people in Chicago thought to report him missing, at which time Herman says it's all a false alarm, that Lamm's out camping on one of the million lakes around there.'

'When in reality, Lamm didn't go up there at all,' I said.

'The truck's the proof,' he said.

'The truck's the pay. Herman got rewarded with a shiny new truck.'

'I've been reassigned,' he said. 'It's part of my training. I'm now working drug investigations on the North Side.'

'Who takes over this case?'

'I've passed my file on to Homicide, but there's no heat on it. They don't see the deaths as murders. They won't follow up.' He reached into his jacket pocket for a white envelope. 'I've now got access to snitch money. In this case, twelve hundred dollars.' He slid the envelope across the table. 'Use it to work confidentially. Report only to me. Find Arthur Lamm. He travels in the same circles as did the dead men. He's got to be the key to everything.'

As perhaps was Wendell, but Delray had the decency to leave that unsaid.

'You didn't go back far enough with Whitman's calendars,' Delray went on. 'I had his secretary pull two more of his appointment calendars. Four years ago, Whitman wrote "C. Club" on two of those special Tuesday nights.'

'That's not much more help.'

He nudged the envelope closer to me. 'Check it out.'

'Is it legal, you paying me?'

'Requisitioning money for one purpose, and using it for another?' He laughed. 'Hardly, but as far as you're concerned, it's expense reimbursement. You don't know I've been reassigned.'

'If I can prove Jim Whitman was killed, and not a suicide, I'll be a rich man.'

'So Debbie Goring said. This money will help you find that out quicker.'

'What's in this for you, if you've been transferred?'

'I'll be seen as riding in on a white horse to save Chicago's most prominent people. My career will be made.'

I admired the kid's candor, but I suspected he was holding something back. 'What aren't you telling me about Arthur Lamm?'

'Nothing. He's disappeared, and he hasn't shown up dead. For now, that's enough to make him a suspect.'

'Why would he kill?'

'Let's find him and ask.'

'And we do that by first finding the C. Club?'

'It's our only lead.'

The kid had a point.

We ate our burgers and talked of Chicago politics. When we got up to leave, I pushed the envelope back toward him. Technically, or maybe not, Wendell was still my client, and Amanda was my first obligation. I couldn't split my allegiances.

I told him Debbie Goring was going to make me rich.

It seemed reasonable at the time.

THIRTY-TWO

I trolled the Internet the next morning for anything that smacked of a 'C. Club' in Chicago and its surrounds. Google spit up a thousand organizations such as the University of Chicago Alumni Association and a curling club that met in the northern suburbs to sweep brooms fast on ice. None looked like they needed to meet in secret.

I then widened my search by including all organizations that began with the letter 'C.' Eleven thousand names popped up, including a women's rugby club in England and an outfit claiming to own the world's largest catsup bottle. Narrowing these down to only those in Chicago didn't help.

Finally, I searched the public donor lists of Chicago's premier civic, charitable and social organizations. Barberi, Whitman, Carson, Lamm and Wendell Phelps had all supported the Union League, the Standard, the Boys' Clubs of Chicago, the Metropolitan YMCA and a dozen others. It was to be expected. They'd traveled in the same do-gooding circles. I switched off my computer. Delray's lead had been a bust.

I knew a Fed in the city. He didn't think much of me because we had history, but I called him anyway and asked my question. He said he could give me five minutes of his time, in precisely one hour, but only in person, in his lobby. He wanted me to fight traffic to ask a question which he might or might not answer. That was understandable, too. Time does not heal all wounds.

I thought about bumpers to bumpers and the impossibility of making it downtown in one hour, which was probably his intent, and I hustled to take the train. As it clattered along, I looked out the window, remembering when Leo and I were in high school and rode downtown, headed for un-chewable, two-dollar steak lunches served up with a spotted, hard potato and a piece of toast smeared with something the approximate color of butter. We'd cracked wise on those rides, at the colors and sizes of the clothes hanging on the lines behind the three-flats, sharing our stunted, sophomoric witticisms with those other passengers who'd not thought to bring earplugs, ear buds or whole buckets of water in which to submerge their heads.

I saw no clotheslines on this trip; basement dryers must be everywhere by now. Nonetheless, my faith in adolescent boys remained. They'd always ride trains, and they'd always find ways to embarrass themselves in public.

Agent Till's offices were on Canal Street. He was an investigator at Alcohol, Tobacco and Firearms. He'd threatened to prosecute me one autumn for withholding information he considered vital to wrapping up a case. He'd been half right – I was withholding – but the information wasn't crucial. The case closed fine without it. Still, we both knew he'd been charitable in letting me skate unpunished.

He came down to the lobby, walked to the granite bench by the window where I was sitting. He was a short, wiry man in his fifties with the wizened, creased face and hunched shoulders of a career investigator. Every time I'd seen him in the past, he'd been wearing a brown suit. Today was no different.

'Five minutes,' he said, by way of an opening pleasantry. He remained standing.

'You appear to be brimming with good health.' The last time I'd seen him, he'd complained about the healthy food his wife was forcing upon him.

'Cut the crap.'

I stood up so I'd be taller than he was. 'I need information.'

'Me, too,' he said, still touchy about that previous autumn.

'Have you heard anything about an investigation of Arthur Lamm?'

'The insurance guy?'

'Yes.'

He shook his head. 'ATF is not investigating him.'

'I think the IRS is.'

'I wouldn't know about them.'

'Could you find out what's going on, and where they think he is?'

'Sure.'

'*Will* you find out?'

'Will you tell me what I've wanted to know for too many years?' he asked.

'The case is closed.'

'It doesn't matter.'

'No,' I said.

He smiled and suggested I do something that, were it even physiologically possible, I would never do in the lobby of a government building, particularly on a bench by a window where passersby could see.

Chuckling, he walked past the guard and disappeared into an elevator, and I headed back to a train not due to depart for another hour.

THIRTY-THREE

The outbound train was a midday plodder that stopped at every crossing on its way west. I could have used the time to review what I'd learned about the men in the heavy cream – the three who died, the fourth who'd gone missing, and the fifth, my ex-father-in-law, whose evasiveness clung to everything, blurring it like thick, black smoke – except I'd learned nothing. So mostly, I looked out the window and let my mind drift back to old times, when laundry was hung on lines and semi-chewable steaks could be served up with rock-hard potatoes and yellowed toast for two bucks.

A black Chevrolet Impala, the kind of car Federal agents drive, was parked a few yards past the turret. There was nobody inside. It didn't matter; I knew who it was. Such a car parked outside my turret was like old times, too.

I headed into the kitchen to rummage in the cardboard box where I keep my dry food. For lunch, I had the choice between Cinnamon Toast Crunch, which I usually ate dry, or peanut butter, which I usually ate sticky. Sparks of culinary creativity, borne of financial deprivation, fired into my skull. I put two scoops of peanut butter into a plastic cup, shook in ten of the little sugared cereal squares, grabbed a plastic spoon, and went down to the river.

ATF Agent Till, who'd just given me a bum's rush downtown, had beaten me back to the turret and was sitting on the bench. A brown lunch bag was beside him. He was throwing scraps of a sandwich at a duck.

It was no surprise that he'd remembered the way. He'd come around often, frequently and futilely, when I'd been recuperating from the lacerations and burns I'd suffered in the explosion Till was investigating. I hadn't wanted to talk, for fear of incriminating those who didn't deserve incrimination. Amanda and a friendly doctor kept him away from me, citing my need to heal.

That did not deter Till. For two weeks, he came every day at noon, to sit on the bench and throw bits of his lunch at the ducks, and to threaten me with his relentless presence. New cases finally forced him to give it up, and he quit coming around.

I sat next to him on the bench and ate the first of my peanut-buttered Cinnamon Toast squares.

The sandwich Till was tearing had little green tendrils poking out from under the bits of wholewheat bread. Each time Till tossed a piece, the duck would circle it, floating in the water. The river was calm that afternoon, barely moving. Bits of sandwich surrounded the duck.

'The duck isn't eating, Till,' I said, after a moment.

'He's waiting for the green things to wash off.'

'What are they?'

'Alfalfa sprouts. My wife says they're good for arthritis.' He ripped off another piece and tossed it at the duck.

'Are you going to throw away your whole lunch?'

'It's called recycling. I throw this into the water, the duck eats it, and converts it to something better: duck shit.'

'But the duck's not eating.'

'Then it's going to get arthritis.'

'And you?'

'I stopped for two chili dogs on the way here.'

'Ah,' I said. I spooned up more peanut butter and Cinnamon Toast Crunch.

'What are you eating?' Till asked after a time.

'What's available.'

'Ah,' Till said.

We sat silently on the bench until all of Till's sandwich lay floating around the duck. Then he folded up his brown bag, put it in the jacket pocket of his brown suit, and stood up.

'Are you going to tell me what I want to know?' he asked, of that long-ago explosion.

'No,' I said.

'Arthur Lamm is in big-time trouble,' he said. 'He took customer deposits from an escrow account holding insurance premiums.'

'Embezzling?'

'Absolutely. Sometimes clients pay their premiums to an insurance brokerage agency. That agency is supposed to put the money into a reserve account for forwarding to the insurance company. Lamm tapped the keg for personal expenses like upkeep on his mansion and beauty treatments for his lady friends, replenishing it with new escrow payments as they came in. The IRS also likes him for giving freebie insurance to his heavyweight pals in Chicago and for not returning client overpayments. They're getting indictments ready.'

'Sounds like reason enough for Lamm to run.'

'Lamm's on the lam.' He laughed, delighted by his wit. 'He hasn't been seen for some time.'

'Isn't the IRS out looking for him?'

'They need warrants first.'

'You found all that out awfully fast,' I said.

'Only took one phone call. I did it in the car, between chili dogs.'

'Thank you.'

'That tree's dead,' he said, looking up at the ash.

'Not yet,' I said.

'Soon,' he said, and walked away.

THIRTY-FOUR

'Your information was correct,' I told the Bohemian. 'Arthur Lamm is being investigated by the IRS. He might be running.'

He sighed into the phone. 'That's good news of a sort, if it means he's hiding out and not dead, a fourth prominent man killed. Fears of a murderous conspiracy are unfounded?'

'I don't know.'

'Your client knows, though, doesn't he?' By now I was sure he'd guessed that I'd been hired by Wendell Phelps.

'Debbie Goring promised me five per cent of any insurance she collects if I can prove her father was not a suicide,' I said.

'You won't tell me your client's name?'

'No.'

'Any chance of helping Debbie collect?'

'Only if I can prove someone else gave her father an overdose.'

'So we *are* back to imagining conspiracy?'

'You're familiar with very private, exclusive organizations?'

'Some,' he said, evading now himself.

'I'm interested in something called a "C. Club". It meets on the second Tuesdays of even-numbered months.'

'That's very specific.' He paused so I could tell him why I was asking.

I didn't. I waited.

'I've never heard of it,' he said finally.

'Perhaps you could contact a few friends.'

'My God, Vlodek; I can't call around and ask whether they belong to some secret organization.'

'Barberi, Whitman and Carson each died on, or immediately following, one of those secret-meeting Tuesdays.'

'This is for real?'

'Real as death, Anton.'

'Then I shall try,' he said.

The Bohemian called back early that evening. 'No one admits knowing anything of a "C. Club." More interestingly, two gentlemen whom I know very well, and who are ordinarily very voluble, actually blew me off by saying they had to take important incoming calls.'

'Dodging you?'

'These are men who talk confidentially to me about all sorts of things,' he said, still sounding shocked, 'but they clammed up, almost rudely, when I mentioned your club.'

'I'm striking nerves.'

'What's going on, Vlodek?'

'Fear. Where is Arthur Lamm's primary office?'

'He runs everything out of his insurance brokerage.' He gave me the address.

Lamm's insurance brokerage was in a three-story building in Oak Brook, several towns of better income west of Rivertown. I got there at eight o'clock. Since it was Friday night, only a handful of cars remained in the parking lot. The back vestibule door was locked, but a woman was coming out.

There was a FedEx box outside, next to the door. I opened the supply compartment, pulled out an empty envelope, and pretended to fill out the label. The woman came out, in too much of a hurry to notice I'd used my shoe to stop the door from closing behind her. I slipped inside and went to the directory by the elevators. Lamm's insurance agency was on the top floor.

My gut wanted the cover of the stairs, but my brain took the elevator because it reasoned I'd look more like I belonged if I rode up. Executives coming back for evening work don't use stairs; they're too tired from spending long days being executives.

The top floor hall was empty, except for filled black plastic garbage bags piled outside several of the offices. Luckier still, Lamm's office was one of them, and his doors were propped open by a metal cart filled with cleaning aerosols, more black bags and rags. I tucked the FedEx envelope under my arm and stepped inside, clever as hell.

A vacuum cleaner was running close by, off to my left. I walked away from the noise, towards the row of offices in the back.

The vacuum cleaner stopped. Footsteps approached from behind, padding softly on the lush carpet. I turned to smile, executive-like.

The vacuuming man wore dark blue trousers and thick-soled black shoes. The pale blue oval on his white shirt said his name was Bill.

I held up the FedEx envelope. 'I forgot to leave this for Mr Lamm's secretary.'

He smiled and went back to the vacuum.

It was that simple.

The doors to the private offices had names lettered in black on their glass sidelights. Lamm's was in the corner. Seemingly studying the FedEx envelope, I bumped up against the knob. It was locked. The glint of a square silver dead bolt showed in the gap between the door and the jamb, too solid for a credit card to pop.

I sat behind the L-shaped secretarial desk closest to Lamm's office, took my pen from my pocket and a yellow Post-it from the pad next to the phone, and pretended to write a note. I stopped to shake the pen like it was out of ink. It was more clever subterfuge, an excuse to riffle the top of the desk. There were phone directories, a dozen folders filled with insurance applications and a file of local restaurant takeout menus, but there were no pens on the desk. And there was no appointment book.

I opened desk drawers, one by one. There were files and note pads, envelopes and paperclips, but there was no appointment diary inside the desk either. There was, however, a pen. I used it to pretend to finish the note on the Post-it, stuck it to the FedEx envelope, and turned it upside down so the cleaning person, Bill, wouldn't see I'd written nothing. Lamm's secretary would throw out the FedEx envelope the next morning, thinking only that somebody had accidentally dropped it on her desk.

It had been a long shot, amateurish, and hadn't yielded a thing about where Arthur Lamm spent six Tuesday nights a year. Nonetheless, I left his insurance agency warmed by the self-satisfied glow of a truly daring and clever sleuth.

THIRTY-FIVE

At seven-thirty the next morning I was lying in bed, admiring my half-built closet from across the room, when someone began banging on my door. I slipped on jeans and a sweat-shirt and hustled down the stairs barefoot.

Two men in dark suits and even darker neckwear stood outside. The older one, about my age, held up a glossy plastic card. Next to his picture were the letters 'IRS.'

'Can you come with us, Mr Elstrom?' he asked.

'It's Saturday morning,' I said, almost giddy with admiration for Agent Till. He'd moved quickly to get his contacts at the IRS to meet with me about Arthur Lamm, even though it was the weekend. I ran upstairs, put on shoes, grabbed my pea coat and was out to their sedan in less than three minutes, ready to be enlightened.

The agents who'd been sent to drive me were close-mouthed. Heading to the expressway, I got only grunts in response to my questions. It was understandable; they were errand boys. Till must have arranged for me to meet with an agent-in-charge. I leaned back and looked out the window.

Halfway into the city, I spotted a tagger high up beneath one of the overpasses. Graffiti artists work silently and anonymously, usually too high up to ever be noticed. Perhaps like a killer preying in the heavy cream.

We got off at Wacker Drive, drove another few blocks and stopped in front of a black glass office building. The agent riding as a passenger got out, opened my door and walked me past the two uniformed guards in the lobby to the bank of elevators. We rode up to the eighteenth floor and went into a conference room that had no pictures on the wall.

'I'll be outside the door,' the agent said.

'I'm delighted to wait,' I said.

The building's ventilation system wasn't on, probably since it was Saturday, and the conference room was humid and stuffy.

Faintly gasping for air, left to stare at walls that had no pictures, anyone with even the mildest sense of claustrophobia would cop to lying on a tax return, just to get out of that room.

Five minutes later, the door opened and in walked two thin men, one in his thirties, one in his fifties. The younger man set a cardboard tray of three cups of black coffee on the table and sat down. He moved one of the cups toward me.

The fifty-something-year-old had a disc in his hand and a mix of patience and distaste on his face. 'My name's Krantz,' he said, walking to a gray metal cart in the corner that held a player and a television. He turned on the television, slipped the disc into the player, and pushed the play button.

The video had been shot from a ceiling-mounted camera in the hall outside Lamm's brokerage. A man wearing khaki pants and a blue button-down shirt, clutching a blue-and-white Federal Express envelope, came down the corridor and stopped at the open glass door of the insurance agency. Taking a slow, guilty look around to be sure the camera recorded that he was up to no good, he stepped inside.

Another camera then recorded the man stopping to cock his head, listening, before turning to mouth silent words to someone out of the picture, undoubtedly a man wearing a white cleaning supervisor's shirt with a name patch that read 'Bill.' After a minute, the cunning blue-shirted intruder smiled, obviously relieved. His shoulders relaxed, and he moved into the general office.

A third camera recorded the blue-shirted man approaching the private offices. He moved jerkily, like an overly medicated person trying not to collapse in a tea room. After pausing several times to take more furtive looks around, he finally bumped to a stop against a door. He pawed the doorknob. The knob didn't turn; the door was locked.

The man walked to the nearest secretarial desk and sat down to write a note on a yellow Post-it. Shaking his own pen as though it had run dry, he picked through the items on the desk, pretending to be looking for another pen but clearly looking for something else. Finding nothing of interest, he opened the desk drawers and, after a prolonged search, came out with a blue ballpoint pen. He made writing motions on the Post-it and stuck the note to the FedEx envelope. The camera was high-resolution, and recorded that the Post-it was blank; the man had written nothing on it. The man turned the FedEx envelope upside down on the desk and sauntered away, a moronic smirk on his face. The screen went blank.

There had been no sound accompanying the video. Clown music, especially if accompanied by a chorus of honking squeeze horns and an uproarious laugh track, would surely have made the video a contender in any short comic film contest.

Krantz turned off the television, sat down and sighed. 'Our man followed you down to the first floor and identified you from your license plates.'

'Bill, the man operating the vacuum cleaner?'

'Actually, his real name is Roger.'

I gestured at the now blank screen. 'You don't see that kind of cleverness very often, do you?'

'Sadly, no,' Krantz said, looking truly mournful. 'If criminals were that inept, we'd have them all behind bars in a matter of weeks.'

He leaned back in his chair and made a come-to gesture with his hands. 'Tell us.'

I had to offer something, having been caught by Feds. 'I think Arthur Lamm is connected to three murders.'

I told him everything I knew, minus any mention of Delray and Wendell. By the time I finished, some of the lazy contempt in their eyes had gone.

'You think Lamm's a killer?' Krantz asked.

'I can't see a motive for that, but I think he might know plenty.'

'You're working for Whitman's daughter?' Krantz asked.

Debbie Goring had become a superb justification for my snooping around, especially useful in keeping Wendell's name out of the questioning. 'She promised me five per cent of her father's insurance proceeds if I can prove his death wasn't a suicide.'

'How will Lamm's appointment book shed light on that?'

'Each of the murdered men was secretive about where he went on the last night of his life. Lamm traveled in their same circles. His calendar might show exactly where they all went.'

Krantz looked at the younger agent, who then got up and left the room. Turning back to me, he said, 'You really think Lamm killed those other three men?'

'That, or he's another victim. What can you tell me about your investigation?'

'Not a damned thing,' he said.

'But you do have men looking for him?' I asked.

'We don't have enough to arrest Lamm yet.' Krantz stood up and opened the conference room door. 'No more illegal entering, Mr Elstrom.'

THIRTY-SIX

Down in the lobby, I realized I'd hustled out of the turret without grabbing my wallet or cell phone. I thought about calling up to Krantz, demanding a ride home, but his demeanor suggested he didn't consider us to be pals. One of the guards in the lobby let me use the desk phone to call Leo's cell.

I hoped this was one of the mornings he'd slept at Endora's, because her condo was close by. She is young and beautiful and his time with her is not to be interrupted, especially by someone who had recently trashed his Porsche and then slipped away without explanation. But this was no ordinary morning.

He answered on the third ring. 'This had better involve my winning a lottery.' His voice was scratchy with sleep.

'Even better. It's your friend for life, abducted this morning by the IRS, now stranded downtown with no money in his jeans and a real hungry expression on his face.' I gave him the address. 'Come pick me up, buy me breakfast, and drive me home.'

He said he would. Or at least that's what I hoped he might have said after he swore and clicked me away. I didn't know for sure until he roared up forty-five minutes later.

'Do not speak,' he said as I slid in. Beard stubble smudged his pale face.

I started to do just that.

He held up a hand for silence. 'And do not rest your shoes on the carpet. Someone disgusting fouled the interior of this fine machine, and clumsily attempted to clean it himself. I shampooed it myself last evening, but it's still damp.'

'I'll pay for a proper detailing—'

'And leave your window down. The whole car smells like an over-treated urinal.'

'I told you: I'll pay—'

'Exactly how much money are you packing these days?'

'I have potential.'

He downshifted, turning onto LaSalle Street. 'Tell me when we get to Min's and I've had coffee.'

Greasy spoon, spotted vest; no term can do proper justice to Min's Café. No words can accurately describe the impact the fat-cat pols and business types who've warmed Min's plywood and pink vinyl booths have had on Chicago, nor can words convey the artery-clogging magnificence Min piles onto her chipped green plates. In a town renowned for its massacres, from Fort Dearborn through St Valentine's, to the latest gang shoot-outs in public parks, Min's entrees have felled more crooks, saints and just plain ordinary folks than any gun-wielding hoodlums or gang bangers ever have. It was an appropriate place to discuss murder. We took a booth under a paint-by-number picture of a forest and ordered Eggs Bud.

Leo held me off until he finished his first mug of coffee. After the waitress came by with a refill, he took another sip and said, 'Now talk.'

'I got picked up on video tape illegally entering Arthur Lamm's office.'

His eyebrows tangoed at my foolishness. 'What the hell were you doing there?'

'Hoping for a peek at his appointment book.'

'You fiddled with locks . . .?'

'The door was open.'

'And inside was a federal crew with video cameras?' He grinned, lighting the morning with a thousand bright teeth. Dumb was dumb.

Before I could answer, our Eggs Bud came. Bud had been the grill man at Min's for ten years. His masterpiece was four over-easy eggs piled atop two English muffins, slathered with sausage, melted cheddar and mushroom gravy the thickness of porridge. Bud died young. No one wondered why.

Leo smacked his considerable lips, lifted a dripping forkful and asked, 'So, you passed yourself off as prospecting for that five per cent Debbie Goring will give you?'

I nodded. 'I said I think Arthur Lamm attended those secret Tuesday night get-togethers.'

'As a killer, or as a victim?'

'I think Lamm's alive,' I said.

'Why do you think that?'

'Because I think that's why Wendell fired me. I think Wendell is covering up for Lamm.'

'How much of this have you told Amanda?'

'She knows her father is withholding.'

'How is it, being close to Amanda again?' he asked, a little too gently.

'We're getting along,' I said. For now, that's all I would allow aloud.

'And Jenny?'

I gave him what I could manage in the way of a grin. 'We're getting along, too.'

'What's next?' he asked.

'Finish my Eggs Bud.'

'And then?'

'Wait for inspiration.'

He sighed.

THIRTY-SEVEN

My wait for inspiration wasn't long.

The younger agent who'd sat wordlessly with us in the IRS conference room, before Krantz sent him out for something, stopped by before noon. He opened a large white envelope and took out a sheaf of photocopied calendar pages. 'All we have is this year's. We think he destroyed the previous ones.'

It was Lamm's calendar. I flipped through the sheets. 'He's got the same notation for each of those second Tuesdays,' I said. '"Sixty-six."'

'As you can see by his other entries, he noted all his appointments with numbers, sometimes followed by a letter or two.'

'Abbreviations for addresses?'

'We think so. Lamm didn't use a driver. He drove himself
around. Those entries were the properties he visited. On those
second Tuesdays, his last stop was always a place with a number
sixty-six street address. It's meaningless and irrelevant to our
investigation, but Special Agent Krantz thought you'd appreciate
a first-hand look.'

He held out his hand, I gave him back his copies, then he said,
'Mind giving me a quick tour of one more floor? I've never been
inside something like this.'

It surprised me. Unlike most first-time visitors, he'd paid no
attention to the craggy walls. 'Sure,' I said, and led him up to the
second floor.

'That cabinet isn't quite level,' he said in the kitchen. He was
looking at the one that had been vexing me for days.

'I'll get it right,' I said.

He stepped out into the large area that would one day be something more specific, like a living room or a study or maybe both.

'This is your office?' he asked, walking up to the card table
where I keep my computer.

'Things are simple here,' I said.

He touched the torn vinyl covering on the card table, smiled,
and said, 'I'd best be going.'

I don't remember whether it was Albert Einstein, Thomas Edison
or Bozo the Clown who said genius was one per cent inspiration
and ninety-nine per cent perspiration. I'm guessing it was Bozo,
because he had to stomp around in huge shoes, something sure to
make him sweat like crazy. Stomping around, sweating, was all I
could think to do next, though mercifully I wouldn't have to do
it in two-foot-long floppy red footwear.

I drove to the corner of Michigan and Walton in Chicago, where
Jim Whitman had been dropped off that last evening of his life. I
parked the Jeep two blocks over, just off State Street, and headed
west on foot. State Street is the dividing line for east and west
addresses, and I figured Arthur Lamm's number sixty-six would
be a block or two east or west of it, and similarly, only a block

or two north or south, since it had to be within easy walking distance for Whitman, a dying man.

North of Walton, I walked east and west along Maple, Elm, and finally Division Street. There were four properties numbered with a sixty-six address: a Thai restaurant, an adult bookstore, a day spa and a private, three-story graystone residence.

I turned around and walked the streets south of Walton. There were only two properties numbered sixty-six down there. Both were three-story graystone homes.

I'd seen nothing, but I knew somebody who might know somebody who knew more. I walked west to Bughouse Square. Its real name is Washington Square Park, but to generations of Chicagoans it's always been Bughouse Square, the place where soapbox orators used to stand on crates to rant about the inequities of the day, real or imagined. For decades it was a welcoming place for activists, lunatics and those who simply liked to watch.

Then the neighborhood went upscale, like so many in Chicago. Some of the old graystones were renovated, but more were bulldozed to make way for concrete towers of condominiums, beige and bland inside and out. Sadly, Bughouse Square became gentrified along with everything else. Its worn, grassy expanse was professionally landscaped and cut with diagonal concrete walks, its loonies chased away to AM talk radio where they wouldn't have to stand on boxes – or for that matter, even wear pants – to orate.

Fortunately, the Newberry Library, across the street from the north of the square, remained untouched. I sat on one of the new benches the city had installed for trendy ladies and well-clipped dogs to share with homeless people and looked up at the fine old building.

I called Endora's cell phone. 'Who do you know that's a wiz on finding obscure private clubs in Chicago?'

'Me, of course. I have access to wonderful computers.'

'I know it's Saturday, but would you care to swing over to the Newberry?'

'I'm already there.'

Her office faced the park. 'Look out your window,' I said, waving.

'I see.' She laughed and said she'd meet me in the third-floor reading room in fifteen minutes.

I tell Leo that the reason Endora adores him can be fathomable only to aliens from more twisted civilizations. She is in her early thirties and has magna cum laude degrees in history and anthropology that she'd financed by modeling upscale clothing in national women's magazines. At graduation, she'd turned down longer contracts with the big New York agencies to work at the Newberry. Beautiful, brilliant and quirky, Endora was devoted to two things: the study and preservation of historical documents, and Leo.

That she loved Leo pleased me immensely.

That she worked at the Newberry assured me that occasionally there is perfect symmetry in the universe. For the Newberry Library, too, is quirky. It was planned on a promise of funding in the 1880s by a Mr Newberry, one of the richest men in Chicago. Unfortunately, before ground for the new library could be broken, Newberry died on board a ship en route to Italy. His traveling companions persuaded the captain not to deep-six the influential Newberry, as was the custom then for on-board expirations, but instead to preserve him in a barrel of whiskey. And so it went. Newberry completed his journey, to Italy and back to America, bobbing in a cask. In fact, even returned to Chicago, Newberry never left his barrel. He was rolled up the hill to Graceland Cemetery and buried in it, pickled and, by then, undoubtedly puckered.

Newberry's heirs squabbled over honoring his commitment to build the new library. Compromise was reached: exactly half of the library would be built. And so it became. Its front and sides are ornate, built of fine stone exactly as planned, but the detailing along its sides ends abruptly, like an ornately frosted rectangular cake sliced smack down the center. The upper cornice work stops crudely, and the back of the building is walled with the cheapest common bricks. Half was half.

Such rudeness aside, there is nothing half-finished about the Newberry's resources. It is renowned for its collections of arcane history, especially about Chicago.

The third-floor reading room is a great old hall of golden oak, arched windows and massive tables lit by pull-chain, green glass lamps. It is a sturdy, safe place. I pulled out a book of old maps of Europe, brought it to a table, and looked at ancient geographies while I waited.

Ten minutes later, a hand lightly touched my shoulder. Endora wore her usual dark, concealing work clothes. Her hair was pulled back in a severe bun, and she wore no makeup. Even dressed so sternly, she was lovely, and I had no doubt that many of her male colleagues spent much time each day imagining what naughtiness with Endora might be like.

'What's up?' she whispered, sitting down.

I handed her the piece of paper on which I'd written the addresses of the buildings I'd just checked out. 'What information do you have about these locations?'

'For ownership or tax records?'

'I'm trying to find a private club.'

We went to one of the computer kiosks where she typed in a query. A moment later, she keyed in another question, and a couple of minutes after that, she motioned for me to follow her out into the hall.

'There might have been such a club, a hundred years ago, at Sixty-six West Delaware, though I can find no current description of it. There's someone else who may know more, and he's in today, too.'

We went through the double doors leading to the private offices. At the end of the corridor, Endora knocked on the wall next to an open door, and leaned in to speak to someone inside. After a second, she stepped back and motioned for me to go in ahead of her. 'Mickey Rosen, Dek Elstrom,' she said.

The office was the size of a utility closet. It was crammed with bookshelves, a small metal desk and a tiny old man seated on a swivel chair. Mickey Rosen was at least eighty-five, and dressed in a pilling orange polyester sweater and maroon pants. He stuck out a small, leathery hand. 'Any male friend of Endora's is an enemy of mine,' he said, leering up at her.

'Dek's got a question about properties around here,' Endora said. 'Specifically, private clubs, with street addresses numbered sixty—'

'Stop!' Mickey held up a liver-spotted hand to silence her, then moved it to his forehead like a psychic. He closed his eyes as a big grin split his face, exposing yellowed teeth. 'Nobody say anything. I'll divine what your friend wants to know.'

I glanced at Endora. She looked stricken.

I cleared my throat. 'Mr Rosen, all I'm looking—'

He moved his hand from his forehead, opened his eyes, and finished my sentence. 'You're looking for an organization of influential people that meets only six times a year, does so secretly, is named with a word that begins with a "C" and has a street number of sixty-six.'

He dropped his hand and looked at Endora. Satisfied with her look of stunned admiration, he asked her, 'Will you sleep with me now?'

'No.' She laughed.

'Just as well,' he sighed. 'My heart beats best in boredom.' He turned to me and winked. 'Do you know a man named Small?'

I shook my head.

'Certainly there's nothing small about him. A heavy man, heavy breather, destined for a coronary event,' he said. 'Anyway, this Mr Small came to see me. Edward, I think he said his name was, or Edwin.' Mickey shook his head. 'He too wanted to know about a property around here numbered sixty-six.'

'How recently?'

'Late February, or maybe the beginning of March.'

'Was he a cop?'

'He didn't show a badge.'

Small might have been the investigator Wendell had hired. 'Were you able to help him?'

Mickey Rosen smiled. 'The Confessors' Club,' he said.

THIRTY-EIGHT

Sixty-six West Delaware was one of the graystones I'd seen south of Walton, an old, narrow, three-story with high steps leading to a black-painted front door. It was in the middle of a mix of residences, boutiques and bars.

I didn't spot any security cameras outside, but some might have been mounted inside the windows. Remembering my obviousness at Lamm's office, I didn't linger, and ducked into a bar directly across the street instead. It was one of those places that catered to the slim, hip, wanting to be noticed. Its front wall was almost all glass, so that people inside could be admired from outside, and people out on the sidewalk could be admired from inside. But all that admiring was for later, after it got dark. Now the bar was almost empty. I stood at a high table close to the window, ordered coffee, and pretended to be slim and hip, but really wishing I had a doughnut to go with the coffee.

I called Delray's cell phone. 'I'm in a bar across from the C. Club,' I said to his voice messaging, right after the beep.

He called right back. 'Where?'

'State and Delaware.'

'What is it?'

'Apparently, a club inside a private residence. How soon can you get a warrant?'

'Any sign of activity?'

'You mean Lamm, puttering about, freshening the lawn for spring? I've seen no one.'

He told me he'd be there soon. I told him I'd wait. By now it was getting dark, and the slim and the hip were beginning to descend on the intersection in slim, hip droves.

There was a restaurant across the intersection trying to pass as a fifties diner. The counter waitress was a cutie done up all in pink, right down to the bubble gum she was chewing with an open mouth. I sat on one of the red vinyl stools, slapped a roll of Tums on the counter and ordered a chili cheeseburger, chili fries and chocolate malt. She gave me an admiring glance, recognizing me as a serious contender who knew to bring antacids to a grease pit.

The chili burger and fries had *cojones*, the malt was too thick to go through the straw and the music was quintessential rockabilly, made long ago by men who'd married prepubescent cousins. I took my time, savoring the malted milk and inbred rock and roll, until seven-thirty when Delray showed up at the corner across the street.

He was dressed in a black silk shirt, black trousers, black silk sport coat and black shoes. Subtract the gelled stuff he slathered on his hair, add two hundred pounds, a beard, and fifty years, and he could have been Orson Welles. Except not dead.

He studied me as I crossed the street like he was checking out a Salvation Army mannequin. 'Is there a story behind you never wearing anything but a blue button-down shirt and khakis?' he asked.

'Not much of one,' I said. 'Where's your team?'

'I'm not assigned to this case anymore, remember? Second, there's no Chicago PD warrant out for Lamm. And third, it's Saturday night.'

'So you're not going inside?' I asked.

He grinned. 'You said it's a residence?'

I knew that sort of grin, and knew that I'd be protected, being in the company of a cop.

'Let's go clubbing,' I said. By now the sidewalks were teeming with people younger than me and older than Delray.

I took him to the bar I'd been in earlier. The guy sitting outside, on a stool, didn't give me a second glance but asked Delray for identification. Delray flashed his open wallet, and we went in to stand in the crush by the window. We shouted an order for long necks to a young girl with really blonde hair.

'Where is it?' Delray leaned to ask, after the girl had brought us the beer.

'Sip slowly,' I said. 'Anticipation is everything.'

'Then tell me about why you wear only blue shirts and khakis.'

'I got in some trouble, had to sell stuff to pay legal bills. It was strangely liberating, and I found I enjoyed it. What I couldn't sell I gave away, including most of my clothes.'

'I read up on you. You were all over the front page of the *Chicago Tribune* for a couple of days before you got cleared.'

'Yes, but I was not cleared on page one. My honor was restored right below notice of a sewer bond recall, well inside the paper where my former clients didn't notice.'

'*C'est le monde*,' he said. Then added, 'That's French for "that's the world."'

'My *monde* is taking a long time getting straight.' I nodded towards the three-story graystone across the street. A single lamp with a multi-colored Tiffany-type shade had been switched on behind the sheer curtains on the first floor. The second and third floors were dark.

Puzzlement furrowed his forehead.

'The Confessors' Club,' I said.

He looked past the throng on the sidewalk. A slow smile had formed on his face.

'It's been there since 1896,' I said professorially. 'It started as a leisure club for the elite gentlemen of the city: dinner, whiskey, underage prostitutes, the kind of place influential men could enjoy basic Victorian debauchery. I doubt the underage prostitutes visit anymore, but I'm guessing that on the second Tuesday of every second month, there's good food and good booze to be had inside, as well as sanctuary for the richest men in town to relax among their kindred.'

'"Confessors?"'

'Supposedly, the club was formed so that its all-important members could relax and say anything – confess anything – and know it would be kept in the strictest confidence.'

Delray waved to the blonde girl for more beer. 'How did you track this down?'

'Sheer, dogged digging through accounts of old Chicago,' I said. I couldn't tell him about the private investigator who'd beat me to the Newberry without implicating Wendell Phelps.

Our second beers came, and as we drank, Delray leaned back, studying me.

'What?' I asked.

'Have you reported anything to Debbie Goring?'

I told him the thought had crossed my mind, but I hadn't done anything about it.

He asked me for Debbie Goring's number and thumbed it into his cell phone. 'Ms Goring? Officer Delmar, with the Chicago police. I'm calling to tell you that Dek Elstrom is being very useful in our examination of the circumstances surrounding your father's death.' He paused, listening. 'Yes, ma'am, though I can't discuss progress yet. No guarantees, but if anything comes of this, you can thank Dek Elstrom. He's a very diligent man.' Another pause, and then, 'Of course we'll stay in touch.' He clicked off, and looked at me with raised eyebrows.

'You're a stand-up guy, Delray. Thanks.'

'With that five per cent from her, you could buy new clothes,' he said.

'And you can be a star in Homicide.'

'Screw Homicide. I'm headed higher than that.'

It was eight-thirty. By now, people choked the sidewalk, bobbing laughing heads. 'The neighborhood is as loud as it's going to get,' I said.

He nodded, agreeing. 'The neighbors must shut their ears to everything.'

'We'll keep our bottles.'

'Why?'

'People look away from wandering drunks.'

We carried our beers outside. April was just beginning, and the young men and women chattering on the sidewalk wore leather appropriate for the evening's soft chill. We crossed to the other side only when I was sure we were out of camera range of anything that might be mounted at the front of Sixty-six West Delaware. We continued down, turned up the side street and walked into the alley that ran behind the Confessors' Club.

'Here's where these bottles come in especially handy,' I said. 'We can't nose around during the day – too many business types and smart young mothers pushing imported prams can see us. But at night, the streets belong to people like you, Delray, hip as hell.'

'And the alleys?'

'After dark, exclusively the territory of the young hip male. No one wants to watch a well-dressed young man, carrying a beer, duck into an alley, for fear they'll hear the splash of his relief.'

We stopped when we got to the chain-link fence at the back of number sixty-six. All the rear windows were dark, but a low-watt bulb shone above the back door. There was no way of telling if there were any rearward mounted cameras.

'Second thoughts?' he asked.

I set my almost full bottle next to the fence and raised the metal latch on the gate. 'I'm with a cop. If anybody comes along, just flash your badge.'

'No chance. I don't have a warrant.'

I pushed open the gate anyway, and we crossed to the shadows at the back of the house. There were basement windows on either side of the door. I started to kneel at the one to the right.

The bulb went dark above my head. Delray had unscrewed it.

The basement window was locked tight. As I straightened up, I heard something jangling. Delray had pulled out what looked like a ring of loose wires.

'A cop with lock picks?'

He didn't answer as he bent to the lock. Almost instantly, the tumblers let go with a short, loud click. He pushed open the door. For a moment, we stayed outside, listening for any sounds from within. But all I could hear was my heart.

He turned and pressed the lock picks into my hand.

'I don't want these,' I whispered.

'They go in your pocket. If we're caught, I can help us more if I don't have them.'

It wasn't a good place for spirited debate. My fingers clenched the slender metal picks and jammed them in my pocket.

I stepped inside.

THIRTY-NINE

The darkness of the house was cleaved, front to back, by the soft reds, greens and yellows spilling into the other end of the long central hallway. The Tiffany lamp I'd seen behind the sheer curtains in the front window was the only light burning on the first floor.

I stopped just inside the back door, straining for the sound of a muffled footfall or the sharp intake of a breath. All that came back was the blood beating in my ears, and the smells of a hundred years of cigar smoke, grilled meat, whiskey. And secrets.

Delray pressed up close behind me. 'Basement,' he whispered. I felt rather than saw him pat his inside jacket pocket. He'd come armed.

The door was against my left shoulder. I stepped away.

He tapped my right hand with slim, cool metal. I closed my fingers around a small flashlight. Lock picks, a gun, and now a flashlight – Delray had come a real scout, fully prepared.

'Keep it low,' he whispered, meaning I should descend into the basement first.

'But you're armed,' I whispered back. Surely proper police protocol demanded that the cop go first.

'Best I stay up here, in case someone comes,' he said low, stepping back.

That did nothing to calm the blood rushing loud in my ears,

but I supposed it made sense. Any threat was likely to come from someone on the first or upper floors.

I turned the knob, swung open the door. Cool, dank air rushed out as though from a long-sealed crypt. I reached inside, feeling for a rail. There was only cold plaster.

Steadying myself with my left arm against the wall, and holding the flashlight with my right, I stepped down onto the stairs. A slightly lighter gray haze lay like a thin fog on the basement floor, streetlight washing in through a basement window. Ten steps down, I got to the concrete floor. Enough light came in from the two side windows to show spindly shapes against the walls, but the center of the basement was pure darkness, as though something hulking was resting there, sucking up the light.

I stayed at the base of the stairs and switched on the flashlight, aimed at the floor. The black mass in the center was an enormous old boiler, hot water pipes extending from it like tentacles from a giant squid. The shapes along the wall were a shovel, a rake, and an old-fashioned, reel-type push lawnmower, manufactured in a time when engines to cut grass had not yet been imagined.

I'd seen enough; there was nothing alarming there. I hurried softly back up the stairs, pressed the flashlight into Delray's hand. He could lead into the next dark place. He had the gun.

I followed close behind as he moved to the open door to the kitchen, just ahead on the right. An old white porcelain sink counter, tinged a ghostly blue from the moonlight coming through the back window, took up most of one wall; on another was an ancient, chipped eight-burner gas stove. Dented, dulled pots hung like steel moons from an overhead rack. The only modern presence in the cramped room, a small refrigerator, was jammed into a corner, an interloper in a kitchen outfitted when ice was kept in a box.

By now my ears had acclimated to the old house's rattling and pulsing every time a car or, even louder, a motorcycle passed by. My eyes, too, were now comfortable in the gloom. I made out ornate, curved shapes of electric light sconces, dark now, set high above the deep grooves in old wainscot paneling along the hall.

Delray stopped a few steps down the hall. A sliver of light ran up the wall on the left. It came from the center seam of a pair of closed pocket doors. I pressed my ear against one of them, but heard nothing above the noises from outside.

'Open the door,' he whispered. His hand moved to the inside of his jacket.

I placed my fingertips at the seam and, when he nodded, slid open the rightmost door.

It was a dining room, lit stronger by the same reds, yellows and greens that were spilling into the hall. Another set of pocket doors had been opened directly into the tiny front parlor. The colored glass Tiffany lamp I'd seen from across the street sat behind the sheer curtains on a mahogany claw-footed table, plugged to a timer. Two red plush settees were set on either side of it.

'Stay away from those parlor doors,' Delray said softly, close to my ear. 'We don't want to make shadows that can be seen through the front window.'

In contrast to the small parlor, the dining room was huge, and almost completely taken up by a long oak table surrounded by more than two-dozen high-backed oak chairs. The whole first floor was meant for dining and drinking.

Delray moved around me, and I followed him into the room.

'Let's have a look at a couple of those,' he whispered, pointing up. Two long rows of tankards hung from rails on the paneling.

It seemed an odd thing to be interested in, but I pulled two off their pegs and held them in the glow coming from the parlor. The mugs were heavy pewter, dented, and old. Each was etched with a different number: I was holding numbers seven and eight. I started to hand one to him. He shook his head. 'How many do you count?'

I set the two mugs on the table and looked up to count the pegs. 'Thirty, all told.'

'Same number as the chairs,' he said softly.

'Thirty members,' I whispered.

He motioned for me to back out into the hall. I started to reach for the two mugs I'd left on the table.

'Go on out. I'll put them back,' he said. He came out a few seconds later.

I crossed the hall, opened a door to a tiny washroom that contained a toilet and a porcelain pedestal sink. A cloakroom was cut in next to it, partially under the stairs. There was no rod, no hangers, just rows of brass hooks on three walls, set high and far enough apart for the sorts of broad coats that would have been worn in 1896.

I started to cross the hall, to take another peek into the parlor, but Delray grabbed my upper arm. 'Remember the front window,' he whispered.

I stepped back, pointed to the staircase. He nodded. I started up first.

Pressing myself against the wall to minimize any creaking, I climbed four steps, stopped, and held my breath to listen. I heard only the sounds of automobiles and motorcycles. Almost certainly, we were alone in the old house. Delray came up behind me and we continued up to the second floor.

A blush of moonlight backlit the gauzy fabric at the rear window, but most of the hall was in absolute darkness. The smell of cigar smoke, mingled with must and old wood, was strong, like below. The air moved next to me as Delray reached into his pocket. A second later the pencil beam of his flashlight broke the darkness at the floor.

It was enough to see the five doors that lined the old corridor. Each was partially open – for ventilation, I supposed.

Motioning me to stay behind him, Delray moved to the closest door. Easing it open with his shoulder, he stepped in quickly and stabbed low at the darkness with his pencil beam. It was the size of a small bedroom, no doubt once shared with prostitutes. Now it was furnished for relaxed conversation, with two pairings of red leather wing chairs, each with its own smoking table and glass ash tray, facing each other. There was no closet for someone to hide in. The graystone was built when clothes were kept in armoires.

Delray stepped back out of the room. One by one, he moved on to the others, nudging their doors with his shoulder, then sweeping his light beam fast and low, searching for feet and legs, arms and guns. All were furnished with chairs, tables and ashtrays, except for the last one, which was a bathroom.

At the staircase to the third floor, he whispered, 'Go back and pull the doors almost closed, the way they were.' He watched from the stairs until I'd closed each door to its previous position, and then we continued up.

The street noise was barely audible at the third-floor landing. We stopped to listen anyway, this time just for a few seconds.

There were only three doors on the third floor. Two were ajar, like those below. The third door was closed tight.

I stood aside as he nudged the first of the slightly open doors. It revealed a small attic of exposed wall studs and roof rafters, empty except for an iron bedstead leaning against one wall and a dusty, galvanized bucket. The other partially open door led to a bedroom furnished with an iron bedstead like the one in the attic, a painted wood dresser, and a metal night table. There was no mattress. It must have been a servant's room, unused for a hundred years.

Delray again raised his hand to the inside of his sport coat, stepped back, and motioned for me to open the closed door. He hadn't yet drawn his gun and the thought that he was readying himself now made me nervous that he'd sensed something I had not. I twisted the knob.

The door was locked. I held out his picks. Handing me his pencil-beam, he worked the old lock open in an instant. We traded picks for flashlight and again his hand moved closer to his gun.

I turned the knob and pushed too hard. The door flew open, banging loudly into the side wall.

'Shit,' Delray muttered, stabbing his light into the room. He inhaled sharply, in surprise.

Only a table sat in the center of the small room. On it were four large, professional quality digital recorders. Thin wires ran from each of them to holes in the floor, likely down to microphones placed throughout the house.

Delray raised his forefinger to his lips, but I already knew. The recorders could have been sound activated.

He swept the flashlight beam swiftly across them, looking for any glow of LEDs or other signs that they'd been triggered by the sound of the door I'd just slammed into the wall. But the machines were still; they'd all been switched off.

The recorders had been labeled: BR1, BR2, BR3 and BR4. I had the inane thought, then, that even when bugging the former second-floor bedrooms, tradition required the eavesdropper to behave as a gentleman. The washroom had not been wired.

'Let's get out of here,' Delray said, snapping off his flash-light.

We padded down the two flights of stairs and through the hall to the rear door. I opened the door and was about to step out when he whispered he should go first, in case anyone was waiting. He stepped outside and I pushed the button lock on the door and pulled it closed behind me.

We didn't say anything as we walked down the alley and around the corner.

'Coffee?' I asked, after we'd crossed Delaware.

'Booze,' he said.

FORTY

There was a bar in a boutique hotel two blocks east of State Street. It was empty except for a bartender watching a television sitcom and two dozen chrome bowls of peanuts. Delray bought us squat tumblers of whiskey and ice, and though the place was deserted, carried them to the plush chairs in the back. I followed with two of the bowls of peanuts.

'Paranoid about being seen committing a crime?' I asked when we sat down, trying a joke.

He took a long sip of his whiskey. 'I have to admit, it's not my favorite thing to do.'

I took my own deep sip. Never before had the cold fire of whiskey tasted so good.

'I'm getting used to it.'

'What do you mean?' he asked.

'I got caught on a surveillance video last night; Lamm's office. I had to tell some of what I knew.'

His face tensed as I told him about my morning at the movies with the IRS. 'You're sure you didn't mention me?'

'Positive.'

He relaxed back into his chair. 'How close are they to finding Lamm?'

'We weren't sharing confidences. The conversation was mostly about me, looking stupid, though one of Krantz's men stopped by later with Lamm's appointments calendar. Lamm went to an address numbered sixty-six on those same Tuesday nights. That's how I zeroed in on the clubhouse.'

'The question is: who set up the recorders?'

'Think about the purpose of those recorders,' I said. 'Likely someone was hoping to grab stock tips, or other insider information, by bugging the conversations going on in those private rooms.'

'That doesn't rule out any of them,' Delray said. 'They all would have had access to the clubhouse.'

'Along the way, whoever bugged the rooms also learned who was vulnerable, health-wise, who had a condition or an illness.'

Delray leaned forward. 'Benno Barberi's heart condition,' he said, seeing where I was headed.

'And Jim Whitman's cancer.'

'Insurance,' he said.

'Barberi came home from the Confessors' Club agitated that some anonymous someone had insured his life,' I said. 'Jim Whitman's daughter had a different insurance concern: there was none that insured suicide.'

'Unless?' he asked, grinning, certain now.

'Unless there was,' I said. 'Someone wrote a policy on Whitman's life that Whitman knew nothing about.'

'Like with Barberi?'

'And like the policy taken out on Grant Carson that named some anonymous entity as beneficiary.' I raised my glass in salute. 'Insurance motives, three times over: Barberi, Whitman and Carson.'

'Arthur Lamm.'

'Arthur Lamm, the insurance man,' I said. 'He owned his own brokerage. He could fake his own medical exams, write his own policies, name his own beneficiaries. Smooth.'

'Why risk murder? Lamm's one of the wealthiest men in the city. Why dose Whitman with Gendarin at the December Confessors' Club when all he had to do was wait to collect on the policy he wrote on the man's life? And why risk pushing Carson out of a car?' He swirled the ice cubes in his glass. His whiskey had gone.

I had no answer for that. I went to the bar and bought us another round. It was the first time I'd had a second drink since I'd been tossed out of Amanda's gated community one sodden Halloween a few years earlier. That Halloween, though, I'd had a lot more than two whiskies.

'How do we find Lamm?' he asked when I came back.

'Let Homicide find him. You've got enough to get them interested.'

'Recording machines discovered during an illegal search? They'll freak.'

'Tell them to start by squeezing Canty. You do remember Canty, up in Wisconsin?' Delray had to be the cop from Chicago the flannel shirts in the bar had told me about.

Delray grinned. 'Yep,' he mimicked.

'Canty had to be the accomplice Lamm needed to kill Carson.'

He shook his head. 'It isn't enough to get Homicide involved.'

'Then call Krantz, tell him you've got a hunch Lamm and the three dead men are linked to that graystone. They don't need to know we went in. They'll get search warrants; you'll still be the hero.'

'No,' he said, staring into his drink. 'I want to find Lamm myself.'

'Career and ambition?'

'Having a rabbi means I have to work doubly hard to prove myself.' He looked up. 'You've got to squeeze Wendell Phelps about Arthur Lamm. Phelps might know where Lamm is hiding.'

I had no illusions about keeping Wendell out of the investigation forever. Sooner or later, Delray or another cop would tumble on to the fact that Wendell had hired a private investigator to nose into the killings before he hired me to do the same thing. They'd pull out all the stops on Wendell, then, and squeeze out everything he knew.

But that time had not yet come. 'That kills the deal for me, Delray,' I said. 'You wreck Wendell Phelps, you wreck me.'

'Because of loyalty to your ex-wife?'

'I put her in the newspapers once. I'm not going to do it again. I'll call Krantz, give him a heads-up on the graystone.'

He stared at me for a long minute, judging whether I'd carry out the threat. He knew as well as I that the Feds always trumped local cops. They'd chase Delray and the homicide cops right off the case.

'OK; no Phelps and no IRS, for now,' he said, backing down. 'I'll go to Homicide, but my way, and on my time schedule.'

'You don't have a schedule anymore.'

'What do you mean?'

'Arthur Lamm might have another insurance policy we know nothing about. He might kill again.' I took a last sip to finish my whiskey and stood up. 'You've got seventy-two hours before the Confessors' Club meets again,' I said.

FORTY-ONE

S unday went calmly before it went to hell.

I awoke late that morning, well rested from knowing that Delray Delmar had alerted homicide cops to the links between Arthur Lamm and the deaths of Whitman and Carson. I had no doubt they'd be all over the Confessors' Club on Tuesday, to stop whatever killing was meant to go down.

And by the early afternoon, I'd achieved success with my troublesome tilting kitchen cabinet at last. I'd loosened every screw, re-shimmed, and re-tightened to get it to hang perfectly straight and level.

Even the butchered ash seemed to stand victorious, out the window, a headless man with both of his arms raised in triumph.

So I was feeling good, sipping coffee and more than occasionally sneaking admiring glances at my perfectly aligned cabinet, when Debbie Goring called.

'Elstrom, you son of a bitch,' she said, sounding almost jovial as she exhaled smoky carcinogens into her mouthpiece. 'Guess what?'

Surely she was phoning about Delray's call, trumpeting my worthiness, but I waited so she could say it and I could act pleasantly surprised.

'I just opened yesterday's mail,' she went on. 'Know what was in it?'

'Not a clue.'

'A cashier's check for a hundred thousand dollars.'

'From whom?' I asked.

'Come on, Elstrom. No need to be coy.'

'Doesn't the check show the remitter?'

'No.'

'It wasn't because of me.'

'A deal's a deal. You shook some big bucks loose. I owe you five per cent, five grand.'

'Hold the dough. It wasn't my work. There's no clue who sent it?'

'One of my father's rich friends, someone you made feel guilty. Stop by and pick up your check. Oh, and Elstrom?'

'Yes?'

'That cop who called me last night? Total unnecessary, pal. I'm good for paying you a commission on everything I get. I got faith that more is coming for both of us, Elstrom. You and the cops will prove my father was murdered.'

A faint squeak came from across the would-be kitchen. I spun around. And froze. The cabinet I'd just tightened so perfectly was starting to tilt.

'Keep plugging, Elstrom; there's big money—'

The cabinet gave up a mighty screech, a horrible, wood-ripping sound, and let go from the wall. I dropped the phone and ran but I did not get there in time. It slammed to the floor and split into a dozen pieces.

Some seconds later, I thought to pick up the phone from the floor and put it back to my ear. Debbie had hung up.

Coherent thoughts about anything in that kitchen were out of the question. I left the cabinet kindling on the floor and went across the hall to my computer and the numbing diversion of the Internet. I started off by Googling hardware sites, searching for miraculous advances in wall-mounting technology. Nothing wondrous appeared. I'd used the right anchors; they just hadn't been right enough.

My mind wandered, then, to Wendell and what sort of investigator he'd hired before he hired me. As I expected, Edward Small was a common name, and there were many of them. A toymaker, a guy who studied earthworms, and another who offered to repair Disney collectibles were just some of those listed. There was no mention of any being a private investigator.

I thought back. Mickey Rosen at the Newberry had said the first name could have been Edwin. I keyed in the new first name, found three different salesmen, an antique car enthusiast, four college professors, and at least two Rotarians – though in different parts of the country – and still no private detective.

I wanted coffee, but not bad enough to face the carnage in the kitchen. I typed in a new first name – Eugene – to delay getting up. My computer screen lit up with listings of lurid stories from the *Chicago Tribune* and the *Chicago Sun-Times*, dating back only several weeks, to the beginning of March.

Eugene Small had been murdered.

The *Tribune*'s website tersely summarized: 'Eugene Small, a local private detective, was found shot to death in an alley on Chicago's north side. His wristwatch and wallet were missing, leading Chicago police to theorize that Small had been robbed.'

Plenty of people get killed in Chicago: dope distributors arguing over deals; gang bangers fighting for turf; addicts slumped too far into a fix; and kids, lots of kids, and other just plain folks dropped by drooling morons shooting wild, not aiming so much as looking to simply make a cry in the night. The robbery and death of a private dick didn't need to mean anything.

Unless it came from the Confessors' Club.

Delray could find out more. I called but got his voice mail. I figured he was still huddled with Homicide. I left a lie for a message, saying I'd known Small from another case, had just heard of his death, and wanted him to find out what he could.

The Internet gave me Small's business address. Being Sunday, mid-morning, I breezed into the Chicago Loop in twenty minutes.

South Wabash struggles to find the sun even more than South Michigan Avenue, one block to the east. Tall buildings still smudged from Chicago's sootiest days a century earlier line both sides of the narrow street, and the elevated train that gave the Loop its name runs high on rusting old scaffolding down its center, casting the pavement in ever changing grids of shadow. Even at midday, when the sun is directly overhead, South Wabash Avenue is perpetually in gloom.

It is a street of ancient enterprises. Second- and third-generation diamond merchants, beef restaurateurs, and seedy clothing merchants operate behind dark doorways. Eugene Small's building was a rickety old warren of tiny offices, catty-corner and down from what used to be Marshall Field's before Macy's bought it, cluttering its aisles and dimming its lights.

The door to the faded gilt lobby was open. The directory on the wall just past a small pharmacy said Small's office was on the fifth floor. I pressed the elevator button, unsure whether the rumbling I then heard came from the elevator or a train passing high on the tracks outside. I waited for a few minutes, then gave it up and took the stairs.

The fifth floor was hushed. Everybody was at home for the weekend. My footsteps slapped loud and alone at green-and-black tiles dulled by too few waxings and too many decades of shuffling feet. The lettering on the frosted glass door panels was old and chipped and hard to read; no lights burned behind them. Another elevated train rumbled outside, shutting out the sound of my footfalls. And then it had gone and the building went silent again.

'Small Detective Agency' was lettered on a door halfway down. The office to the right advertised loans for people who had no credit; the glass on the door to the left was blank.

I remembered how easy it had been for Delray to pop the lock at the Confessors' Club, and realized I'd forgotten to give him back his picks. They wouldn't have done me any good even if I'd thought to bring them. I was strictly zero-tech when it came to illicit entering; all I was packing that morning was a Visa card.

Nothing clicked as I pressed the card between the door and the jamb. I didn't even turn the knob. The door simply swung open.

FORTY-TWO

I bent to look at the jamb. Orange chewing gum had been pressed into the recess to prevent the bolt from sliding shut. Someone wanted easy access for a return visit.

Small's desk was old scratched oak, littered with papers, a Starbucks cup, and a tipped over Dunkin' Donuts box. The green vinyl on the desk chair was cracked; the red vinyl visitor's chair held an old blue IBM Selectric typewriter. A half-dozen cardboard file boxes lay in a ragged row on the floor near the wall.

I sat at the desk. The green desk chair had been dished by a substantial man, and groaned as I reached to move away the Starbucks cup that still stank of the cream, dried now, that Small must have used to keep his weight and cholesterol up. One doughnut remained in the tipped Dunkin' twelve-pack. It was sprinkled with coconut and somewhat intact, missing one human-sized bite and a few hundred smaller rodent nicks. Probably a few mice or rats were anticipating coming back to finish it, as had Eugene Small, I supposed.

The papers scattered next to the black phone were copies of invoices sent to furniture stores and used-car dealerships. Someone had pawed through them.

I re-sorted them into numerical order, reading as I went. Eugene Small had been a small-time repo man, grabbing back patio furniture and reclining chairs when he couldn't get work repossessing cars. The invoices charged flat rates, three hundred for a car, fifty for a sofa, and twenty-five for a patio set.

One invoice was missing from the sequence. Judging by the dates of the invoices preceding and succeeding, it had been dated around the first of March, a few days before Small was killed. It seemed likely that the man who'd jammed gum into the office door lock thought that particular invoice was worth taking.

There was nothing in the desk drawers except a stapler, a full box of red-capped ballpoint pens boosted from an Econo-lodge, and a small pad of note paper with a trucking company logo on it.

I scooted the chair to the ragged row of file cartons. Most of the folders had been used several times, their tabs erased and re-lettered in pencil. That they'd been jammed roughly into the cardboard boxes might have meant simply that Small was a slob, except they were not in alphabetical order. Likely they'd been hurriedly searched and jammed back by someone who knew Small was never again going to return to his office.

There was no file for the Confessors' Club, no file for Arthur Lamm or any of the dead men. Most especially, there was no file for Wendell Phelps. I felt no relief at that. I was certain Small was the detective Wendell had hired. Whoever had searched Small's office knew that now, too.

I stood up, went to the closet. Four wire hangers dangled empty on a rod. An enormous pilled polyester cardigan sweater hung on a fifth. It smelled of gin and sweat and, like the worn, reused files in the cardboard boxes and the empty desk, was another marker of a guy who'd haunted the poorer alleys of town, grabbing back unpaid-for used cars and discount furniture.

A guy who might have stepped out of his league and into the path of someone killing in the heavy cream.

I'd seen enough of nothing to be sure I'd seen enough. The office had been looted.

I paused at the desk on the way to the door. I don't like creatures that scurry, and saw no point in making their dinner easy. I dropped the foul smelling Starbucks cup and the remains of the coconut doughnut into the trash basket and was about to toss in the stained, crumb-littered paper desk-top calendar when I noticed its corners. The top sheet, January's, was blank – nothing had been written on it. But the pad's corners were creased from being turned up. I shook the candy sprinkles into the wastebasket and flipped to February's page.

For a big man, Eugene Small wrote tiny; the little numbers and initials scribbled inside the squares beneath the coffee rings were almost indecipherable. Only the dollar sign at the top of the sheet was big. He'd retraced it so many times that the tip of his black ballpoint had cut through the paper. I flipped to the next page.

He'd filled the first days of March with tiny numbers and initials, too. They stopped on March 8. Small had been killed the next day.

Many of the initials matched the Bohemian's list of those in the heavy cream. One pair of initials – A.L. – appeared most of all. Arthur Lamm.

Something rustled inside the closet. It was feeding time at the rat ranch. I grabbed the desk calendar and left.

I called Delray when I got outside but again got his voice mail. 'Eugene Small's office was tossed,' I said. There was more to say, but I'd say it when he called me back.

Small's intruder, likely his killer, had missed something important.

FORTY-THREE

I studied the calendar for an hour back at the turret, and then I called Leo.

'I've broken and entered twice more since we last spoke,' I said.

He groaned. 'As skillfully as you did at Arthur Lamm's agency?'

'Even stealthier.' I told him about Arthur Lamm, and the recording equipment Delray and I had found at the Confessors' Club. And then I told him about Eugene Small.

'You think Small got killed because he was working for Wendell?' he asked.

'Everything else the man did was small-time repo, not worth being killed over. I need you to look at something of significance.'

He said he was headed downtown to Endora's, but always liked being delayed for significance. He told me to come right over.

Light showed from the window of his basement office. I tapped the glass six times with the toe of my shoe – three taps, a pause, then three more, our code since seventh grade – and went to sit on the front steps. He came to open the door a minute later, wearing a huge blaze-orange T-shirt with a black deer head on it, the sort a 300-pound hunter would wear on a warm autumn day. Pressing his index finger to his lips to let me know Ma was still asleep – Saturday night was late-night dirty-movie night on her favorite cable channel, and she often didn't stagger to bed until almost dawn – he led me through the front room to the kitchen.

Leo poured coffee into Walgreen's mugs and we sat at the kitchen table. I placed Eugene Small's calendar between us and flipped past the blank January sheet to February, littered with small markings and the enormous dollar sign, traced and retraced, at the top. I pointed to a small, almost microscopic 'W.P.,' with an equally small huge dollar amount written next to it: '$5,900.' I told Leo of the one invoice copy that was missing from the small pile on Small's desk.

He laid his finger on the tiny markings. 'These are Eugene Small's billable hours?'

'And surveillance record.'

'You think the missing invoice was Small's copy of one he sent to Wendell for fifty-nine hundred?'

'It's a good guess.'

'Why would someone want to take the invoice?'

I pointed again to the most obvious mark on February's page, the enormous dollar sign inked over and again, so obsessively that the pen had almost torn through the page. 'I'm worried someone else besides Small sees big bucks in going after Wendell.'

'Blackmail, over what Small learned about the Confessors' Club?'

I could only nod.

Leo picked up the calendar. 'Let's put this under better light before we draw too many stupid conclusions.'

We tiptoed down the basement stairs, not speaking as we passed the cartons of Leo's old school books, the spindly little plastic tree they stuck on the television at Christmas, and the model train tracks we'd screwed on green-painted plywood when we were kids.

His office didn't have a door, just a roughed-in opening to unpainted drywall, bare concrete and mismatched filing cabinets in black, gray, tan and orange. He set the planner upside down on the light table and pulled over the long-armed Luxo magnifying light.

'Sale stickers,' he said, pointing to two little red tags stuck to the cardboard back. 'One for four dollars, then one for two dollars.'

'As I said, Small was a repo man who grabbed furniture and cars. He didn't need such a large calendar until the very end of January, or perhaps the beginning of February, when he had to keep track of lots of pairs of initials, and lots of billable hours for Wendell. By then, calendars were on sale.'

'Excellent, for such a modest mind,' he said. He turned the calendar right side up and began examining February's sheet through the magnifying lens of the Luxo. I sat in the sprung over-stuffed chair that had been his father's favorite up to the moment he'd died in it. For all his flippancy, for all his finger-clicking, hipster mannerisms and outrageous clothes, Leo Brumsky was recognized as one of the best ferrets in the country when it came to examining historical documents and pieces of art.

He worked slowly, examining each inch of the February sheet, saying nothing. After thirty minutes, he switched to a stronger lens on the Luxo and bent down again. 'Who's R.B.?' he finally asked, straightening up after he'd spent another twenty minutes on the marked-up quarter of the March page. 'Those initials appear most frequently, always appended to other initials.'

'Look at which sets of initials they're always closest to.'

'A.L.'s. I already noticed. Arthur Lamm?'

'I'm thinking Small hired R.B. to tail Lamm so that Small could tail the others.'

He switched off the Luxo. 'If Small indeed worked for Wendell, then only two people know what Small learned,' he said.

'R.B,' I said, because it was easiest.

'And Wendell Phelps,' he said.

FORTY-FOUR

I called Wendell's home as I pulled away from Leo's. The woman who answered had a Latin accent. She said he wasn't home.

'Call him on his cell phone. This is urgent.'

'He not to be disturbed.'

'Delores, then. Is she home?'

'She with her pigs.' She pronounced it 'peegs.'

'I need to talk to Wendell now.'

'No.'

'You're going to lose your job.' It was the cheapest of false threats, and remarkably ineffective. She hung up on me.

I called Amanda. 'I need to speak to your father.'

'What's going on? What have you learned?'

'A couple of small things.'

Her voice got scared in an instant. 'What small things?'

'Damn it, Amanda. Your father is still my client.'

'He's playing golf.'

'Where?'

'Crest Hills, north of the city. I think he teed off at ten o'clock. He switches his phone off when he's out there, so your best bet is to catch him in the bar, afterward.'

She started to ask a question. I told her I had to run.

Better she worried about what I didn't say than about what I did.

I'd passed by Crest Hills Country Club several times in the past, seen the colorfully clad players driving slowly in electric carts as their white-uniformed caddies followed on foot. Though the golf bags were in the carts, I supposed course rules required that every player be tended by someone to replant the huge chunks of turf that golfers launch when flailing at such little balls, though the folks hustling behind might be better termed gardeners rather than caddies. I'd heard it cost half a million dollars to join Crest Hills, plus tens of thousands more each year for dues and fees. If I'm ever that rich, I'll go dig holes for free in a prairie somewhere, and spend the money instead on employing a world-class pastry chef.

I drove through the stone arches and parked in the lot adjacent to the white stucco clubhouse. The bar, a room of dark paneling with a wall of glass facing the course, was in back. Wendell sat at a table with three other men who were all drinking clear drinks made with sparkling cubes of ice and slices of preternaturally green lime. He wore a lavender shirt and pale blue trousers, and had a yellow bucket hat tilted back on his head. His colorful clothes and sun-pinked skin combined to remind me of an Easter egg.

Oddly, I got right to him. There were no security men hulking anywhere in sight.

'Mr Elstrom,' he said, frowning but not surprised. One of his secretaries, or even Amanda, must have given him a heads-up that I'd be rolling in. He didn't stand, or extend his hand.

The other three men at the table were also dressed in country-club pastels. Together, the entire foursome suggested a giant basket of jovial, decorated eggs. They turned to Wendell, expecting to be introduced. Wendell said nothing.

'Dek Elstrom,' I said to them. 'I'm here to repossess Mr Phelps's car.'

That popped Wendell from his chair to grab my elbow and hustle me outside through a service door.

'Was that necessary?' Most satisfyingly, his face had gotten darker under the pink.

'Tell me about the Confessors' Club.'

'I don't know that club.'

'How about you and I have a glance at your day planner? If you attended other engagements on the second Tuesdays of even-numbered months, I'll back off.'

The red beneath the pink darkened even more.

'Or you can tell me about Eugene Small,' I went on, after he said nothing.

'Ineffective,' he said.

'Particularly now that he's dead?'

I watched his face, looking for change, but it stayed tight, in control. He knew.

'Small's office got tossed,' I said. 'If it wasn't you, then someone else took one of the invoices he sent to clients. I think that person also took a file. I'm guessing both had your name on them.'

Surprise hit his face, but it could have been shock, or fear. He said nothing.

'Do you understand, Wendell? Someone has now linked you to Small, and what he knew. Maybe what he knew got him killed. Maybe it will get you killed.'

'Let this alone,' he said.

'Where are your guards? I breezed right in.'

'Unnecessary.'

'Unnecessary because you now know your friend Arthur Lamm's been behind the killings? Or unnecessary because he's gone into hiding?'

'Don't be a fool,' he said, but his voice was wavering.

'Did you send Whitman's daughter that anonymous hundred grand from guilt, or are you hoping she'll drop her interest in her father's murder?'

'You're fired, Elstrom,' he said, starting to turn.

'You already did that. When did you first suspect Lamm was behind the killings?'

His back stiffened as he headed toward the clubhouse.

'The cops have discovered that third floor,' I called after him.

He stopped cold and turned, confusion on his face now. 'What the hell are you talking about?'

'The room with all the recording equipment, in the house on Delaware Street. Were you listening, too?'

The pink had drained away from his face. I'd gut-punched him with something he didn't know. He headed into the clubhouse, walking jerky-legged, like he'd just torn a ligament. Or ten.

I let him go. He was no ordinary ex-client. He was Amanda's father.

I walked back to the Jeep. For a time I sat behind the wheel, drained too. And wishing that somehow I'd managed to fly to San Francisco, and lost my cell phone on the way, before Amanda had ever thought to call me about her father.

Time passed. Then, ten or fifteen minutes later, loud laughter came from the portico of the clubhouse. Wendell's three fellow colorful eggs were coming out. He lagged several paces behind them, shuffling like a ninety-year-old man. He reached in his pocket, came out with keys and fingered a remote lock.

His car chirped and flashed its headlights.

I knew Wendell drove a vintage Mercedes. Not today. The car he got into wasn't expensive. It was a medium-priced sedan, the kind of car that retirees, merchants and countless thousands of other ordinary people drive.

It was older and tan, the one I'd seen in Wendell's garage the day I'd first gone up to speak with him. The kind of car that had swerved in front of me on South Michigan Avenue, wanting to trigger that memory.

The kind with holes on the side, the kind Mrs Johnson had seen Jim Whitman coming home in the night he'd been murdered. A Buick.

Wendell Phelps had driven Jim Whitman home the night Whitman was murdered.

FORTY-FIVE

Monday: the day before the Confessors' Club was to reconvene.

I woke at six, light on sleep but heavy with what I knew should be done.

I should pull photos of Buicks with portholes from the Internet and forward them to Mrs Johnson to identify – for me to then forward to the police – the precise model and year of car that had driven Whitman home. The cops would then run a list of all such Buicks, in tan, registered in the Chicagoland area. Even if the car was titled to some corporate entity, some enterprising young cop – perhaps Delray, perhaps not – would probe deeper, and link Wendell to the Buick, and from there to Jim Whitman.

This I did not do.

I should call Delray again, in hope of getting him and not his voice mail, to tell him of a mysterious associate of Small's whose initials were R.B., someone who might know important things about the secret meetings of the men in the heavy cream. It was a useful lead, one that should be tracked down before the cops converged to watch the Confessors meet the following night.

This, at least, I tried to do, several times, but each time I got Delray's voice mail. Finally, I called the main number of the Chicago Police Department. 'Delray Delmar, please.'

'Which department?' a woman said.

'Special Projects.'

She hesitated, then said, 'Hold please.'

She came back on a moment later. 'We have no department named Special Projects.'

'He reports to the deputy chief.'

'You mean deputy superintendent?'

'Sure.'

'Which one?'

'There's more than one?'

'Of course.'

'I don't know.'

'Hold please.' This time she didn't come back for three minutes. 'Officer Delmar is in Traffic, but he's on leave.'

She transferred me to Traffic, and I asked the crusty voice that answered how I could contact Delray.

'You a friend?'

'Yes.'

'You're a friend, and you don't know he's on leave?'

A thousand charged needles began prickling the top of my head, thinking he'd been hurt. 'What's he on leave for?'

'Look, pal, if you're a friend, ask the family.' There was a question now in his cop voice. He hung up.

I called the main police number again, asked to be transferred to Traffic. Luckily a different voice, young and female, answered. 'I'm from Haggarty and Dunn, jams and jellies out of Napa, California?' I said. 'Someone, a Mr Delray Delmar, gave this phone number when he placed an order. I can't read the delivery instructions. What time will he be in?'

'This has to do with police work?'

'No, ma'am. This has to do with a gift he wants to send.'

'We don't give out home phone numbers.'

'I should leave a message with you?'

'What the hell, call St Agnes in Chicago.'

None of it made sense. Delray had said nothing about working in Traffic; he'd just been reassigned to Narcotics on the north side. More troubling, he was now in the hospital. And that might have meant he hadn't tipped Homicide about the upcoming meeting at the Confessors' Club.

A new spring storm had raged up suddenly outside. I ran out to the Jeep through rain drops hurling down as big as nickels. The Eisenhower was the most direct route to St Agnes, but the sewers built to drain the expressway were collapsing, like so many in Chicago, and had begun clogging up, stopping traffic in monstrous puddles whenever it rained. I sped as best as I could through the side streets, blowing through stop signs, running the red lights. It took an hour to make what should have been a thirty-minute trip.

The kindly lady at the hospital's front desk said it was too soon for visiting hours. I asked for Delray's room number, said I wanted to send him flowers. She smiled and said he was in 518, and that he was fortunate to have such a considerate friend.

I went out the main door, came back in through the hall from Emergency, and took the elevator up.

A pushcart holding breakfast plates under stainless steel covers was outside 518. Above it, the slip-in name holder by the door read 'Delmar, D.' I peeked in. The bed closest to the door was empty. A woman in a yellow uniform was by the window bed, taking a plate from a rolling table. The occupant of the bed was concealed behind the curtain. I smiled at her when she came out. She didn't smile back. I went in.

'Delray—' I began, but stopped when I got past the curtain. The man in the hospital bed eating scrambled eggs was at least fifty years old, and had gray hair.

'Sorry; wrong room,' I said, and started to back out.

'I'm Delray,' he said in a surprisingly robust voice.

I moved forward to the edge of the curtain. 'Delray Delmar?'

He nodded.

'Chicago police?'

'Twenty-eight years,' he said.

'I'm looking for your son.' There was nothing else to think.

The man set down his fork. 'No son; just two daughters. What's this about?'

I turned and walked out of the room. At the nurses' station, I said I was the old man's nephew in as steady a voice as I could manage. 'I just learned about my uncle's condition. How long has he been here?'

The nurse checked a chart. 'His bypass surgery was last week, but there were complications. His lungs started—'

'He's lucid?'

'Of course. No problems with that . . .'

I walked away before she could finish, on legs that felt like they weren't mine.

Outside St Agnes, the rain had stopped, but the sky had gotten even darker, as if it too knew that hell was coming to Delaware Street tomorrow and that all the notecards I'd made in my head had been reshuffled and thrown into the wind. The air felt too heavy to breathe. I walked across the street to the garage and leaned against a cold concrete column. Delray Delmar, the boy cop, was no cop. The kid was a fraud and maybe a killer.

I called the IRS. A sweet voice said Krantz wasn't in. I asked if I could speak with anybody who was working on the Arthur Lamm case. Sweet Voice said she couldn't confirm which cases the IRS was working on. I said bullshit. She asked if I would leave a number and I said I damned well would, that the matter was extremely urgent.

I hurried to the Jeep, but made it only a block before the sky opened up again. The earlier rain had filled the sewers. The new downpour was now turning the streets to rivers, the intersections to lakes. Worse, every form of road cholesterol had come out to clog my way, from distracted, pokey drivers too intent on cell phones to the truly timid, frozen by the deluge and waiting, I supposed, for a white-bearded man in robes to part the waters and show them the way to the ark. I swore at every damned one of them, cut up an alley, across another, and finally got free several blocks later.

I pulled into a gas station and called the IRS again. This time I insisted on speaking with someone who worked directly with Krantz. A man took the call, said Krantz was in Washington. Hell was coming down, I told him; Krantz had to call me. The man said Krantz was in meetings.

'There's a murderer out there, maybe two!' I yelled. I hung up, realizing I'd sounded too deranged to warrant pulling Krantz out of any meeting.

The rain had slowed to a drizzle by the time I got back to the turret. I walked down to the river, to have one last think at what seemed to be my only remaining option.

The Willahock agreed. It was angry, kicking up white spray over the banks and onto the crumbling riverwalk. Lightning lit the sky to the west, promising another storm, and the wind snapped hard at the two-armed ash. The ground around the tree was littered with young, green leaves, dead now forever. I didn't need the leaves to tell me the world had turned into a dark tempest, and that the kid cop imposter, and Arthur Lamm and his caretaker, Canty – and R.B., whoever he was – were swirling right in the middle of its dark heart. It was four-thirty. Barely twenty-four hours remained before the Confessors were set to meet the next evening, when another of them might be killed. And Agent Krantz, the only person I could hope to trust, was too busy in meetings to call me.

I phoned the bastard who'd trashed my life.

'John Keller,' the voice said.

'This is Dek Elstrom.'

He gave me a contemptuous sigh. 'Listen, Elstrom, you gotta put this behind—'

I cut him off. 'I'm not drunk this time, calling to rant about how you shafted me in your columns. I've got a story, maybe the biggest story you'll ever get. It's ideal for you, Keller, because I can't prove any of it. You're going to have to go with speculation.

But you like that, Keller. All I ask is that you lead with it in tomorrow's column – "details to follow," your usual crap.'

'I'll listen,' he said.

'You better do more than that, or people are going to die.'

FORTY-SIX

Tuesday morning. Confessors' Club day.

All night, one storm after another had thundered through Rivertown, pounding the ground, roiling the river. I wouldn't have slept much anyway, not the night before the Confessors were to gather.

I got out of bed at six, finally, because there was no reason not to. I started coffee, slipped into my yellow rain poncho and stepped out into the downpour. In the faint light of the streetlamps, Rivertown looked like it had been shaken by a furious giant. The ground was littered everywhere with branches, and several trees were down in front of city hall. Rivertown, being Rivertown, would not field a city crew to clear the streets until well past noon. The lizard in charge of municipal services owned one of the tonks on Thompson Avenue, and spent most nights until dawn drinking deeply from his own inventory.

I pushed the end of a spindly limb off the Jeep's hood, and then ran across the spit of land and Thompson Avenue to buy an *Argus-Observer* from the blue box in front of the Jiffy Lube. Ducking beneath the eave below the sign advertising full lubrications, it struck me, because my mind so often speeds in unnecessary directions, that full lubrications were the essence of Rivertown. During the day, cash greased the palms of the town's fathers to ease sticky zoning violations or troublesome brushes with what passed for the law in Rivertown. At night, cash bought lubrication of an entirely different sort, from the sweet-smelling women who worked the darker patches along Thompson Avenue. I gave a mental nod to the red-and-white sign lit bright in the rain; it was a perfect beacon for the town.

I flipped the paper open to 'Keller's Korner' only long enough to be sure he'd led with my words, then tucked it under my poncho and ran back to the turret. The coffee was ready. I caffeinated my travel mug and read what I had wrought.

Keller had headlined his column with his typical hysteria: 'FEDS AND CHICAGO PD COVER UP SECRET BLACKMAIL MURDER CLUB.' The smaller print below continued in his usual breathlessness: 'According to the agent of a well-known local businessman, a secret blackmail and murder society has been operating in the city for over a century. In the past six months, several prominent Chicagoans have been snuffed out after attending meetings in the society's secret headquarters in a graystone off the Mag Mile. And just one month ago, a private detective who discovered recording machines set up for high-stakes blackmail and worse in the ancient den was killed before he could spill what he knew. Still to be fathomed: another club member, a prominent insurance man with big-big connections to the very top-ola, has gone missing while CPD dithers and Federal boys bungle. Details to follow.'

'Details to follow,' was Keller's signature tag line, and since there were rarely any details to begin with, almost none ever would follow. He was a master at frenzied innuendo, a jester at journalistic integrity. He'd distorted what little I'd given him, used only words that would sizzle in print. He'd not named the Confessors' Club or its precise location, nor the Federal agency that was involved, the supposed murder victims, or Lamm. He'd written nothing of substance, and he'd done it as magnificently as I'd hoped. Now it was time for tens of thousands of Chicagoans to read 'Keller's Korner' online or in print, and without realizing it, they'd begin to fill in the blanks themselves. Newsreaders abhor vacuums, and in talking the story up in office corridors, over store counters and on the phone from their homes or their cars, they'd add their own little suppositions that they were sure to be true. And by noon, a hundred versions of the story would have spread to half the people in town. It was Keller's particular genius, setting roaring fires with so few tiny twigs.

I knew, because I'd been burned by those same flames. 'POWER SON-IN-LAW DETECTIVE WHINES HE WAS DUPED TO CONSPIRE' had been my bold print when Keller ridiculed me as a stupid schlep that conspired to falsify evidence. That I'd been stupid was true. That I'd conspired was false. But I was the son-in-law of Wendell Phelps, a major Chicagoan, and that got me the big ink. No matter that I'd never met Wendell, no matter that I'd been fooled by some very expert forging. No matter even that the charges against me were piled thick to obscure some very sloppy prosecution. None of that saw print in 'Keller's Korner.' My details to follow, in the form of a full exoneration, never had followed in Keller's column, and only in tiny print in the back pages of Chicago's other newspapers.

I walked to the window. Lightning lit the Willahock, heaving and frothing in the storm. Amid a hundred lesser fallen branches, the butchered ash stood as though raging in the rain, angrily thrusting its two contorted, rain-slicked limbs at city hall. I had the hope that other, more human limbs were being contorted farther to the east, in the city. By now, someone at the IRS had read Keller, and had called Krantz in Washington, and I wondered if Krantz would order that I be run downtown for some extended, repetitive questioning, if only as retribution in advance for the ridicule his snail-paced investigation was soon to receive. The Chicago police would be slower. They'd have to play catch-up, frantically call the various Federal offices in Chicago to find the agency that knew who'd made them look stupid. I had no doubt that when they rang the IRS, Krantz's crew would cough me up in a heartbeat, understanding that the Chicago cops needed their piece of me, too.

So be it. What mattered was that Keller's words would render the Confessors' Club toxic to its members. No one would dare go there that evening for fear of Feds, cops and killers. And in the coming days, other reporters, more conscientious than Keller, would dig. The names of the Confessors would be revealed, the house on Delaware would be pictured, and the graystone nest would be poisoned for all time. Nobody would ever return. Nobody would ever again be killed because of what had been recorded there.

Or so I thought, that morning.

FORTY-SEVEN

The first response I got wasn't from Krantz's men, pounding on my door. It was Wendell calling, and he was smoked.

'What the hell are you doing, Elstrom?'

'Your name isn't in the column. Neither is mine.'

'You should have checked with me first.'

'You walked away from me, remember?' I paused, then said, 'What was Jim Whitman doing in your car on the last night of his life?'

He ignored the questions. 'Somebody at the IRS or the Chicago police is going to track this to you, and then to me.'

'Too late; the IRS already knows me. That's why I can't talk long. I want to be available to make sure they get the spelling of your name right.'

'You're a son of a bitch, Elstrom.'

'Tell me how deep you're in with Arthur Lamm.' I needed to tell him more, that there was a cop imposter also chasing Lamm, but he didn't give me the chance. He hung up.

It was time to make the call I'd been dreading, but she called me before I could punch in her number. 'The acquisitions committee is meeting at the Art Institute all day,' Amanda said, her voice amazingly calm. 'Dinner tonight at five, on the cheap, at the Corner Bakery across the street?'

Even now, after the dust from our divorce had long since settled, she had the power to charm and transfix me, no matter the turmoil. I supposed that would never change.

I went into the would-be kitchen for more coffee. The cabinet that had fallen lay now in pieces on the makeshift counter. It had taken me hours to tap it apart. I'd salvaged what I could, but still it needed new structure. I'd considered scrapping it, making a new cabinet from scratch. But there are times when starting over seems unwise.

Krantz finally called. 'Care to have lunch?' he asked, though his tone made it clear I had no choice.

'I thought you were tied up in meetings in Washington, discussing ways to harass innocent taxpayers.'

'I'd like to say I flew back first thing after hearing about your friend Keller's column. But the truth is, I'd already landed at O'Hare when I got the news.' He named a Chinese restaurant close to his office and told me to be there at one.

I took a noon train that got me to the restaurant at the tail end of the lunch rush. Krantz was waiting at a table in the corner. A copy of the *Argus-Observer* lay on the table, opened to Keller's page.

I set my rolled peace offering on another chair and sat down. 'No muscle with handcuffs?'

Krantz peered through his reading glasses at the newspaper. 'I love this: "Federal boys bungle."'

'I knew you wouldn't be upset.'

'About you broadsiding a federal investigation, blowing us wide open before we could assemble all our facts?'

'You're not identified.'

He looked over his glasses like I was some sort of exhibit. 'Actually, I suppose I'm pleased. You've speeded things up. As we speak, I have an agent in a judge's chambers. It won't take long to get warrants now.'

'Warrants for what?'

'To search the so-called Confessors' Club at Sixty-six Delaware.'

He'd referred to it by name. 'You knew about it?'

'Of course. Arthur Lamm writes the property insurance for it, and collects a rather sizable management fee for its maintenance. We've known, too, that they gather on the second Tuesdays of even-numbered months. But until now, that's been no cause to go inside and search.'

'Tonight's a second Tuesday.'

'Your reason for going to Keller was to protect your father-in-law?' he asked.

'Ex-father-in-law,' I corrected, 'but no, he's not involved. I did it to make sure nobody got killed tonight.'

'We'll be watching the place to make sure,' he said, 'along with the Chicago PD.'

'The word's out?'

'Maybe not about everything,' he said. 'A private detective was murdered?'

'Eugene Small, hired to do surveillance on the members.'

I had the sense Krantz already knew about Small, like he knew all about the Confessors' Club.

I took the thin roll of paper I'd brought and put it on the table. 'Small's desk calendar. It details the dates, hours and initials of his surveillance targets.'

'How did you get it?'

'Someone dropped it on my doorstep, anonymously.'

Krantz frowned. 'Who hired Small?'

I looked around for a waitress, any waitress, to let me veer away from the questioning by ordering lunch. Only one was in sight, and she was coming toward us carrying two small brown bags.

'I already ordered for us.' He leaned forward across the table. 'Same guy who hired you?' he repeated.

'I don't know who hired Small.'

'I'm going to interview your client as soon as I can.'

'Debbie Goring?'

'Don't be a smart-ass. You're in this because Wendell Phelps hired you. Phelps is a prominent guy. So is his business partner, Arthur Lamm.'

'Not business partner, Krantz. Wendell invested in a couple of real-estate ventures with Lamm. Rich guys do that. To them, it's just playing Monopoly.'

'I've only just started looking, Elstrom. I'll learn more.'

I told him about Delray Delmar, the young cop imposter.

He didn't seem all that surprised, but I supposed by then he wasn't surprised at any of my fumblings.

When I finished, he asked, 'The supposed cop really told you, with a straight face, that his name was Delray Delmar? Wasn't that enough to tip you the guy was a fraud?'

The waitress stopped at our table and set down the two bags. 'To go, so you don't starve,' Krantz said, smiling.

FORTY-EIGHT

I understood the moment I stepped out to the sidewalk. Two Chicago police detectives sitting in a dark sedan waved badges, motioning me over.

The driver gave a smiling Krantz a thumbs-up as he walked away with his little bag of lunch. He'd saved them the legwork of finding Keller's source, even reeled me in by summoning me downtown. Such was his revenge for my calling Keller.

'Mind if I check out your IDs?' I asked the two cops, giving them what I hoped was the intelligent smile of someone newly smart about such precautions.

'Might be a good idea, considering,' said the cop behind the steering wheel, showing me his wallet ID. His name was Pawlowski. The cop riding shotgun was Wood.

I moved a few steps away and called the Chicago police main number. In seconds I received emailed photos of Pawlowski and Wood. I walked back to the car.

'So now tell us,' Pawlowski said, gesturing with his thumb at the back passenger door.

I told them just about all of it, in the car, by the curb, excepting anything about Wendell.

When I finished, Wood sniffed the air. 'We're missing lunch,' he said to Pawlowski.

'You need to work with our artist,' Pawlowski said. 'As we drive, you can give us a better description of this Delray Delmar.'

Wood turned his bulk to look at me sitting in back.

'Chinese,' I said, handing my brown bag forward. Wood opened it, took out the chopsticks, and began eating sweet-and-sour chicken from the white container. He was remarkably agile with the sticks, dropping little as we hit potholes that likely wouldn't be repaired for months, since most tax money, by court decree, was now being given over to replenish the city's looted pension accounts.

I described Delray's thin build and boyish looks for Pawlowski.

'A damned preppie?' Pawlowski asked.

'Right down to his polished Weejun loafers.'

'You ever see other cops dressed like that?'

I couldn't see Pawlowski's tie, but Wood's had a fish on it, right below a fresh speck of sweet-and-sour sauce. 'I took Delray to be typical of your fine fashion expertise.'

Pawlowski glanced at the chewing Wood. Cops have heard most things, from fools, at least twice.

As we headed south across the Congress expressway, I asked, 'How did you two happen to catch this case?'

'Lots of people caught this case. You made us all look stupid.' Pawlowski stopped the car at a nondescript office building a block down from Buddy Guy's blues club. I used to go there, back when I was young, cool and financially stable, and had to look elsewhere to find the blues.

'This is a police station?'

'We're using a freelance sketch artist. Ours got cut back to part-time.'

We got out, went through a tiny, brown-painted lobby to a door marked 'Art School of Chicago.' Adjacent to it was a door marked 'Hair Salon School of Chicago.'

'Budgets,' Pawlowski said.

Looking sorrowful, Wood dropped the empty white food container in an open trash barrel, wiped his hands on his pants, and pushed open the door. The foyer had been converted into a break room, and we took a moment to select those scuffed orange plastic chairs that contained the smallest residues of dried colas.

'I'm still not understanding the fuss about these Tuesdays, and Barberi, Whitman and Carson,' Wood said. 'Heart attack, self-administered overdose, hit-and-run.'

'All three men died after getting together on second Tuesdays,' I said. 'That can't be coincidence.'

'You're saying where?' Wood asked.

I hadn't yet mentioned the Confessors' Club by name, though I figured by now everyone in law enforcement knew it, since Krantz had said it at lunch. He'd also said there would be a heavy police presence there that evening.

'An old graystone at Sixty-six West Delaware,' I said, to be sure. 'You need to have people there tonight.'

'This private dick you mentioned – Small?' Wood asked. 'Who hired him to watch these rich guys?'

'I have no idea,' I said, 'You should send a guy up to sweat information out of Lamm's caretaker, a guy named Herman Canty.'

'And this young punk cop imposter, the one you're going to help us draw a picture of, who hired him?'

'I think Small did. Then the kid started working for himself.'

'He's a killer, this kid?'

'He could have killed Small.'

'Why?'

'To get Small out of the way, so he could shake down someone, likely Arthur Lamm.'

'The kid tricked you into finding this Delaware Street meeting place?' Wood grinned.

'Only the outside. I tricked him back by not finding out much else.'

Pawlowski shifted on his chair, fixed me with the beady eye they teach at police school. 'What's Wendell Phelps, your father-in-law, going to tell us?'

For sure Krantz had passed along Wendell's name. I gave Pawlowski my own beady eye back, the one I practice in the mirror. 'Ex-father-in-law,' I corrected.

'Come on, Elstrom.' Pawlowski smiled. 'What's Wendell Phelps going to tell us?'

'Same thing he tells everybody: his daughter is well-rid of me,' I said.

FORTY-NINE

The sketch artist, an instructor at the art school, finished a passable cartoon of Delray at four-thirty. Pawlowski and Wood took it and disappeared out the door without offering to give me a ride. I didn't object. The Corner Bakery, where I was to meet Amanda, was just a few blocks away.

Jenny had called while I'd been inside. I returned her call once I got out.

'A huge story is coming out of Chicago,' she said, right off. 'A secret society in a creepy old mansion, and dead rich guys exactly like your father-in-law.'

'Ex-father-in-law,' I corrected.

'Is this the case you're working?' she asked fast, still in a rush.

'I blew the whistle.'

'You didn't call me?'

'You're in San Francisco.'

'This story is going national.'

'Conflicting obligations,' I said. 'Old father-in-law.'

'Ex-father-in-law,' she corrected, laughing.

We were well. I told her everything, on deep background.

'And Amanda? You're protecting her, too?' she asked, when I was done.

'Of course.'

'Are you wearing the purple bow tie I sent you?'

'Not at this moment, but I'll put it on when I get back to the turret.'

She said she had to take another call and that we were not done.

'I hope so,' I said.

I walked north. I wanted to feel good. I'd rung the alarm bell, alerted everybody to the danger up on Delaware Street. Cops would soon mobilize there, and every one of the Confessors, wherever they were, would be on guard from now on. Arthur Lamm might be on even greater guard, too, though for different reasons. I still couldn't fathom why that exceedingly rich man would resort to killing for insurance money, if indeed he had. But that was for cop minds to determine, not mine.

With luck, too, the investigations would prove that Jim Whitman had been fed pills. And that might make Debbie Goring the recipient of some insurance proceeds, at last.

And some of that might trickle down on me, but it would feel like dirty rain. Wendell was playing too tight with Lamm. He'd driven Whitman home an hour or so before he died; he'd hired a private detective who'd gotten killed. Wendell's secrets put a darkness over everything, and that might well envelope his daughter. Damn the man, Wendell Phelps.

Keller called. 'I'm going to make you a star, Elstrom.'

'I'm tapped out. You've gotten everything I'm going to give you.'

'Who came knocking after this morning's column?'

'Ours was a one-shot deal. We're done.'

'You're sure you won't need me again?'

'You'll always bite at anything sleazy.'

'The Chicago police?'

'And the IRS,' I said, folding like a paper tent.

'Give me the agent-in-charge.'

'Krantz.'

'What's with Wendell Phelps, your father-in-law?'

'Ex-father-in-law,' I corrected, 'and he's not involved.'

'Wendell's involved; his daughter Amanda is involved.' He laughed, though it was more like a cackle.

'You're a bastard, Keller.'

'Details to follow,' he said, and hung up.

Amanda was waiting in the Corner Bakery at what had been our favorite table, farthest from the window counter, before we got married. She'd gotten me a roast beef sandwich on a jalapeño roll, a Diet Coke and a brownie – my dinner of choice, back in the day.

A copy of the morning's *Argus-Observer*, opened to Keller's column as Krantz's had been at lunch, lay on the table next to her salad.

'This unnamed "agent for a prominent businessman" is you?' she asked as I sat down. Her voice was calm.

'Should I eat the brownie first in case I have to run?'

She didn't smile.

'You've talked to your father?' I asked.

'Mostly he apologized for being absent when I was growing up.'

I touched the newspaper with my forefinger. 'Your father is furious with me, but I had to sound an alarm before someone else died.'

'That club.'

'It needs to be exposed.'

'My father has placed all voting authority of his common and preferred stock in my name. Worse, he's begun transferring owner-ship of the stock itself to me as well. He says it's in accordance with some tax plan his accountants and attorneys had long been planning to put in place, but I don't believe him. He's acting like a man about to die.'

I looked again at Keller's column lying open, a battlefield I'd strung with landmines that even I couldn't see. 'It's going to come out that your father is a friend of Lamm's.'

'I figured Arthur was Keller's "insurance biggie." How exactly is my father involved?'

'I think your father belongs to what's known as the Confessors' Club, a group of wealthy, influential men. I think he hired Eugene Small to tail some of the other club members because he was afraid some of them were being targeted, like Barberi, Whitman and Carson had been. When Small got killed, your father got truly scared. He hired bodyguards. You noticed that anxiety, and pressured him to hire me. He agreed because he still wanted answers, and he could control my investigation. When he realized that Lamm, his closest friend, might be behind the killings, he fired me.'

'My father went along with murder, Dek?' The words came out of her mouth dry and hoarse.

'I'm pretty sure your father drove Whitman home the night he died, which might not mean anything other than it was an act of a friend. I'm also pretty sure your father sent Debbie Goring a hundred thousand dollars anonymously, because she'd gotten none of her father's life insurance.' I tried a smile. 'That seems like the act of a friend, too.'

She turned to look at a family at the next table. The little girl was putting a potato chip in her father's hand.

'I don't understand any of this,' she said. 'What now?'

'We hunker down and let the investigations run their course.'

She leaned back, pulled a tissue out of her purse, and dabbed at her eyes. 'My father and I were estranged, and then we were not . . . I wonder if I know him.'

She didn't ask any more questions, and I didn't offer any more speculation. We ate a little, and talked of other things a little, and then she took a cab to her condo, and I hoofed it to the train station.

And both of us headed away remembering when our evenings didn't end that way and we understood so very much more than we did that night.

FIFTY

D reading that Keller had done a follow-up mentioning Wendell or Amanda by name, I hustled out early the next morning to get the day's *Argus-Observer*. But I did not go out early enough.

I'd just grabbed a paper from the box in front of the Jiffy Lube when two vans with local television logos pulled up in front of the turret. Keller could have identified me in the paper I was holding, or Krantz – or any number of angry Chicago cops – could have made calls. What was certain was that television vans had rolled up. I was now in the light and the circus was about to begin.

Going back directly meant video. I walked a half-mile down on Thompson Avenue, crossed, and came up the river path. The turret has only one door and it faces my stub of a street, so the short stretch around to the front required a sprint. Key in hand, I charged like Teddy Roosevelt up San Juan Hill, unlocked the door and ducked inside before the news folks even thought to set down their lattes.

Angry hands began beating on my door as I climbed the stairs to my would-be office. The red light on my answering machine was flashing. Another light glowed constant: though I'd only been gone an hour, the recording tape had already maxed out. I listened to the first few messages. All were the same. Television and print reporters from as far away as Minnesota were requesting phone interviews. I left the machine full, so it couldn't record any more.

By now the incessant banging on my timbered door had taken on an arrhythmic, irritating quality that set my circular metal stairs, loose at points, to ringing in an unsympathetic vibration that pulsed through my head like an infected tooth.

I have a large gray plastic wastebasket. It is thin, and tall, and rectangular. I used it to catch leaks before I got the roof fixed. I ran into the kitchen, filled it with cold water, and added a long spritz of dishwashing soap for color and bubbles. Forcing away any thoughts of restraint, I cranked open the slit window directly above the entry.

Though lousy for admitting light, my windows are medievally correct for raining down liquids like boiling oil on marauding pillagers. And also, I hoped, for sudsy water. I upended the wastebasket out the window. The frigid soapy water cascaded magnificently down onto the door-bangers, bringing forth much yelling and swearing. The pounding stopped. It had been the minor gesture of an immature mind, and I retreated from the window a satisfied child.

I scanned Keller's column and saw no mention of the Confessors' Club. The day's new allegations concerned short-pours by crooked concrete contractors at a city park. Typical Keller: yesterday's news was yesterday's news. He'd flung a grenade and moved on. Details to follow.

Not so the websites of Chicago's main daily newspapers. All offered up new details, including speculation from unnamed law enforcement types that I was Keller's unnamed agent, recaps of my involvement in the phony-check trial years before, and brief mentions of my marriage to Amanda Phelps, daughter of Wendell Phelps, a wealthy Chicagoan.

None of the reporters had dug deep enough to mention the Confessors' Club by name. Nor were there any references to Delray Delmar, though I supposed Krantz and the Chicago police were keeping a lid on him in the hopes of grabbing him, unawares.

All the reports did note that Agent Krantz of the IRS would be holding a press conference at noon, to discuss matters that bore on the case.

It would be a good day to not answer the phone or look out the window. I put sandpaper into the block, Robert Johnson into the ancient CD player, and worked on rebuilding my most troublesome kitchen cabinet.

An hour later, a car horn sounded outside. Three blasts, a pause, and three more. It was the secret staccato from seventh grade.

I peeked out the window. Leo and Endora had gotten out of his Porsche and were making their way through a cluster of the now seven news people thrusting microphones and aiming video cameras. Leo wore a black suit, black shirt, white tie and a cream fedora, and looked like a perfect miniature of a twenties-era gangster. Endora, much taller, was dressed as a flapper, in a pale blue beaded shift and a red cloche hat. Each of them carried a carton filled with groceries.

I ran down the stairs, ringing the metal. No one bringing food has to wait at the door of my turret. I unlocked it, eased it open a crack.

'Now,' I yelled, tugging the door open all the way.

Leo and Endora ran at the door, laughing. Endora came through, but Leo paused at the threshold. 'Not only did Elstrom grab the Lindbergh baby,' he yelled out, 'but he killed Archduke Ferdinand to start World War One. And I have it on good authority that he's personally responsible for the last two earthquakes that hit California.'

I pulled him in and slammed the door on the shouting news people.

Endora, still laughing at the theater of it, handed me her carton. It was filled with celery, carrots, apples and oranges, bottles of fruit juice, a head of lettuce, and some low-sodium microwavable meals. 'It was my idea to bring you food, since we knew you'd be hunkering down. It was Leo's idea to dress up.'

'Good thing we'd gone to a costume party last fall,' he said, setting his carton on the floor. He'd brought Twinkies, Oreos, Ho Hos, peanut butter and Cinnamon Toast Crunch, and several two-liter bottles of Diet Coke. He is my friend.

'I'll get us coffee,' I said.

'Laced with sawdust?' Leo blew at the dust mites floating in the narrow beams of sunlight crisscrossing the room. 'No. We only drink bathtub gin,' he said, still in character, 'and we don't even have time for that. Endora has to be at work, and I've got a plane to catch.'

They moved toward the door.

'Ready?' I asked.

'Twenty-three skidoo,' Leo shouted, and out they went.

I slammed the door shut behind them and ran up the stairs to watch from the window above the entry. Leo marched towards his Porsche with his arms outstretched like a pint-sized southern governor. He held the car door open for Endora, the perfect moll, who paused to curtsy before getting in. Grinning, Leo went around, got behind the wheel, and drove them away with a loud blast of exhaust.

FIFTY-ONE

Semi-reclined in the electric-blue La-Z-Boy, the micro-television resting on my lap, I was ready. My hands balanced coffee, a stick of celery and a two-pack of Twinkies. It was exactly noon, the time Krantz was to hold his televised news conference.

Krantz apparently wasn't ready. He was late.

The WGN noontime anchor, a trim fellow with a tanned face that likely had never been smeared with a Ho Ho, began to ad-lib to fill time.

'While we wait, we have some . . . ahem . . .' He lit his tan-toned face with a slightly trembling, professionally whitened smile, as though he were about to be overcome by something momentous. '. . . rather bizarre footage, shot earlier this morning outside the residence of one of the people allegedly involved in the newly unfolding secret club mystery.' He nodded at some unseen technician, and the screen switched to tape.

A videocam zoomed in on the window that was opening above the newsmen beating on the turret's door. My face materialized from out of the gloom, pale as Marley's ghost, followed by my hands, then arms, all struggling to tip a thin but obviously heavy wastebasket down at the ground below.

'Vlodek Elstrom,' Tan-tone narrated, 'allegedly a source cited by John Keller in his newspaper column yesterday, apparently took offense to some news people seeking to interview him this morning . . .' Tan-tone paused to let the video carry the spectacle.

On the screen, my arms swiveled to upend the gray plastic wastebasket.

'Whereupon, as you can see, well . . .' Tan-tone chuckled softly, professionally overcome by the ludicrousness of what was unfolding.

The water came. Soapy and glistening, it gushed down in a torrent of a million sparkling colors, drenching the two dark-suited reporters and setting them to jumping up and down and shaking their fists up at the window over their heads.

The usually stern voice of Tan-tone dissolved into perfectly

modulated laughter, and was joined by the guffaws of his always
jocular sportscaster and the station's newest weather sweetie, a
hip Latina. Normally the little news-at-noon band offered fake
laughs at the end of the show, to leave their viewers happy despite
the murders and war deaths they'd just reported. There was nothing
fake about the howls that day. Real tears of laughter were running
down their cheeks. I would have laughed too, if it hadn't been me
on the screen, starring as the perfect jackass.

'Let's . . . replay . . . that . . .' the almost hysterical voice of
Tan-tone managed. But the screen cut abruptly to a shot of Agent
Krantz standing at a podium, and I was saved.

'I have a statement, and then I will take questions,' Krantz
began, adjusting his reading glasses. 'Approximately four months
ago, we began investigating allegations of accounting irregularities at the Lamm All-Risk Insurance Company. Based upon the
information we obtained during this careful and thorough investigation, we have now issued warrants for the arrest of Mr Arthur
Lamm, charging him with failure to maintain mandated premium
accounts, use of premium balances for personal expenditures,
illegal reimbursement of political donations, providing illegal
discounts, and falsifying policy applications. Other charges may
follow.' He took off his reading glasses and attempted to smile.
'If there are any questions, I will be happy to take them now.'

He'd just announced charges for the sorts of business irregularities that never headlined the news and said nothing about what
had drawn the reporters: the killings coming out of the graystone
on Delaware.

Everybody shouted at once. 'Is Arthur Lamm connected to the
secret society?'

'The so-called Confessors' Club?' Krantz asked.

'Confessors' Club?' several people yelled. The name was new
to them.

For a moment, Krantz appeared flustered. 'It's what some people
call it, I've heard. Mr Lamm's brokerage carried the insurance on
the property.'

'That's the only relationship?'

'We believe he also managed the maintenance of the property.'

'Come on, Krantz; this isn't important enough to hold a press
conference.'

Krantz shrugged.

'Lamm ran this Confessors' Club?'

Krantz shrugged again.

'Where is Lamm now?'

'As I said, we have issued warrants for his arrest,' Krantz said.

'You're not interested in the deaths of the businessmen and the private eye?' the well-creased political reporter for the local ABC affiliate shouted.

The room went quiet as everyone strained to hear.

Krantz's face acted confused. 'Chicago homicides are never our purview.'

'You're saying you're only investigating Arthur Lamm for income tax?'

'We're the Internal Revenue Service. That's our job.'

'And in this matter, you're only interested in Arthur Lamm?' someone shouted.

'Well . . .' Krantz said slowly, as coy as a young girl in gingham being asked on a first date. 'There is another individual.'

'Give us a name, Krantz.'

'I'll only say that he is a business partner of Lamm's. We're not ready to name him at this time.'

And there it was, squeeze theater, performed for an audience of one: me. Krantz would go public with Wendell's name, and innuendo, unless I got more cooperative.

The shouting got louder. The press was ravenous for the new name and was yelling for more angles into the Confessors' Club.

'Ladies and gentlemen,' Krantz yelled, 'you are asking me questions about murders.' He flashed a humorless smile, tossed out a quick 'Thank you very much' and strode abruptly from the podium.

He'd completed his mission artfully. He'd used a bland statement about the ongoing IRS investigation to limit its responsibility to income-tax issues only. The IRS should not be blamed for any lack of progress in a murder case.

And he'd called out the name: the Confessors' Club.

He was the only one who'd used it.

He'd used the name, too, during our lunch at the Chinese restaurant. I supposed that needed to mean nothing. Krantz was way out in front of Pawlowski and Wood and all the Chicago cops who hadn't yet known the name. He'd been investigating Arthur Lamm for months.

Still, I wondered how Krantz had learned the name. He'd used it so easily, so familiarly, at our aborted lunch. He'd known its members met on the second Tuesdays of even-numbered months. He seemed to have known about Eugene Small, and about Delray Delmar, too.

He'd been investigating for months, I told myself again.

Still . . .

I thought then of how promptly Krantz had dispatched one of his agents to the turret with copies of Lamm's appointments calendar. And the agent's almost dutiful request to see a little more of the turret, and how I'd shown him the second floor, the floor where I worked at a card table, the floor where I did most of my talking on the phone.

I pushed myself out of the La-Z-Boy and went to feel under the card table.

It was just a little bump, a tiny piece of plastic no bigger than a nickel stuck to the underside. I left it alone.

The agent had also gone into the kitchen. The second little bump was stuck beneath a cabinet. I spent the next hour searching the second floor. I found no more.

Two bumps; two bugs. Krantz had been listening to what I'd said on the phone, mostly talking to Leo, but also to Amanda and Debbie Goring. I hadn't said it much, but I'd said it enough: The Confessors' Club, second Tuesdays, even-numbered months. No doubt I'd said other things, too.

I wanted to run down to the river and drown the little bugs, but that would tip Krantz that he'd been discovered, and might prompt him to pick me up to sweat me harder. Better to leave his bugs alone, so Krantz would leave me alone, in hopes he'd hear more.

I thought about spending the afternoon working in the kitchen, trying to soothe my nerves with working wood. But I didn't have the calm for that.

I called Gaylord Rikk from outside.

FIFTY-TWO

'You said you were going to help us recapture our payout,' he said.

'I've got a new lead, but I have to know where the money went.'

'I've been reading between the lines in the papers, Elstrom, and watching television. You're thick in the middle of everything, yet you tell me nothing.'

'Did Arthur Lamm write the policy on Carson?'

'Lamm's agency is huge. He writes a lot of the people we insure. Give me other names, so I can see if we got screwed over with them, too, and maybe I'll tell you a little more about Carson's policy.'

'Benno Barberi, James Whitman.'

I heard his fingers typing at a keyboard. 'No go on both.'

Lamm had spread the policies around, to avoid attracting attention. 'The check on Carson has gone out?'

'Some days ago.'

'Who was the beneficiary?'

'A guy from Chicago PD called just an hour ago, asking the same thing.'

'The police, and not the IRS?'

'The police. Now you. The IRS will be next. Sometimes it takes the Feds longer, is all.'

'Did the cop leave a name?'

'Come to think, no,' he said. 'Just some guy, younger.'

'You knew to stonewall him, didn't you, Gaylord? You didn't give him the beneficiary?'

'I told him that information was confidential, like I'm telling you. He said he'd get a subpoena over, but I'm doubtful.'

'He was no cop, but maybe you already figured that.'

'Damn right I did, just like I'm trying to figure your motives this very moment. Why do you need the name of the Carson beneficiary?' he asked.

'I want to see who's collected on running Carson down. You'd look dumb, Gaylord, if you blew a chance to recover the payout.'

'Meaning what?'

'Meaning you let an opportunity slip by to stop the Carson check.'

'We're an insurance company. We can't go grabbing back checks because there's an insinuation of a crime.'

'Not even from the killer?'

'Oh, hell, Elstrom, I don't want to know anything more,' he said, speaking fast now. 'It was a two-million-dollar term life policy, payable to a Second Securities Corporation.' He gave me an address on North Milwaukee Avenue in Chicago.

'Thank you, Gaylord.'

'Up yours,' he said.

Jenny called me as I headed to that north part of the city.

'Though a most interesting story out of Chicago has gone national,' she said, 'and I've been on intimate terms with the man at the center of it . . .' She faked a cough. 'And I've been anticipating becoming even more intimate . . .' She let her voice trail away.

'I'll tell you almost all of what's new,' I said, and did.

'What about Wendell Phelps?'

'I don't know the truth about Wendell.'

'Do you know your truth about Amanda?' She wasn't asking about the case.

'I think so,' I said, but it might have been after a hesitation.

'You're still coming to San Francisco?'

'Soon,' I said, but I wondered how long it would take to know the truth about that as well.

FIFTY-THREE

blew past the place twice before I saw the tiny numbers. They were tarnished, almost invisible on a dark brick building wedged between a dry cleaner's and a quick loan place that had gone out of business. I parked around the corner on a residential side street and walked back.

A rusting bracket looked to have once held a barber pole, and the front window next to it had been filled in with glass blocks. The front door was full glass except for the mail slot cut into the metal scuff plate at the bottom. There was no name anywhere, or anything else that made it look like the legitimate recipient of a two-million-dollar insurance payout. I went in.

A young girl, nineteen or twenty, was talking to a glitter-encrusted cell phone that lay on a small wood desk. She was chewing spearmint gum and painting the nails on her right hand with silver glitter that matched the phone, the sequins on her black sweater and the sparkle of the silver studs piercing her ears, nose, and one cheek. Even her dark hair had been dusted with silvery specks. I didn't imagine all that sparkle was problematic during the day, but come nightfall, any driver catching her million glints in his headlights would likely be blinded and driven off the road.

She had no computer, no typewriter, no papers, and no desk phone. The walls were also blank, except for a closed door in the wall behind her.

Her thick eyelashes rose and then sagged, probably from their own caked weight, as I sat on a ripped vinyl chair and smiled.

'I'll call you back, Arnold,' she said, releasing more spearmint into the air. Mindful of her wet nails, she touched a button on her cell phone with only the tip of a glistening little finger.

'Can I help you, sir?'

'I'm here to see Mr Lamm.'

'I'm sorry. We have no . . .' She'd already forgotten the name.

'Lamm.'

'Like in "Mary Had A Little—?"' She ground harder at the spearmint gum, working the thought.

'No. L–A–M–M.'

She shook her head, confused. As she did, she caught sight of her wet right nails, still suspended like pincers splayed up in the air. She laid them down carefully, nails up, on the surface of her desk.

I replaced my smile with an officious frown. 'This is Second Securities Corporation?'

'Just a minute.' With her left forefinger, she hooked open the center drawer of her desk, read something, and said, 'Yes, this is Second Securities Corporation.'

'I'm with the Department of Verification,' I said, trying to intone like Tan-tone did on the news at noon. 'My office set up an appointment with Mr Lamm.'

'I'm sorry, sir—'

'Sorry won't cut it.' I stood to loom over the poor girl. 'If Lamm thinks he can avoid this, he is sadly mistaken.'

'I don't know Mr Lamm,' she said, her chair scraping back on the tile floor as I made for the door behind her.

The faintest of foul smells came as I reached to turn the door knob. It was locked.

'What's back there?'

'A garage full of rats, I'm thinking. Some alive, some dead.' Her voice, frightened, had shot up an octave.

'Where's Lamm?' I demanded, louder than was necessary.

A tear began descending in a black rivulet. 'I don't know any kind of lamb. My ma never cooked it. I'm just supposed to sit here and take in the mail and not look at it and put it in the desk.' She tugged at a right-side drawer handle, mindless now of her wet nails, and pulled it open. It was stuffed with flyers and catalogues. 'Somebody comes by at night to pick it up.'

I reached past her, grabbed a handful. All of it looked to be junk: grocery flyers, ads for cosmetic dentists, sales at a tire discounter. There were no first-class business envelopes in the pile.

'This looks like more than a day's worth,' I said, handing it back.

She took it, sniffling. 'They must be on vacation. They haven't been by for a few days.'

'I have to get in back,' I said.

My cell phone rang. I pulled it out.

'Dek?' It was Amanda. Her voice was high pitched, almost shrill. 'An Agent Krantz—'

'Department of Verification,' I said officiously, for the glitter girl's benefit.

'Dek, he says—'

'Hold please,' I said, cutting her off again. I nodded curtly to the glitter girl and started for the front door. 'Tell Lamm I'll be back. He can't hide forever.'

'Tell him yourself,' she sniffled behind me. 'I haven't been paid in over a week, and I don't need this shit.'

I strode out, pompous and erect, a bully. And sure of the obvious: Second Securities was a front, a mail drop, a place set up only to receive an insurance payout.

I clicked Amanda back on. 'Sorry; I was role playing.'

'An Agent Krantz just phoned . . .' More words came, but they were muffled, indistinct, lost to the traffic rumbling along Milwaukee Avenue.

'Yell, Amanda,' I shouted.

'He says my father's going to jail!' she screamed.

FIFTY-FOUR

Amanda's condo tower is for the very rich. She'd called down to the guards in the lobby, and one of them whisked me right into an elevator. Amanda was waiting for me in the hallway outside her door.

'I just don't know what's going on,' she said, 'but I figured I better get away from the office in case Krantz showed up.

'Your father is stonewalling everybody.'

'But why?'

'Arthur Lamm is his best friend?'

She nodded.

'I just came from Second Securities, a mail drop Lamm set up to receive insurance payouts like the Carson check. There was a girl there, a receptionist, who doesn't do anything except wait for the mail and put it in a desk drawer. I don't like the set-up; it's crooked. I'll go back after dark for a more thorough look around.'

'You think this has to do with my father?'

'I think I'd like to know how close he is to Arthur Lamm.'

'Let's go to Second Securities now,' she said.

'The girl will still be there. I'll go alone, tonight.'

I didn't want Amanda along. My mind, or rather my nose, had slipped back to that noxious smell coming from behind the locked door at Second Securities. It could have been rats. It could have been something else.

She stood up, grabbed her purse and her cell phone. 'I have a plan for her.'

There was no mistaking the resolution on her face.

'Good deal,' I said.

Thirty minutes later I sat in the Jeep, waiting. I'd parked at the edge of a drugstore lot, mostly hidden but angled for a good view of Second Securities across the street. Amanda had gotten out a block away, so she could walk up to the drugstore alone.

Amanda came out of the drugstore. With her back turned to the building across the street, she stopped at the trash receptacle on the sidewalk to thumb off the price stickers before dropping the lipsticks into the small case she'd brought. When she was done, she turned and, without a glance at me, crossed Milwaukee Avenue. It wasn't a sophisticated plan, but we didn't have time for sophistication: she was selling cosmetics, door-to-door, and anxious to hire an assistant, even a gum-chewing, glittered-up assistant, right on the spot.

She pulled the door handle at Second Securities, and stopped. It was locked. She pressed close against the glass to peer in and began knocking. After a moment she started to turn away, but as she did her purse fell out of her hand, spilling its contents against the door. Making a gesture of disgust, she knelt down, her back to the side-walk, the street, and me. She took an incredibly long time to pick up her things. Finally she stood up, and walked down Milwaukee. I started the Jeep and followed her around to a side street.

'Nobody home,' she said, getting in. She was perspiring lightly.

'Let's drive around, check for a back door.' I started to pull away from the curb.

She held her hand out. 'We'll use the front door, like we were invited.'

I hit the brakes. In her hand was a key.

'I got lucky,' she said. 'I saw the key through the glass, lying on the floor. There's a mail slot at the bottom of the door. It took me forever to fish it out.'

'I scared the girl away,' I said.

'Enough for her to drop the key back inside the mail slot before she took off.'

'You wait in the Jeep while I go inside.'

'We'll go together,' she said.

'Let's check around back first.' I drove around to the alley. There was a dented, gray steel garage door at the rear of Second Securities. I jumped out quickly and gave the handle a tug. The door was locked from the inside.

'Likely enough, the garage is full of rats,' I said as I got back in the Jeep.

'I don't care. We're going in together,' she said.

Remembering what had appeared to be a solid interior door leading to the garage in back, I drove to a Home Depot we'd passed a mile down Milwaukee Avenue and bought a short jimmy bar, a sixteen-ounce claw hammer and, after a second's consideration, a pair of thin work gloves for her, a pair of thicker yellow rubber gloves for me. I wasn't only thinking fingerprints; I was recalling smell.

I parked on the side street. Amanda put the Home Depot things in her purse and we marched up to Second Securities like we had an appointment. A turn of the glitter girl's key and we were in.

The place still smelled of her spearmint chewing gum and cheap perfume, but the other smell – the dead smell – had grown stronger in the hours that the place had been shut up.

Amanda sniffed the air. 'What is that?' she whispered.

'Rats, as I told you,' I said. After a moment's hesitation, I switched on the overhead fluorescents and pointed to the desk. 'Sit at the desk like you belong and search every inch inside for an envelope with a check in it, even behind the drawers. Try to keep your hands out of sight because I want you to keep your gloves on. If anybody comes in, say your friend asked you to fill in for the day.'

I didn't expect Amanda would find anything; Lamm would have grabbed the Carson check by now. But I wanted her away from whatever wasn't right in back.

I took the hammer, gloves and pry bar from her purse.

'Maybe I should first go with you, to the back, to help you . . .' She stopped as I shook my head. She didn't want to follow that smell, not really. She put on the thin gloves I'd bought for her.

I pulled on my own gloves and went to the door.

I slipped the jimmy bar between the door and the jamb, just above the lock, and struck it with the hammer. The solid-core door splintered around the lock at the fourth blow, releasing the scent of hell.

Behind me, Amanda caught her breath. 'Oh, Dek, that's not rats.'

I pushed open the ruined door. Enough light filtered in from the office to show a car shape at the center of the garage. I found the light switch and closed the door behind me. The overhead fluorescent fixture buzzed, sputtered and caught.

The car was several years old, a small, white two-door Ford made faintly green by the fluorescent light. It was filthy, except for the crumpled front fender that was strangely dulled.

I walked up to it. Fine scratches crisscrossed the damaged fender. Someone had flattened the car's finish with steel wool. Likely, I thought, to remove Grant Carson's blood.

The car's doors were locked, and it had no license plates, no temporary dealer tag or windshield parking stickers. It could have been bought for cash in a bad neighborhood, or simply stolen.

The garage was stuffy and hot from being closed up. Trying to breathe in only through my mouth, I pressed against the glass to look inside. The interior appeared empty. Whatever was fouling the air wasn't coming from the passenger compartment.

I turned away from the car and swung the hammer backwards, exploding the driver's side window into a million tiny green-edged bits. I opened the door and was brushing some of the glass off the seat when Amanda stepped into the garage. She'd heard the shattering glass.

'Dek?'

'Go back. If anybody comes, keep them in front.'

She didn't argue.

The dead smell was worse inside the car. A key was in the ignition. I took it out and went around to the back. The key didn't work the trunk. I leaned back into the car, replaced the key in the ignition, and searched beneath the seats, under the floor mats and in the glove box. There was no second key, nor any interior trunk release.

I slid out. The trunk seam was narrow. Jimmying the bar into it only slightly bent the lid. I'd have to go in through the back seat to see what was dead in the trunk.

I climbed in behind the driver's seat and began hacking at the back of the rear seat with the claw end of the hammer. The vinyl upholstery came away in chunks, still attached to its foam padding. The rank smell of death came at me stronger with each new blow, sticking thick in my throat and nose. I whacked faster at the seat back; I wouldn't be able to stay in the car much longer.

The last of the upholstered seatback tore away, but the metal springs behind it wouldn't budge. They'd been fastened tight with a pneumatic wrench on an assembly line.

I swung blindly at the rear shelf now, crazed by the ever stronger foulness rising from the trunk. The fiberboard dented and at last split apart. I ripped at the pieces, threw them out of the car, and reached down into the trunk.

I touched cold metal, ribbed and hard. Reaching past it, I found something just as cold, but not quite as hard, wrapped in thick plastic. My gut twisted. It was what I knew I'd find. Rigor.

I pulled my hand back, felt again the cold metal. It was a case of some sort, wedged between the seat back and the corpse. I found the handle and tugged it through the hole where the rear shelf had been. It was an aluminum metal briefcase. I dropped it on the front passenger seat and stuck my hand back into the hole.

I was sure I was touching death, perhaps days old. I felt along its shape, found a shoulder, and then the curve of an arm locked in place, unyielding. And a knee, tucked up under the chest.

I wanted to run, get free from the stench, the death. But I had to know. For myself. For Amanda, more.

I sunk the teeth of the hammer's claw into the plastic shrouding the death, ripping it. The purest fumes of hell came at me, searing my nose, constricting my throat, pulling up bile. I held my breath, afraid I'd vomit. I found a belt and followed fabric – denim, wool or cotton; I couldn't tell through the yellow gloves – past a dead hip to the small raised square that I was hoping to find. A wallet in a back pocket. An answer.

I eased it out with my fingers, backed out of the car, and dropped it on the hood. I poked it open with my index finger. The driver's license was in a plastic window.

Herman Canty, PO Box 12, Bent Lake, Wisconsin.

The body exhaled behind me, a soft sound of gas escaping through the rips I'd made in the plastic. I grabbed the metal case from the front passenger seat, left the wallet behind, and ran to the ruined door that led to the office.

FIFTY-FIVE

'Oh, hell,' Amanda said after we'd sped down the first mile of Milwaukee Avenue. 'I forgot to leave the key.' She looked stricken at the thought we'd have to drive back and slip the key through the slot in the door.

After the briefest glance at the cash inside the metal case, we'd fled Second Securities unnerved, sick from the smell of death, barely able to remember to lock the door behind us.

'Put it in the ashtray,' I said. 'I'll get rid of it later.'

'Why did we take all that money?' she asked, gesturing at the metal case I'd tossed in back. Her hands shook as she dropped the key in the ashtray.

'To see who comes after it.' It was all I could think to say. I had no plan that involved grabbing cash. I hadn't expected it would be there. 'Canty must have been Lamm's partner in running down Grant Carson. Lamm must have killed him to silence him for all time, then left the money with the corpse, thinking it would be safest there, while he went north to tidy up a last detail.'

'What last detail?'

'Canty's girlfriend, Wanda. Lamm must be thinking Canty told her some things. Do you know how to block your number when you make a call?'

'Sure,' she said.

'Get the number of the sheriff's department near Bent Lake.

Leave an anonymous tip that Wanda over at Loons' Rest might
be in trouble.'

It only took her a couple of minutes. Then she asked, 'I still
don't understand: if Arthur needs money badly enough to kill for
it, why risk leaving it in that garage?'

'Guys like Lamm and your father, they don't fly commercial,
right?'

'Lear jets, chartered out of Midway Airport,' she said.

'Then Second Securities is the safest short-term place he knows.
Nobody knows about it except Rikk at the insurance company
. . .' I let the thought trail away.

'Dek?'

'And anybody else he might have told. He swore he didn't tell
Delray when he called, posing as a cop. But you never know.'

'Does that matter?'

I thought for a moment, and said, 'I don't think so. Delray's got
to be thinking the check was picked up and cashed somewhere.
I'm pretty sure the only person who's going to be shocked at Second
Securities is Arthur Lamm, when he comes back. He'll be light the
two million dollars he needs for fleeing in a corporate jet.'

'Are you going to tell Krantz to keep watch for Arthur to show
up at Second Securities?'

'I owe your father more than that. We're going to tell him about
the money we just found. That ought to make him talk about his
friend Arthur.'

'And then?'

'We find a way to give it to the cops without implicating your
father.'

'Damn it,' she said. 'I wish my father didn't get rid of his
security detail. Too much cash is being tossed around.'

'He believes he has nothing to fear from his old friend Arthur.'

'I'm going to call my father when we get back to my
apartment.'

We drove in silence for another five minutes, until she told me
to pull over in front of a discount men's clothing store.

'My treat,' she said. I stunk of the death I'd found in the small
battered Ford, and I'd torn one knee of my khakis, ripping my
way into the car trunk. She was out with a bag in five minutes,
and we were back on our way.

Upstairs in her condo, she handed me the bag.

'Ah, new duds,' I said.

'But the same you,' she said. 'Cheap khakis, de rigueur blue button-down shirt in cotton polyester, socks and underwear. Thirty-six fifty for the whole outfit. Once you've showered, you'll smell and look like new.' She forced a nervous laugh, but she was firing on all pistons, in control. 'Guest bath is waiting. While you're showering, I'll call my father, see if we can meet him in an hour or so.' She handed me a paper bag for the clothes I was wearing. 'Incinerator chute is outside, in the hall.'

Shampoo and soap were in the shower; I needed nothing. Yet previous lives occasionally demand a fast indulgence. Inside the medicine cabinet were wrapped bars of soap, two fresh tubes of toothpaste, a sealed toothbrush, and nothing else. Most especially, there was no man's razor, shaving cream, or deodorant.

She'd mentioned Richard Rudolph, socially impeccable silver-haired hedge fund manager and investor, only in passing, saying he was in Russia, doing a deal. I'd mentioned Jenny the same way, just as reluctantly and also only in passing. I'd supposed our vagueness was normal, an offering of respect for the past and probably nothing more.

Now, in her guest bathroom, surrounded by her soaps, her linens, things didn't feel so firmly rooted in the past.

I opened the linen closet, looking for a towel, and got a soft jolt. An inch of familiar red and blue striped terry showed bright behind the stack of white towels. I pushed the towels to one side and was sure. It was the robe she'd bought me right after we married. That she'd kept it wanted to set off too many conflicting thoughts, and I showered trying not to think about any of them.

I emerged twenty minutes later, studiously scrubbed, garbed in fresh polyester and smelling swell. I dropped my paper bag of clothes into the incinerator chute down the hall, came back, and went into the kitchen. She'd made us coffee, and set cups on the kitchen table.

'My father is in meetings,' she said.

'I'll leave the two million here,' I said. 'You've got all the building security it needs.'

We drank the coffee, then she walked me to the door and told me she'd call as soon as she heard from her father.

FIFTY-SIX

Amanda didn't call, and I fiddled away all of the next morning and the earliest part of the afternoon on the Internet. News sites everywhere had seized upon the gray-stone they were all now calling the Confessors' Club, used only six times a year for the secret meetings of wealthy men. Facts were in short supply, so many of the reports offered Keller-like speculations of wild drunkenness, sexual debauchery, political manipulations and, of course, murderous plotting. It seemed that the farther the news organization was from Chicago, the wilder was the prose it used on its website.

Close to home, the reporting was more responsible. The *Tribune*'s site ran a story about the IRS investigating Lamm next to a history of the Confessors' Club, leaving no doubt that the two stories were related. The IRS story reported the likelihood that Lamm had high-tailed it out of Chicago to escape his impending indictment. Unnamed federal authorities, Krantz or one of his subordinates, said that the search for him had shifted to Sarasota, Florida, where Lamm had another home, and to a small, unnamed Caribbean country, where he might have transferred funds.

The Confessors' Club article was historical, and featured a photograph, taken around 1900, captioned as being the only one known to ever have been taken of its members. It showed thirty men, in high collars and walrus mustaches, sitting stiffly at the long dining-room table, staring unsmiling into a camera that must have been set up in the parlor. The story noted that no record had been found of the club ever participating in civic or charitable endeavors, despite the prominence of its members, and seemed to have always conducted its activities in secret.

There were short sidebar biographies of Barberi, Whitman and Carson, noting that the deaths, though still presumed to have resulted from natural causes, excepting Carson's, were being re-examined as part of the Lamm and Confessors' Club investigations.

No site mentioned Delray Delmar, or offered the police artist's sketch of Delray I'd been hauled in to help create. The lid was still tight on the cop imposter. I supposed it didn't much matter. It was the other stuff that was big news, and no real news at all.

Amanda called at two-thirty, but not with news that we were to meet with Wendell. Her words were perfectly precise with rage. 'The man from the IRS is now here at my home. He's the one who called yesterday. He says his name is Krantz. I'm wondering if you might stop by.'

'What's he saying?'

'Sleazy innuendo that I'd rather you heard first-hand.' Undoubtedly Krantz was within hearing distance.

I told her I'd get there in a hurry, and I did. She was waiting out in the hall. We shared a brief hug and I followed her inside.

Agent Krantz was standing in the center, looking tiredly at the framings on the wall. If he knew art, he recognized the names on the oils. If he didn't, chances were he at least recognized the bold signatures on the big Manet and the small Renoir. And if he didn't know a Manet from a Monet, like me before I met Amanda, he still would have guessed from the heavy security in the building that he was staring at big-dollar art.

'Ms Phelps has been educating me about light and brush strokes, and backgrounds and shadows and colors,' he said to me, instead of saying hello. He turned to Amanda. 'May we proceed now, Ms Phelps?'

Amanda ignored him and smiled at me. It was a smile that could have cut steel. 'I asked Secret Agent Krantz if—'

'That's *Special* Agent—' Krantz cut in.

'Whatever.' Amanda changed her smile to a glare. 'I asked this *man* if he wouldn't mind waiting until you got here, Dek. I didn't want you to miss one word of his slimy accusations.'

'Now wait . . .' Krantz started to protest again, but Amanda had already turned to go into the kitchen. Krantz and I followed and sat at the table. It was the one she'd had at her multi-million-dollar house at Crystal Waters before it blew up – cheap pine, poorly enameled, and chipped from years of use. If Krantz took any meaning in being led from fine art to sit at a garage sale table, he didn't show it. Coffee that smelled fresh came from a high-end

Braun maker on the counter. Amanda, an able gameswoman when angry, sat down without offering to pour us any.

Krantz took a long breath, which only built more tension in the room, and began. 'I stopped by to ask Ms Phelps if she knew where her father was. Ms Phelps told me that she did not. I asked her if she knew about her father's business relationship with Arthur Lamm. Ms Phelps said she wanted you here. I've just spent thirty-eight minutes learning things I do not need to know about fine art.'

Amanda cut in before I could answer. 'Secret Agent Krantz is implying all sorts of things—'

'That's *Special*—'

'Wendell is missing?' I asked Krantz.

'My father often travels on business,' Amanda cut in.

'According to his housekeeper,' Krantz said, 'he never went into the office this morning. He threw clothes in an overnight bag and left about eight o'clock, telling her he'd be gone for one or two days.'

'Secret Agent Krantz is implying my father fled town rather than speak to him.'

'I was to interview Mr Phelps this afternoon at his office,' Krantz said. 'When I got there, I was told he'd left. Ms Phelps confirms she hasn't seen him today.'

'He's only been gone for a few hours. Our offices are on different floors,' Amanda said.

'When did you set up the appointment?' I asked.

'Day before yesterday, Tuesday.'

Tuesday, Confessors' Club day.

'You talked to him directly, to set up the appointment?' I said.

'It took a while to get past all the secretaries, but yes.'

'How did he sound?'

'Unappreciative.'

'How about today? Did you speak to his wife?' I asked.

'Apparently his wife didn't see him leave. She was home at the time, but off . . .' He paused to look at Amanda, perhaps afraid she'd come across the table at him if he used the wrong words.

'Tending pigs,' Amanda said.

'Exactly,' Krantz said, wincing only a little. 'I only spoke to the housekeeper.'

'Secret Agent Krantz is implying that my father took off to avoid being questioned,' Amanda said.

Krantz sighed. 'I merely informed him of his responsibilities when we spoke, day before yesterday. We're not much interested in this so-called Confessors' Club, the murders that were supposedly set in motion there, or even why your fingerprints are everywhere inside, Elstrom.'

I started to say something, offer up some lie about why I'd failed to mention I'd been inside the graystone, but he waved it away. 'The Chicago police are pursuing all that, Elstrom. I want to interview Mr Phelps because of his shared business interests with Mr Arthur Lamm.'

'My father serves on many boards,' Amanda said. 'And he bought shares in some of Arthur's real-estate ventures.'

'Your father bought half of Lamm's insurance brokerage last fall.'

Shock widened Amanda's eyes. It linked Wendell to the insurance agency's enormous IRS problems. Worse, though Amanda couldn't realize it yet, it tied her father to any killings Lamm might have done.

I rested my hand lightly on her wrist. 'Buying into an insurance agency doesn't link Wendell to any of Lamm's alleged frauds.'

'For Christ's sake.' Amanda stood up and walked out of the kitchen. A moment later, a door closed down the hall.

Krantz looked at me across the chipped table. 'As I've been saying, we've been investigating Lamm for all sorts of tax law violations. It's not hard to imagine he was also instrumental in the deaths of James Whitman and Grant Carson, but that's for the cops. Our focus is on income tax evasion, and that must include Wendell Phelps, because he owns half of Arthur Lamm's brokerage.'

'But you said Wendell only recently bought into the agency.'

'Phelps is tight with Lamm, damn it. He owns half of his insurance brokerage, belongs to the same secret club. Lamm has gone missing. So has Wendell Phelps. Even if Phelps is completely innocent, Lamm is dragging him down. Phelps can help himself if he tells us what he knows.' He leaned back in the chair. 'As can you, Elstrom.'

'Meaning what?'

'That Confessors' Club on Delaware Street.'

'How is it you knew its name before anyone else?'

'We've been investigating Lamm's activities for months,' he said, lying, with an impressively straight face.

'Maybe you should have tipped the cops about that club. Maybe you could have saved lives.'

'Maybe you should explain what you were doing inside.'

'I went in with a guy I thought was a cop.'

'Where the hell is Phelps?'

'I don't know.'

'Where's the supposed cop?'

'*Supposed?*'

'Maybe he doesn't exist,' Krantz said.

'Why don't you get the cops to release the sketch I helped their artist develop?'

'They're touchy about someone passing as one of their own. They think people will end up not talking to any of them.'

Delray had gone to Wendell's house, but I didn't want to bring Wendell any closer into this conversation. 'The kid posing as Delray Delmar is real. Whitman's daughter spoke with him,' I offered instead.

'Your fingerprints were on pewter mugs left on the dining-room table in that graystone.'

'Delmar had me take them off a wall rack. He left them out so they'd be printed.'

'CPD also pulled your prints off a lot of doors.'

'Delray was careful to leave no fingerprints of his own. He was setting me up to become a fall guy, someone to pin everything on.'

'Why?'

'Maybe to use as leverage, to get me to do something.'

'What?'

'I have no idea.'

Amanda came back into the kitchen, but stood facing the coffee maker, as though waiting for Krantz to leave before she poured herself a cup.

Krantz stood up. 'Encouraging Wendell Phelps to come forward will deflect some of the glare off you, Elstrom, and help your father, Ms Phelps.'

I walked him out because the set of Amanda's back showed she wouldn't turn around to look at him.

At the door, Krantz looked at his watch. 'I'm thinking twenty-four hours.'

'Until?'

'Until I ask the Chicago police to pick you up for questioning. They can lose records long enough to sweat you for forty-eight hours if I tell them you're withholding information in their murder investigation.'

'That's crap.'

'That's notoriety for your ex-wife, and legal fees you can't afford.' He stepped out into the corridor. 'Play tough with me, Elstrom, and there'll be "details to follow," to quote your favorite columnist.'

I slammed the door as he walked, whistling, to the elevator.

'You left us to call Lake Forest?' I asked, coming back to the kitchen.

'My father raced out of there this morning with a suitcase, just as Krantz said. No one's heard from him since. Delores is frantic.'

'Did he leave by cab?'

'No. He drove himself.' She took coffee cups from a cabinet and was about to pour coffee when suddenly she shook her head. She set down the coffee pot and reached over to the counter for a corked bottle of Shiraz.

'In that tan Buick?'

She spun around. 'Why shouldn't my father give Jim Whitman a ride home? They were friends. They served on boards together.'

'As I said before, giving Whitman a ride home the night he died doesn't mean your father killed him.'

'My father was better friends with Arthur,' she said, her voice quieting.

'I don't like your father buying into Lamm's insurance brokerage.'

'Arthur must have really needed money.' She smacked the bottle hard as she started to fill one of the coffee cups. 'Where's my father?'

'No wine for me,' I said. 'I'm driving.'

She looked up, startled. 'Where?'

'The only place I'm thinking your father would need to take a suitcase.'

'Bent Lake,' she said.

FIFTY-SEVEN

My first run north, by borrowed Porsche, had been a breathtaking mix of German engineering, fast speeds and precise, road-hugging turns. I'd had time, and something of a plan. Now I was clattering to upper Wisconsin in an aged Jeep Wrangler that shook and trembled in perfect accompaniment to the fear and confusion playing tag in my gut.

I'd lied to Amanda. I had no belief that Wendell was innocent of anything. He and Lamm were friends, going way back. Some sense of loyalty, or just as possibly some sense of greed, might well have gotten Wendell to fold himself into whatever Lamm was up to, including buying into the scams Lamm was running from his insurance brokerage.

I could only blunder around blind. I'd ask around town to see if anyone had seen Wendell, or Lamm. I'd confront Wanda, the hostile girlfriend of the dead Canty, or at least see if the sheriff's department had protected her from Lamm.

Only as a last resort would I come up on Lamm's camp to see if he, or Wendell, was there.

Amanda demanded two things before I left her apartment. The first was that I take the two-million-dollar Carson payout along to Bent Lake, for no other reason than Arthur Lamm wanted it and it might be leverage, somehow, in keeping her father safe.

Her second stipulation was simpler: if any danger arose, I was to call Krantz.

I phoned when I got to within an hour of Bent Lake. She answered on the first ring.

'No word from my father,' she said.

I told her I might lose cell phone contact in a few miles, hung up, and went back to hoping Wendell wasn't involved up to his neck in whatever Lamm was doing.

I got to Bent Lake later than the last time. It was now pitch black. The used-to-be service station was closed, its concrete island, shorn of pumps, looking like a casket vault left low and forgotten in the shadows. Of more interest was the phone booth next to the service bays. It had been awhile since I'd seen one, but then again, it had been awhile since I'd been any place where cell phone reception was considered so unpredictable.

Like last time, though, the Dairy Queen across the street was bright with lights and lust, and the same carb-swelled high school lovers were framed, embracing, in the order window beneath the yellow bug lights. Such was their intensity that neither looked up as I drove by.

I passed by the neon Budweiser sign beckoning in the middle of the block and pulled to a stop in the gravel lot of Loons' Rest. As I'd feared, it was dark. But there was a note handwritten on lined tablet paper taped to the inside of the front window. 'Closed for a while,' it read. 'Off for New Adventures.'

I drove back to the gas station, parked in the dark next to the pay phone, and took the aluminum case for a walk to the bar down the block. My footsteps echoed off the deserted store fronts, loud and alone, though I imagined the Bent Lake Children's Club would soon come to fill the evening air with joyous sounds of beating brooms and stomping feet. It felt like a night for death all around.

The same three flannel shirts were perched at the bar, talking with the bartender. All four remembered me. In appreciation, I slapped a five-spot on the bar and bought short beers for the house.

'Come back for more excitement?' the beard behind the bar asked. I wondered whether he knew I'd been shot at during my last visit, or was just being witty. I played it like he was a comedian.

'The excitement's already started,' I said. 'There's a note taped at Loons' saying it's closed.'

'Wanda and Herman took off,' the bartender said.

The faces above the flannel shirts nodded in agreement.

'Who would know where they went?'

'Who would want to?' the bartender asked.

The flannel shirts laughed.

'I don't suppose Arthur Lamm's been by?'

The bartender shook his head.

'How about this guy, drives a tan Buick?' I set an Internet photo of Wendell Phelps on the bar.

The bartender's eyes narrowed. No longer was I some fisherman pal of Lamm's. Now I was a guy asking too many questions.

I laid another five on the bar for a second round, and tapped the photo. 'This is my girlfriend's father. He's a friend of Lamm's, too. I think he came up here looking for him.'

The bartender relaxed, and they all shook their heads. The second five-dollar bill disappeared, and more beer was poured.

I put the photo back in my pocket. 'I'm afraid I know the answer to this, but is there a place I can stay for the night?'

'Yep,' the bartender said. 'Chicago.'

That brought outright guffaws from the gents in the flannel.

'How about the ski lodge?' Red Flannel asked.

'Closed by now, I think,' Green Flannel said.

'No place within thirty miles, mister,' the bartender said. He poured me another beer, set it next to the second I hadn't yet touched. 'On the house. Just kidding about the Chicago part.'

'No offense taken,' I said, and took a sociable sip of one of the beers in front of me. 'You're sure there's nobody watching Loons' for Wanda, someone who might rent me a room?'

'Like I said, she ain't got nobody,' the bartender said, 'exceptin' Herman.'

'Best I get looking for a room elsewhere,' I said, getting off my stool.

'What you got in that metal case, mister?' one of the flannel shirts at the end of the bar asked as I started towards the door.

'Two million in cash,' I said.

It dropped them. They were howling as I walked out.

FIFTY-EIGHT

I went back to the Jeep. Across the street, past the bug bulbs and the greasy plastic of the order window, the young man stared deeply into the girl's eyes as his hand rustled at the pulled-out hem of her DQ blouse. I envied him his youth and his certainty that miracles could be touched so simply.

I drove to the sheriff's office. A different deputy was on duty.

'I'm looking for this man, Wendell Phelps, drives a tan Buick.'
I handed him the Internet photo of Wendell.

'Who might you be?'

'His son-in-law. If you need to verify, you can call his daughter.'

He shook his head. 'What was he doing up here?'

'Looking for Arthur Lamm.'

'Man, that Lamm must be in some big-time trouble. Federal
guys called about him a couple of days ago. Likewise a Chicago
cop, all of them wanting us to look around. I went to his place
myself. Lamm wasn't there.'

'I heard his car is there,' I said, like I didn't know.

'Damn shame, a fine Mercedes taking bird doo, tree sap and
stuck bugs.'

I held up Wendell's picture again. 'Any chance you or the sheriff
could run out to Lamm's place with me tomorrow, take another
look for this guy?'

'Your father-in-law is law enforcement?'

'He's just a friend of Lamm's.'

'He got Alzheimer's?'

'No.'

'Then no can do. There's just me, another deputy, and the sheriff.
We got plenty to keep us busy, busting up bar fights and scraping
drunked-up teenagers off the roads, without looking for Chicago
people who might be up here, visiting friends.'

At the door, I turned back to look at him. 'I was hoping to stay
in Bent Lake, but I heard the woman who runs the motel might
have run off with Lamm's caretaker, some guy named Herman.' I
tried to make it sound easy, like I was just making conversation.

The deputy grinned. 'Don't that beat all? They been rocking
the cot back of Loons' office for damn near ten years. Now, all
of a sudden, they get the urge to see the world? Don't know a
thing about it, mister.'

'You don't suppose they're in trouble?'

'Am I missing something? I thought you were up here looking
for your father-in-law.'

'Where's the nearest place to sleep up here?'

'This is a dead time, too late for snowmobilers, too early for
summer people. Lots of places closed.'

'How about the ski lodge?'

'Oh, they're always closed up by this time of year. Best you call around, if you can get your phone to work.' He was done providing information.

It was dark like it never got in Rivertown, except inside closets. I drove back to Bent Lake along deserted roads, unchallenged by anything except an occasional stop sign and hundreds of pairs of eyes, low to the ground, watching me from the edges of my headlight beams like I was dinner.

Bent Lake had become a veritable festival of beacons since I'd left for the sheriff's office. White lights swarmed along the sidewalk like frenzied giant fireflies. The young broom beaters were out with flashlights, aiming up, then after a little jig, down at the soles of their boots, to admire what they'd turned to goo.

I nosed the Jeep back into the darkness alongside the gas station and found, by jockeying the Jeep around a little, that I could raise enough service bars to use my cell phone. I called Amanda.

'Anything?'

'Nothing.'

'I haven't found anyone who's seen your father, which I'm hoping means he didn't come up here. I'll have a good look around tomorrow.' I gave her the number of the pay phone. 'In case my cell phone gives up from weak reception, I'll hear the pay phone from the Jeep.'

'That's not the number at the motel?' she asked.

'I'm sleeping in the car, next to a pay phone. Wanda is not here.'

'Dead?'

'Not so anyone has noticed. She left a note taped to the window, implying she's run off with Herman.'

'Is that town safe?'

I glanced down the street, at the white lights of flashlights crisscrossing up into the canopies. 'This place is so quiet, the teenagers bring out brooms at night, just for something to do.'

'Just be careful,' she said, too distracted by worry to tell me I must be exaggerating, and hung up.

Romeo and Juliet separated when I materialized into the DQ's yellow light. Juliet came to the order window, hurriedly jamming her wrinkled blouse into her jeans.

I showed her the picture of Wendell Phelps, said he drove a tan

Buick. She shook her head twice. Romeo came to the window and shook his head, too. They were earnest and nice and so focused on each other that they wouldn't have noticed Attila the Hun thundering by with his herd of marauders.

I had two burgers, fries and a chocolate shake at the picnic table, and left weighted sufficiently to withstand even the fiercest of windstorms, should one arise. I climbed in the Jeep and fell asleep more easily than I would have thought, beside the aluminum case that, until recently, had shared its nights with a dead man.

Despite a thunderstorm that rolled in, I slept almost until six the next morning, when my cell phone beeped with a text message: *Still got my picks?*

FIFTY-NINE

For sure, the guy had brass in his pants.

Delray? I typed.

He messaged back instantly: *good name as any*

Who are you?

u took

Turn yourself in.

u only 1

I don't understand, I texted, but of course I did. Either Delray was working with Lamm, or he'd found out about Second Securities on his own, perhaps through Rikk. No matter; he'd known to go to Second Securities, to look for cash. But what he'd found was a splintered door, a trashed Ford, and the realization that, with my extensive insurance company contacts, I'd gotten the address of the Carson beneficiary, and beaten him to the money. I shivered, realizing we must have missed each other by only a few hours.

u bring, he wrote.

Bring what? I texted, still playing dumb.

we trade

For what? I wrote, like I didn't know.

wp

And there it was. Likely enough, Wendell had driven right into his own abduction.

I'll have to call Wendell, I texted.

noon bl will tell u where then

I don't understand, I wrote again.

wp not where u think

I need more time.

He didn't respond. He had gone.

I called Amanda.

'Delray's in it with Lamm. They've got your father.'

She inhaled sharply. 'How do you know?'

'Delray just texted me. They want to trade your father for the payout, up here at noon.'

She paused, thinking. 'We should call Krantz?'

'They've anticipated that. Delray wrote that your father's not where I think he is, meaning not at Lamm's camp. Since there's two of them, they can operate from two locations.'

'What do we do?'

'We've got a big advantage. They don't know I'm already up here. That buys us six hours, time enough for me to sneak out to Lamm's camp, to see who's around before I call the sheriff.'

For a minute, only the rain made a sound. 'You're sure this is the best way?'

'If I knew that, I wouldn't have spent the night sleeping in a leaking Jeep in the rain.'

SIXTY

A faded brown Chevy Malibu pulled into the DQ and parked next to the overhang above the restrooms. I needed that overhang, too, and I needed hot coffee. I drove across the street, wondering what the hell I was doing, considering a new kind of insurance.

A fiftyish woman with stringy blonde hair dangling limp from her scalp and an unfiltered cigarette dangling just as limp from her mouth got out of the Malibu and ran for the door as I pulled up, covering her mouth so the rain wouldn't extinguish her smoke. I backed up as close as I could to the overhang.

I got out when the inside lights came on and jumped over the growing puddles to the order window and tapped on the plastic. She nodded and slid open the window, offering up the smell of old grease and new cigarette smoke. I ordered coffee and eggs on muffins. I wasn't hungry, but I needed to get her away from the window long enough to work at the back of the Jeep. She told me in a hoarse voice that the griddle wasn't warm yet. I said I could wait, and went around to the side, first to the Jeep, then, after five minutes, to the men's room. It was puddled too, though I did not linger to determine whether that had resulted from the rain. Fresh from a cold water rinse of my face – there was no soap – I went back to the order window. My coffee was sitting outside on the counter, cooling in the downpour. I took the cup to the picnic table under the side eave, sat, and watched the red clay beside the cement slab dissolve and run toward the road.

'Up here fishing?' the woman rasped through the screen.

I went to press as close as I could to the window, out of the rain. 'I came up here looking for a guy who came up here looking for a guy.'

'Huh?'

I showed her Wendell's picture. 'Have you seen this man?'

'He was here,' she said, lighting a fresh unfiltered Camel. It was the same brand Debbie Goring used to hoarsen her own voice.

'You saw him?'

'Yesterday. I worked a long shift.'

'He drove a tan car?'

She nodded. 'Parked right where you did, ordered coffee.'

'At night?'

'Huh?'

'He came in at night?'

She exhaled smoke. 'I don't work nights. Teenagers work that shift because they like to screw when things are slow.'

'Afternoon, then?' That would have fit, time-wise. Krantz had said Wendell packed a bag at eight in the morning.

The Camel hung limp from the edge of her mouth, confused.

'The man came in the afternoon?' I repeated.

'About three o'clock. Not that I mind a little screwing.' The

Camel was rising between her lips. Her eyebrows had risen, too. Her hair, though, stayed limp.

'This man, did he say where he was headed?'

'I don't expect much,' she added, after giving me a head-to-toe look.

I had to look away. 'Anything you remember will help,' I said to the clapboards next to the order window.

She pointed down Main Street in the direction of the road to Arthur Lamm's fishing camp. 'He gave me a five-dollar bill, told me to keep the change, and shot out of here like his britches were on fire.'

I nodded. It was not hard to fathom.

She went to pull my two egg muffins off the grill. She wrapped them in paper, slid them through the little window. I gave her a five-dollar bill, and told her to keep the change because I was no slouch either.

She said I owed another buck seventy-five.

SIXTY-ONE

The rain came down in sheets of gray glass beads, dissolving my headlight beams into mist and blurring the trees alongside the road into seamless dark curtains. Every few seconds, great jagged spears of lightning gave me enough of a snapshot of the narrow gravel road ahead to speed forward another hundred yards before everything went dark again, and I had to drop back to my snail's safe crawl.

So it went, for an hour, until a fresh flash of lighting lit the tall, narrow Tinker Toy shape coming out of the gray. The rickety bridge was twenty feet ahead. I downshifted to first gear, unzipped the driver's curtain so I could see to orient myself with the left side rail, and eased onto the old wood. Lightning flashed again, bringing a huge stutter clap of thunder that shook the ancient span like loose sticks. The rail next to me swayed in the sudden light. It was barely a dozen feet above white caps frothing in roiling water. The river was rising.

Ice needles blew in through the open curtain, stinging my face as I watched the rail to my left. It was the only way I knew to drive straight. But drift too close and I could catch a front tire, knock the left side loose and plunge over the side. Drift too far the other away, I might hit the right rail, and drop off that side.

Lightning flashed; I was halfway over. I squeezed the steering wheel tight and, holding my breath, punched the car forward. After what seemed like an hour, my tires crunched gravel. I'd made it across.

Still, I dared speed up only when lightning cracked to give me a view. Finally, at what seemed like the twentieth flash of lightning, or perhaps the hundredth, the fire lane appeared for an instant. I stopped, downshifted into the ultra-low gear that off-road Jeep crazies use to assault steep hills, and waited. At the next flash of lightning I gunned the Jeep down into the slush of a gulley and up through the gap in the trees, and cut the engine as the woods darkened again into invisibility. I could only hope I'd pulled far enough in to conceal the Jeep from the road.

I found my black knit hat under the passenger's seat, but left behind the yellow poncho. Yellow would light me up like neon every time lightning flared. Telling myself that courage can only be strengthened by adversity, I stepped out into the rain.

There was a thick tree fifteen paces directly perpendicular to the Jeep's right front wheel. The soft loamy compost at its base went deep enough to easily bury the aluminum case. I pulled back the loam, dropped the case, and covered it with wet leaves. By now my khakis and shirt were soaked clear through with freshly strengthened courage.

Though the rain was beating harder, louder, the woods felt suspended beneath the din, as if every living thing within it – every bird, every squirrel, every insect – was holding its breath in fear of what was about to happen.

I ran to Lamm's camp. My footfalls barely sounded above the rain invading the trees, but to my ears now every twig snapped like a gunshot, every breath called out as loud as a shout.

The Mercedes rested in its same place, still filthy with its fuzzy carpet of sap, pine needles and a thousand pats of green-white bird guano. But here and there the hard rain was loosening the crusted blanket into spots of bubbling paste that had begun to run down the sides of the car in dirty little rivulets, like the car had become something evil, molting, shedding its skin.

There were no other cars there, no tan Buick. The clearing and the back of the cottage appeared deserted, yet something flashed bright in the gloom, down by the water. Staying inside the trees, I moved to the shore. An orange rowboat with an outboard motor attached to its stern bobbed high, despite the rain, at the end of Lamm's dock. I edged closer to see into the water. The barely floating boat I'd bent to look at last time, the instant before I'd been shot at, had gone. Canty had said it had been a second boat. I hadn't believed it then; I didn't believe it now. There'd been no other boat. Someone had bailed out the one I'd seen earlier, attached an outboard motor, and used it to go off somewhere.

'We're gonna be rich!' a man screamed in a strange, singsong voice from inside the cabin.

I crouched, and moved back deeper into the woods. I knew the voice. It was Delray Delmar, no doubt yelling at Wendell.

I pulled out my cell phone to dial 911. There were no bars. No service.

I backed farther into the woods. Still no bars.

I did the minutes in my head. Fifteen to run back to the Jeep, maybe forty-five minutes to make it through the storm either to the sheriff's department or to the pay phone in Bent Lake. No matter which way I chose, the sheriff might not get there for two hours.

Still, the cops would arrive well before noon, when Delray told me I had to be up in Bent Lake.

'Son of a bitch!' Delray screamed.

I turned to run back into the woods, to the Jeep.

A bolt of lightning lit the dark sky, and a second later, thunder shook the ground.

A gunshot fired.

I turned around, charged the back door, twisted the knob and shouldered it open.

And got clubbed on the back of the neck with a million-pound bat.

SIXTY-TWO

I came to on my belly, trussed like a hog. My wrists were tied together behind my back with rope that was then crisscrossed down to tug up my ankles before it was knotted behind my knees. A blanket was thrown over my head. I could barely breathe through the suffocating wool. I couldn't see a thing.

'Dek Elstrom to the rescue.' The unnaturally high voice giggled faintly.

'You're a shit, Delray,' I said to the floor.

'You've brought treasure?' His voice was skittish, insanely wrong.

'Wendell Phelps.'

'The money, honey,' Delray sang.

'Wendell,' I called into the floor.

In an instant, a steel rod, likely the barrel of a gun, was jammed through the wool into the center of my neck. It surprised me. I thought Delray was across the room.

I didn't resist, concentrating instead on keeping my body loose. There was play – an inch, maybe two – in the rope. Tugging would only tighten the loops around my wrists and ankles.

He pressed down on the big knot. Pain like I'd never known shot through my shoulders and legs as they were drawn closer together. I shut my eyes, and tried to focus on sucking more air through the wool.

'The money!' Delray screamed, so seemingly distant. Strangely, he'd said nothing about me arriving hours early.

'Wendell!' I shouted. 'Tell me where he is, and I'll tell you where I've got the money.'

He pressed harder on the knot, ripping new pain into my shoulders, knees and legs. But there had been a lag for just a fraction of a second. For sure there was play in the rope.

'The money,' he called out in that faraway voice.

'Wen—'

A gun fired just above my ear, shattering glass somewhere and filling my head with thunder.

I yelled fast, for surely Delray had gone insane. 'Follow the road to town, go into the fire lane. My Jeep's there. I buried the case at the base of a tree, fifteen paces perpendicular to the right front wheel.'

'See?' Delray shouted from far away. 'All is good!'

Footsteps, loud in heavy boots, thudded across the plank floor. The door creaked open.

The gun fired twice, something thudded, and the door slammed shut.

The thud, I was sure, was the sound of a body falling. Wendell.

'Damn you to hell, Delray; damn you to hell,' I managed, in little more than a whisper, beneath the wool. 'Damn you too, Wendell; damn you as well.'

I had to get away. Delray would come back to kill. Ten, fifteen minutes was all he'd need to get to the Jeep, walk off the paces, paw through the leaves and find the metal case. He'd check it and he'd come back, wild-eyed and furious, eager to torture. He'd want everything, and then he'd want me dead.

'Delray!' I shouted, to be sure.

No answer. He was gone. I was alone, but only for a few minutes more.

I tried to roll up onto my side, to shake away the suffocating blanket. Pain tore at my shoulders as the weight of my legs tried to tug them from their sockets. I teetered up for only an instant before I fell back on my belly, still covered by the blanket, and now even more desperate for air. I counted one, counted two, and lunged again. This time, I made it up on my side and held. The blanket fell away.

He was slumped against the front door. Laying on the floor, all I could see were his pants, his shoes. And the fresh blood puddling back toward the center of the room.

I took in a breath, and another. Another precious minute had gone, maybe two. Delray was pacing off the steps to the tree by now.

I flexed my shoulders back. Daggers shot deep into my back and arms, but the rope slipped an inch. I flexed again and my legs dropped another inch. I raised them back up, as tight to my back as the pain would let me. It was enough. The rope slacked enough to get my thumbs inside the loop around my wrists.

My mind flitted to the dark fury that would be contorting

Delray's face when he returned. I bit at my lip, pushed the image away, and kept working my thumbs. They were numb, unfeeling stubs, but somehow the cord around my left wrist loosened even more, and then my left hand slipped free. I pulled the cord from my right wrist, and then from my legs. I almost wept.

I rolled onto my knees and started to stand. Too soon. I fell back. I crawled across the room.

The body had two gunshots: one to the head, one to the heart, leaking red on the floor.

Not Wendell.

Delray Delmar looked back at me through dead eyes.

SIXTY-THREE

There was no time to make sense of it, only to get away. Surely Lamm – for it had to be Lamm; Wendell wouldn't hunt me – was coming back with hellfire in his eyes. By now he knew what I'd done.

I staggered out the front door on trembling legs, braced for the sudden bark of a gun, the cold fire of a bullet tearing into my skin. Incredibly, nothing sounded in the now softly falling rain. I still had a minute, maybe more. I looked back. The Mercedes was still parked there; he'd gone through the woods. I hobbled down to the water and into the trees, for it would be the fastest way back to the Jeep. I could only hope to spot him and drop down before he saw me; he had the gun.

I stumbled into a jog along the shore. When Lamm returned to the cabin and saw I'd escaped, he'd race back to the Jeep. He'd run better than me, quicker. I had to get to the fire lane first.

Sooner than I dared hope, the red of the Jeep appeared faintly through the gray of the rain. I dropped to the sodden ground and crawled the last few yards to see.

To my left, the fire lane stretched clear back to County M. It was lined thick enough with trees to hide anyone waiting to squeeze a few shots into the Jeep. But Lamm couldn't be there. He'd be racing back to the cabin.

I moved forward a few yards, enough to see that the leaves had been clawed from the base of the tree. Lamm had found the aluminum case. He would have opened it, to be certain.

He would have seen.

I ran for the Jeep, holding the ignition key in front of me like a sword. Jumping in behind the wheel, I fired the engine and ground the gears, shifting loudly into reverse. The Jeep slammed back into a tree, killing the engine.

I spun around to look. The spare tire was pressed too hard against the tree. I jumped out; I had to know. The spare was still solid on its bracket. Back in, I restarted the engine, and shot up the fire lane and onto the gravel of County M. My tires grabbed at the stones, spraying them back into the wheel wells, rat-a-tat, like machine-gun fire that must have been loud a mile away.

Though the rain had slackened, County M was even more blurred now with fog, and Lamm was somewhere close by, in the murk of it, enraged, with a gun. There was no time for caution. I sped into the gray, foot hard on the gas, arms rigid, not daring to use my headlamps for fear of giving him lights to shoot at, wherever he was.

I'd gone only a few hundred yards when headlamps rose up faint out of the mist at the side of the road ahead, like some dim-eyed primordial beast trying to claw itself free from a steaming swamp. I slowed as the car in front teetered up at an angle, its fang-like grill aimed at the sky, shaking and rumbling before its front end dropped, its wheels caught, and it lurched forward, kicking back dark spray like it was venting its own entrails. It fish-tailed for an instant, straightened and took off down the road.

It was a tan car with dark, tinted windows. A Buick.

Lamm, in Wendell's car. Or Wendell himself.

I pressed down on the accelerator and switched on my head-lights. He was going to damned well see my face.

Red brake lights flashed for an instant; he'd spotted my headlamps.

He sped up, surging and sliding on the gravel, fighting to keep the car straight, speeding forward. I pressed down harder on my own accelerator. Jeeps aren't worth much on highways. They vibrate like blenders, chuck and skitter at the smallest bumps and potholes. But shifted into four-wheel drive, on the loose marbles of County M, the Jeep charged straight forward like it was on rails.

The distance between us closed; three hundred feet, two hundred feet, then a hundred. From somewhere close by, I heard a man yelling. Only in the next second did I realize it was me.

Fifty feet separated us when the Buick's window powered down. A pistol came out, wavered, then steadied, pointing backward at me. It might have fired, I couldn't tell. We were speeding through gray mist, and I was deaf to everything except the gravel blasting up beneath the Jeep and the rain beating on my hood and vinyl top.

His tapped his brakes, slowing for a steadier shot. I dropped back a few yards and tucked in directly behind him. The gun recoiled once, and again. No starbursts appeared on my windshield; no glass exploded. I was in his blind spot. He sped up. We raced on.

County M dipped us into low-lying thick fog for an instant, and then the road rose up. And when it did, the black, spindly one-lane wooden bridge filled the soft rain in his headlights. His gun wavered, firing back at me. He wasn't looking ahead.

His brake lights flashed. He'd turned and seen the frail timbers rushing towards him, but it was too late. He hit the right edge of the bridge at thirty miles an hour. The Buick reared up like a frightened horse, then slammed down hard on the loose planks and inched forward, its still-spinning front wheels tugging him tighter against the right side rail.

Some faint part of my brain shouted to slam on my own brakes: I was charging a one-lane bridge that was already filled with a car. There was no room.

But I, too, had gone insane, at least a little. I needed vengeance. I had to see the eyes of the man who'd trussed me like a pig, the man who'd just tried to shoot me. And he had to see mine.

I aimed for the narrowing space between Wendell's Buick and the rickety rail to my left. He had to go over the right side, to crash on the boulders below.

I hit him on his left rear fender, sending up a thousand sparks as the Jeep tore into the Buick. I tugged the steering wheel all the way to the right and pressed harder on the accelerator, grinding the Jeep further up into his car. The sagging side rail only a foot to my left was too frail to prevent my own plunge to a wet death on the boulders below.

It was no matter. I fed the Jeep's engine more gas; he had to die. But my wheels wouldn't move. The Jeep and the Buick were pinned between the uprights at the entrance to the bridge, trapped together like they were welded.

The Buick groaned as it shifted forward. His right front wheel dropped off the right side of the bridge. He turned to look back over his shoulder at me, wide-eyed and frantic.

It was Herman Canty, and he was seeing the Devil and his own death reflecting off my eyes.

He pulled at his shift lever, struggling to raise it into reverse. Lurching backward would be his only escape.

The whine of my engine was deafening, the stench of my spinning tires acrid in the rain. The Buick slid forward another foot. He let go of his steering wheel, turned for something on the seat.

The gun.

I tugged harder at my steering wheel. Only another foot or two would send him off the bridge, but the Jeep's wheels were spinning uselessly. I shifted into ultra-low, the mountain-climbing gear, and let out the clutch. The Jeep shuddered for an instant, and then began grinding slowly forward, one inch, then two, pushing the Buick farther off the edge.

Wood snapped, not loud, but almost gently, and the right side rail beyond his windshield fell away.

Canty didn't see. His hand had come out with the gun. I ducked down below the plastic passenger curtain, keeping my right foot on the gas pedal, my left above the brake, tugging the steering wheel hard to the right to keep grinding into the Buick. A shot ripped through the plastic curtain, another sparked off the roll bar above my head.

And then the Jeep lurched forward several sickening feet. I slammed on the brake and pulled myself up, terrified I was about to plunge over the right side.

The nose of the Buick had slipped all the way off the bridge and was angling slightly downward toward the rocks in the river below. The frail wood uprights to either side of the teetering car were snapping away almost lazily, one after the other, as the Buick was slowly being tugged off the bridge by its own gathering momentum.

Canty had dropped his gun and was scrambling to push himself out of the driver's side window. His eyes locked on mine, pleading, begging.

A great new scream of ripping wood filled the air and the entire right side of the bridge fell away. The Buick's nose went down after it, the car's trunk rising now like the stern of the *Titanic*, gently, almost beautifully. The Buick creaked, and settled backward, its left rear tire catching between my bumper and my hood, stopping its slide over the edge.

Canty was now halfway out of the open side window, not four feet from my face, kicking at the steering wheel to propel him the rest of the way out before the car fell into the river.

His frenzy shifted the balance of the Buick, and it again began moving slowly over the edge. The Jeep began sliding with it, hooked by the Buick's rear wheel.

I jabbed hard at the brake, but it was no use. The Jeep was going over the edge, too.

I fumbled open the driver's door and pushed myself backward out of the Jeep. Fire shot up my left arm as first my shoulders, and then my back hit the planks. I dug my heels into the wood and scrabbled backward, kicking back from the carnage.

Herman Canty was still only halfway out when the car's trunk rose up to the sky. Gravity had trapped him, pulling him back into the car.

The Buick's front door disappeared over the side as its rear wheel, rising higher, gave a last tug at the Jeep's bumper and then broke free. The Buick's rear bumper vanished over the side of the bridge.

Canty screamed until the car crashed onto the rocks.

I lay on my back, frozen in the new, sudden stillness, afraid to move. The rain beat down on me as the river frothed high beneath the planks. At some point I reached to touch my left arm and found sticky wetness. I'd been shot. I'd not ducked down far enough. I laughed.

After a time I stood up and walked along the center of the bridge, careful to look only forward until I got safely to the solid ground on the other side. Even then, I walked another ten feet before I dared to turn around to look at the river below.

The Buick lay upside down, pinned between two boulders in the churning, swollen water. Its roof had been crushed by the fall.

I am told that I pulled off my belt and cinched it around my left arm above where the blood was the stickiest. I don't remember. Nor do I remember the man in the flatbed truck who slowed behind me as I wobbled down the middle of County M, by then a mile from the bridge. He saw the blood on my shirt and the vacancy in my eyes, and raced me to an emergency medical clinic in a town I'd never heard of.

SIXTY-FOUR

While I was being stitched up, an enterprising nurse thought to try the last numbers in the call memory of my phone. She got both Leo and Amanda. They drove up together and arrived at the clinic about the time the sedatives began to lift.

Amanda sat beside my bed and took my good hand. Leo sat in the corner, a blur of tropical colors.

'I don't know about your father,' I said to her – but I did, or at least I was afraid I did.

She didn't ask whether I was talking about Wendell's whereabouts or his complicity in Arthur Lamm's crimes. She merely sat for a moment, silently squeezing my hand like she was afraid of letting go. I told her to go find a sheriff's deputy, to see if they'd learned anything. I wanted to talk to Leo, because I was running out of time.

Agent Krantz materialized in the doorway before I could say a word. He must have been lurking in a side corridor, waiting for Amanda to step out.

'You got here fast,' I said.

'It is standard procedure to notify the sheriff about a gunshot wound. This particular sheriff remembered you'd stopped by, asking about Lamm and, more interestingly, your father-in-law.'

'Ex-father-in-law,' I corrected.

'The sheriff also remembered our own inquiry about Arthur Lamm's whereabouts, so he called me. I've filled him in with some particulars, but I've left my concerns about you vague. For the time being, he's agreed to let me be your only law enforcement contact.'

'Feds trump locals,' I offered.

'Every time.'

Leo got up from his chair and came to stand by the bed.

Krantz made a show of looking closely at Leo's clothes. Leo was wearing an outrageous medley, a shirt of pink parrots and lavender orchids on a yellow and black background, lime green trousers, and brown-and-white wingtip shoes with orange soles. 'You are?'

'Mr Elstrom's advisor,' Leo said.

'Advisor for what?'

'Haberdashery.' He fingered the hem of his shirt, having noticed Krantz's scrutiny of his duds, and then said, 'Along with everything else.'

'Does this seem eerily familiar?' I asked Leo.

Leo smiled, whitening the entire room with teeth. He, too, was remembering Sweetie Rose. 'Same state, different cop.' He turned to Krantz. 'We've done this before,' he said, signaling we had previous practice and were real sharpies at admitting nothing to law enforcement officers.

Krantz frowned and turned to me. 'He's quite odd,' he said as Leo went back to sit in the corner.

I shrugged as best I could using only my right arm, the left having been shot. 'I need him to speak for me because I've been sedated and can't be responsible for anything I say.'

'You're worried about vehicular manslaughter?'

'Nah.'

Krantz sat down in the chair Amanda had vacated. 'We have no body.'

I started to sit up, but the torn ligaments in my legs, and my shot left arm, tugged me back like I was on a leash. 'What the hell, Krantz?'

'We found a handgun and an aluminum case full of money, but no sign of Canty.'

'He was stuck half out of the driver's window when the car went over.'

'We don't yet know if it was Canty, Lamm or Phelps who was driving that Buick.'

'Why would I lie?'

'To protect Phelps.'

'Let's not talk until you find Canty's body.'

'Relax,' he said. 'I believe you. That river is running fast from the storm, and it might take a while to find him downriver, or in one of the lakes that feeds off it. But when they do, they'll compare his fingerprints to those on the gun they recovered. The bullet they took out of your arm also looks to match one found in a dead young man in Arthur Lamm's cabin, and together they will tie to the gun. You're in the clear, Elstrom, so tell me everything.'

'I went to Lamm's camp, looking for Wendell, and got clubbed going in the door,' I said. 'I woke up to hear someone firing a shot, but I was trussed and covered by a blanket. I couldn't see anything.'

'Why were you left alive, Elstrom? Why didn't Canty shoot you, too?'

I'd expected he'd ask that one. I couldn't admit it was because Canty needed to be certain I'd brought up the Carson cash, so I said, 'Charm,' because it was all I could think to say.

Only Leo laughed, from the corner.

Krantz pulled out his smart phone, selected a picture. 'This is the young man we found in Lamm's cabin.'

It looked like an Illinois driver's license photo. 'Delray Delmar,' I said.

'Richie Bales,' Krantz said. 'A small-time repo man out of Chicago Heights. He did collections and auto repossessions. Ring any other bells?'

It rang a big bell. 'He must have been the "R.B." on the calendar I gave you.'

'Phelps hired Small, and Small hired Bales,' he said. 'For what?'

'As I've told you, Wendell never told me who he hired, but I do believe it was for surveillance. Wendell's friends were dying. His goals were noble; he wanted to stop it.'

'Wendell Phelps killed Small, for what he found out.'

'There you go again, fencing with me about Wendell. Someone else killed Small, for what he found out.'

'Who?'

'Either Arthur Lamm, because Small discovered his scheme, or Canty, on Lamm's orders, or Richie Bales, to get Small out of the way so he could extort big money out of Lamm.'

Krantz reached for the little bronze-colored Thermos on my bed tray and poured coffee into the matching bronze cup.

'No coffee, thanks,' I said.

Krantz smirked and took a sip. 'Arthur Lamm's brokerage wrote insurance policies on the lives of Benno Barberi, Jim Whitman and Grant Carson, each in the amount of two million dollars. Remember who owns half of Lamm Enterprises?'

'You told me in Amanda Phelps's kitchen.'

'Your father-in-law, Wendell Phelps,' he said anyway.

'Ex-father-in-law,' I corrected anyway, adding, 'Wendell's the good guy in this, Krantz. I think he bought half of Lamm's brokerage to help out an old friend who had problems.'

'Money problems?'

'IRS problems.'

Undeterred, Krantz went on 'Each of those life insurance policies was from a different company, but they all named something called Second Securities as beneficiary. It's not listed as a business anywhere, but I'm thinking you've heard of it.'

Once Krantz got a whiff inside Second Securities, he'd open up the small Ford, see he had another murder on his hands, and come at me like a locomotive if he suspected I'd been there and hadn't admitted it. And come at Wendell, because of his half-share in Lamm's insurance agency, if Wendell was still alive. I needed to talk to Leo.

'I've heard of it, yes,' I said, feeding out some truth in case Krantz's agents had already questioned the glittered receptionist.

'Phelps told you about Second Securities?' he said, watching my face, still testing.

'I got the name from an insurance company contact.'

'Did you get an address?'

'I'll check my file.'

'Cut the crap, Elstrom. Second Securities is on Milwaukee Avenue in Chicago. They wired the Barberi and Whitman payouts to a bank on Grand Cayman. That money is gone. But the Carson check was converted to cash at an outfit laundry in Chicago.'

'An *outfit laundry*?' I asked, as though I'd never heard the term for a mob-controlled bank that converts checks into cash for people with connections.

'We're thinking that since Lamm's been hiding out, it was likely his partner Phelps who ran the check through the laundry.'

'You're trying to pin things on the wrong guy, Krantz.'

'If Phelps is so innocent, then where is he?'

'Maybe dead,' I said, thinking of the car at Second Securities. I really needed to talk to Leo.

A faint, smug smile had formed on his face. He might have had more against Wendell; he might have been bluffing. I wanted to smash that smugness with a hammer, but all I had were words.

'You put a brick on Lamm's passport?' I asked.

His smile broadened from smug to obnoxious. 'Some trouble with Homeland Security.'

'Bricking Lamm's passport was your way of preventing Lamm from going to Grand Cayman to get at the Barberi and Whitman payouts?'

'Four million, total. Damned shame,' he said.

'When did you put the brick on his passport?'

'First of this year.' He wanted to crow.

'Wait until Keller reports that you singlehandedly got Carson killed six weeks later. You made Lamm hang around to kill again – Carson this time – for new getaway cash. If you hadn't bricked Lamm's passport, he would have been long gone to Grand Cayman, and Grant Carson would still be alive.' I smiled. 'Details will be following.'

The maddening smile flickered, but not his self-righteous calm. His hand was steady as he poured himself more coffee. 'About that Carson cash . . . that money I said we found in Phelps's Buick?'

'A million.'

Leo shifted abruptly in his chair, Krantz's smile widened, and I knew, in an instant, that I'd slipped.

Krantz pounced. 'I never said how much was in that case.'

'I've been sedated,' I offered, too feebly and too late.

'I just told you the Carson payout was for two million, Elstrom. We found only half of that in the Buick. We're thinking that was Lamm's share, fifty per cent, which Canty got by killing Lamm. Question is: who's got the other million? Answer: Wendell Phelps.'

'Wendell doesn't need a new million. He's got hundreds of them already.'

'It was Phelps's car you pushed in the river.'

'That day you called Wendell, to set up an interview?' I asked.

'He blew me off.'

'How hard did you lean on him? Did you threaten him, tell him he would do time for Lamm's crimes?'

'I might have.' Still the bastard smirked.

'You set Phelps off like a live grenade, Krantz. He didn't simply skip his appointment with you. Most likely, he charged right up here to confront Lamm, a man who'd been his friend for years, for setting him up. Knowing Wendell just a little, he probably planned on throwing Lamm in his trunk and driving him back to Chicago to deliver to you.'

'Nice try, Elstrom. Phelps didn't leave until two days after we set up our appointment. Phelps came up here to collect his half of the Carson payout.'

'Then Richie Bales enticed Wendell to drive up to help his old friend. Remember, there was nothing on the news that Richie, the infamous Delray Delmar, was impersonating a Chicago police officer when Wendell took off from home. So far as Wendell knew, Delray Delmar was a real cop.'

'You're trying awfully hard to come up with excuses for your father-in-law.'

'Find Lamm. And find Wendell, if you can find him still alive.' I looked away.

'We're getting warrants to search Second Securities,' he said, to the back of my head.

'Enlightenment looms,' I managed, through teeth that surprisingly had not started chattering.

Amanda came into the room.

Krantz, the gentleman, stood up. 'Ms Phelps,' he said.

'Secret Agent,' she said.

Krantz turned to me. 'I'm going to think about what you've told me,' he said. 'Very carefully. I'll be back tomorrow.'

He nodded at Leo and Amanda and started to leave. But he stopped at the door. 'Any news about your father, Ms Phelps?' he asked.

She frowned. He left.

'There's a ski resort two miles outside of Bent Lake,' Amanda said. 'Plenty of rooms.'

'I heard it was closed,' I said.

'They were thinking about closing for the season, but changed their minds when I said we'd need lodging.'

Leo's eyebrows rose.

'Dek won't be staying there at all,' she said, mock-frowning at Leo, ever the romantic. She turned to me. 'Leo and I will stay there tonight. The doctor said you can leave tomorrow. Leo will drive you home and I'll stay on up here, until something is learned about my father.'

'I'm getting out of here now,' I said.

'You can't,' Amanda said.

'You're nuts,' Leo said.

'I'm ready,' I said, because now I had no choice.

SIXTY-FIVE

It was night, just past nine o'clock, before I got out of the clinic and then only with dire warnings of my likely demise from infection.

'I expected Amanda would be hauling you back to Rivertown horizontally, like truck-smacked venison,' Leo said, explaining the long Cadillac Escalade he'd rented for the drive up. Amanda had parked it behind the Jeep at the front of the clinic.

'I don't know if I trust you driving my Jeep back to Chicago,' I said.

'It's a wonder it still runs,' he said. 'Or why.'

I maneuvered myself up onto the Cadillac's passenger seat and handed him my crutches to toss in back. My wounds weren't much – a gunshot that missed bone in my left arm and ligaments torn in both legs from straining to throttle the Jeep into the Buick while trying to lie beneath Canty's gunfire. But working the Jeep's clutch and shifter was out of the question for a couple of weeks.

'You noted the extent of the Jeep's damage?' Leo asked, trying for light as I closed my eyes, waiting for the pain to go away. 'To restore it to its previous, uh, condition, you'll have to find a used fender in cracked, faded black plastic; a used front bumper, also faded black, but in rusted metal. You'll need a radiator cover and a hood in the same tarty red, if you can find one mottled with enough of the aforementioned rust to match the rest of your heap. The whole repair shouldn't set you back more than two hundred bucks.'

Amanda would be coming out at any moment. 'You forgot to take off the spare tire,' I said.

'Ah, yes, the spare.' He left me to hustle forward in the Escalade's headlamp beams.

Amanda came out of the clinic holding a big white envelope with my medical instructions and pills. She went up to Leo, who'd taken out a lug wrench and was removing the Jeep's spare tire. He shook his head and jerked a thumb back at me. She shrugged, gave him a hug, and came to slide in behind the wheel of the Cadillac.

'He won't tell me what he's doing,' she said.

'Putting my spare tire into the back of this thing for the night,' I said.

He came back and tossed the Jeep's spare in the back of the Escalade.

'Why?' she asked.

'The tire is out of air.'

'Is that supposed to make sense?' she asked.

'Must be the meds,' I said, patting my pockets like I was missing something. 'I think I left my phone in my room.'

'I'm not sure they should have released you,' she said, managing a laugh. She went back inside.

Leo shut the rear door and came around to the passenger side.

'You're clear on what to do when we get to the ski lodge?' I asked.

'Let me do it alone. It'll save me another round trip up here.'

'The less you know . . .'

'You're being irrational. It's Lamm in the trunk of that car at Second Securities.'

'Who knows what Canty and Delray were thinking? I have to be sure it's not Wendell, and if it is, I want him moved, away from such a link to Lamm.'

He gave it up. 'That nurse that called Amanda and me?'

'Yes?'

'She also called Jenny's cell number. Jenny called me from

California, and made noises about flying in. I said you'd had a slight accident, nothing serious.'

'I'll call her when I'm done.'

'If we haven't been arrested.'

I held up my phone as Amanda came outside. 'Had it after all,' I lied, by way of explanation.

'Meds,' she said, accepting, and we drove away.

Fifteen minutes later, she pulled to a stop under a stone-pillared canopy. The resort was old, made of logs darkened by tens of decades of winters and moss-covered, rough-hewn roof shingles. She told me it had gently sloping halls, a restaurant with wide booths, and firm leather couches that were easy to get out of. They were used to people on crutches.

'I can bird dog the sheriff by myself,' she said, for the fifth time.

And I agreed, for the fifth time, telling her I knew she was perfectly capable of harassing the sheriff until he found her father. Her worst fear, and my second-worst fear, was that Wendell was lying dead somewhere in the surrounds of Bent Lake.

They walked, and I hobbled, to the registration desk. The lobby was deserted.

'You said three rooms for tonight, then two for the next week?' the desk clerk asked.

From old habit, Amanda hesitated. So did I. So did Leo.

'That's correct: three for tonight, then two,' she said.

'As I told you on the phone, I can only do coffee, cold cereal and milk in the morning,' the desk clerk said. 'Our handyman goes home at three. After that, I'm the only one here until the next morning.' She smiled at me. 'You'll have the run of the place,' she said to me, offering a joke about my crutches.

Amanda said we'd manage. She and Leo were given rooms down the long hall, in the new wing. The desk clerk gave me a room just four doors past the lobby, saying it had been fitted with thick grab handles and wider doors should a wheelchair become necessary, of which she had two, right on the premises.

The desk clerk handed us old-fashioned, square steel keys. I walked, of a fashion, the few steps to my room. Leo went ahead, as if to go into his room.

'You'll sleep?' Amanda asked.

'I've been well medicated,' I said, offering a yawn as proof. I unlocked my door and went in.

I waited a minute, then stuck my head out. The hall was empty. The door to the back parking lot was only a few feet away.

Leo had pulled the Jeep around to the back. He pushed open the passenger door; I put in my crutches and got in.

'*Que?*' he asked in Spanish. It is a language he does not know.

'*Pronto*,' I responded in kind, sounding every bit as fluent as him.

SIXTY-SIX

'I'm here merely to shift your gears; I get that,' he said after we'd driven a dozen miles in silence. 'You're sure you'll be able to drive the little Ford?'

'It's got an automatic transmission. No shifting.'

I repeated what I'd outlined quickly in front of the clinic while we waited for Amanda. 'Total turnaround time will be less than twelve hours, most of it in darkness.'

'Except the last few, when I cart you back to the ski resort in broad daylight.'

'We alibi each other. We went out to hunt up doughnuts.'

'What about cell tower pings? I saw on TV that cell phones can place people at a site of perpetration.'

'*Perpetration?*' I asked. 'That's a stretch of a word, even for you.'

'Don't obfuscate. You didn't think of that little detail, did you?'

'I've only got tonight to perpetrate.' I told him where I wanted to be picked up so we wouldn't have to use our phones and risk being identified as perpetrators. Still, he handed his over and I removed the batteries from both our phones.

He reached to rattle the key in the Jeep's ashtray. 'This time, remember to leave the key on the floor,' he said.

I took it out and put it in my pocket. 'I hope I'll feel it was a good thing I didn't, the last time,' I said.

'How did Canty get in after you'd been there?'

'Or Delray?'

'Or Delray,' he agreed.

'They must have used Lamm's key,' I think I mumbled, before I fell asleep.

Five hours later, Leo tapped my neck. Thanks to the lingering meds, I'd slept all the way down to Chicago. He'd stopped around the corner from Second Securities. I grabbed the yellow gloves from the back, planted my crutches on the asphalt, and slid out of the Jeep.

'Wondering about surveillance cameras?' he asked.

'I have to risk them,' I said, pulling my knit hat low and tugging up the collar on my pea coat. 'Krantz will probably have his search warrant later this morning.'

I slipped on the gloves and started down the short half-block to Milwaukee Avenue. I hobbled more than I walked, and scraped along more than I hobbled. Ligaments in both legs were torn, and it would be some time before I got the hang of the crutches.

The middle of the block was dark, and I kept my head down as I unlocked the door, but I didn't imagine Krantz would have any difficulty identifying me from surveillance photos, if any were being taken. Men on crutches aren't often out in the middle of the night.

The scent of the glitter girl's cheap perfume and spearmint gum had gone; the place now smelled only of the stench I'd set free when I'd cut through the dead man's plastic shroud. I locked the door behind me and dropped the key to the floor. I wouldn't be going out that way.

I went through the door I'd splintered and into the garage. The smell of death was so thick it stuck to the back of my throat like rotten paste. I pushed what was left of the door closed behind me.

I needed a fast, clear look. I switched on the overhead fluorescents. The car sat in the center of the garage, rank and dented, exactly as I'd left it. I switched off the lights, crutch-walked across the garage to the overhead door's power switch and raised the door. Moonlight flooded into the garage.

I hobbled back to the car, slipped in, twisted the key I'd left in the ignition and backed out into the alley.

I wanted badly to speed away; a corpse was rotting in ripped

plastic just three feet from my head. But an open door would draw
cops too soon, and I was clutching at the faint hope that time
would dissipate the smell before Krantz showed up with his search
warrants. I got out, reached in to push the door button, got back
in the car and drove to the end of the alley.

Leo was waiting around the corner, as we'd agreed. He must
have been crazed with worry as he followed me deeper into the
city. I was driving the Carson kill car, with someone else's body
in the trunk.

He stayed well back when I turned off and parked on a side
street in a run-down neighborhood on Chicago's west side. It was
the middle of the night but I knew there were a hundred eyes on
me, and him. It couldn't be helped. What I was doing was done
often enough, on those blocks. I shut off the engine and left the
key in the ignition. Leo shot forward, I got in, and he drove us
west to the tollway north to Wisconsin.

He told me to unzip my side curtain as he did the same. I'd
brought the stink of the death in that small Ford with me. After a
few minutes I started shivering, from the cold and from worry that
I'd left some trace of my DNA behind.

'What's wrong with you?' he asked.

'My DNA.'

'I've always worried about that, too,' he said.

SIXTY-SEVEN

Amanda and I met for breakfast at ten the next morning.
The dining room was empty except for us, a pitcher of
milk, a Thermos of coffee, and several little boxes of barely
sweetened, nutritious, thoroughly uninteresting cereal.

'My room is charmingly ancient,' I said, chattering light. 'Real
porcelain handles on the pedestal sink, cast-iron bed stand and a
scratched maple dresser. Still, this place is quiet as a tomb, optimal
for sleeping.'

She poured us coffee. 'What time did you and Leo get in this
morning?'

'How did you know?'

She shrugged, trying to grin. 'Your rusted muffler is quite distinctive. I heard it start up ten minutes after we checked in. At first I thought it might be Leo, moving it to park in back, but when I looked out, I couldn't see it anywhere. It wasn't hard to guess that he might have driven off, or who'd gone with him. The only question is why you didn't take the Escalade.'

'We were being clever, and worried you'd go out to the Cadillac for something. Seeing the Jeep gone, you'd simply assume Leo was off in search of doughnuts.'

'Why did you go back if there was no chance for a peek in the trunk?'

'Eliminate a link.'

She touched my wrist. She realized I'd gone to separate Wendell from Lamm, if only a little, if Wendell had even been there at all.

'The other scenario is no better.' I told her about the orange rowboat I'd seen, bailed out and bobbing high on the water at Lamm's camp.

'It's why I'm waiting up here. I'm expecting he could be in a lake,' she said, looking away.

Her eyes were clear; her chin was raised. In that instant, I could see the chief executive she was destined to be. 'My father drove Jim Whitman home,' she said.

'I take that as proof of his innocence. Your father is not stupid. As I told you before, he wouldn't have risked driving Whitman if he'd had any part in killing him.'

'You're sure?'

'As much as I'm sure Whitman's death shocked your father into hiring Eugene Small at the end of January.'

'Two weeks later, Carson got killed.'

'And Eugene Small was murdered two weeks after that. It made your father frantic.'

'Richie Bales killed Small?'

'I told Krantz it was either Bales, looking to get Small out of the way so he could extort money from Lamm; Lamm himself, because Small had learned too much; or Canty, on Lamm's orders. Each had motive.'

'Why did my father come up here?'

'I told Krantz that either Krantz's threat to prosecute him for

Lamm's crimes sent him into a rage, to come up and confront his false friend, or Richie Bales got to him, still posing as a cop, demanding your father come up on one pretext or another, perhaps to help Bales locate Lamm.

'There's no chance my father is still alive?'

The soft way she was asking sent my mind back to the small photos I'd seen in Wendell's study, of the little girl she'd been, clutching a small cluster of blue balloons. The balloons would have soon gone away; there was never any helping that. Just like there was no way of helping her much now.

She said she was anxious to drive back to Bent Lake, to track down the sheriff. It was more likely she wanted to be alone, to prepare herself for a call from the sheriff. As I hobbled to walk her to the lobby door, we heard the resort manager yelling from a private office. 'I don't care where the hell he is. You tell him to get out here now with glass and new locks.' A desk phone was then banged down in anger.

'Tell the sheriff about that bailed-out rowboat,' I said by the front door, 'though he's already searching the lakes for Canty.'

'What's worse, Dek? Finding my father in a car, or in a lake?'

I shook my head. There could never be an answer to that.

SIXTY-EIGHT

Leo found me at twelve-thirty in the lobby, eating unsweetened Cheerios, dry, and watching television. There had been no report of a corpse being discovered in a car in Chicago, nor on the websites I'd snagged on my cell phone. Then again, it had been that kind of neighborhood.

He curled a forefinger for me to stand up, and went to the front desk to check out. 'Excellent beds you have here; I can't remember the last time I slept a solid twelve hours,' he said, as though he hadn't just done a round trip to Chicago to partake in the felonious transport of a corpse.

'You hear anything last night?' the resort manager asked. It was the same question she'd asked me, after Amanda left.

'I was out cold for twelve hours,' he said again. 'What happened?'

'Damned kids, looking for booze. They broke in the kitchen door.'

'Did they get away with much?'

She shook her head. 'That's just it: I can't see where anything was taken, other than maybe a box of crackers and a jar of peanut butter. Damn, dumb bored kids, looking for a thrill.'

Outside, I said to Leo, 'Clever, you saying that about being asleep for the whole night. Twice.'

'Cleverness is one of my many middle names,' he said.

'Amanda heard us leave.'

'Let's hope the desk lady did not,' he said, cleverness draining from his face. Then, 'No news?'

'Nothing on television or on the Internet.'

'I checked the Internet, too, after I went out to the Escalade earlier. No word of a car being found, boosted and stripped, with a body in the trunk.'

We went outside. 'Don't blow a tire; you're driving with no spare,' I said, peering into the back as he climbed into the Jeep. He'd put the Jeep's spare in the back, and covered it with my yellow rain poncho.

'Caution is another of my middle names,' he said, and took off for Chicago.

I called Jenny from the terrace.

'Leo had implied your vocal chords were healthy enough to call before now,' she said.

'It's been hectic.'

'Yes, that story,' she said. 'Tell me.'

'It's unresolved, and potentially damaging.'

'You're worried about Amanda?' she asked.

'And her father.'

'Where are you exactly?'

'A ski resort in the piney woods of Wisconsin.'

'Alone?'

'Amanda's here. Leo just left.'

'I'm going to be so proud to not ask the next question.'

'Separate rooms,' I said.

'This is so like high school.'

'You rented rooms in high school?'

Jenny laughed before the newswoman, never far away, took over again. 'Give me something for the future.'

I told her all of it.

'The wires out of Chicago have barely scratched the surface of this,' she said when I was done.

'I need you to watch those wires.'

'For a stolen car found stripped, with a body in the trunk.'

'With luck, they'll find it today, and then we'll know.'

'Are we still talking about you coming to San Francisco sometime?'

'Seafood on the Wharf.'

'There could be that,' she said, hanging up and leaving me to wonder why I'd ever want to waste time going to the Wharf.

SIXTY-NINE

A manda got back just before dark, red-eyed and hollow-cheeked. She'd been gone eight hours, but she said it seemed she'd been gone twenty. We sat at the bar in the deserted, dark lounge and had drinks – a whiskey and water for her, a med-friendly ginger ale for me – that the resort manager had come in to make for us.

Amanda had brought two bags. One was plastic, and contained a loaf of rye bread, a jar of Dijon mustard and an orange brick of Wisconsin's official sustenance, cheddar cheese. The other bag was paper, and well worn. She'd ducked into an antique store that displayed used books in the window, and bought a collection of poems by somebody I'd never heard of, a guide to making soups, and a history of World Wars One and Two condensed into one hundred pages. She tried a big smile as she took out the last book, an old British mystery novel that she said was written when sexual activity was described with vague movements of eyebrows and fluttering hands, though she promised to take that one away if it set my own eyebrows and hands to twitching.

'How rough was your day?' I asked.

'Too many lakes,' she said.

'Maybe moving the car was dumb.'

'No; it was risky, and daring, and I love you for it.' Then, likely realizing she'd said something she didn't mean to say, she added, 'I called my office every hour. I said only that my father was up here and might have gotten stranded on one of the small lakes. Of course, they've been watching the news . . .'

'Not unusual. Most people in Chicago are following the Confessors' Club story.'

'No one said anything, but it would be impossible for them not to assume my father's caught up in all of that.'

We tried making jokes about what I might learn from the books she'd bought but mostly we just made silence.

Agent Krantz found us at eight o'clock, lapsed into sitting stiffly at the bar like two strangers on a train. He had to perch on the other side of Amanda because I'd taken the stool at the end of the bar so I could lean against the wall. The manager came in and Krantz ordered a low-carb beer. It figured.

'I assumed you'd gone back to Chicago,' I said, by way of an enthusiastic greeting.

'I promised we'd talk again today, and I didn't want to disappoint,' he said, taking a pull at the beer and not grimacing. 'There have been developments.'

Amanda glanced sharply at him.

'No news about your father, I'm afraid,' Krantz said quickly.

'Herman Canty?' I asked.

'Nor him, either, though the sheriff's people did find a note that Canty's girlfriend, a Wanda something, taped to the door at the Loons' Rest. It said she was off on an adventure of some sort.'

'That's a development for sure,' I said, agreeably.

'Except Canty's truck was found parked on a side street.'

'In plain view?'

He nodded.

'Wow,' I said. 'There's been some ace sleuthing done.'

Undeterred, he said, 'One of those tool bin things is bolted inside the truck bed, behind the rear window. Want to guess what was in it?'

'Not tools,' I said, 'because people around here say Canty never did much.'

'There was a freshly packed duffel bag inside. Our Mr Canty was planning a trip.'

'With the lovely Wanda, as her note said?'

'Could be, or not could be. That is the question.'

I groaned, but said nothing to spoil the taste of his low-carb beer.

'There was a fresh set of tire tracks in the fire lane closest to Lamm's camp, made by tires almost bald of tread,' he said. 'Jeep tires, just like yours, Elstrom. And just a few feet away, we found evidence that someone had been digging at the base of a tree.'

'I told you I got trussed up in Lamm's cottage. The fire lane was where I parked. As for the digging, there are beavers and raccoons up here.'

'One of my men had a peek inside your Jeep earlier this morning.'

'I've been meaning to clean out all those hamburger wrappers.'

'Why is your spare tire inside, instead of mounted on the bracket on the back?'

'It's out of air,' I said.

'And why was the hood warm?'

Amanda inhaled sharply, but stared straight ahead.

'From the sun,' I said, patting the crutches I'd leaned against the wall. 'Obviously I can't drive.'

He leaned forward so he see could more directly past Amanda. 'My warrant came through to search Second Securities.'

'What did you find?' I leaned back so he'd either have to almost lie across the bar to maintain eye contact, or lean backward and risk tipping over. It was immature and felt appropriate.

He chose to lean back. 'Not much except the identity of a girl who worked there. She told an odd story. The front door is all glass, and has a mail slot in the metal at the very bottom. She hadn't been paid the wages she was owed, so she walked out, pushing the key inside the mail slot after locking up for the last time. Later, she realized she'd left behind a bottle of black nail polish. She went back to reach in for the key so she could retrieve the nail polish, but the key was gone.'

'Another employee opened up, and took the key?'

'She was the only employee. Here's the odd part, Elstrom: When my agents arrived there this morning, the key was lying inside the locked front door, right where the girl said she'd left it.'

'Obviously, the key was there all the time,' I offered reasonably. 'The girl just got confused.'

'Or an intruder showed up after the girl quit, snagged the key through the mail slot, used it to go in the front door, locked that, and left by the garage. Since there were no signs of forced entry, it's a plausible explanation, especially since . . .' He let the thought dangle, prompting.

'Yes?' I asked.

'There were signs of forced entry inside. Someone smashed the inner door to get in the garage. The girl said it hadn't been that way when she worked there, and that it was always locked.'

'What did you find in the garage? More tire treads?'

'Fresh ones, pulling out. And little rubber cuppy marks.'

'Little rubber *what*?'

'Concentric circles, three of them, totaling an inch and three-quarters in diameter.' He pointed to my crutches, leaning against the wall. 'Exactly the sort of marks made by the rubber caps they put on the tips of crutches, to prevent them from slipping.'

I could see Amanda had caught her breath. I wanted to hold my own, too, for fear Krantz was going to ask to see my crutches.

'Trouble is, almost every crutch manufacturer uses those same caps,' he said, looking straight at my eyes. 'That garage smells like something's been dead in there for quite some time.'

'What was it?'

'We found nothing . . . yet.' He took another maddeningly delighted pull on his beer. 'Still, you know what's even more bothersome than that?'

'Apparently not your low-carb beer,' I said.

He frowned, but only a little. Obviously they spent hours teaching self-control at IRS Agent school. 'It's the two-million-dollar cash payout on Grant Carson's life.'

'Why?'

'Only one million dollars was found in that case in the Buick.'

'You said that at the clinic.'

'A number which you confirmed at the time.'

'I was medicated and confused.'

'I was in the local tap in Bent Lake, having a brew with the locals—'

'Low carb?' I interrupted.

'They didn't have any—' He caught himself and stopped. Then, 'They remembered you, especially your wit. Seems you came in carrying a metal case that looks exactly like the one we recovered from the Buick. When they asked you what was in it, you cracked them up by saying you had two million dollars in there.'

'That's right.'

'That's right?' Krantz set down his beer.

'My wit did sparkle that evening,' I said.

Amanda laughed, just once, but continued to stare straight ahead at the glasses gathering dust above the bar.

'I could haul you down to Chicago, keep you for forty-eight hours.'

'I had my briefcase in the bar that night. Somebody stole it from my Jeep when I was in the clinic.'

Krantz looked at me, and looked at Amanda. He stood up, knocked back the last of his de-carbed beer and left, looking less happy than when he'd arrived.

'What's the deal with the second million he keeps asking about?' Amanda said.

I shook my head; I was paranoid about a sticky microphone Krantz might have left behind. We ate cheese and bread and talked about World Wars One and Two, and then we finished our drinks and went outside where there would be only cheese-fed, native Wisconsin insects and not bugs imported from Chicago, made of plastic, batteries and bits of metal.

She touched my hand, questioning. 'What happened to the other half of the two million we found at Second Securities?'

'I held that half back to bargain with, in case I got double-crossed about where your father was,' I said.

'And now?'

'Somebody's owed something out of this,' I said.

SEVENTY

T he meds couldn't put me to sleep that night. I eased onto my good side to read the bedside alarm clock. If it was close enough to dawn I'd quit struggling to sleep and get up to read about soups and wars and sleuthing Brits.

No red numerals shone from the top of the nightstand. The alarm clock had died.

I reached to switch on the lamp. The lamp didn't work. The power to my room was out.

I found my phone. It was four-fifteen.

A moment after I laid back, I heard something click faintly, one-two, in fast succession, out in the hall – followed, after a delay, by a third, softer sound, a thud. Perhaps someone was out there, checking on the power. Then I remembered that there was no staff in the resort, except for the manager, and she'd likely be asleep in her rooms. It was the middle of the night.

There were no other guests, either, except for Amanda, probably also sound asleep.

And me, sleepless, with jitters that would jump at anything.

One-two; another pair of clicks came, followed again by the third sound, the soft thud.

I grabbed my crutches from the other side of the bed, and levered myself to stand. Moving had set the stitched bullet wound in my left arm and the torn ligaments in my legs to throbbing. I waited until I'd steadied and hobbled to the window.

The resort was dark. The entire building had lost power. No one was awake to notice.

Except for me.

Click-click; the new sounds seemed slightly louder now. Again, they were followed by a strange soft thud. I started toward the door.

The fourth pair of fast clicks came when I was still only halfway across. Definitely louder, definitely closer.

By the time I got to the door and pressed my ear against it, I was sweating like a man standing under a hot August sun. Fifth and sixth sets of noises had come, increasingly louder. By now I'd recognized them for what they were: doors were being unlocked with one of the big, square-cut metal keys. The first click was the sound of the lock bolt retracting, the second the sound of the bolt snapping forward after the door was opened. The soft thud following each delay was the sound of the door being gently closed.

Rooms were being searched.

'Damned dumb, bored kids, looking for booze,' the resort manager had called the intruders who'd broken in.

Damned dumb, bored kids didn't search an empty resort, room by room, looking for booze.

I pressed my eye to the magnified peep-hole. A light flashed for an instant, out in the hall. Tiny prickles shot across my scalp as I understood. Someone was using a pencil beam flashlight to quickly scan the rooms.

A new pair of clicks came loud. And, after only a second, the thud.

He'd spotted my Jeep parked in the lot, broken in for food, and for sanctuary. Until everyone was asleep.

The next clicks came loudest of all. I could hear him through the wall. He'd opened the room next door. Too soon, the soft thud came. He'd closed the door.

I could hear him breathe, out in the hall.

I pressed against the wall, steadying, seeing the faint low shape of the bed – my unmade bed. In an instant's flash of his light, he'd know I was there.

Metal scratched on my door. He'd slipped the master key into my lock.

I leaned one crutch against the wall, pressed back to brace myself, and raised the other crutch like a bat.

First click; the bolt retracted.

Second click; the bolt sprung back out. The door was opening.

His breathing was heavy, labored, not two feet from my face.

The pencil beam of light moved unsteadily, low across the carpet toward the bed.

The beam halted. He sucked in air. His flashlight had found my shoes, next to the bed.

The floor creaked as he stepped softly into the room.

SEVENTY-ONE

I swung my crutch like I was swinging for the moon, aiming high where I hoped was a head. I hit him with such force that the impact knocked the crutch out of my hands and slammed me back against the wall.

He shrieked, dropping his flashlight, but he didn't go down. The black shape of him turned on me like a monster, stretching his arms out for me like giant bat wings. I pushed off from the wall and half charged, half fell onto him. We went down with me on top, beating at his face with my good right fist, once, twice, three times, until I connected with something small. It crunched. I'd caught his nose, shattered a bone.

Exhaling hard, whistling wet through his nose, he raised up his hands to flail at my head.

I had no strength; my body was on fire with pain. I had to get away. But his giant hands reached up and found my neck. I beat down at his smashed wet nose again. He pushed me off, rolled on to his side and then onto his belly, to get up, to kick at my head.

I clambered on his back, put a knee into the small of it, and grabbed the hair at the back of his head with my good right hand, to force him down on his chest.

He reared back to raise his knees to buck me off. I dropped my hands around him, down to the carpet to steady myself, and found aluminum with both hands. The crutch that had been knocked from my hands now lay perpendicular under his chest. Tugging at the crosswise crutch with both hands, I forced my knee deeper into his back. My gunshot arm and torn legs raged in pain. But to let up was to die.

He took in a great breath, raised his head and got his knees up, six, eight inches, contorting into the beginning of an arch, but it was no good. I had him pinned. He slammed down face flat on the carpet, except now the front of his neck lay on the crutch.

Pushing all my weight through my knee deep into the small of his back, I tugged the crutch hard up under his neck. Hot blood flooded down my left arm; my stitches had torn loose from my flesh.

His right hand fluttered up, weak, trying to loosen my grip.

'Die, you son of a bitch,' I heard myself scream to the body writhing beneath me. 'Die!'

Something snapped loudly, wonderfully. The hand that had been flailing up to find me fell limp. I did not let up. I let the blood run hot down my left arm; I let my torn legs rage in pain. I tugged on both sides of the crutch until I could tug no more. And then I counted to a hundred.

Finally, I had nothing left. I fell off him and began to crawl out of my room. I could hear nothing but the frantic gasping of my own breathing.

At some point I tried to rise, at least up to my knees, to head down the hall, to find Amanda. Surely he'd found her first. But I had no strength. I slumped back to the floor and sort of rolled, kicked and crawled the dozen yards to the lobby.

There was a fire extinguisher mounted on the wall. And a fire alarm. I reached up and managed to pull the red handle down on the alarm.

Horns on, battery back-ups sounded down both halls. White lights flashed like lightning strikes.

I fell back; I could do no more.

'Dek?' Amanda's voice sounded after a time, from far away. Her breath found my cheek, on the floor. 'He's here?'

She didn't ask who; the blood running out of my torn left arm had already told her.

'The Escalade,' I managed to whisper. 'Get us inside, lock the doors, drive us away.'

Surely the man could not be killed. Surely he was still alive.

She ran to get her keys, knelt to help me up, and half dragged me out the lobby door and across the parking lot to the Escalade.

'Just lock the doors,' I said, after I'd crawled up onto the seat. Bright white lights were flashing everywhere, under the eaves, on the walls, out through the windows from inside.

I passed out.

SEVENTY-TWO

'd killed.

I'd snapped Canty's neck with my crutch; his back with my knee. With time, I'd feel something more about that. For now, all I felt was numb.

After being re-stitched and re-bedded for the rest of the night at the clinic, Amanda was allowed to return me to the ski resort the next afternoon. However clumsily I'd walk-hobbled before, I was now bound to a motorized wheelchair, since I could only use my right hand. The resort manager's niece had moved us into a nice, wheelchair-accessible two-bedroom suite, just off the lobby. No charge for the upgrade or the motorized wheelchair, the niece said, though I was sure she would have been happier if she'd been allowed to tow me to the top of the highest ski run and push me over the back edge. I'd brought horror to the log resort. After cutting the resort's power and telephone landlines, Canty had beaten her aunt senseless before taking her master key.

Amanda and I slept well enough, separately. I supposed she was as unsettled as I by our close proximity, and how easily some of the old mannerisms and rituals we'd shared in marriage wanted to return. But she had much bigger worries, waiting for word of her father. There had been no news, either from the local sheriff, or from the cops in Chicago reporting a body found stuffed in a stolen car.

And we slept safe. Sheriff's deputies from two surrounding counties, supplemented by a special detachment of two armed special agents from the IRS, were now staying at the resort. I quickly grew fond of the deputies; they brought doughnuts, freshly fried and often topped with sprinkles.

Krantz's special agents, though, were another matter. They were a grim-faced pair, dispatched ostensibly to be vigilant, but more likely sent for what they might overhear. Krantz's frustration with me was growing exponentially. He was certain I knew plenty, but without Wendell around to squeeze, and nothing otherwise to link me to Eugene Small, Arthur Lamm or the Carson payout, he'd resorted to posting the two agents to hang around the lodge and pretend they weren't listening.

I'd found their bugs right away, one stuck under my nightstand, another stuck under Amanda's. I was tempted to reposition them on either sides of the toilet, to offer a stereophonic listening experience, but I left them where I'd found them. Amanda and I made sure to never discuss anything of substance in our small suite, for I was certain Krantz had planted more bugs.

The waiting drove Leo nuts, too, back in Rivertown. He enlisted Endora, no stranger from her modeling days to changing her look, to rent a car and look down the street where I'd abandoned the small Ford, while he rode ducked down in back. He then called me from an unfamiliar number.

'Burner phone,' he whispered. 'Forty bucks at Walmart. I'll toss it after this call.'

'But you called me on my regular phone,' I said, wanting to laugh for the first time since Canty.

'The eagle has flown,' he murmured.

Meaning the small Ford was gone. I could only marvel that Chicago's car thieves were as strong-stomached as its gang murderers. They'd boosted the car, likely stripped it, and with luck, turned it into a recyclable steel cube, albeit one that was slightly leaking.

Amanda said nothing of it. Or much about anything else. She left early each of the next three mornings to check on the sheriff's search plans for the day. After that, I think she just drove, or stopped somewhere. I never asked, and she never offered. She expressed no rage at her father, or at the world, or at me. She ate next to nothing, and I think slept little. Her hands trembled almost continuously. It was like that, waiting.

Krantz took a room at the lodge. He visited my mouth, in the wheelchair, in the lobby, twice a day in hope the new meds I'd been given had relaxed it enough to offer up more of what he was sure I knew.

'Where's Phelps?' he asked right off on the first, second and third mornings and afternoons after I'd killed Canty.

'The television news says Lamm has left the country,' I said, each time.

'Did I tell you the receptionist at Second Securities remembers you?'

'The one who couldn't remember her nail polish, or where she'd left a key?'

'I'll be bringing her in to look at you through a mirror.'

'No need. I went there, but I didn't break in, Krantz. I walked in through the front door.'

'Spewing some cocked-up story about being an inspector. You didn't say anything about that when we first spoke at the clinic. Withholding information from a federal investigation is prosecutable.'

'Meds,' I said. 'They made me forgetful.'

And so it went for those three mornings and three nights. Then, very early on the fourth day, the sheriff called to give Amanda directions to a tiny lake.

We packed what little we had and went out to the Escalade. I got behind the wheel. The stitches in my arm were holding, and the new fissures in my torn leg ligaments were healing. It was not a day for Amanda to drive.

'The sheriff will let you leave, afterward?' she asked, after we'd gone a mile.

'He termed what I'd done to Herman Canty "justifiable." I might not even have to come up for the inquest.'

'And Krantz?'

'He said he'll arrest me in Chicago.'

'He was kidding?'

'Krantz has difficulty with humor.'

'That low-carb business,' she said, struggling, looking straight ahead. No one should ever be required to be strong enough to look at someone fished dead from a lake.

Parked on the dirt road leading to the water were two county cruisers, Krantz's black Crown Victoria, an ambulance and the county medical examiner's van. The sheriff walked over, opened my door and leaned in. 'Mr Elstrom can handle this, Ms Phelps.'

'Yes, but who has ever been able to handle Mr Elstrom?' Her voice was surprisingly calm, forcing the new joke. She remained seated.

The sheriff had a high-wheeled off-road vehicle brought up and a paramedic got in with us. It was a rough five-minute drive through tall weeds to the edge of a small lake.

'No one ever comes to this lake, because they can't get to it,' the sheriff said. 'It's more like a retention pond that fills when there's been a lot of rain, and only then does it connect with the lakes to the north.'

They helped me stand, and we walked, of a fashion, to the shore. By then I was sweating.

They had them face down; two bodies on two tarps dragged from the edge of the lake, covered with other tarps. The paramedic bent to pull back the one covering the corpse closest to me.

Wanda screamed back at me in silent rigor.

'Not that one, you idiot,' the sheriff yelled at the paramedic. Then, to me, 'She knew too much, and with a million dollars, Canty must have figured he could afford better.'

The paramedic moved to uncover the body lying past Wanda.

I'm not good with ruined corpses. To buy time for a few deep breaths, I focused on the watch on his wrist. A Rolex with that much gold cost more than ten thousand dollars, and it looked to still be keeping perfect time. I supposed that would be expected. Certainly it was water resistant to a depth far greater than the shallows at the raw end of the small lake, and the gentle lapping of the water through the rushes was more than enough to engage the self-winding mechanism. It was a gentleman's wristwatch, designed for a wealthy man, a man of nuance, a man who need make only subtle gestures, even in death.

He had dressed well, his last day. His gray gabardine trousers were of the finest wool, light for the warm temperatures. Looking for identification, they'd turned back the label on his white shirt. It was from Pink's, on Jermyn Street in London. The shoes, I knew from Amanda, were English, too: lace-up broughams of sturdy leather that would have once held a high polish.

The clothes and shoes, of course, had not fared as well as the wristwatch. The press had gone from the trousers, and here and there tiny bits of milky flesh protruded where the wool had been abraded by the barky texture of the water reeds. The shirt was now a putrid green, mossed and dirtied by the muck at the shore. And the leather of his shoes had puckered and blistered, for even the finest of leathers, no matter how well oiled, are not meant to withstand submersion.

They turned him over. That part of his face closest to the bullet hole was gone, nibbled away in tiny bites by the sunny fish and microscopic urchins that worked the shore of the small lake.

I nodded and the paramedic covered him again.

'They were both shot somewhere else, then dumped in this lake by someone in a boat.' Krantz had come up to join us.

'An orange rowboat, recently bailed out,' I said.

The sheriff looked at me and nodded. 'Canty, in Lamm's boat,' he said.

The medical examiner held out two spent bullets for the sheriff to see. 'We'll have them tested,' he said, 'but they're the same caliber as those we found in Bales, and in . . .' He gestured toward me, the meat that had also caught a bullet from Canty's gun.

'Canty, for sure,' the sheriff said.

'Can you identify time of death?' I asked the medical examiner, to be certain.

Krantz looked sharply at me.

'Actually, yes, for both,' the medical examiner said.

And then I turned on my crutches, and started the slow walk back down the pressed tracks we'd just made, alone. No one had thought to offer to help me back. And that was good. I needed to understand all I'd just heard. And all I now believed.

At the car, I slid my crutches in back, and got in behind the wheel.

Amanda said nothing, the gold flecks in her eyes impossible to see behind the tears.

'Time to go back to Chicago,' I said.

'Do not start the car,' she said.

SEVENTY-THREE

'Tell me what happened up here, all of it, right now,' Amanda said in a surprisingly strong voice. 'In this, his last place.'

I let my hand fall away from the ignition switch. 'He's dead. One bullet.'

'Who shot him?'

'Canty. Delray was never a killer,' I said, sure of that and most everything else, now.

'From the beginning at Second Securities then, as best you see it.'

'Canty must have driven Lamm down to Chicago to convert the Carson check to cash, and probably to help Lamm leave the country from there. Except Canty saw an opportunity to change his own life instead. He killed Lamm, stuffed him in the trunk of the Carson kill car along with the cash, and came back up here to erase the only other person who knew what he'd been up to.'

'Wanda.'

'Unfortunately for Canty, Richie Bales was up here by then, looking for Lamm. He surprised Canty, maybe as Canty was bailing the boat to take Wanda on her last ride, or maybe when Canty got back to the dock after disposing of her. Canty must have breathed a huge sigh of relief when Richie told him he wanted half the payout. Don't forget, Canty still thought Richie was a cop, and saw him as one who could be bought off.'

'So they drove down to Second Securities to split the money?'

'Where, surprise, surprise, Canty saw the splintered door and the trashed car and thought the money had gone forever, and with it his hopes for getting out of the country a rich man. Richie, though, took a broader view.'

'Meaning he saw how you could have learned through your insurance contracts that Second Securities was the Carson beneficiary, and gotten to the money ahead of them.'

'And he saw how he could use your father to get that money back.'

'All he had to do was lure my father up here to hold as hostage,' she said.

'I'll bet checking your father's phone records will show your father received a call from a burner phone just a few minutes before he left Lake Forest for work that Thursday morning. That would have been Richie, who your father still believed was a cop named Delray Delmar, telling him some of his and Arthur's legal problems might go away if he'd come up to Bent Lake to talk to him and Arthur.'

'Krantz had already frightened my father when he'd called for an appointment, threatening to prosecute him for Arthur's crimes because my father owned half of Lamm's agency.'

'Between Krantz and Richie, it was enough to induce sudden panic in your father. He shot up to Bent Lake with no hesitation.'

'When was my father killed?'

'As soon as he arrived up here, according to the medical examiner's timeline. They didn't need to keep your father alive to lure me up here with the money.'

She looked out the window. 'What could anyone have done?' she asked.

It was the question I knew she would ask, and the one I most feared. I took a breath. 'I wish I'd moved slower.'

She turned to look at me. 'That Tuesday, Confessors' Club day?'

'No. The day before, Monday, when I'd been in such a rush to call Keller.'

'You were in a panic; worried that Lamm would kill again the next night.'

'I didn't know Lamm was already dead, so I called Keller on Monday. On Tuesday morning, early, your father called me, furious. I got furious right back at him, saying he'd kept what he knew to himself for too long. He hung up on me before I could tell him that Delray Delmar was a fraud.'

'Because if he'd known Richie was no cop, he never would have come up here?'

'Yes.'

I waited for a moment and then for another, but there was nothing more to say. And so I started the engine and swung around to head back to Chicago.

Neither of us spoke the whole way down.

SEVENTY-FOUR

D ebbie Goring came by a week after I'd gotten back from Wisconsin. It was eleven in the morning and I was on the bench by the river, watching Leo up in the purple ash. He was sawing off one of its main limbs. I'd come back from up north to find seven more leaves curled on the ground, but I fought the idea of cutting down the tree. There'd been too much death that spring.

She tossed a thick, letter-sized white envelope on the bench next to me and sat down. 'I was expecting to hear from you,' she rasped.

'I was vacationing, up in Wisconsin.'

'So I read in the newspapers. You got shot, pushed a killer off a bridge with your car and then snapped his neck and broke his back a few days later.'

'The vacation brochures are right: there's always plenty to do in Wisconsin.'

Debbie looked up at the ash. Leo, wearing an orange Sesame Street T-shirt, had begun hamming it up like a monkey, waving his bow saw at the front of the turret. Someone else had arrived.

'What's wrong with him?' she asked.

'His clothes, mostly.'

She turned back to me. 'Even though I received that anonymous cashier's check for a hundred grand—'

'Wendell Phelps sent you that check, though it need never be proved,' I interrupted.

'Then it's a shame, his death,' she said. 'Anyway, that check was a damned fine thing to receive, don't get me wrong, but I was still bummed thinking no one would ever be prosecuted for killing my father,' she said. 'Then I heard about your little foray into the woods. Now, at least, it might become obvious that my father was murdered.'

'It will never go to trial without Lamm. And Small and Richie Bales are dead.'

'Arthur Lamm has escaped, scot-free?'

'That's what everyone is saying.' Only Leo, Amanda and I knew that Arthur Lamm had escaped nothing. The Carson kill car had never been recovered, and by now I was daring to believe that it had been compressed to a small steel cube in a scrap yard friendly to car thieves, and that Lamm was on his way to becoming a doorknob spindle or perhaps part of a toaster.

She turned to look into my eyes. 'Everybody's saying also that Lamm escaped with a million dollars that's missing from Grant Carson's insurance.' She lit a Camel and blew smoke at the Willahock.

Up in the ash, Leo was smiling down. Amanda had come around the side of the turret followed by a thickset man in a black suit. Wendell's corporation had lost no time imposing a security detail on its new largest shareholder.

Amanda and I had not spoken one word since leaving Bent Lake, and when she dropped me at the turret, I was not sure she'd ever speak to me again.

'I told myself that I'd have to live with Lamm's permanent disappearance,' Debbie went on, 'but then, this morning, a messenger from a bonded delivery service brought me a box.'

Amanda glanced only briefly at me and went on talking up to Leo.

'Want to guess what was in the box I got?' Debbie asked behind a puff of smoke.

'Flowers?'

'Something that smells even better. Here, take a whiff.' She picked up the envelope, opened the flap, and fanned the contents inside with her thumb.

I made a sniffing noise, but kept my eyes on Amanda. She'd opened a small rectangular box and was holding up its contents to show Leo, whose face had turned serious.

I turned back to Debbie. I couldn't smell anything other than cigarette smoke.

'Smells like a tire, doesn't it?' Debbie said.

'Why would it smell like a tire?'

'Look closely, Mr Elstrom. They even have little bits of rubber dust on them, like from the inside of a tire.'

'Interesting,' I said.

'Got any idea why these might have been inside a tire?'

'Not a clue.' I pushed myself up to stand. I'd been off the crutches for three days, but that was more from temperament than prudence. I needed to walk, to take steps to get on with my life.

'Me, neither.' Debbie Goring flicked her cigarette butt in the river and stood up, too. 'Two million in insurance was what I had coming, but a million cash, even smelling like the inside of a tire, made me a damn sight happier than when I first woke up.' She reached for my wrist, slapped the thick white envelope into my hand and started to walk away.

'Wait,' I said. I looked closely into the envelope. There were eleven packets of currency inside. Fifty-five thousand dollars.

She came back. I extracted one packet – five thousand – and jammed it into my khakis. I held out the envelope to her.

She backed away. 'No, no, Elstrom. Our deal was five per cent. You earned that, off the cashier's check and the contents of this morning's delivery.'

'The papers mentioned an IRS agent named Krantz?'

She nodded.

'He'd planned on making a big, career-boosting arrest of Arthur Lamm for income tax evasion. He'll seize many of Lamm's assets, but Krantz will be criticized for letting four million dollars get sent to Grand Cayman, where it can never be seized by the IRS. Krantz did recover a million dollars from Wendell Phelps's Buick, but there's no proof that it was the Carson payout, so he'll never be able to seize that either.'

A huge grin lit up her face. 'The newspapers are saying Lamm used the other half of that insurance money to get away. You saying you can't always believe what you read in the papers?'

'Krantz will hunt for that missing million for the rest of his days because he doubts that Lamm got away. He thinks I know something about that, and he'll be watching me and my tax returns for years. If he finds me with money I can't explain, he'll redouble his efforts to nail me, along with anyone else he thinks might know something.'

'Meaning me?'

'Meaning anyone connected with the case that shows sudden signs of wealth.' I pressed the envelope into her hands. 'Be prudent, Debbie. Hide it all in a dozen places, trickle it out in small amounts over a lot of years, for clothes and tuition and a vacation every once in a while.'

'As my father would have wanted.'

'Yes.'

Her eyes got wet, and she stepped forward like she was going to kiss me. But reason took hold, and she turned. 'You're not half bad, Elstrom,' she called back, as she disappeared around the front of the turret.

I started towards the ash, un-crutched but wobbling. Amanda met me halfway.

'I noticed your spare tire is back on your Jeep,' she said.

'It just needed new air.'

'I'll bet. That happy woman was Debbie Goring?' she asked.

'She gave me five grand.'

'How much did she want to give you?'

I looked up the hill, past the turret. A black limousine was idling at the curb. No doubt the driver was armed, just like the bodyguard who'd followed her down the hill and now stood a few vigilant steps away. Her new life had begun.

When I didn't answer, she said, 'I checked my father's incoming calls. He got a call from a burner phone thirty minutes before he left for Bent Lake.'

'Delray Delmar, the fake cop,' I said. 'Your father was a good man.'

'You always find the good, don't you, Dek?'

'You're going to do fine as a tycoon,' I said.

'There will be bumps. The Pig Lady's lawyer called this morning, saying she's going to sue for all of it. Otherwise, he said, she's going to go hungry.'

'Send her lettuce and tomatoes. Properly frugal, she can have BLTs for years.'

Amanda laughed at that, a good, long, healing laugh. She handed me the small white box.

A great creak came from the tree. Leo had stopped sawing.

'How many leaves remain?' she asked.

'Six,' I said, 'per this morning's count.'

'You're cutting off only one limb?'

'It's a minor setback, nothing terminal.'

Leo kicked the limb. We watched it fall. The tree, now with only one limb, looked like the hands on a clock, set at ten to six.

She kissed me, maybe longer than she'd ever kissed me before.

I looked at the gold flecks in her eyes.

'I need to accept that I never knew my father,' she said.

'You know enough.'

I walked with her, and the bodyguard behind us, up the hill.

'That ash will survive, Dek?' she asked, at the limo.

'Perhaps stronger than before.'

The bodyguard opened the front passenger door.

'Aren't you going to open your gift?' she asked.

I did.

She got in front, next to the driver. The guard closed her door, and got in back. In time, she'd learn to ride in back.

Her car pulled away, and in a minute it had disappeared. I looked down at the sunny-colored, yellow bow tie, wondering if it was more of a declaration than a gift, and thinking of my other bow tie, the purple one hanging on a nail in my almost-finished closet.

I started back down to the river, to look some more at the water and at Leo up in a tree, moving as best I could, one step at a time.